CW00829077

WELL I'LL BE DAMNED

MARC X GRIGOROFF

This is a work of fiction. Names, characters, places, and incidents either are the product of the author's imagination or are used fictitiously. Any resemblance to actual persons, living or dead, events, or locales is entirely coincidental.

Excerpt from "High Flight" by John Gillespie McGee Jr.
Public Domain

ISBN 979-8-9920651-0-7
First Edition: 2024
Other Side Books

For Noah and Zoë. Always.

You cannot force a man to believe.
You can only force him to pretend to believe.

– Pindar Plifner

Well I'll Be Damned

1

Glazed

I don't like God. The grumpy one from the Bible, anyway. I'm saying that right up front because I know that for a lot of people this is a deal breaker. They'd rather be caught surfing gay porn than consort with a heretic, someone who not only refuses to worship the Creator of Heaven and Earth, but openly professes a dislike for Him. The truth is, I don't even believe in God. Unlike the devout, however, I accept the remote possibility that I could be wrong, that despite the overwhelming lack of evidence, there might be a Supreme Being peeking into my mind to check for impure thoughts. And if there is, well, I don't like Him.

God's been on my mind a lot lately because my daughter Joey has been asking questions about Him. Apparently, she's attempting to unravel the nature of existence. She's only four years old, so I was unprepared when she walked up and demanded, "Why are we here?"

"Where else should we be?" I responded defensively, assuming I'd forgotten a birthday party or a doctor's appointment.

"No," she said condescendingly, "I mean why do we exist?"

"You're asking me why we exist? Like philosophically?"

She nods.

"I don't know. We just do."

"That's not a very good answer."

"You have a better one?"

"Because God made us?"

"You believe that?"

"I don't know. Do you?"

"I'm not comfortable discussing theology with you."

"Why not?"

"Because you're four years old."

"Almost five."

"Why don't you go watch TV?"

Joey eyed me warily. She knew what I was doing, throwing her off the scent with a diversion, but after a few seconds she put her existential journey on hold and went searching for the remote.

Over the next few days, she peppered me with questions about the Supreme Being.

"If God made us, who made God?"

"What does God look like?"

"If God is a man, does that mean he has a penis?"

Her last question intrigues me.

It turns out that Joey's curiosity about God had been piqued by our Filipina neighbor, an amazingly resilient woman on whom life has dumped more excrement than anyone I've ever met. Ironically, it is Bernadette's horrific past that has strengthened her faith to the point where my cynicism bounces off her like beer off a raincoat. Indeed, whenever I offer my sincere, though arguably pessimistic, interpretation of life, she smiles at me with fervent brown eyes and says, "Oh, Mister Max, God loves you too!"

"Does God have mucus?" Joey wants to know.

I don't really like mucus either.

In fact, I don't have much affinity for any of the bodily fluids, though I can appreciate the functions of most of them. But mucus? Yes, it helps protect us from fungi and bacteria and whatever. But couldn't the Master of the Universe have come up with a better defense mechanism than the green goo that constantly runs out of my daughter's nose?

This is one of the many reasons I don't like God. He did such a half-assed job designing human beings.

"You think you could have done a better job?" I'm asked whenever I articulate my dissatisfaction in the presence of a believer.

"No. And I can't play the soprano sax as well as Kenny G, but I'm highly critical of his musical output."

"I'm going to pray for you."

"No thanks."

"You're going to end up in hell."

"Will you be there?"

"Of course not! I'll be in my heavenly home with God and Jesus and Mary and all the saints and the prophets and my dog Booty, who got hit by a car when I was thirteen."

"Will your Christian friends be there too?"

"All those who've accepted the Lord Jesus Christ as their personal savior will achieve their heavenly reward."

Hearing the roster of those who won't be in hell always makes it sound inviting.

Joey pulls on my hand. I look down and see that she's still waiting for an answer.

"Yes, God has mucus."

I feel a twinge of guilt because she believes me. At this point in her life, she believes everything I tell her. It's not unlikely that she'll walk around for the rest of her days absolutely certain that God has mucus. I had the same sort of relationship with my dad. At four, I asked him, "Who's the greatest singer in the world?" He thought for a moment and said, "Bing Crosby." That was it. For the rest of my life the answer to "Who's the greatest singer in the world?" will be Bing Crosby. I fight it, I really do, but whenever the subject of preeminent vocalists pops up, the first person to enter my mind is Der Bingle.

"Daddy, can *Ate* Bernadette come to my ballet recital?"

Joey prefaces Bernadette with *ate*, which means *elder sister* in Tagalog, the language most widely spoken in the Philippines. Bernadette taught her to use this familiar form of expression, which I find rather charming. Although *ate* has the same spelling as the past tense of the English verb *to eat*, the Tagalog version has two syllables and is pronounced *AH-tay*. It would be inappropriate for me to employ *ate* before Bernadette's name because she is neither my sister nor my elder. I'm in my late forties and Bernadette is only twenty-eight, although she looks a lot older. No, that's not true. She doesn't look older. She just seems older. Maybe it's because of all the shit she's been through. In fact, it's a miracle that she's even alive.

Bernadette was impregnated at thirteen by her forty-three-year-old cousin Raoul, who claimed she seduced him. In fact, Raoul had gotten her drunk by spiking the Coca-Cola he'd brought her—the first she'd ever tasted—with bootleg rum. Naturally, her parents sided with Raoul, and Bernadette was banished from the family home and forced to live on the streets. A very sickly girl with a cleft palate was born five months later, but to Bernadette, Christina was the most beautiful child she'd ever seen. The infant stopped breathing a few days after her birth, and although Bernadette was heartbroken, she understood it to be God's will.

Three years later, she was induced to marry her third cousin Pacifico, also forty-three, who beat her with savage regularity. Despite the constant cruelty, she stayed with him for two years, as it was God's will. Their union produced no children, because Pacifico's idea of intercourse involved an orifice that had no direct connection with the human reproductive system. One morning, after a long night of drinking and whoring, he came home and attempted to cut off Bernadette's feet with a machete. His reasoning, he explained as he chased her through the house, was that amputating her feet would save him the cost of buying her shoes. At this juncture Bernadette realized that staying with him would be suicide, and suicide was most definitely not God's will.

She made her way to Manila and found work as a nurse's aide in a hospital for the poor. The work was long and hard, and the pay was laughable, yet Bernadette was truly happy helping those less fortunate than she was. Her happiness abruptly ended the night she was gang raped by a mob of patients high on homemade liquor. Her injuries were so severe that she would never again be able to bear children. Although Bernadette believes this too was God's will, for the first time in her life she asked Him why.

After months of rehabilitation, Bernadette found work on an American airbase two hours north of Manila. There, she met a young airman from a small town in east-central Illinois. Timothy Shelter was neither rich nor particularly good looking, but he was a truly decent human being who truly adored her. Although they both believed they'd found the love of their lives, Bernadette sadly explained that they could not be together because she was still married to Pacifico. Even worse, due to the powerful influence of the Catholic Church, divorce is not permitted in the Philippines. The only possible way for Timothy and Bernadette to wed—making her eligible for a US visa—was to have her marriage annulled. But like so many possibilities for happiness in the Philippines, annulments are the province of the rich; thus, pursuing this course of action never even occurred to Bernadette. Eventually, Timothy discovered the loophole himself and insisted on paying for the annulment using his own savings. Bernadette was horrified and refused to let Timothy throw away his money. She had absolutely no sense of her own value, for no one had valued her even a fraction as much as Timothy did.

"What would you give to have Christina back?" he asked her gently.

"Everything," Bernadette whispered, "I would give everything."

"That's what I would give to be with you," he whispered back.

That evening, Bernadette wrote to her cousin Eduardo, the only member of her family with whom she was still in touch, and asked him to contact Pacifico to see if he would agree to the annulment. Eduardo's reply came two weeks later, and in it he explained that an annulment would be unnecessary. Pacifico's most recent girlfriend, a prostitute named Joy who had survived the brutality of the Subic Bay sex trade, took exception to his penchant for beating the woman in his life and sliced off his *boto*. Before saying goodbye to her blubbering ex-boyfriend, Joy called the local medical clinic—she really didn't intend to kill the worthless piece of shit—but Pacifico managed to lock the doors before the doctor arrived and refused to let him into the house. The doctor pleaded with Pacifico, explaining that if he didn't receive medical attention immediately, he would bleed out. Unmoved, Pacifico declared that he'd rather be dead than dickless. Fourteen minutes later he was both.

Bernadette accepted her husband's death as God's will and this time felt no need to question it. She and Timothy were married shortly before his transfer back to the US, which is how Bernadette de los Santos Bonifacio Garcia Reyes became Mrs. Timothy Shelter. After several months of the inevitable visa complications, she joined her husband in the heartland of America.

Things were fine, more or less, once the locals got used to an "oriental" living in their midst. Bernadette was surprised to learn that the Americans she encountered made little distinction among Asians. Chinese, Japanese, Vietnamese, Korean, Filipino—they were all the same to Bernadette's new neighbors. She would actually smile when some of the neighborhood children yelled "Jap" and "Chink" as they sped by on their bicycles. Her obvious amusement seemed to confuse her would-be antagonizers, and before long the name-calling ended.

Her first four years in America constituted the happiest period of Bernadette's life. She was safe. She was married to a man who loved and respected her—a man who never touched her in anger. And although far from rich, Bernadette was no longer poor.

Timothy was diagnosed with pancreatic cancer a week after their fifth wedding anniversary and died three months later. This constituted the saddest period of Bernadette's life. It was worse than the beatings and the rapes and even the death of her child. She had lost the only man she would ever love, the only man who would ever love her, and she knew this with absolute certainty.

Joey and I moved next door to Bernadette about a year ago, and I've managed to piece together her biography over time. It doesn't come out as a single, continuous narrative that follows a chronological sequence. It's more like a series of loosely connected anecdotes, all of which are used to buttress her unflinching belief in the benevolence of her Creator.

"He doesn't sound very benevolent to me," I tell her.

"Oh, Mister Max," she beams, "God loves you too."

This is another reason I have no fondness for the non-existent God. No matter how many horrible things befall humanity, it's never His fault. Of all the holocausts and calamities and disasters and pain and suffering and sorrow that virtually define human life, not one of them can be blamed on God. The nun teaching my second-grade catechism class explained it this way: "It's like God is on top of a tall building. He looks down and sees a car speeding toward an intersection. Then He sees another car on another street speeding toward that same intersection. There's going to be a horrible crash because they'll reach it at the same time. Almighty God sees everything and knows everything that's going to happen, but it's not His fault that the cars crash." My skepticism must have shown, for when I raised my hand to ask for clarification, Sister Mary Shut-the-fuck-up hit me on the head with a ruler. This short-tempered celibate who spent every class period filling our heads with tales of God's omnipotence now expected me to believe He couldn't conjure up a couple of traffic lights?

"Yes, Bernadette can come to your ballet recital."

I check my watch.

Joey's ballet class begins in thirty-three minutes, so she'll be no more than ten minutes late. She hates being late, but it's not a big deal to me. I'm the one paying, so I'll finish my work and email it to Japan before we leave. Unfortunately, I won't have time for a doughnut. Parental sacrifice is endless.

Joey waits patiently as I extricate myself from my piece-of-shit Chevy. It's not much of a car, but at least I can afford it. She takes my hand, and we walk into the shopping mall.

The receptionist at the dance studio frowns at me but smiles at Joey.

"I'll be back in an hour," I say.

"Forty-five minutes," the receptionist says smugly.

I start to retort, but Joey shoots me a look, then disappears into her classroom.

I turn to leave.

"Have a nice day," the receptionist chirps with the sincerity of an extended middle finger.

"It can only get better," I mumble over my shoulder.

I hate shopping malls.

And yet, I don't mind shopping. I mean the activity, not the lifestyle. For me, shopping involves going into a store and buying something. Maybe checking out a couple of different stores if it's a big-ticket item like a desk lamp or a smoke detector. The same way you might shop around for a second opinion if you were diagnosed with rectal cancer.

Without choosing a destination, some inner navigational device guides me to the doughnut shop on the fourth floor. I look over the shiny items on display and order two glazed, a cup of coffee, and a glass of water. I'm not one of those people who like to dunk; a glazed doughnut is perfect in and of itself, and submerging it in coffee compromises that perfection. So I wash my doughnuts down with something neutral, like a glass of water, and then have the coffee for dessert.

My obsession with doughnuts is genetic, by the way. My dad worked in a bakery during high school, and apparently there was an accident one morning as he injected filling into a tray of Bavarian Creams. I don't know if it involved radiation or some other DNA-altering substance, but there was definitely chromosome damage. Thus, he passed on to his progeny a predilection for sugarcoated fried dough. It has yet to express itself in Joey, though I have no doubt it will—probably about the time she becomes concerned with her weight.

I do my best to wipe away the sticky flakes of glaze that surround my mouth, but the waxy napkin bearing the store's logo is useless. I get as much as I can with my tongue and then head back into the mall. As I step off the escalator, I recognize the mother of one of Joey's classmates hurrying toward the studio. She has a significant lead, but if I can get there before her, I won't be the last parent to show up. I increase my pace to a trot and then to a full-on sprint. The door to the fabric shop opens so quickly I only have enough time to get my hands up before making contact. I attempt to flatten myself across the door's surface because if my body is concentrated in too small an area, I'll almost certainly bust through the glass. I hit it with such force that it propels the woman exiting the store several feet before she crashes to the ground. It knocks the wind out of me, but instead of "oomph" or some other innocuous grunt escaping my lungs, I hear myself yell "FUCK!"

I slide away from the door, adjust my glasses, and stumble over to help the fallen woman, noticing, as I do, that the other parent has already reached the ballet studio.

"Fuck!"

I really didn't mean to say it this time either. The woman on the floor takes a swing at me as I lean down to help her, but I'm able to feint back far enough so that she only hits the tip of my nose.

"Fuck!"

Again, involuntary.

"Don't you swear at me, you son of a bitch!" the woman says through gritted dentures. "You're the one who knocked me over!"

"I'm sorry, ma'am. It's just that the door opened so quickly…"

"Oh, so it's my fault, is it?"

"That's not what I mean…"

"You come tearin' down that hall and smash into the door and almost kill me, and you got the gumption to say it's my fault?"

The woman is not young, probably in her late sixties, and she's a bit heavy, though not nearly as overweight as most of the mall-walking, grand-slam-breakfast-eating American public. A crowd is starting to gather, so I decide to do my penance and move on as quickly as possible.

"It was all my fault," I say as sincerely as possible, "and I'm very sorry for any inconvenience I might have caused you."

"Inconvenience?!!!" the woman screams back at me. She says it with such fury that I might as well have called her a cunt. I'm now certain that any words of apology I offer will be taken in the same spirit, so without speaking I try to help her to her feet.

"You get your goddamn paws offa me!"

I feel a hand on my shoulder. An elderly man with a kind face squats down. A retired sociology professor perhaps, or a man of the cloth. Definitely someone who will help me calm this psychotic.

"Sir," he says in a voice reserved for the learning disabled, "don't you think you've caused this woman enough distress?"

I hate these trick questions. If I say *yes*, I admit I've been an asshole. If I say *no*, it implies that I haven't yet finished being an asshole. Eddie Granger used to do the same thing. Eddie had the distinctive honor of being both the meanest and the ugliest kid in my high school. Perhaps there was a correlation. He would single out someone small and weak and then shove his victim up against a wall and demand, "Have you ever sucked a sweeter peter than mine?" Back in those days, *peter* was one of the many synonyms for the dangling male appendage. Perhaps it still is. I'm not sure why Eddie opted for this particular one, for there were certainly more colorful and aggressive terms at his disposal. Cock. Prick. Dick. Schlong. Tool. Pecker. But he chose *peter*. I can only assume he was charmed by the fact that it rhymed with the adjective preceding it. In any case, the question had no safe answer. *Yes* meant that you had performed fellatio not only on Eddie but also on any number of other individuals, some of whose peters you found to be sweeter than his. If you answered *no*, it could be inferred that of the many peters you had sucked, Eddie's was indeed the sweetest. Most kids said *no* without considering the implications of their answer. This made Eddie happy, and he usually let them go with no more than a slap to the back of their heads. I, on the other hand, attempted to explain the unfairness of his inquiry. Eddie patiently heard me out and then kicked me in the balls.

The sociologist is now holding the fallen woman's hand, and they are gazing at each other as if caught up in some sort of geriatric foreplay. It's my chance to slip away unnoticed.

Joey is sitting alone on an upholstered bench in the reception area of the dance studio. Her face lights up when she sees me, which makes me feel like I've opened a package addressed to someone else. I get the expected judgmental glare from the receptionist, who magically appears just as I'm about to hurry Joey out the door. Her face is transformed by a warm smile as she bends to give Joey a hug.

"I hope you know how special your daughter is," she says, looking me in the eye.

I hold her gaze.

"I would have been here sooner, but I had to help a woman who fell and was seriously hurt. The paramedics told me I probably saved her life."

The receptionist is taken aback, and I can see that she is having second thoughts about judging me so harshly. Joey, however, isn't buying it. Although she believes everything I tell her, she's learned to doubt the things I say to others. She takes my hand and pulls me out the door.

"You want to get a doughnut?"

"Can we just go home?" she says flatly.

We walk to the elevators instead of the escalator because I have no desire to cross paths with the woman I upended. Joey runs ahead and pushes the down button. As we wait for the elevator to arrive, she looks up at me and says, "You shouldn't tell lies."

I start to explain that it wasn't a complete lie, but when I see how earnest she is, I nod my head and say, "I know. I'm sorry."

She smiles and takes my hand. A few seconds later the doors open and we step inside. Joey pushes the ground-floor button, and for a moment nothing happens. Then the doors slide shut and we begin our inevitable descent.

2

God's Face

When I think of God, I picture a very fat Japanese man with Down syndrome. Coincidentally, I lived in Japan for three years, working at one of the biggest advertising agencies on the planet. I still do the occasional job for them, though I now work from my home office in Illinois—if a six-year-old iMac on an Ikea particleboard table constitutes an office.

I'm a copywriter, which is to say I'm responsible for coming up with words for the ads and commercials that define our civilization. Within the industry it's considered a creative job, though it involves more copying than writing. Copywriters take from other ads, taglines, slogans, songs, movies, TV shows, poetry, prose—making minor changes in order to claim originality—hoping to bamboozle clients into thinking we've found the mystical combination of syllables that will compel consumers to acquire the new and improved version of their pointlessly redundant products.

Several years ago, just prior to my stint in Japan, I arrived at work in central New Jersey, and Angelica, my Italian-American officemate, was performing her morning ritual: reading the help-wanted section of the *New York Times*. An otherwise talented copywriter, Angelica is cursed with a terrible flaw: she is driven. Being idle made her crazy, so I knew she wasn't searching for a position that would offer more flexible hours or a lighter workload or a higher salary. Angelica was desperately seeking a greater challenge. I, on the other hand, am not driven. I lived for the days we didn't have any work and was often able to convince myself there was nothing to do despite an overflowing inbox.

"Here's one that's perfect for you," she said as I slid into my chair.

"Perfect what?"

"Perfect job, you moron."

"I'm not looking for a job."

"I didn't say you were looking for a job. I said it was perfect for you."

"What is it?"

"What do you care? You're not looking for a job."

I swivel to face her.

"What's it say?"

She holds my eye for a moment then looks at the paper and reads, "Wanted: copywriter. Must be willing to travel internationally."

It *was* perfect for me. Because what I love even more than not working is not working while traveling internationally.

After I promised to pay for lunch, she gave me the phone number.

The guy who answered sounded like he was speaking in slow motion. It wasn't just the deep, mournful voice; his words seemed to go on forever.

"Helllooooo?"

"Hello, I'm calling about the copywriting job advertised in the *Times*."

"Dooo yoou haavve aanneee chiiiilllddrrrenn?"

"What?"

"Doo yoou haavve…"

"No. No kids."

"Aaarre yooou maarrrrreeed?

"Married? No. I mean, well, I have a girlfriend."

"Aaaaahhhhh."

"Is that a problem?"

"Weelllll…"

"I can dump her if it's a problem."

"Weelllll…"

"Really, it's not working out anyway."

I noticed a flutter of motion in my peripheral vision and glanced up to see Angelica giving me the finger.

"Iitt's beeettter iifff theee caandiiddaate iissn'tt ohhvverrlee enncummberrrd byyy perrrsonalll reellaashuunsshiiipps."

"I'm not! Jesus. I'm totally unencumbered. Totally. I'm… cumberless."

"Thaaat's aaa gooodd oonne, haaaaaaaaaa haaaaaaaaaa."

"Uh, can I ask what kind of job this is? I mean, you guys usually want to know about qualifications."

"Theee suuucseessfuulll caanndiidaate wiill beee reeequiiirred tooo reelowcaaatte tooo Jaaappaaann."

Japan?

Fuckin' A!

Shit! Did I say that out loud?

No response.

"I see," I said calmly. "What's the company?"

He said some Japanese-sounding name and probably expected me to be familiar with it, but knowing nothing about Japan other than what I'd seen in war movies and the display cases of electronics stores, I fell back on stereotypes and assumed they manufactured cameras or some miniature device that was improved—but not invented—by their spectacle-wearing staff of loyal-to-the-death engineers.

"Oh, they're a great organization," I blathered, "Truly excellent."

"Theeyyy neeeed uuhh coppiiwrriittterrr."

"Well, I'm a copywriter, and Japan is my favorite country."

I considered modifying that last statement, because if my interviewer was the patriotic sort, he might be offended by the fact that I hadn't said "second favorite."

"Aarrr uuuu iiiinnterrrreesstted?"

Fuckin' A!

"Yes sir, I am interested."

He gave me a number and told me to fax my résumé. Just before hanging up, I thought to ask his name.

"Jooosefff Mmowwshuunn."

Joe Motion.

Jesus.

I hung up the phone and looked across my desk. Angelica was staring sadly at me.

"You're going to Japan."

"No way," I replied. "Do you know how hard those people work?"

Just before lunch I faxed over my résumé, an inspired work of fiction laced with just enough truth to provide plausible deniability should the story of my success be called into question. Two hours later he phoned and informed me that I had an interview scheduled for Thursday afternoon at the Essex Hotel in Manhattan. I'd be meeting with the head of the Overseas Creative Department, a Japanese man who was, he promised, fluent in English. In the meantime, I was to send him my portfolio.

I told Angelica that I'd be calling in sick the day after tomorrow, and she reminded me that I was required to attend an important presentation in the morning.

"I don't want to miss the interview," I whined.

"What time is your interview?"

"At four-thirty."

"In the afternoon?"

"No, four-thirty in the morning. The Japanese are early risers."

"You are such an asshole. Just take the afternoon off."

"Hey, that's a good idea."

"It's not an idea. It's common sense."

The next day I spoke to my supervisor, a former nun named Margaret, and arranged to take leave the following afternoon.

"Where are you going to?" she asked.

I felt an immediate surge of anger. It wasn't her nosiness that irritated me. It was the fact that she'd ended her sentence with a preposition. It annoys me when people do this, particularly if they employ the completely unnecessary prepositions that do nothing but add to the word count, thereby extending the amount of time I have to spend listening to their shitty English. Perhaps I'm being a bit severe, but why couldn't she have just said, "Where are you going?" Did she really believe it wouldn't make sense without that extra syllable?

"Where are you going?"

"I'm sorry, Margaret. I don't understand your question."

"I mean, 'Where are you going to?'"

"Ahh!"

I am far more forgiving (not that anyone asks for my forgiveness) when the terminal preposition, however misplaced, is at least useful. For example, "Where are you from?" wouldn't mean the same thing if the preposition were omitted. The same is true with "What is it for?" Of course, these sentences could be rearranged or reworded so that they follow the acceptable rules of grammar, but I digress.

"Where are you going to?" Margaret asked.

"Japan," I replied.

"You know, you don't always have to be such a smart aleck. It's the sign of an insecure personality." Then she gave me one of those smiles that suggests, *I'm only saying this because I care about you*. I gave her a nod in return, the one that says, *I acknowledge your concern and will rein in my sarcasm*.

"I have an appointment with a proctologist in New York for a full rectal screening."

Margaret waited several seconds before responding, looking for some indication that I was once again exercising my insecure personality.

"I'll have to clear it with William," she finally said, referring to her own boss, a short, strangely introverted man who collected guns and never washed his hands after using the toilet.

"So?" Angelica asked when I returned to our office.

"Margaret's going to check with William, but it shouldn't be a problem."

"See? Common sense."

An hour later the phone rang. It was Joe Motion, calling with more information about the interview. After seven mind-numbing minutes, he said he'd meet me in the lobby of the Essex at four-fifteen. Just before hanging up I asked, "How will I know you?"

"I'lll bee thuuh sixxx-ffffoottt, sixxx-iiinnchh peaarrr-shhaaaapped mmaaann."

I was unable to acknowledge his description. Several seconds of silence followed.

"Imm haarrrddd tooo mmmiiiisss."

"Alrighty then," I said in the perky voice used by waitresses who've just been insulted by a bitchy customer but are still angling for a tip, "we'll see you tomorrow."

"Who's we?" Angelica demanded after I hung up the phone.

"What?"

"You said 'we'll see you.'"

"It's just an expression."

"Oh, you mean you're so fucking amazing that a singular pronoun won't cut it? You need we to capture all your greatness?"

"What the fuck are you talking about?"

"Never mind. What time are you leaving tomorrow?"

"I'm not even sure if I'm going."

"What? You get the afternoon off and now you're not going?"

"The guy told me he's six and a half feet tall and shaped like a pear!"

"So?"

"So what the hell is that? I don't know anything about this guy. It could be some kind of scam."

"Because he's pear shaped?"

"It could be a thing."

She rolled her eyes and made a rude gesture indicating that I should continue.

"He told me that after they finish in New York they're interviewing in Chicago. Jesus, I'm up against copywriters from New York and Chicago, and I can barely cut it in New Jersey. There's no way in hell I'm getting that job."

"Then it's perfect, you fuckhead," Angelica said excitedly.

"What do you mean?"

"You've got nothing to lose. You go to the interview knowing you aren't going to get the job, so you don't give a shit. It'll be fun. They might even have a sushi tray."

"I've never had sushi."

"Then it'll be a new experience for you."

"What if I don't like it?"

"Spit it into a napkin."

"I can't do that during an interview."

"But you're not going to get the job anyway! And when the interview's over, you can hang out in the city. Maybe get yourself a Rolex."

Angelica was right. The opportunity to hang out in New York on a weekday afternoon was reason enough to go through with the interview. In my hometown, the highest manmade structure was the Lacy brothers' tree house, and it was barely tall enough to cause serious damage to a falling body. Jeremy, the elder of the Lacy twins, fell out and only suffered a broken elbow when he hit the ground. (There might have been some incidental brain damage, but where I grew up that sort of thing was difficult to diagnose.) Thus, any building rising more than a few stories remains impressive to me. This made visiting Manhattan not unlike stepping into a science fiction movie. I am in awe from the moment I exit the Holland Tunnel to the moment I reenter its bowel-like embrace and am excreted back into New Jersey. A real New Yorker (or anyone pretending to be a real New Yorker) would never have walked down the street as I did, head swiveling back and forth, completely mesmerized by everything from the Flatiron Building to the man without pants arguing with a pizza. It's especially entertaining when tourists attempt to minimize their status as outsiders by feigning street smarts. In Battery Park I once overheard a conversation between a chubby Caucasian-American and a grim-faced Nigerian watch vendor. The Nigerian was carrying his merchandise in a briefcase that he could flip open and use as a display. Chubby was standing before the proffered case, fondling a garish timepiece. After several moments of thoughtful deliberation he proclaimed, "This isn't a real Rolex."

The salesman rolled his eyes.

"It's eight fuckin' dollars, mon," he snorted, "of course it's not a real fuckin' Rolex."

Chubby dropped the watch and made a beeline for one of those machines that, for a dollar, will flatten a penny while embossing it with an image of the Statue of Liberty. As the Nigerian closed his case, he noticed me observing. I gave him an insider's nod, the universal sign of *I'm with you, brother*. In fact, we were kindred spirits, this ebony stranger and I. Like him, I was forced to suffer through a world full of dipshits and tourists and bad grammar. Then it occurred to me: maybe I'd been too hard on myself. Maybe I have a little New Yorker in me after all.

"You wanna buy a Rolex?" he asked.

I shook my head. (They aren't real, you know.)

"Then fuck off."

"So you'll go to the interview?" Angelica presses.

"Like you said, I've got nothing to lose."

Eight months later, I was walking through Shinjiku, one of Tokyo's most ridiculously overcrowded and hyper-frenetic wards, completely mesmerized by everything from the fresh-faced prostitutes of Kabukicho to the glass-eyed gazes of pachinko-parlor patrons. After half a year in the Land of the Rising Sun, I was still as excited and overwhelmed as I was when I first stepped off the plane. Japan, and Tokyo in particular, plays full-tilt boogie with every one of your senses, and a few others you might not even know you have.

People were everywhere, endless thousands of them, some rushing, some lingering, some shopping, some searching, and some, like me, surrendering to the incessant flow of the crowd as it moved along its unpredictable path.

And then I saw her.

An old Japanese woman, nondescript as old Japanese women go, with nothing about the way she looked or the way she was dressed or the way she was behaving that would make her stand out from the crowd.

And yet I saw her.

Father O'Connor, the parish priest of my childhood, once gave a sermon that managed to keep me from sleeping. He spoke of the time Jesus—along with the twelve handsomely bearded men—was making his way through a frenzied crowd that was anxious to see some indication he was the son of You-Know-Who. All at once Jesus stopped and demanded, "Who touched me?"

The apostles and everyone else within earshot found this question rather odd, since Jesus was being touched, patted, grabbed, fondled, and high-fived by everyone he passed.

"Someone touched me," Jesus insisted.

A woman stepped forward and said, "It was me, Lord."

And Jesus replied, "You mean, 'It was I.'"

She looked at him blankly. Jesus continued, "When a pronoun follows a linking verb, it should be in the nominative case." (I've always assumed the Son of God would be a stickler for grammar.) What Jesus actually said—or what the English translation of the Latin translation of the Greek translation of the Hebrew translation of the Bible maintains he said—was "Daughter, your faith has healed you." Evidently, the woman had been suffering from some medical condition that involved incessant hemorrhaging, but the moment she touched the hem of his garment, she was cured.

I'm getting to the point now.

Out of all the hands that touched him, Jesus felt that woman's. He felt the one that was special. He felt the hand of faith. Now, I'm not making any claim to divinity, but this parable does a pretty fair job of describing what happened to me that afternoon in Shinjuku two millennia later. Think about it: of the thousands and thousands of human beings surrounding me—including a significant number of young women wearing school-girl outfits, a staple of the Japanese porno industry—it was an all-but-invisible old woman who held my attention.

She was standing at a small kiosk, talking to the man behind the counter. After several moments, the man turned and disappeared from my view, but the woman remained, waiting patiently. As I studied her, I discerned an expression of anticipation on her face and a kind of reverent stillness in her posture. It reminded me of my days as an altar boy, of the people kneeling at the communion rail, waiting for the body of Christ to be placed on their tongues.

When the kiosk man returned, he was holding something just out of my view, but the old woman saw it and her face lit up so intensely it seemed to glow. She gave a slight nod and then slowly reached out her hands. What could he possibly be selling her to elicit such awe, I wondered. Some ancient Buddhist artifact? A relic from the divine emperor? She passed the man some money then pulled her hand into view. I felt myself smile. Her purchase had nothing to do with cultural icons. She was holding an ice cream cone. It was a double scoop, chocolate and vanilla, and I waited for her tongue to appear, just as I had anticipated the tongues of communicants when I held the paten beneath their chins. But the old woman did not lick the ice cream. Instead she slowly turned, her face still aglow, and extended her arm.

A massive man came into view. He was over six feet tall and had the build of a sumo wrestler. He leaned forward to take the cone from his mother—his hand incongruously small, his fingers short and stubby—and that's when I got a clear look at his face. He was Japanese, of course, but something else was apparent: he had ended up with an additional twenty-first chromosome. This giant of a man had Down syndrome.

A photograph taken by W. Eugene Smith flashed to the front of my mind. Smith was the brilliant photographer who documented the horrific effects of the poisoning of Japan's Minamata Bay. The tragedy occurred at the hands of the Chisso Corporation, a greed-soaked entity that had been dumping tons of mercury compounds into Minamata Bay since 1925. The soulless pricks in charge were immediately aware they were wreaking havoc with the environment, for the thousands of dead fish made it impossible to pretend otherwise. But like most right-thinking corporate douchebags, rather than end the deadly practice, they paid off the fishermen. Before long, people began to notice that cats hanging around the docks for fish scraps were dancing for their meals. It was a *danse macabre*—seizures that preceded their inevitable deaths. Soon, the people of Minamata began to recognize such symptoms among themselves. Slurred speech. Numbness in the limbs. Constricted vision. Seizures. Brain damage. Insanity. Paralysis. Coma. Death. The wonders of mercury poisoning. And all in a day's work for the fine men of the Chisso Corporation. Oh, they did make changes once they were no longer able to contain the fallout: they stopped dumping into Minamata Bay and started dumping into the Minamata River. In fact, the

Chisso Corporation didn't refrain from poisoning the waters of Minamata until 1968, and even then it was only because their method of production had become outdated.

Smith's photograph shows Ryoko Uemura holding her sixteen-year-old daughter, Tomoko, in a Japanese bath. Tomoko is naked in the photo, her severely deformed body a heartrending reminder of the human cost of insatiable corporate greed. But despite the tragic nature of the image, it is utterly transcendent. The look on Ryoko's face as she gazes down at her helpless daughter is a sublime expression of love, and it defines, at least for me, the very essence of motherhood.

It was this expression—this glow—that I observed on the old woman's face as she handed the chocolate-vanilla ice cream cone to her gargantuan offspring. Her little boy.

And yet, it was what I saw in the son's face that caused me to rethink, if only temporarily, my conclusion that we were alone in the universe. Never before had I beheld such absolute joy. Such total contentment. Such infinite love. In fact, what radiated from his countenance was so powerful I almost looked away. But I managed to keep my eyes fixed on that exquisitely overweight son, watching as he drew the ice cream cone closer and closer to his mouth. To the tongue that protruded ever so slightly from between his thick, half-parted lips. Watching as his rapture intensified. And suddenly I understood: if God had a face, it would look like this.

3
Baptized

My mother was Irish Catholic and my father a Bulgarian convert. This is not a particularly good combination for a child who viewed Father, Son, and Holy Ghost in the same light as Sandman, Tooth Fairy, and Santa Claus. Both parents were extremely devout and ensured that my sister and I were too—that we attended Mass every Sunday, never ate meat on Friday, and always felt superior to non-Catholics. Yet, despite their abiding faith in God, they seldom spoke of Him; Jesus came up quite a bit, as did the Virgin and a few of the more popular saints, but the Supreme Being remained a shadowy background figure. It wasn't until I started attending catechism class that God came into focus. Catechism is the Catholic version of Sunday school, though it can take place any day of the week. For me, it was Monday, a full hour of after-school religious instruction from a squishy, red-faced celibate named Sister Mary Cherry. Like most nuns in teaching positions, she was in a foul mood whenever children were present, though she did bring God out of the shadows. "There is no end to His love for you," she proclaimed to the class. "It is infinite. Eternal. It goes on and on and on and then keeps on going. He loves you a million times more than your mommy and daddy." Her unsettling demeanor notwithstanding, I was impressed. This God fellow, He seemed like a pretty good guy.

Then she dropped the other shoe.

God would damn us to hell if we missed Mass on Sunday, lied to our parents, showed disrespect to a nun, or went to a movie condemned by the Catholic Legion of Decency. These and countless other mundane offenses—mortal sins, all—would ensure that we spent eternity burning in the fires of hell. And then she made a startling revelation: the fire in hell is black. It is darker than the darkest night, for God would allow no illumination to ease the suffering of the damned.

The class went quiet, stunned. Sister Mary Cherry smiled, her face glowing with satisfaction as it always did when she frightened children. But I wasn't frightened. I was too fascinated by the concept of black fire. It sounded like something from a comic book, something an evil genius would come up with to destroy Captain America. I began to see God in a new light.

"You have something to say, boy?" the nun snapped.

I looked up. Sister Mary Cherry was glaring at me.

"Uhhh," I struggled to think of something, "so God hates us too?"

She jumped back as if I'd spat at her. Quickly recovering, she reached across three rows of first graders and slapped me in the face. Her own face, tightly framed by her wimple, was so contorted by rage she looked like a cartoon character. Grasping my right ear, she pulled me to my feet.

"Class, pray silently until I'm back!" she hissed.

"I'm sorry! I'm sorry!" I pleaded as she dragged me down the hall, though I had no idea what I'd done to make her so angry.

"You will die and go to hell, you ungrateful little heathen!" she seethed. "And you'll never see your mommy or daddy or brothers or sisters or friends or anyone else because you'll be burning in the black fire for all time."

"I don't have a brother," I corrected.

"Shut your heathen mouth!"

When we reached the base of the stairs, she stopped to adjust her grip, and in that moment of calm, I was emboldened.

"Sister Mary Cherry?" I asked.

"What?!"

"How do they make the fire black?"

I saw hesitation in her eyes: indeed, how do they make it black?

The door to Father O'Connor's living quarters was open. He was sitting in the living room watching a nature documentary. Rather than ring the doorbell, my captor called out his name in a singsong voice.

"What is it?" the priest demanded without turning away from the duck-billed platypus swimming across his screen.

"Father, it's Sister Mary Cherry," she said and let go of my ear.

Father O'Connor turned and saw the two of us standing on the doorstep. Sister Mary Cherry actually blushed.

"My goodness, is that the Androv boy?" he lilted. He did not acknowledge the nun.

Seemingly unaware of the slight, Sister Mary Cherry nodded and said, "He told me that God hates us."

"Oh no!" the priest gasped in mock horror as he stood and ushered us into his expensive-looking living room. "Do you really believe that, young man?"

I knew enough to keep my mouth shut.

The priest squatted down so we were eye to eye.

"God is our creator. Our Heavenly Father. He loves us. And His love is infinite," he chirped.

"That's what I told him!" the nun blurted out.

The priest shot her a look. She retreated a step. He turned back to me, clearly expecting a response.

"Okay?" I said timidly.

"Okay, what?" he persisted.

I hesitated.

"God is our creator. Our Heavenly Father. He loves us. And His love is infinite."

The priest looked at me blankly for several seconds. Every kid knows this expression. It's worn when an adult is deciding whether to smack you for being a smartass or to pat you on the head for being a good learner. Eventually his eyes refocused, and he reached out and tousled my hair.

"That's right, Androv."

I relaxed.

"That's not what he said in my class, Father," the nun pleaded. "He said God hates us."

"Why would you think God hates us, Androv? Our loving Father who sent down His only son to die for our sins?"

Behind the priest, Sister Mary Cherry was grinning like a hyena.

"The...the black fire." I stammered.

"The black…?" Again, he shot a look at Sister Mary Cherry. "Oh, I see. You wonder how a loving God could punish the wicked in the fires of hell."

I nodded, thinking it was the right thing to do.

"Well, that's only for bad boys and girls," he replied as if this explained everything.

I nodded again.

"And you're going to be a good boy, right?"

A third nod.

He continued to stare at me, and I realized that this time a non-verbal response would not suffice.

"Yes," I said softly.

"Yes what?!" the nun barked, infuriated that I was wriggling out of the predicament.

The priest's eyes never left mine.

I was confused for a moment.

"Yes, *Father*," I ventured.

"Good," he smiled.

Rising, he turned toward the nun. "There you are, Sister."

"Oh, thank you, Father," she gushed, as if he'd just bought her a new pair of shoes.

She hurried over and I flinched, assuming she was going to grab my ear. She acted surprised at my fear, then gently placed her hand on my back and scooted me forward. Father O'Connor gave a little half-circle wave, the kind favored by Middle Eastern dictators, then hurried back to the platypus. As soon as we were out the door, the nun cuffed me on the back of my head and said, "You're not fooling me, you little heathen."

Though she often called me a heathen, I didn't know what it meant. Something bad, obviously, but I wondered how bad. As if sensing my curiosity, Sister Mary Cherry smiled and said, "God hates heathens."

"God loves me," Joey declares as she jumps onto my bed, desecrating my Sunday-morning slumber.

"Joey, I'm trying to sleep," I say without opening my eyes.

"God loves you, too."

"That's unlikely."

"He does. *Ate* Bernadette told me."

I pull the covers over my head and wait for her to go away. It's a ploy that usually works, but on this morning she tugs them down and proclaims, "God loves everybody."

"Not if you're a heathen."

"What's a heathen?"

"Someone who wants to go back to sleep."

"That's silly. God doesn't care if you sleep."

"He does if you're sleeping instead of going to Mass."

"What's Mass?"

"Church."

"But we never go to church."

"That's why I'm a heathen."

"Am I a heathen too?"

"It's too early to tell."

"I don't go to church."

"You don't have to. You're not baptized."

"What's baptized?"

"Jesus, Joey, are you gonna let me sleep or not?"

"Is it like hypnotized?" she asks suspiciously.

Joey is currently fascinated with hypnosis. Several times a day she'll dangle some trinket in front of my eyes and chant, "Your eyes are getting heavy. You're going into a deep, deep sleep." Then she'll turn me into a dog or a cat or a chicken and I have to make the appropriate animal noises. She finds this terribly amusing, and since it requires minimal effort on my part, I generally go along with it. Unless I have something better to do. Like sleep.

"It's nothing like hypnotism."

"What's it like then?"

"You're four years old. You're not supposed to know all the answers yet. Now leave me alone."

"But Daaaadddeeeee…"

The image of a six-foot-six-inch pear-shaped man floats into my head.

"Baptism is the sacrament that washes away original sin."

"What's original sin?"

"C'mon, Joey, I wanna sleep!"

"What's original sin?"

"It's the sin we're all born with because Eve couldn't keep her hands off the apple God told her not to touch. And you can't get rid of it until you're baptized."

"You mean I have an original sin on me?"

"It's not…"

"I want baptism!"

"It's not even real. Original sin is just some myth the Catholics made up so people would join their church and give them all their money so the pope could afford big hats."

"I don't want original sin on me!"

"You don't have any sin on you! Except the one for not letting me go back to sleep!"

"Are you baptismed?"

"Baptized. Jesus, Joey, you sound like a hillbilly. Yeah, I'm baptized, but that happened when I was a week old. My parents didn't give me a choice."

"Is *Ate* Bernadette baptized?"

"Probably."

"Then I wanna be baptized, too. I don't want an original sin on me."

"It doesn't even exist!"

"I wanna be baptized!"

"I'm not gonna..."

She starts crying.

I am unmoved. Kids cry when they don't get their way. It's no big deal. But Joey has incredible stamina when it comes to shedding tears, and I want to go back to sleep.

"Okay, you can be baptized!"

"Yay!!!"

"Now, beat it."

"Okay, Daddy," she says brightly, kissing me on the cheek.

I listen to her pad across the floor but don't relax until I hear the door click shut.

When I wake up a few hours later, Bernadette is in my kitchen washing dishes. She often comes over on Sunday mornings after returning from Mass. Joey talks to her over the fence, and then Bernadette volunteers to straighten up the house and make breakfast. This morning she made Joey banana pancakes, her

36   •   MARC X GRIGOROFF

favorite. Me, I hate them. Why ruin a perfectly good pancake with mushy fruit? I sit down at the little dining table, and Bernadette puts a cup of hot black coffee in front of me.

"You want banana pancakes, Mr. Max?" she asks sweetly.

"As long as you hold the bananas."

"I'm sorry, Mr. Max, I don't understand."

"Yes, I want banana pancakes, but hold the bananas."

"You want me to hold the bananas?"

"I want you to hold 'em between your knees," I sneer in a shitty Jack Nicholson imitation.

She looks at me apologetically, assuming she is being obtuse.

"Sorry, Bernadette. I was paraphrasing a line from an old movie."

She looks even more confused.

"Never mind. I just want some plain pancakes. I don't like bananas."

"Oh, so sorry, Mr. Max," she says sadly, "bananas already in the batter. Joey loves bananas so I think you love them too."

"It must have skipped a generation."

She looks as if she's about to cry.

"It's fine. I'll just have a doughnut."

I start to rise but then remember I'd eaten the last Krispy Kreme before going to bed.

"Dammit. I guess I'll just have some eggs and bacon."

"I make for you!" Bernadette exclaims, and I know she sees this as a form of penance, a way of atoning for not anticipating my dislike of bananas.

"Great."

I take a sip of coffee. It's not bad, though a little strong for my liking. If you take your coffee black, as I do, it doesn't have to be particularly strong to be flavorful. The thing is, I actually like the taste of American coffee. A cup a joe. The kind you get in an old-fashioned diner. Or a red-blooded truck stop. You walk in with an empty quart-sized thermos and walk out with a full one. Now you're set for the next three hours or two hundred miles or as long your bladder holds out.

"I'm sorry the coffee is so weak," Bernadette apologizes.

She cracks a couple of eggs, and a moment later I hear them sizzling in the pan.

"Make the eggs over easy," I tell her.

Bernadette spins around, a deer-in-the-headlights expression on her face.

"Over easy?"

"Relax, Bernadette. Just cook them a little on one side, then flip them over for a second and they're done. But don't break the yolk."

A smile lights up her face. "Ballcaino eggs!"

I have no idea what she's talking about.

"That's what Joey calls them," she explains. "Ballcaino eggs. Like Mount Pinatubo. Because when you push the fork down they squirt out like a ballcaino."

"Yeah, that's it, ballcaino eggs."

She turns back to the stove, and soon I hear the music of frying bacon. God, how I love that song.

"Mr. Max," Bernadette says, interrupting the musical interlude, "I think it's wonderful what you gonna do for Joey."

Again, I have no idea what she's talking about.

"Joey's baptism!" she declares, grinning at me like I'm Father of the Year.

Oh fuck.

"Baptism?"

"I think it's wonderful! You making her so happy. And you making me so happy, too!"

I wonder how happy they'll be when I tell them I have no intention of letting Joey get baptized, that I only said she could because I wanted to go back to sleep.

"She might have misunderstood what I said."

"Oh no, Mr. Max, she very sure what you said," Bernadette beams. "I tell her this is so wonderful because now she won't have to go to leembo."

"Go where?"

"Leembo."

Leembo?

Limbo?

I vaguely remember hearing about limbo in some theological context, but it's been replaced by the disturbing image of overstuffed people on cruise ships trying to squeeze themselves under a bamboo pole.

"The place where you go when you die if you're not baptized."

Ah, yes. Not good enough for heaven, not bad enough for hell. So you're sentenced to limbo, land of eternal boredom.

"You told Joey that she'd go to limbo if she wasn't baptized?"

"But I only said it after you tell her she gonna be baptized," Bernadette responds happily.

Before I can point out the fault in her logic, she places the ballcaino eggs and two strips of still-sizzling bacon in front of me. The aroma is so intoxicating it almost lifts me out of my chair. Thoughts of limbo and baptism are relegated to a less active region of my cerebral cortex. A few moments later she completes the meal with two diagonally cut pieces of buttered toast. I grab one of the triangles and use it to sop up the yolk from the ballcainos, then swallow it in two bites. I see Bernadette observing me. Loretta, a former girlfriend, used to watch me this way. As if she were witnessing a feeding frenzy at the zoo.

"You don't eat your food, you inhale it," she declared.

Loretta was a dainty eater, tiny bites and with long intervals in between, but she managed to tolerate my gusto. Until the night we passed a bakery on the way home from a movie. It was an old, family-style business, and the smells wafting down the sidewalk were as tangible as the appendage-like representations in old cartoon shows, irresistible fingers of aroma that beckoned Tom or Jerry toward some dangerous delight. I pressed my face to the front window and beheld a cornucopia of pastries, lovingly made by hand, including some of the most seductive doughnuts I'd ever seen.

"Can we stop here for a quick dessert?" I pleaded.

Loretta seemed perplexed but nodded her assent.

I ordered a half-dozen glazed and a bottle of water. She asked for a chamomile tea. I offered her one of the doughnuts, and when she declined I was quietly pleased.

It took me less than five minutes to ingest all six, and when I lifted my head she was staring at me the way people who've never lived with a cat stare at a hairball.

"Six doughnuts in five minutes?" she demanded.

"Yeah, but there's that big hole in the middle," I offered in my defense.

Loretta rose from the table and moved toward the door. I knew better than to follow.

"Could I get a dozen to go?" I asked the baker as the door swung shut.

He nodded and with his tongs carefully procured twelve doughnuts and expertly arranged them in a white paper sack. Placing the sack on the counter, the baker glanced toward the door and then back at me. He seemed to understand that I'd made a choice.

"It's genetic," I said.

He nodded sympathetically, then reached into the case, took out an additional doughnut, and placed it amongst its twelve brethren. A baker's dozen. I walked out the door and quickly headed back to my place, the weight of the bag reassuring me that I wasn't really alone.

"Are the eggs okay?" Bernadette asks nervously.

So she isn't being judgmental after all. She just wants to be sure I'm pleased with the breakfast.

"Mmm," I nod.

She smiles. "I make you more?"

"No, I'm good."

Joey explodes into the room.

"Daddy, we have to go to the mall!" she cries breathlessly.

"Why do we have to go to the mall?"

"To get my baptism dress!"

She hasn't been this overtly happy in a long time, and I hate to put a damper on it, but I am not about to sell her soul to the Catholic Church.

"Joey..." I begin. Her face falls. A single word and she understands I'm going to disappoint her. But before I can confirm it, Bernadette chimes in.

"I buy it for her. I buy the dress."

"Bernadette..."

"Please. I want to buy Joey her baptism dress. My Christina went away before I could get her baptized. This is something I never forget, and I never forgive myself for. Please let me buy the dress for Joey."

No wonder she's so excited about Joey being baptized. The poor woman has been carrying around a load of pointless guilt for more than half her life, and now she has an opportunity to atone.

No.

That isn't it.

Bernadette wouldn't see Joey's baptism as an act of atonement. To her, it's an act of love. She's excited for Joey, but she's also excited for me, excited that I'll never know the pain of a losing a child to limbo. Joey leaps into her arms and hugs her with the ferocious intensity children generally reserve for their mothers.

"Thank you, *Ate*! Thank you, thank you, thank you!"

"No, no! Don't thank me!" Bernadette exclaims. "It's your daddy you must thank. He's the one who letting you get baptized."

Bernadette lowers her to the floor, and then Joey scampers into my lap and covers my face with kisses.

"Jesus, Joey, I'm trying to eat!"

"I love you, Daddy! Thank you for letting me get baptized!"

As Joey continues to express her gratitude, I look up and see that Bernadette has tears in her eyes. Is there no stopping this train?

I play my last card.

"Joey, if you get baptized you'll have to get up every Sunday morning and go to church and miss all your cartoons. No exceptions. You can't change your mind. For the rest of your life. You won't have to worry about going to limbo any more. Now you have to worry about going to..."

"I take her with me, Mr. Max! You don't even have to get out of bed!"

"Yes, I want to go to church with *Ate*!"

The room falls silent. I look at my daughter's face. And then my neighbor's. They wear identical expressions of joyful anticipation that, I'm quite certain, many would find heartwarming. I quell an impulse to smack them both with a banana pancake.

"Can I get some more coffee?"

Joey and Bernadette exchange a puzzled look.

Bernadette takes the carafe from the warmer and pours me a fresh cup. I rise from the table, grab the cup, and walk back toward my bedroom.

"Daddy?" Joey calls after me.

I turn back just as I step into the room.

"I thought you two were going to the mall," I say and then shut the door before they can respond.

It takes a few moments for them to understand my capitulation. Once they do, I hear them jumping up and down, thrilled beyond reason that Joey will receive her first sacrament. I don't want any part of their celebration. I'm not being a good parent. I'm being selfish. This is my way of ensuring I can sleep in on Sunday mornings. But Joey, she's going to become a Roman Catholic. She will be subject to the endless rules, regulations, prohibitions, threats, declarations, fabrications, denials, hypocrisies, idiosyncrasies, and other whimsical mandates of an endless parade of pompous male celibates. No, I'm not in any mood for celebration, because I know one thing with absolute certainty: sooner or later, Joey is going to miss her original sin.

Bernadette asks if I want her to come along when I meet with the priest, Father John Franklin, or "Father John" as he liked to be called. I give her an appreciative nod but make it clear that her presence is not required. To Bernadette, Father John is a man of God, a saintly figure who shepherds his flock toward the gates of heaven. To me, he's just some single, middle-aged guy who doesn't date.

I leave Joey in her care and drive the few blocks to St. James Catholic Church, the Chevy coughing and wheezing like a two-pack-a-day asthmatic. The parish parking lot is almost deserted, but I pull into the space with RESERVED boldly painted between the yellow lines. The car continues to gasp and sputter long after I pull the key from the ignition. I'm halfway up the stairs to the rectory before it makes a final throaty rattle and dies.

The residence is connected to the back of the church, giving Father John one of the world's easiest commutes. I ring the doorbell and immediately hear shuffling from within. The door opens a few seconds later, and a regular-looking guy with wavy black hair stands smiling before me. He is about my age, average height and weight, and wears a black tunic, white collar, blue jeans, and yellow Converse tennis shoes.

"Please come in, Max," he says.

I've never met Father John (assuming this *is* Father John), and since I'm nearly half an hour late, I wonder how he can be so sure that I'm his eleven o'clock appointment. As I step across the threshold, I once again notice his footwear. What kind of a dipshit wears yellow sneakers?

"Is anything wrong?"

"No. Sorry I'm late," I respond with total insincerity.

"Oh, don't worry about that."

I wasn't worried, I almost say.

"Please, have a seat."

He leads me across the room to a pair of comfortable-looking chairs that probably cost more than my piece-of-shit Chevy, but before I can sit he extends his right hand.

"I'm Father John," he says smiling, "I've heard so much about you from Bernie."

It takes a moment for me to realize he's referring to Bernadette. I find his use of a diminutive annoying. Bernadette is a saint; Bernie is some guy who drills holes in bowling balls. Then it occurs to me that I might be looking for reasons to dislike this priest. Fuck it. He's the one wearing yellow shoes. I grasp his extended right hand with my own. His firm grip does not impress me. I return a feeble squeeze and break the connection.

"Nice to meet you, John."

He gives me a puzzled look.

"I'm just not big on the whole *Father* thing."

"Bernie told me you were Catholic."

"Even so."

"You're not comfortable calling me Father John?"

"Not at all."

"May I ask why?"

"Sure."

I wait for him to catch up.

He smiles.

"Okay then, why are you uncomfortable calling me Father John?"

"It just seems hypocritical."

"How so?"

I know what he expects me to say, that he's not my father. That I'm not the fruit of his fruitless loins. But despite its validity, such a response is far too obvious. Instead, I go biblical on him.

"Matthew 19:23."

I assume he's familiar with the passage, as it's widely quoted by Protestants and anti-papists throughout the world. However, he seems to be a bit behind in his Bible studies, so I smugly recite, "Call no man your father on earth, for you have but one Father, who is in heaven."

"That's Matthew 23:9."

Clearly I've lost the upper hand, but I shrug like it's no big deal.

"But you do bring up a good point," he concedes as he sits.

I settle into the chair opposite him. It's even more comfortable than it looks.

"Do you really think Jesus meant that literally?" he asks, wearing the sympathetic expression the righteous reserve for their spiritual inferiors.

"It seems to me that a literal interpretation of the Bible is fine when it serves your purpose," I respond, "but now that it doesn't, you tell me Jesus was being metaphorical."

"Think about it. Does it make sense that Jesus would want to prohibit Joey from calling you her father?"

His inclusion of Joey in our conversation, even though she is the subject of this meeting, pisses me off.

"Well, John, there's a lot of stuff Jesus said that doesn't make sense to me. Like plucking out your eye and cutting off your member. And speaking of not making sense, doesn't it seem a bit odd that I have to call you, a mere mortal—you I have to call Father. But when it comes to the Son of God, the Messiah, the walk-on-water, Sermon-on-the-Mount, die-on-the-cross savior of all mankind, him I can refer to as plain ol' Jesus? I mean, not even mister."

"Mister Jesus?" he says, as if it had never occurred to him.

"And you know what? I'll call you mister if you like. Mr. John. Or Mr. Franklin."

"Mister Jesus," he repeats thoughtfully.

"Or I could call you John-san. It's the Japanese honorific. It means honorable. The Honorable John. To me, that's even better than Father."

Suddenly the priest smiles and says, "Max, I don't care what you call me. Whatever makes you comfortable."

"This chair sure is comfortable," I say, changing the subject.

"Isn't it? I picked them up at a rummage sale for ten dollars each."

"Ten dollars?"

"They were in pretty bad shape, but I reupholstered them."

I examine the chair more closely. The work is professional. "You did this yourself?"

"My father made furniture. He was very good at it. I guess a little of his skill rubbed off on me."

My opinion of the priest is starting to soften, but then he crosses his legs, and I am once again focused on the yellow tennis shoes.

"By the way, do you know why priests are called…"

"It's in recognition of the spiritual fatherhood of the priesthood," I interrupt.

"You might be a better Catholic than you think."

"I ask too many questions to be a good Catholic, at least that's what the nuns told me."

"What about Joey? Does she ask a lot of questions?"

"Incessantly. Complex ones that never even occurred to me."

"And still you want her to become a Catholic?"

"What?"

"You want your daughter to become a Catholic despite the fact that you think she'll question it even more than you do?"

"I don't want her to be Catholic."

Again, he looks puzzled.

"*She* wants to be Catholic. It was her idea to get baptized, not mine."

"And she's only four years old?"

"Going on twenty-five."

"Still, that's an important decision for someone so young. Why do you think she feels the need for Holy Baptism?"

"She doesn't want to go to leembo."

He looks at me blankly.

"Leembo. It's how Bernadette pronounces it."

The priest breaks into a warm smile.

"She does have a charming way of speaking."

Charming?

"How do you feel about all this?"

"Like I said, I don't want her to be baptized, but she's made up her mind. It's been two weeks now, and she's resolute. I told her about all the shit she's subjecting herself to, and that once you're in, there's no going back, but she knows that I'm baptized and Bernadette's baptized, so she wants to be baptized, too."

"But you won't be playing an active role in her Catholic life?"

"I won't be playing any role in her Catholic life except sleeping like a wombat when Bernadette takes her to church on Sunday mornings."

"And you really think she's in for a lot of…shit?"

"C'mon, Father John, you know as well as I do what she's in for; it's just that in your case you believe it's worthwhile…what?"

"You called me *Father John.*"

"In recognition of the spiritual fatherhood of the priesthood, and the fact that you said 'shit.'"

He laughs. A moment later he becomes serious.

"I'm not sure if Joey should be baptized with you feeling the way you do."

I am about to retort, but he holds up his hand so politely I decide to let him finish.

"I'm not challenging your position. I believe you have every right to your feelings, your opinions, your attitudes, your beliefs. That's the essence of free will. I'm just concerned that it might be confusing to Joey, with you being so at odds with the fundamental teachings of the Church."

"Jesus, man, life is confusing. That's what keeps you in business. But I won't be challenging the things Joey learns. I won't have to. She'll be the one doing the challenging. Besides, Bernadette will be there to guide her along on this spiritual journey."

"Yes, Bernie is certainly…"

"Her name's Bernadette," I say sharply.

For the first time since we began our conversation, the priest is taken aback. He looks surprisingly vulnerable. "You keep calling her Bernie, but her name's Bernadette. After all she's been through, I don't know. Bernie. It diminishes her."

The priest regards me with the same expression he wore while contemplating Mr. Jesus. Finally, he shakes his head.

"It never occurred to me."

He leans forward in the chair and closes his eyes.

"Bernadette," he says softly, "patron saint of the sick and the poor."

"That's her."

He opens his eyes.

"Thank you."

I shrug.

"So, are you going to baptize Joey?"

"I'll have to think about it."

"Bernadette will be her godmother."

He nods politely, as if he didn't already know.

"And the godfather?"

"No, I just want Bernadette. I read somewhere that only one godparent is required."

"That's true."

"Besides, when it comes to faith, it'd take a half dozen saints to match hers."

"You have a lot of faith in Bernadette."

As long as she leaves the goddamn bananas out of my pancakes, I think.

"It's ironic that you have such disdain for Catholicism, while holding a woman with unflinching faith in God and the Holy Mother Church in such high regard."

"You think I'm being hypocritical?"

"No, I think you're tired of hypocrisy, and in Bernadette you've found someone whose faith is matched only by her humility."

We sit quietly for what seems like a long time.

Then he shifts his legs, and the yellow sneakers come back into focus.

"They were a gift from a parishioner," he says.

I look up and try to approximate an expression of befuddlement.

"She's coming by a little later, the woman who gave them to me, and I just wanted to let her know I appreciate the gift."

"That's sweet," I mumble sarcastically, but the priest, who's shown such perceptiveness up to now, takes me seriously.

"Yellow is her favorite color," he adds.

Ten minutes later, I'm walking across the parking lot to my piece-of-shit Chevy. Father John stands politely in the doorway. Our meeting has gone far better than I imagined possible, and

I'm actually a little less troubled by the idea of Joey renouncing Satan. But just as I'm about to open the car door, I'm struck by a question of immense theological significance—one that has plagued me for the past forty-two years. Slowly, I turn and take a few steps back toward the priest, who is eying me curiously. "Hey Father John," I shout, "how do they make the fire black?"

4

Vaya Con Dios

God works in mysterious ways. There are other explanations
for why I stood shivering on the shoulder of the New Jersey
Turnpike wearing nothing but a pair of black socks and purple
Fruit of the Loom mid-rise briefs, but for the sake of brevity,
let's attribute it to divine intervention. Cars were honking as
they raced by my pasty winter whiteness, and, while I wasn't
bothered by the attention, knowing one of them might kill me
was troubling. There's a phenomenon known as target fixation,
whereby drivers who lock their eyes on an object tend to steer
toward it. Thus, if you're trying to avoid hitting the guy in his
underwear, look the other fucking way.

I felt a crawling sensation on my arm and glanced down
to see my ten-year-old Timex fall to the pavement. The band
had come apart again, shiny black electrical tape still clinging
to one end. Angelica was constantly harping on me to buy
a new one and chided me for being a cheap bastard when I
ignored her counsel. I tossed the twelve-dollar chronometer
onto the hood of my '72 Dodge Dart—another piece of shit
in my transportation lineage—noting that it was three-thirty
p.m. This gave me almost an hour to get to my interview with

the Japanese, which was plenty of time, providing some dipshit didn't run out of gas in the Holland Tunnel.

The Japanese.

That's the secular explanation for why I was nearly naked on the turnpike. Then again, I could blame Angelica. She was the one who talked me into wearing a suit, even as she reassured me I had no chance of getting the job. But I'd never dressed formally for work, and suddenly showing up in my blue-gray ensemble from J.C. Penney would have aroused suspicion, particularly since I'd told my boss I needed to leave work early for a proctology exam. I daresay, even a fashionista like Margaret would dress down for a rectal probe.

I picked up my discarded jeans, dug out the car keys, and popped the trunk. My suit was draped across the bald spare tire. A car honked as I jerked pants from hanger and pulled them on. They were ugly and baggy and made me feel like I should be in church. Next came the white dress shirt. I fumbled open the top button and tugged it over my head like a T-shirt. After tucking it in, I reached for the jacket. It was the least offensive component of my outfit. Worn with jeans and a T-shirt it was completely innocuous; seeing it paired with matching pants felt like a betrayal. Finally, the shoes. Selecting the appropriate footwear had been problematic for I had only two choices: a pair of Converse high tops and an older pair of Converse high tops. Then I recalled the black, steel-toed oxfords from my stint as a factory worker two decades earlier.

It was during my gap year—the one between graduating from high school and flunking out of college—that I made an unsuccessful foray into the blue-collar universe. My job was to operate an overhead crane that lifted trailer shells out of the assembly pits once the sheet-metal front and sides had been riveted to the roof. This involved using a handheld control with four directional buttons: up, down, left, and right. Even the high-school graduates of my Midwestern school district were able to negotiate the complexities of this space-age instrument. The only real challenge was to make sure the clamps that held the shell in place were removed before pressing the *up* button. If not, you'd bend the trailer in half and one of the clamps could come flying off to impale a fellow drudge. I was diligent the first couple of days and made a dutiful walk around the pits before sending the shell skyward. But as the hours went by, complacency set in and my dutiful walk gave way to a cursory glance. One afternoon while raising a shell, I heard muffled shouts—muffled because we all wore heavy-duty earmuffs due to the dangerously high decibel levels. Looking up, I noticed several agitated people but was unable to make out their words.

"Stop, you asshole!"

That I could lip-read.

I took my finger from the *up* button and squinted at the shell. It looked fine from my vantage point, but when I walked to the other side, I discovered it was bent into a V shape, thanks to the forgotten clamp still anchoring it to the middle of the frame. A crowd quickly gathered, though no one approached me. I had ruined a semi-trailer shell worth several thousand dollars, wasted the labors of the men and women who'd fabricated it, and was about to get my ass chewed in half by our shift foreman, the rapidly approaching Junior McBride.

Junior looked at me, then the trailer, then back at me. "You worthless, shit-crusted asshole," he screamed, "You're gonna goddamn well pay for this, you pathetic bucket of fuck." Junior's language became progressively less cordial, so I tuned him out. This was fairly easy to do, as my noise-suppressing earmuffs were still in place. The shitstorm would have probably blown over had I kept my eyes down and my mouth shut, but fate had other plans. In my peripheral vision, I spotted Milo Braggen, who'd been working in the factory since the week after his father committed suicide. The elder Braggen put the barrel of a twelve-gauge shotgun into his mouth minutes after forfeiting the family farm. Although I never cared for the old man—he was a mean drunk and a lousy farmer—I went to his funeral because Milo was a friend. You'd think a guy used to working on a farm, outdoors and unsupervised, would hate the confined monotony of a factory, but Milo didn't seem to mind it at all. He walked around with a perpetual smile on his face, though I'm pretty sure that's because he was perpetually stoned. Unlike his father, Milo was a very good farmer. He stood a few feet behind the crowd, pointing his finger at me and laughing. I felt a ripple of amusement, which I quickly suppressed as Junior raged on, flecks of his saliva accumulating on the surface of my safety goggles. Then Milo fell to the floor. He was lying on his side, kicking his feet, and might have been in the throes of a seizure. But I knew what was coming. Sure enough, he began rotating like the second hand of a clock, mimicking Curly from the Three Stooges when he needed a hit of cheese.

Goddamn you, Milo.

Suddenly I was laughing so hard I couldn't stand up straight. Junior stared at me in utter disbelief, as did the other fifty or so onlookers. He didn't say another word. Didn't have to. We both knew I'd crossed the Rubicon. Still laughing, I handed Junior the yellow control box. "Sorry," I said with as much sincerity as I could muster, but since I was laughing it came out as "suh-ha-ri," which didn't sound sincere at all. As I headed toward the exit for the last time, I passed by Milo, still on the floor. When he noticed me, he sat up and his expression became serious. After a few moments he nodded his head, as if he were agreeing with some controversial statement I'd just made. I nodded back, and then, in my shiny black steel-toed shoes, left factory life behind.

I quickly stepped into them, hoping to give my freezing feet a respite from the cold; however, due to the excellent thermal conduction properties of the steel plates in the toe section, any trace of heat in my lower extremities was immediately sucked away. I slammed the trunk and hurried into the Dart, which was already cold, as it had died the moment I'd shifted into neutral. It started on the third attempt, and the heater roared to life. It's a beautiful sound, that whoosh of warm air surging through the vents, and it comforted me while I waited for an opening in traffic. Then I noticed my precious wristwatch on the other side of the windshield. I opened the door and jumped out just as a semi-trailer roared past, its diesel-fumed turbulence blowing me halfway across the hood. I grabbed the Timex and got back into the car, which, of course, had died again. It started on the second try, though it was two minutes before I was able to accelerate onto the turnpike. I put that time to good use by repairing the watchband with tape I found in the glove box. Success, I truly believe, is all about good time management.

There are those who might wonder why I didn't pull into a gas station and use the toilet as a changing room. It sounds like a legitimate alternative, and for some it might be. But most gas stations on the turnpike lock their toilets, and the attendant won't hand over the key unless you buy something. Moreover, the males who use turnpike bathrooms aren't particularly vigilant, and I had no desire to slosh through puddles of chilled urine in my moisture-absorbent socks.

I didn't put on my tie until after leaving the parking garage on Ninth Avenue. Shaking it loose in the breezy cold, I was startled to see a lisping, orange-beaked sociopath sneering up at me. A gag gift from a former colleague that I'd grabbed by mistake. *Fuck it*, I thought as I slipped it under my collar, *if I keep the jacket closed, no one will notice.* Despite the fact that I seldom wear ties, I am very good at tying them. On this occasion, I opted for the classic four-in-hand knot, as I preferred its sassy lopsidedness to the formal symmetry of a Windsor. I stopped in front of a store window to make a few adjustments and after several moments noticed a man glaring at me through the dusty glass. His eyes were dripping with hatred, as if he considered my position before the window some unforgiveable trespass. I mouthed an apology and then turned and walked on down the road.

I was seven minutes early when I stepped into the lobby of the Essex Hotel and immediately beheld an enormous, pear-shaped human filling one of several overstuffed chairs. He noticed me too, which was surely related to the fact that I was the only other Caucasian in the room. Everyone else appeared to be Japanese.

"Mr. Motion, I presume," I said idiotically.

He remained seated even as I extended my hand, which I did not take to be a slight. The man was carrying a lot of weight, and I surmised that rising from a comfortable chair was something Joe Motion would postpone until absolutely necessary.

"Yyyyyoooo mmuuussst bbeeee Mmaaaaaxxx."

Not this shit again.

Conversing with him in person was far worse than by phone, for it was no longer merely a slow-motion assault on my ears; I was now forced to witness the complex play of fatty tissue and facial musculature involved in creating the vibrations that constituted his speech. I nodded, hoping that by responding nonverbally he might do the same and allow the rest of our conversation to proceed without words.

"Havvvveeee uuhhhhh sseeeett."

For the next five minutes, the corporate headhunter briefed me on what to expect from my Japanese interviewers, though at his pace it contained no more than a few seconds' worth of information. One statement that stood out had something to do with his bowels. Perhaps he was trying to crack a joke, for it was followed by a series of unpleasant grunts and snorts, not intelligible enough to be speech, yet not desperate enough to require the Heimlich maneuver. Ergo, he must have been laughing. I was exhausted by the time he rose from the chair—a process that required my participation—and began moving down a long hallway. The big man was surprisingly light on his feet, his steps more like a little dance than anything resembling a walk. He stopped in front of a door near the end of the hall and gave it a quick, backhanded rap as if he were a Romanian count. Seconds later, the door opened and a Japanese man stood in the entranceway. Before I could introduce myself, a foghorn-like bellow filled my ears.

"Koooonniiiiiiiichhiiiiiiiiwwaaaaaaaa."

When Joe Motion finished his greeting, he started to fall forward. Factoring in gravity, inertia, and his planet-like mass, there was no way to keep the pear-shaped colossus from crashing to the floor. To my amazement, however, he returned to an upright position. The Japanese man returned the bellow, albeit at normal volume and speed—*Konichi-wa*—then executed the same body movement, which I now understood to be a bow. So Joe Motion hadn't been briefing me on the state of his lower digestive tract; he was telling me I should be prepared to bow. So I did. Having not performed this function since I was, oh, nine years old, I placed my left palm on my abdomen and the knuckles of my right hand against the small of my back and then leaned forward—just as my music teacher had instructed. Joe Motion offered a condescending smile, but the Japanese man remained inscrutable: either he accepted my Christmas-pageant bow or was too polite to show disgust. I was about to offer an explanation when he slapped me on the back and drawled, "Y'all must be Max." Too stunned to respond verbally, I could only nod as he ushered me into the room. I expected Joe Motion to follow, but he did another one of those gravity-defying bows then turned and danced away.

It was identical to every hotel room I'd been in, except not so run down. There were two beds, both made, facing a large TV cabinet. To the right of the cabinet was a small desk on which sat an important-looking binder embossed with the hotel logo, no doubt containing riveting information about how to order a grilled-cheese sandwich or what time the exercise lounge closed. There was also a small memo pad with one of the hotel's personalized pens lying next to it. A souvenir, I promised myself. Near the curtained back wall, two chairs were facing one another. An older Japanese man occupied one of them. He sat perfectly still, staring at the chair opposite him despite the fact that no one was in it.

"That's the boss," the younger Japanese man twanged from behind me. "And I'm Brad!"

Brad?

"Now I know what yer thinkin'," he continued. "How come a Japanese guy's named Brad? Well, there's two reasons fer that. First, I'm only half Japanese. Second, I was born and raised in Bull Shoals, Arkansas."

"Bull Shoals," I repeated, trying to sound impressed.

"Yep. And we always say exactly what's on our minds."

It was several seconds before I realized he wanted me to take the bait.

"How's that?"

"'Cause we don't bullshit in Bull Shoals."

What an idiot.

"Would y'all like somethin' to drink?" he asked, turning away before I could respond.

"Sure, I'd love a cup of…"

He handed me a bottle of water. It felt warm and the label bore the hotel logo. Great, I thought, mineral water from one of the fine artesian wells of Manhattan.

"The fridge is on the fritz," he explained.

Again, he turned away, so when I said, "That's okay, I like it warm," I was talking to his back.

"I called the front desk 'bout two hours ago," he said, pointing at the small refrigerator, "but they still haven't done a thing." It was pulled out from the wall, and it looked as if he'd been trying to repair it himself. The beer, soft drinks, and mineral water that fine hotels generously offer their guests at a ten-thousand-percent markup were scattered around it.

"My daddy's an electrical engineer, so I know a bit about refrigerators and such," he said, arms akimbo. "When I called the front desk, they said check and see if it's plugged in, like they're talkin' to a civilian, and I'm tellin' 'em their expansion valve probably needs replaced or maybe even the compressor. I'd know for sure if I took it apart, but I didn't brang my tools, so I just told 'em to come fix it or replace it, but like I said, that was purt' near two hours ago and they still haven't done a thing, and that's how come yer water's warm."

I looked over to see what the elder Japanese man thought of Gomer's monologue, but he was still fixated on the empty chair.

"Have a seat, and I'll tell y'all 'bout the job."

I started toward the seating area, where I assumed the actual interview would take place, but he plopped down on the edge of a bed and patted the one opposite him. Resigned to yet more weirdness, I undid the two buttons of my jacket and sat where he'd indicated. Brad surprised me by not launching into another rambling monologue. Instead he stared at me, a smile on his face and a twinkle in his eye. He began to nod.

"I got a *good* feelin' 'bout you, Max Androv," he said, still smiling.

Despite the incongruous accent, I was happy to hear those words.

"I been workin' over there two years, and it's time to move on to another challenge."

I nodded understandingly. As if to contradict me, he shook his head.

"And it has been a challenge. But one y'all won't hafta face."

I won't? You're dismissing me? What about that good *feelin'?*

My consternation must have shown, for Brad quickly added, "What I mean is y'all *look* American. Me, I don't. I look Japanese, and that's not what the bosses in Japan wanna see. When you walk into a meetin' and tell the clients this here's the American writer who's gonna be takin' care of y'all's account, they wanna see a white face. Not a Japanese one."

"Well," I stalled, searching for an acceptable reply. "You certainly don't sound Japanese."

He grinned and was about to say something else, perhaps to further extol the virtues of being Caucasian in Japan, when a shout filled the room: "Da-fi-da-ku!"

Startled, I shot a look over Brad's shoulder and saw that the older Japanese man was now on his feet and gesticulating wildly.

"Da-fi-da-ku!" he shouted again.

I rose from the bed, as did Brad, while the boss continued to wave his arms. He seemed fixated on my chest, so I looked down, thinking maybe my shirt was on fire.

"Da-fi-da-ku!" he shouted for the third time.

And then I understood, for staring up at me was the source of the Japanese man's excitement: Da-fi-da-ku.

Daffy Duck.

He hurried over to where we were standing and, after a quick bow, reached into his jacket pocket and retrieved a business card. Holding it in both hands, he offered it to me oriented so that it was readable without my having to turn it; thus, I could see that his name wasn't Dwayne or Lonnie or Jerry Lee or Jim Bob or any other moniker endemic to places like Bull Shoals, Arkansas. The name on the card was Shinya Yamakawa. I took it from him and decided to return the bow, but since my hands were now encumbered, I was unable to get them into the proper position. So I imitated what Shinya Yamakawa had done and bent slightly forward at the waist. It worked out pretty well. Then he bowed back to me. And I bowed back to him. And then he to me. This went on for several seconds, and it occurred to me that our movements were very similar to the courtship ritual of a species of waterfowl I'd seen profiled in an award-winning BBC documentary. When the bowing finally came to an end, he straightened and said, "Yamakawa-desu."

Upon hearing the man say his own name, I quickly deduced that we were in the introduction phase of our courtship.

"I'm Max Androv. Nice to meet you."

To which he responded, "*Hajimemashite. Dozo yoroshiku onegaishimasu.*"

However, what I heard was, *Haaggsssssshhhhhhhiiimmmsu.*

Brad explained that this translates to "It's nice to be meeting you for the first time. Please do everything you can for me."

I thought this a bit odd, asking someone to do everything they can for you so early in the relationship. Later, I learned that the phrase is actually an expression of humility, a highly valued trait in Japan. A more accurate translation would be: "I am a truly worthless piece of shit who is incapable of even the most meager accomplishment without the assistance of someone as intelligent, good looking, talented, and compassionate as yourself. So please, do everything you can for me."

Then Shinya Yamakawa did a curious thing. He unbuttoned his suit coat and whipped it open, an unspoken *VOILA!* hanging in the air like a hot-air balloon.

"Da-fi-da-ku," I said.

"*Hai,*" he echoed, "Da-fi-da-ku."

He was wearing the same tie.

I looked over at Brad, who shrugged and said, "Yamakawa-san really likes Daffy Duck."

Well, no shit, Brad.

Yamakawa-san put his hand on my elbow and led me to the seating area. Brad sat down on the bed and began perusing the help-wanted section of the *New York Times.* It seemed like an omen. I settled into the chair Yamakawa-san indicated, but instead of taking his place opposite me, he went to the desk and picked up a small green box. It was one of those disposable Fuji Film cameras that were, at the time, all the rage. He lifted it up and down a couple of times, which I understood to mean he wanted to take my photograph. Involuntarily, my hands went to my hair and I puffed it up and smoothed it down and pushed it to the left and then to the right and patted and scrunched and rubbed and flattened and puffed it up some more. There is no point to this ritual, and my hair does not look any more photogenic than it did before the fondling, but whenever a camera is pointed my way, I inadvertently have one of these seizures. Yamakawa-san seemed to understand and waited patiently as I went through the various phases of my styling regimen. Satisfied, I dropped my hands and tried to smile without looking like an idiot. He held the camera to his eye and took a shot. Immediately after the click, he pulled it away from his face and examined it closely, as if mystified by what had just happened. A few seconds later, he wound the film forward and once again raised the camera up and down. Consequently, my hands shot to my hair and I made all the necessary readjustments. We repeated this sequence four times. Portrait session complete, Yamakawa-san sat down in his chair and we were at last face to face. I smiled and nodded, signaling that I was ready, but the solemn-faced Japanese man didn't say a word. After a minute or so, I looked over at Brad, but the hillbilly had his nose buried in the newspaper and remained unaware of my mounting desperation.

I turned back to Yamakawa-san.

Another minute went by.

And then another.

"I had a Japanese friend in the third grade!"

Jesus Christ. Did I just say that?

It's true. I had a Japanese friend in the third grade. His family name was Watanabe, but we called him Koko. He was in my class for about three months while his father, a visiting professor from Keio University, taught a seminar. Though he seemed nice, Koko was a sneaky little bastard. He taught me to count to ten in Japanese, but when I proudly recited the numbers to his mother at a school function, she looked as if I'd just pissed on her shoes. She grabbed her snickering son and dragged him from the room. It turns out Koko had taught me ten synonyms for *penis*.

When I mentioned to my own mother that I had an interview with a Japanese company, she said, "Make sure to tell them about your little Japanese friend."

"Now, why would I do that?"

"Because it shows how openminded and multicultural you are," she said as if I were an imbecile. "Not everyone has forgiven the Japanese, you know."

Many Americans of her generation remained distrustful of those responsible for the sneak attack on Pearl Harbor.

"Well, I don't think all the Japanese have forgiven the Americans."

"Forgiven us for what?" she demanded.

"Hiroshima. Nagasaki."

"The atomic bomb *saved* lives."

"Firebombing Tokyo?"

"We were at war."

"The Japanese internment camps?"

"There were spies and saboteurs among them."

"But most of them were American citizens."

"They didn't look like Americans."

It was at this point that I decided to capitulate; I needed to borrow money from her and was only a couple of facts away from a funding freeze. "You know, you might be right. Having previous experience with the Japanese could give me an edge, so maybe I will mention Koko."

"You should," my mom proclaimed triumphantly.

I had no intention of augmenting my bullshit credentials by recounting a three-month association with an eight-year-old smartass, but after all that smiling and staring, it just came out.

Yamakawa-san nodded thoughtfully, as if I'd just said something wise.

"His name was Koko," I added, seizing the moment.

Another two minutes passed.

Screw it.

"So this is for a job in Tokyo?"

Like most English speakers, I pronounced all three syllables of the Japanese capitol, even though it's a two-syllable word. This is ironic, because the Japanese are notorious for adding syllables to English words. "Daffy Duck" becomes "Da-fi-da-ku." "Building" becomes "bi-ru-din-gu." And my name triples its syllabic content, going from "Max" to "Ma-ku-su." There's a simple explanation for this: the Japanese language ends each phonological building block with a vowel sound, the exceptions being those terminating with an N or an M sound. This works fine in Japanese, because their syllables conveniently adhere to this rule. But foreign sounds aren't so accommodating. They frequently end with a consonant, so the Japanese tack on a vowel, creating an additional syllable. Thus, for a cheap burger, you go to Ma-ku-do-na-ru-do.

"*Hai*," Yamakawa-san answered, "To-kyo."

I waited for him to continue.

He didn't.

Which was a problem.

Because the best way to nail an interview is to keep your mouth shut. It might sound counterintuitive, but it's foolproof. Do not make small talk. Do not volunteer information. Do not attempt to establish rapport. Do, however, hang on to your interviewer's every word, nodding enthusiastically at whatever he or she says. Most interviewers (particularly those in advertising and other professions of negligible social value) are seeking esteem: they do not care about your qualifications; they simply want to know that you're impressed with theirs. Limit your contributions to "Wow!" and "That's amazing!" and you'll do fine. When asked a question, answer slowly. This is not to make you sound thoughtful and contemplative; it's to provide the interviewer with a better opportunity to interrupt you with his or her own answer.

"Ma-ku-su-san."

Thank god.

"Do you like *bi-ru?*" he asked.

"Do I..."

What the hell is bi-ru?

"He's askin' if y'all like beer," Brad chimed in, peeking over the top of his newspaper.

My first impulse was to lie: *No, sir, I refuse to drink anything that could potentially compromise my work performance.* Then again, I wasn't going to get this job even if I'd founded the temperance movement.

"I..."

Fuck it.

"...love beer."

Yamakawa-san nodded thoughtfully and after a few seconds rose and extended his hand. The interview was over. Between us, we'd spoken fifty-eight words, thirty-five of which were mine. I walked over to where Brad was sitting and noticed my portfolio on the bed, partially obscured by the newspaper he'd been reading.

"Is that my book?" I asked him.

"Sure is," he said without lifting his eyes from the paper. "Joe Motion brought it over yesterday."

When interviewing for a copywriting job, it's standard procedure for the interviewee to take the prospective employer through his or her portfolio of work. This happens in one of three formats, each contingent on the personalities of those involved. In the first format, the candidate is aggressively confident and takes full credit for anything that is good while blaming the client, account servicing team, production coordinator, traffic manager, or art director for anything bad. In the second format, the interviewer tells the interviewee that his or her copy is worthless and goes on to explain how it should have been written. This is the preferred format, for all you have to do is nod in agreement as the interviewer shits all over your work. He will, in turn, be impressed with your willingness to embrace his wisdom and is likely to hire you on the spot. (See *How to Nail an Interview.*) The third format is extremely rare and involves the interviewer and interviewee thoughtfully discussing the copy in a way that allows each to learn something about the other. The copywriter becomes aware of the kind of people he or she would be working for, what they expect from a writer, what the writer can expect from them, and so forth. The interviewer can determine how the copywriter approaches a problem-solving situation—how he or she uses words to craft a message. In this scenario, the interviewer looks over an ad and asks a question or two. The interviewee provides a succinct answer and does not rationalize it with some bullshit theory of communication. He or she may then call attention to some aspect of the work, but only once or twice per interview; if an ad requires explanation, it's a shitty ad.

What I found insulting was the fact that they hadn't once referred to my work. Breaking my keep-your-mouth-shut rule, I asked, "Did you want to go over it with me?"

"Nah," he said.

"Nah?" I repeated incredulously.

Brad looked up from his paper. He held my eyes for a moment and then set the paper aside. "Yer work's fine," he said with a sigh. "Yamakawa-san asks me to look through all the books and tell him if I think the guy can write. He barely speaks English, so he depends on my assessment. And I looked at yer book and told him y'all were a purty good writer."

Oddly, this sounded reasonable.

"You must have seen quite a few good writers in the past few days."

"Not so many as you might expect."

"But New York..."

"Thing is," he interrupted, "the best copywriters in New York City don't wanna leave New York City. That's why we gotta interview in Chicago, too. And it's the same thing there. The best ones wanna stay. So we're lookin' fer the purty good ones."

It's possible Brad meant that last statement as an insult, but I chose to believe he was just being honest. In any case, it filled me with joy. *The best need not apply! We're lookin' fer* purty good*! Fuckin' A! I just might have a chance after all!* I nodded to where Yamakawa-san was still sitting and whispered, "What was that all about?"

"That's just his way," he said. "The boss is lookin' fer somethin' more than just copywritin'. See, workin' in Japan isn't fer everybody. Communication's really difficult with the Japanese, even if they speak English. They have a whole different way 'a lookin' at the world, and it shapes the way they express themselves. I'm half Japanese, speak the language purty well, an' I'm still lost half the time. Anyway, I'm here to handle the copywritin', and Yamakawa-san determines whether or not y'all can fit into the complex corporate culture of Japan."

"The complex corporate culture of Japan," I repeated, unable to resist the alliteration. "And he can determine that from taking my picture and asking me if I like beer?"

Brad was about to respond when there was a knock at the door. He leapt to his feet and hurried to the entranceway. After putting his eye to the peephole, I heard him mutter, "Well, it's about damn time."

When the door opened, a small Hispanic man—I assumed he was Hispanic because he looked Hispanic and because the badge on his shirt indicated his name was Hector—stepped into the room pushing a cart. On it was a mini refrigerator, just like the one Brad had been attempting to repair.

"There's a good chance yer expansion valve's shot," Brad told him. "Or it could be yer compressor. I'd know fer sure if I took it apart, but I didn't brang my tools. And I can see that you didn't brang yers neither."

Hector was clearly mystified, and from the nervous way he nodded, I'd wager he didn't understand a word Brad was saying. In fact, I believe he thought the hillbilly was speaking Japanese. He kept up his nervous nodding until there was a break in the monologue, at which point he gestured toward the malfunctioning mini fridge and said, "Change."

"Fine," Brad said, clearly disappointed that Hector hadn't branged his tools. "I'll git that one," he said flipping his arm toward the spoiled unit, "and you git this one."

Hector cocked his head like a bird. Evidently, he was struggling to make sense of the mysterious sounds Brad was making—to decipher the dramatic gestures. Surely, the Essex Hotel, like most hotels out of my price range, has a policy that discourages guests from lifting their rooms' heavy appliances, particularly when a maintenance man is on site. Perhaps Brad wasn't aware of this policy. Perhaps his Bull Shoals upbringing compelled him to believe if he wanted something done right, he had to do it himself. Or perhaps he was just an idiot. He bent over the broken mini fridge and, lifting with his back rather than his legs, hoisted it a few feet off the ground. It was heavier than he'd anticipated, and he staggered to one side. Hector hurried over to help, but no-bullshit Brad would accept no assistance. He twisted away, putting himself between Hector and the fridge. The little man tried to step around him, but Brad turned again. In my peripheral vision, I saw Yamakawa-san stir. He held my eyes for a moment, as if gauging my reaction to the slapstick taking place a few feet away. Hector was now behind the hillbilly, who pushed his body backwards, pinning the maintenance man to the wall. Before Brad could exploit his advantage, Hector slipped out and got his hands on the prize. They looked like a couple of Christmas shoppers from 1983 fighting over the last Cabbage Patch doll. With a final burst of strength, Brad twisted his body away from Hector and directly toward me. Unfortunately, the laws of physics finally had their say, and the energy required to execute this maneuver, coupled with the weight of the mini fridge and the corresponding inertial force, far exceeded Brad's capacity to control it. He lost his grip, and the appliance was airborne.

Until it came crashing down.

Onto my right foot.

The room went instantly quiet, as if a mute button had been pressed. Brad and Hector wore identical looks of horror, waiting for my scream to break the silence.

I wondered about that.

The pain.

And why there was none.

Then I remembered.

I was wearing steel-toed shoes.

Mysterious ways, indeed.

Suddenly Brad and Hector were squatting before me, lifting the refrigerator off my foot.

"Sorry, Max!" Brad cried, "Are you okay? Wanna go to the hospital? I'm purty sure the hotel's got insurance."

What an asshole.

Hector was mumbling something over and over, which I took to be some sort of apology. He was scared shitless and probably thought he was going to lose his job. Maybe get deported.

"I'm okay, Hector. *Estoy bien.*"

At the sound of Spanish (two of the twenty-three words in my working vocabulary), Hector froze. Slowly, he raised his eyes to mine.

"*Madre de dios,*" he whispered, then made the sign of the cross and kissed his thumbnail. He continued to stare at me, as if I were an apparition of the Virgin. It didn't take long for his adoration to become uncomfortable, so I waved one of those mid-air blessings I'd seen Father O'Connor execute when he was in a hurry. It did the trick. Hector crossed himself and went back to work.

Brad looked disappointed as the little maintenance man effortlessly lifted the replacement mini fridge from the cart and slid it into place. He plugged it in, replaced the beverages, and set the broken mini fridge on his cart. Without waiting for a tip, he began pushing it toward the door.

"Hector," I called out.

He stopped but did not turn back.

"*Vaya con dios.*"

He crossed himself yet again, then disappeared into the hallway. When I looked away from the door, I found myself face to face with Yamakawa-san.

"Ma-ku-su-san," he said, "than-kyu."

He put his hand on my shoulder and guided me into the hallway.

"See ya, Max," Brad called from behind.

I turned and waved, but the hillbilly already had his nose buried in the newspaper. Yamakawa-san and I stood face to face, silently appraising one another. I was about thank him, to say goodbye—something—but he gave his head an almost imperceptible shake, making it clear that nothing else need be said. Instead, we bowed. And then he was gone.

For several seconds, I stared at the door, shaking my head like a swimmer trying to dislodge water from his ears. Despite my earlier optimism, or perhaps because of it, I now felt defeated. Slowly, I turned and began shuffling down the long, lonely hallway. My eyes were downcast, so I was able to discern a slight indentation in the toe of my right shoe. A few steps later, I jerked to a stop. *Goddammit!* I'd forgotten the hotel pen! Now I had nothing to show for the ordeal but a dent in my shoe. My mood sank even further. As I moved into the lobby, though, I experienced a surge of excitement. There, on a small table next to one of the overstuffed chairs, was an identical hotel pen. Ignoring the danger, Ma-ku-su-san sprang into action! I grabbed the pen, bolted past the bowing concierge, then burst through the revolving doors and into the freezing embrace of New York City.

5

Playclothes

As a child, I might not have hated going to church so much if my parents hadn't made me wear such awful clothes. My mom and dad might have thought I looked smart in my navy-blue dress pants, burgundy turtleneck sweater, and plaid sport coat, but as soon as I put them on, the world ceased to be a happy place. I wasn't allowed to move lest I wrinkle them, stain them, or fall down and make a hole in the knees.

"Just sit still and think about the Lord Jesus and how He suffered and died for your sins," my mom would suggest as I fidgeted on the couch.

I'd look over at the crucifix hanging on the living room wall, and there was the Lord Jesus, suffering and dying for my sins. But at least He didn't go out in a burgundy turtleneck.

"Can't I just wear my school clothes to church?" I'd plead.

In my house, there were three categories of clothes: Sunday clothes, school clothes, and playclothes. Sunday clothes were my "best" clothes and were reserved for the most excruciating events: Sunday Mass, weddings, funerals, and family portraits. I wore my Sunday clothes until I grew out of them, at which time they were replaced by a new, equally insufferable set. If I'd had a little brother, the old ones might have been passed down to him, but since I didn't, they were donated to the church so some less fortunate kid could have the fun sucked out of his Sunday.

School clothes were much more comfortable than Sunday clothes. Typically, I would go to school in blue jeans, a button-down shirt, and a pair of white socks with two stripes circumnavigating the top. My shoes were sneakers in the warm months and clunky leather boots when the weather turned cold. Clodhoppers, my dad called them. Unfortunately, school clothes also had a dark side. When I was a kid, there was no such thing as prewashed. A new pair of blue jeans was so stiff they could be used as a weapon. This made them incredibly uncomfortable and caused embarrassing friction noises every time you took a step. Ten or fifteen washings were required before the stiffness went away and you could walk around without sounding like a robot. And it might be months before they faded from purple-black to a respectable shade of blue.

Playclothes, on the other hand, set me free. They were old and soft and faded and comfortable, the way clothes are meant to be. I couldn't wait to get home from school or the cemetery or the Olan Mills photography studio and trade the agonizing exoskeleton of formal wear for the comforting embrace of playclothes. It didn't matter if I got them wrinkled. Or dirty. Or torn. Best of all, they were never, ever new. You never took playclothes out of that crunchy cellophane wrapping and removed pins or tore off tags or had to wash them dozens of times before they became your friends. Playclothes were generally school clothes that had grown so worn and comfortable they no longer met my mom's rigid standards for academic attire. So when I asked her if I could wear school clothes to church, it was my idea of a compromise. She didn't see it that way: "You're going to God's house! The very least you can do is dress up for Him."

God's house.

Even as a six-year-old, this phrase struck me as peculiar. What the hell does God need with a house? There are millions of churches all over the world. Does He inhabit all of them? And what about heaven? I thought that was supposed to be His primary residence. Even if He does keep a home on Earth, why would He opt for a dark, dreary, manmade church? Why not the Grand Canyon or Mount Everest or a fjord in Norway? That would make sense. What doesn't make sense is dressing up for Him. Do people really think the Supreme Being is interested in human fashion? That He whispers to Jesus or the Holy Ghost or whomever He hangs out with on Sundays, "Ooh, check out the corduroy jacket in the third row. Bet he got it at Nordstrom."

Dressing up was even more challenging for girls, who were expected to wear modest dresses, sensible shoes, and looks of piety. Yet, this wasn't enough to appease a fashion-conscious deity. Any female entering a Catholic church was also required to keep her head covered. If she forgot to wear a hat, she was forced to pin a Kleenex to her hair. (Back then, all facial tissues were Kleenexes, just as all photocopies were Xeroxes.) Matilda Jansen happily obeyed this rule by sporting a faded St. Louis Cardinals baseball cap, which caused immense consternation among the nuns. According to the Sisters of Style, ball caps were decidedly unfeminine and had no place in a girl's wardrobe. Once during a special Mass for children, Sister Mary Cherry decided to remove Matilda's cap and replace it with a Kleenex. Matilda saw her coming and ducked out of the way. It became a standoff, the two of them staring angrily at one another, and although Matilda was only nine years old, I could see Sister Mary Cherry was intimidated. Then Matilda reached down and pulled her shapeless gray dress out to the side, never taking her eyes from the nun. She let the fabric slip from her fingers and it drifted back down to her scab-covered legs. The message was clear: *You got me to wear a dress; don't even think about taking my ball cap.* After a few moments, Sister Mary Cherry capitulated and the crisis was over. When the nun moved on to intimidate someone less capable of defending herself, I walked over and said, "Wow, Matilda, you really showed her." She slugged me in the stomach with such force I nearly vomited in the holy water font. "The name's *Mat*, you little faggot," she corrected, and then walked down the aisle to receive Holy Communion.

Joey's baptism dress is pink. It's her favorite color. Always has been. It made me wonder if an affinity for pink is somehow programmed into the female genome. Before Joey came into my life, I considered pink an acquired taste—that girls grow to love it because of its ubiquity. From the moment they enter the world, it surrounds them: pink wrist tag, pink baby gown, pink pacifier, pink bottles, pink clothes, pink wallpaper, pink dolls. But Joey didn't face that kind of indoctrination. I don't like pink. So she was surrounded by my favorite color: black. And black isn't even a color. It's the absence of color. Black is mysterious. Black is beautiful. Black is cool. Black is practical. Black never gets dirty. Black clothes never clash. Unfortunately, the makers of baby paraphernalia don't share my enthusiasm for this exceptionally versatile non-color. I did manage to find her a black blankie at the laundromat. And I got her a black (African-American) doll. Of course, there was some color in her life, but I minimized the role of pink. Then one day I asked her, "What's your favorite color?"

"Pink."

"Bullshit."

She waits for me to continue.

"Pink?"

She nods.

"But pink is ugly."

"No it's not."

"What about black?"

"I don't like it."

"What about your blankie?"

"It's not a blankie. It's a towel."

"Really? Okay, you like your towel, don't you?"

"No."

"No?"

"I want a blankie. A real blankie."

"But they don't make black blankies."

"I want a pink blankie."

"You disappoint me."

Nothing.

"What about your doll?"

"What do you mean?"

"You have a black doll."

"She isn't black."

"Sure she's black. I mean, you know, African American."

"She's brown. Like me."

I look at the doll and then back to Joey. The doll is only marginally darker than she is.

"Do you like my baptism dress, Daddy?" Joey chirps, floating into my bedroom office like a pink cloud.

"Yeah, it's nice."

"You didn't even look!"

I spin around in my chair.

Bernadette is standing behind Joey beaming like a proud mother. I look closely at Joey's pink dress.

"It's nice," I repeat.

Joey's mouth forms a kind of pucker. She turns and looks at Bernadette.

"Oh, Mr. Max," Bernadette says, "She look more than nice. She look bee-yoo-tiful!"

Of course *she* looks beautiful. Joey always looks beautiful, no matter what she's wearing. That's just the way it is with some kids. You don't need to dress them up to make them attractive. Joey can rock a vomit-stained Cookie Monster T-shirt. But I'd been asked to comment on the dress, not on how she looked in it. And, not being particularly invested, *nice* was the adjective that popped into my mind.

"That's what I meant," I agree, rather than chastising them for not being more specific.

Joey's mouth remains in a pucker.

A psychologist once told me I was self-absorbed. My response was, "Is that supposed to be a problem?"

"Depends on your circumstances," he replied.

I never really understood that statement until Joey came along. For most of my life, I was perfectly happy being self-absorbed. Friends of yore would enthusiastically inform me that I was a selfish asshole focused solely on my own needs, and I would concur with equal enthusiasm. Self-absorption? It worked for me. Sure, it had a less-than-positive impact on my relationships with women. But there are billions of females on this planet alone, and I was relatively confident that sooner or later I would find one who embraced the charm of my egotism.

Once you have a kid, especially one you have to raise on your own, you're screwed—at least in terms of self-absorption. Even a half-assed parent like myself is forced to make compromises and, on occasion, put the child's needs before my own. Joey was just three weeks old when her enchanting mother Naoko—a Japanese beauty I'd foolishly fallen in love with while working in Tokyo—decided she'd rather backpack through South America with her bisexual, yoga-instructor boyfriend than stick around and help raise the fruit of her womb. (*And I'm self-absorbed?*) Thus, the responsibility for feeding her, changing her, comforting her, taking her to doctor's appointments, buying her clothes, and all the rest of the never-ending minutiae involved with caring for an infant fell to me.

Fortunately, there was a transitional period after Naoko split. My sister Mary came to Japan and stayed with us for a few weeks. Evidently, she feared that I would be unable to raise a child on my own. Mary is two years older than me and has always resented the pleasure I take in my self-absorption.

"You're not the only person at this table," she'd declare as I reached for the last doughnut during the Sunday breakfasts of our childhood. "Other people like doughnuts, too."

"Not as much as I do," I'd respond.

She'd continue ranting, and if my mom or dad were at the table, I'd have to apologize for being such a pig and offer it to her. Fortunately, Mary would never eat food that someone else had touched, so I'd loop the doughnut onto my middle finger and hold it out to her, knowing she couldn't possibly accept.

"This is karma," she declared upon her arrival at Narita Airport. "What goes around comes around. As you sow, so shall you reap."

"Nice flight?"

Mary fell in love with Joey the moment she saw her. She doesn't have any kids but enthusiastically embraced the role of temporary mother and permanent aunt. She was surprisingly good at it. I had no idea my big sister could be so tender and loving. I'd certainly never seen that side of her. Then again, I seldom bring out the best in people.

Mary is a police officer in our hometown and has never been married. She's had a few relationships over the years, but nothing serious. I once asked her if she was a lesbian, and she responded by pulling out her gun and laying it on the table in front of her. She just sat there, staring at me over her Smith & Wesson. Her sexual orientation remained a mystery.

"You know you're going to have to do all this yourself when I go back," she reminded me one morning as she changed and then fed baby Joey.

"It's not *that* difficult," I said.

As she did when the pistol was on the table, Mary just stared at me, and I knew that had she not loved her niece so fiercely she would have walked out the door right then. Instead, she crossed the room (two-and-a-half steps in my typically tiny Japanese apartment) and gently placed Joey in her bassinet. Then she came back to where I was standing, shook her head, and slapped me across the face with such force it knocked me sideways. It stung like hell, but I was more surprised than anything else. I started to ask her what the fuck she thought she was doing, and she hit me again, even harder this time. When I stood back up, I was experiencing a series of emotions someone unfamiliar with my complex psychological makeup might have misinterpreted as fear.

"It *is* difficult," she said with surprising calm. "It's difficult and it's monotonous and it's tiring and it's endless. It's one of the hardest jobs you'll ever have to do. But you will do it. Every day. No matter how difficult it gets. Because she's your daughter, and once I leave, you're all she has. And everything you do, you're going to do with love. I know that seems impossible right now, because you've never loved anyone but yourself, but you will love your daughter. This beautiful, innocent, adorable child that you and your nutjob girlfriend brought into the world. You will love her more than anything else, including your own pathetic self. You will put her needs first, because, from now on, her needs *are* your needs. You're her father, for heaven's sake. And at least for now, you're going to be her mother, too."

A few moments of silence passed, and I figured it was about time to salvage some dignity, so I demanded, "Are you finished?"

"No," she said softly, but did not continue.

I waited for several uncomfortable seconds. Finally she leaned very close to my ear and whispered, "If you don't, I will come back and shoot you in the scrotum."

I had never heard my sister make even a fleeting reference to the male genitalia, so her target selection was almost as disconcerting as the explicit sincerity of the warning. Then again, Mary is a devout Catholic, so it's hardly surprising that she would use the threat of violence to facilitate love. It is the Christian way, after all: love God or burn in hell forever; love your daughter or be shot in the testicles.

Over the next few days, my sister taught me all the things I would need to know in order to take care of my daughter. And I was right. It's not all that difficult. In fact, I was far more prepared than I realized. This is because I've lived with a cat most of my life. Not the same one, of course; they die off every few years, and then you get another one. Even so, I'm not what you'd call a *cat person*; that label suggests a certain fanaticism, a devotion to the species that I simply do not possess. I just like having one around. At any rate, if you're responsible for a cat, you have to feed it. And give it water. And listen to it whine. And offer it affection. And scoop shit out of its litter box. And accept the fact that your efforts, while always expected, are never appreciated. Thus, it was not difficult for me to spoon baby formula into a bottle, mix it with hot water, screw on a plastic nipple, and maneuver it into Joey's mouth. It was not difficult for me to change her diaper, conscientiously cleaning her bottom by wiping the fecal matter—far less offensive than its feline equivalent—from front to back, away from her private parts. It was not difficult for me to alleviate Joey's discomfort by picking her up and singing a lullaby—usually "The Passenger" by Iggy Pop—until she stopped crying. So despite Mary's dire prognostications, I did not find it difficult to take care of my infant daughter. At least for the first few hours.

On the day of her departure, Mary was as sad as I'd ever seen her, and that includes the day of our parents' double funeral. But at least then I understood why she was so upset. We said goodbye at Tokyo Station, one of the busiest transportation hubs on the planet, and for a minute I thought she was going to take Joey with her. That would have solved several of my problems at once, although I don't think she would have made it through customs, even with her law-enforcement credentials. But just before the Narita Express was scheduled to arrive, Mary set Joey in the stroller and kissed her a final time.

"I guess you're really going to miss her," I said, trying to sound sympathetic.

"You can be so thick," she replied, tears rolling down her cheeks.

Jesus, what'd I do now?

"You two are the only family I have," she sobbed, "I'm going to miss you both."

She gave me a massive hug and then hurried through the gate.

"Mary!" I yelled after her.

She stopped and turned, a hopeful look on her tear-stained face. Clearly, she was anticipating some expression of brotherly love.

"Would you really shoot me in the balls?"

A look of disappointment flashed across her face, but a moment later she smiled.

"I don't know if I'm that good of a shot."

"Joey?" I say.

"What?"

Her lips remain in a pucker. Almost a pout.

"You know how I feel about pink."

"You hate it."

"And you know how I feel about baptism."

"You think it's so the pope can buy hats."

Over Joey's shoulder, Bernadette is eyeing me nervously.

"In spite of those reservations, I think that's the prettiest baptism dress I've ever seen, and you look like an angel."

Her puckered expression gradually morphs into one of joy—a flower blooming in slow motion. It's amazing how easy it is to make a child happy. Unless, like me, you're a self-absorbed asshole focused solely on your own needs. But every once in a while, I get a tingling sensation down below. A warning of sorts. And I think of my sister's promise to shoot me in the nether regions. Suddenly I become more aware of the people around me. Of their needs. And of my responsibilities to satisfy them. I become the father Joey deserves. The good man Bernadette believes me to be. I am transformed into a loving, caring, nurturing, devoted, tender, affectionate, understanding, open-minded child of God.

That is, I become someone else.

But if that's what it takes to make Joey happy and to keep my reproductive organs intact, I will be whoever I have to be.

"You two get out of here now. I've got work to do."

"Thank you, Daddy!"

"You a good man, Mr. Max."

Yeah, I'm a good man.

"Hey, Joey, bring me a couple of doughnuts and a glass of water?"

"Okay, Daddy."

"I make you some coffee," Bernadette says with a smile.

"That'd be great."

Off they go.

They're happy.

Good for them.

But what about me? Is it too self-absorbed to wonder about my own state of mind? Am I, in fact, happy?

Doughnuts and coffee are on the way.

Happiness can wait.

Despite the sadistic nature of her sartorial choices, my mother passed on to me the single most important rule of fashion. It's so simple even a three-year-old can employ it effectively, as Joey has exemplified since she began choosing her own attire. Unfortunately, a disturbingly large number of humans are woefully ignorant of this basic directive, and that ignorance is on display whenever the unenlightened venture into public. They're easy to spot, because they all look like dorks. Yet they are oblivious to their status. Who are they? What are they wearing? And what is this magic rule that could have prevented it?

I found out when I was eight years old. It was late summer, and I was leaving the house to play wiffle ball with a neighbor. I was wearing a pair of shorts my mom had acquired from Betty, one of her church friends. Betty's son had outgrown them, so they were passed on to me. They bore a plaid motif and fit nicely into my playclothes rotation. I was also wearing a red-and-blue-striped T-shirt, one of my favorites. My ensemble was completed with gym socks and an old pair of PF Flyers.

"You're not going out like that!" my mom commanded.

I stopped in my tracks.

"Like what?"

"Like that!" she said, pointing an accusatory finger at me. "In that shirt and those shorts."

I was confused. She'd passed me the clothes herself and witnessed me wearing them many times. Now I was committing a sin?

"But they're my playclothes," I said meekly, "and I'm going out to play."

"Max," she said, "The clothes are fine. You just can't wear them together."

This made no sense.

And then she told me the rule.

"You never mix patterns."

"What?"

"You never mix patterns," she repeated. "You never wear plaid pants with a striped shirt. Or a plaid shirt with striped pants. Or a plaid shirt with plaid pants."

"What about checks?" I asked, trying to be helpful.

"Same thing. Checks are a pattern. They can't be mixed with stripes or plaids or even other checks. You can only wear a solid."

"A solid?"

"Something without any pattern. No checks or plaids or stripes. Just a solid color."

"So I can wear these shorts with a white T-shirt?"

"That would be fine."

"Or this shirt with a pair of jeans?"

"Of course."

"But I can't wear them together."

"No, you can't."

"Why not?"

"Because you don't mix patterns."

"Why not?"

"Because if you do, you look like a dork."

And just like that, I was enlightened.

It's amazing how many dorks are out there walking around, most of them men without wives or girlfriends. And because of the way they dress, their relationship status is unlikely to change. It's interesting to note that the most significant expansion of fashion dorkdom occurred with the advent of Casual Friday. Originally an attempt to elevate the morale of white-collar office workers trapped in the 1950s, it didn't really catch on until twenty or so years later. On Casual Friday, the office dress code is relaxed and formal business attire gives way to smart-casual, whatever the fuck that is. Thus, to the male white-collar worker, Casual Friday means making choices about what to wear. I specify men because women are used to making choices. Their office attire extends well beyond business suits. And even if a woman does decide to cloak herself in the female version of corporate manhood, she is likely to include accessories: a scarf, earrings, nylons, perhaps a tasteful, rhinestone-studded broach—all of which involve choices. A man in a suit, on the other hand, makes no choices. Okay, he has to pick a necktie, but how hard is that?

As long as we're on the subject, have you ever stopped to consider how profoundly perverse neckties are? A length of silk (or in my case, high-grade polyester) tightly knotted around the human neck. Its function is strictly decorative, although in reality it serves to make one as uncomfortable as possible. Don't believe me? What's the first thing a man in a suit does when he wants to get more comfortable? He loosens his tie, that's what. And in the words of my college literature professor, a devoted Freudian, "Why would a grown man want to wear a penis around his neck?" Something to think about the next time you're twisting Mr. Winky into a Windsor knot.

One of the upsides of wearing a suit is that the pants and coat are already matched. So aside from the silken phallus, the only thing a man wearing a suit is required to choose is his shirt, which, to paraphrase Henry Ford, can be any color as long as it's white. You see? It's not really a choice at all! But on Friday, these seemingly tasteful businessmen who've impressed co-workers and clients all week with their office finery must now don a set of clothes that are not pre-matched. Consequently, a large number of corporate leaders reveal themselves to be garden-variety dorks. It took a while, but eventually they caught on, and Casual Friday was phased out. The memo would explain that the return to formality was out of respect for clients, but everyone knew it was so the boss could go back to hiding behind a suit.

Bernadette offered to buy me a suit for Joey's baptism.

"I would give you one of Tim-o-thee's," she said, referring to her late husband, "but it would be too little for you."

A laugh escaped before I could suppress it.

"Mr. Max, you must look your best for Joey's baptism," she persisted. "She in her beautiful pink dress and you in your beautiful new suit. It will be wonderful."

It dawned on me that the only time I'd seen Bernadette display any signs of obstinacy was when she was trying to do something nice for someone else.

"Don't worry, Bernadette. I'll just wear my school clothes."

I could see this statement confused her.

"Trust me, I'll look fine."

Bernadette was not reassured. She'd seen what kids in the neighborhood wear to school.

"But Mr. Max, you not going to school. You going to Joey's baptism. You have to look nice. Please. I will buy a suit for you."

"That's very generous, but I don't wear suits. I don't think they make you look nice. They make you look like you have no imagination. Who decided the only way a man can be taken seriously is by wearing a suit? It's absurd."

Bernadette was silent for several seconds and then looked at me with an odd expression.

"Yes!" she exclaimed, as if she'd just solved a Rubik's cube.

"Yes, what?"

"I have the idea!"

She started laughing. A moment later Joey ran into the room.

"What's so funny?" she asked, then joined in the laughter without waiting to find out.

"The joke's on me, I guess," I said with a touch of petulance.

"I have the perfect clo-thes for your daddy to wear to your baptism," she said to Joey.

"Yaaayyyy!" Joey chirped.

"I already told you, I'm not wearing a godda…a suit."

I was starting to get angry. As long as I didn't mix patterns, it was nobody's business what I wore.

"I'm gonna get you a barong," she said triumphantly.

The room went silent.

"A what?"

"A barong. It's what the Filipino men wear to get dressed up for something special like a wedding."

"A wedding?"

"Or a baptism," she quickly added.

"I'm not wearing anything formal!"

"No, no, it's not so formal. It's just like a shirt. You can wear it over your jeans and T-shirt, but now you will look very nice."

"Oh, Daddy's gonna look nice for my baptism," Joey sang.

"In his barong!" Bernadette chimed in.

"In his barong!" Joey echoed.

Then she took Bernadette's hands and the two of them danced around the room.

Later that evening, I turned to Google. As Bernadette had been trying to explain, a *barong tagalog* is an embroidered shirt traditionally worn by Filipino males on formal occasions. Oddly, a barong is so thin it's transparent. It was rumored that Spanish invaders made Filipinos wear barongs to keep them from concealing weapons, though this is now considered apocryphal.

In any case, should I agree to wear a barong to Joey's baptism, I will be forced to enter the church unarmed.

Though I believe this is a concession I can live with.

Because it's far less objectionable than Sunday clothes.

Or having a penis wrapped around my neck.

6

Fuck the Marlboro Man

"I...put out my hand and touched the face of God." This startling claim first came to my attention when I was eight years old. It's from the poem "High Flight" by John Gillespie Magee, Jr., a Royal Canadian Air Force pilot during World War II. Young John composed this ode to flying when he was just nineteen. He would not live to see twenty. My familiarity with his work should not be construed as a childhood predilection for Canadian poetry; rather, it is a by-product of my addiction to American television. One of the local stations used it as part of its nightly signoff, the recitation followed by "The Star-Spangled Banner" and several hours of electronic snow. I still think of that uplifting verse each time I step onto a plane, though I am anything but uplifted. What the voice in my head recites as I prepare to slip the surly bonds of Earth is, "Step into this eager craft, and you will die."

Had I considered that the *New York Times* help-wanted ad Angelica read to me that fateful Monday morning would eventually necessitate an intercontinental voyage in a winged aluminum tube, I can say with absolute sincerity that I never would have made the corresponding phone call; never would have established that mind-numbing connection with the molasses-mouthed Joe Motion. Indeed, had my Italian-American co-worker said, "Here's one that's perfect for you, Max, although should you be hired, it will oblige you to spend fourteen hours soaring thirty-six thousand feet above the Earth's surface," I would have told her (politely) to fuck off.

Honestly, I never believed I had a chance of landing that job. When I left the interview, I assumed the hotel pen would be my only reward. And frankly, it would have been enough. So the following morning when I arrived at work, everything was just fine. I exited the elevator, and there was Margaret, smiling beneficently. "How's your rectum?" she asked.

"Fine, how's yours?" I replied a split second before realizing she was referring to my fantasy rectal exam, the excuse I'd provided as a means of securing a half-day's leave.

"I mean, it's good," I quickly recovered. "In fact, the proctologist said I had nothing to worry about as long as I continue to maintain a vigorous regimen of healthy rectal care. You know...brushing...flossing...that sort of thing." I turned and walked on before she had a chance to respond.

Angelica was waiting for me when I stepped into our office, the look on her face making it clear she was desperate to know how the interview went.

I ignored her.

Five minutes later she broke the silence.

"You are such a fucking jerk!"

"It went fine," I said.

She nodded and waited for me to elaborate. I did not.

"So?"

"So what?"

"So did you get the job?"

"Get the job?"

"Yeah, did you get the fucking job?"

"What do you mean? You're the one that told me I didn't have a chance. Now you're asking me if I got the job?"

"I only said that because I knew you'd fuck it up if you thought you actually had a chance."

"So you thought I had a chance?"

"Of course I thought you had a chance. Why else would I tell you to go to the interview?"

"All that about it being a good experience and eating sushi and enjoying New York? All that was bullshit?"

"It wasn't bullshit. But I still thought you had a chance."

"So you think I'm a good enough writer?"

"No, I think you're a good enough bullshitter."

I nodded. She had a point.

"I didn't get the job."

"How do you know?"

"I could tell. They didn't ask me anything about writing. They didn't say anything about the job. It was really weird. There was this old Japanese guy who was asleep most of the time. All he wanted to know was if I drank beer."

"I told you to put that on your résumé."

"And this other guy, some weird Japanese redneck."

"Japan has rednecks?"

"I don't know. It doesn't matter. But at least I got this."

I held up the hotel pen.

"That's impressive," she said.

"I got something else, too. Something I think you'll really appreciate."

Angelica looked at me suspiciously. I held up my left arm. It took a moment for her to catch on.

"I don't fucking believe it!" she laughed.

She stood and walked over to my side of the desk to take a closer look at my new watchband.

"What made you do it?"

"I don't know. I wasn't thinking too clearly after the interview, so I just started walking. After a while, I ducked into a store on Eighth Avenue to get warm, and the next thing I knew a whole case of watchbands was staring me in the face."

"How much?"

"Four dollars."

"Did they have an installment plan?"

"I paid cash."

"Wow, Max, you really are evolving."

Angelica stood there a moment longer waiting for some sign that our conversation was over—something tangible, like that sucking sound at the end of a milkshake. I could tell she felt bad for me, that she wanted to say something encouraging. Finally, she patted me on the shoulder and returned to her desk.

Less than a minute later the phone rang.

Angelica picked up the receiver.

"Yeah?" she said in an irritated voice, maintaining her high standard of phone etiquette.

"Hunh?" I heard her say a moment later.

A flash of movement caught my attention, and I looked up to see Angelica offering me the receiver, her arm fully extended.

She was holding it in a way that suggested she found it repugnant, as if it were smeared with bat guano or some equally unpleasant substance. I leaned forward and took it between my thumb and middle finger. There were no obvious signs of excrement, so I put it to my ear and said, "Hello?"

"Huuuullllloooo, Mmmaaaaaxxxx."

"Who is this?" I demanded, as if it were a prank call.

"Iiitttt'ssss Joooooe Mmmmmotion."

"Sorry, Joe, I didn't recognize your voice. What's up?"

"Thhhhheeeeeeeeeeeeyyyyyyyyy saaaaaaaaaiiiiiiiiiidddddddddd aaaaaaaaiiiiiiiiiiiiiiiiiiiiii sssssaaaaaaaaaaaavvvvvveddddddddd thhaaaaaaa bbbbeeeessssstttt ffffffooooooorrrrrrrrrr lllllllllaaaaaaaaaaaaaasssssssssssssst."

"Hey, Joe, we must have a bad connection. Could you repeat that? Only like…ten times faster?"

There were several seconds of silence on the other end of the line. Then, a deep sucking sound, the gurgly kind one associates with a plethora of mucus. It was brutally unpleasant. And then I understood. The pear-shaped man was attempting to fill his lungs with air.

"Thheeyyy saiiiddd IIII ssaaveddd thaaa bbeesstttt ffoorrrr llllaasssssttt."

They said I saved the best for last.

It made no sense.

Another deep sucking sound.

"Yyouuu wweerrree thaaa llllllaasssttt innttttterrvviieeww inn Neeewwww Yooorrrrrrkkk."

I was the last interview in New York.

What was he trying to tell me?

A categorical syllogism quickly formed in my mind:

Major premise: They saved the best for last.

Minor premise: I was the last.

Conclusion: I am the best!

It took the big man several minutes to communicate the following information, because he was no longer able to accelerate his speech by drawing in large quantities of air. In fact, I suspected he'd depleted the ambient supply and his respiration was now dependent on a roomful of foul-smelling carbon dioxide. In any case, after I left the interview, Yamakawa-san invited Joe Motion into the room and suggested he'd saved the best for last. The headhunter was delighted to hear this, for should I be hired, his commission would be equivalent to twenty percent of my first year's salary. The two of them continued their discussion—both perfectly at ease with the other's idiosyncratic speech patterns—and, after several minutes, had probably exchanged no more syllables than those found in your average *haiku*.

Upon learning I aced the New York interview, I allowed myself to believe I had a chance of living in a land where office workers too drunk to find their way home can sleep it off in a hotel room the size of a horizontal phone booth. I emphasize the word *chance* because Yamakawa-san and Hillbilly Brad were off to interview a second batch of candidates in Chicago, one of America's great advertising towns. The storied Leo Burnett Company is based there, and they came up with what is widely considered to be the most successful advertising icon of all time: the Marlboro Man. Even though I'd scored in New York, the job was by no means mine. It just meant that it wasn't completely unreasonable for me to entertain a little hope.

"I fucking told you!" Angelica shouted when I hung up the phone.

"What?"

"You got the fucking job!"

"No, I didn't."

"Bullshit. I can see it on your face!"

"That's not it. He just told me I was the top candidate in New York."

"So you got the fucking job!"

"No, Angelica," I said as if talking to a six-year-old. "Now they're going to do interviews in Chicago."

"Chicago?" she said as if she'd just stepped in shit.

I nodded.

"What are you worried about?"

"The Marlboro Man?"

"Fuck the Marlboro Man!"

There was a rapping at the door, and a moment later Margaret stuck her face into the room.

"Everything okay in here?" she asked in the condescending voice people use when they want you to "lower the volume."

"Max's rectum is still a little sore," Angelica explained before I had a chance to respond.

Margaret looked at me and nodded sympathetically.

"He was telling me the doctor had really big fingers."

I watched Margaret's face for several seconds, her look of befuddlement gradually giving way to a grimace of understanding.

"You bastard!" Angelica said the moment we were alone again.

"What?"

"You're going to Japan."

When I got home that evening I told my girlfriend, Annette, there was a fifty-fifty chance of me landing the job. That's how I saw the race at this point: even odds for the New York–Chicago matchup. Up until then, she'd believed, as had I, that my chances were more like one in a million.

"Oh my god," she exclaimed in her lilting Hungarian accent, "we could go to Australia!"

Annette had come over from Budapest when she was twenty-three to study animal husbandry at the University of Illinois. It wasn't long before she lost interest in the purification protocols for bull semen and managed to secure a transfer to Rutgers University in New Brunswick, New Jersey, where she pursued a degree in criminology. As part of her studies, she was required to do several ride-alongs with patrol officers of the New Brunswick Police Department. That's how Annette and I first made contact. She happened to be in the patrol car the night I was pulled over for suspicion of driving under the influence. It was all a misunderstanding. I'd recently consumed a shredded-beef taco, and one of the shreds had become lodged in the recesses of my upper left wisdom tooth. I'd been trying to work it free with my tongue, but after several minutes of fruitless struggle, I flipped on the dome light and attempted to catch a glimpse of the errant strand in the rearview mirror. Since I was driving down Raritan Avenue, one of New Brunswick's main thoroughfares, I glanced through the windshield every few seconds in order to make course corrections and avoid oncoming traffic. Upon the third glance, I was dismayed to see that the car in front of me, a late model Chevrolet Capri, had come to a stop. Based on the blinking taillight, I deduced that the driver was preparing to make a left turn, which, at that moment, seemed exceptionally inconsiderate. I slammed on the brakes and managed to stop just before our bumpers made contact. The Capri completed its left turn and drove off, oblivious to the accident that had barely been averted. I put my foot on the accelerator and returned to the excavation of my wisdom tooth. Seconds later a patrol car swooped in, lights flashing, and forced me to pull over.

As I passed my license and registration to the painfully thin police officer, I tried to explain the reason for my momentary spate of erratic driving, supporting it with visual effects by opening my mouth and indicating the tooth where the taco remnant had taken refuge, but it was obvious from his jaded expression that he'd already heard this story—or some bullshit variation of it—a million times and nothing would convince him of my sobriety short of successfully completing his curriculum of foolproof acrobatics: stand on one foot, hop up and down on it, stand on the other foot, hop up and down on it, walk a straight line, and touch my index fingers to my nose. The cop was just beginning to believe I might be telling the truth when a beautiful woman stepped from the passenger side of the patrol car. She appeared to be in her mid-twenties, slim with dark hair and mysterious, deep-set eyes.

"You should stay in the car," the officer said sternly.

"I'm not afraid of him," she said in a soft, eastern-European accent.

"Annette," he said as she walked up to me, his voice now more pleading than authoritative.

"Hey, boy," she said when her face was no more than a few inches from my own, "are you a drunk?"

I had no idea what role she was playing in this unfolding saga, but since she was authoritative, foreign, and somehow connected to the police department, I wasn't about to mess with her. Thus, the first words I ever uttered to the woman I was about to fall in love with were, "No, ma'am."

"I believe him," she said to the police officer without taking her eyes from mine.

Then she leaned in close and whispered in her charming accent, "Do you want me to frisk you?"

I opened my mouth to say something—I have no recollection what those words might have been—but found myself unable to speak. A moment later she smiled the most beautiful smile I'd ever seen, and that was it. Head over heels.

"I think we should let this one go," she proclaimed.

The cop shrugged like he didn't give a shit and climbed back into the patrol car. She looked intently at me for several seconds, and I actually felt my body temperature begin to rise. Then, without another word, she turned and started walking back toward the cruiser.

"Annette?" I said tentatively.

She spun around, a surprised look on her face, then seemed to recall that the cop used her name. Gradually, her surprise gave way to another beautiful smile.

"I'll be at The Trattoria at nine-thirty," she said.

I nodded. The Trattoria was one of the best Italian restaurants in the area—delicious, reasonably priced Italian pasta and pizza with a corkage fee of only three dollars. As soon as the patrol car's taillights disappeared, I drove to a liquor store, bought a mid-priced bottle of French wine, and went home. It took me half an hour to dig the sinew out of my tooth, which left me just enough time to shower, dress, and make it to The Trattoria by nine-thirty.

Annette slept at my place that night, but we didn't have sex. We just held each other and kissed and talked, and it was just as good as having sex—or so I thought until the next night, when we did have sex and it was infinitely better than not having sex, although we still spent a lot of time holding each other and kissing and talking. Three years later we were still having sex, but we didn't do much holding and kissing and talking any more. Our relationship had moved into that soulless phase where we co-existed in a state of mutual apathy—not loving, not hating, not sure why we were still together. Ultimately, Annette and I just weren't that compatible. We had different dreams and wanted different things out of life, but neither of us could muster the energy to break up. Angelica once asked me why we stayed together, and I told her it was inertia—the propensity of a body in motion to continue moving in the direction of that motion until acted on by an external force.

"Bullshit," Angelica had retorted. "You just like fucking her."

I nodded. She had a point.

Then she added, "In fact, your whole story is bullshit. You keep saying *we* when you talk about her, but you really mean *I*. It's all about you. I'll bet you don't have a clue how she feels."

"So you're on her side now?"

"I don't give a shit about your Bulgarian trollop."

"She's Hungarian."

"Good for her. All I'm saying is why stay together if you're not happy? You're not married, for Christ's sake. You don't have any kids to screw up."

Inertia, that's why.

I was waiting for the arrival of an external force.

Japan.

Now there's an external force.

"What do you mean we could go to Australia?" I asked my Hungarian trollop.

"I mean if we move to Japan, we could go to Australia because it's so much closer than New Jersey."

I found this sentence troubling on a number of levels.

While it's true that Japan is significantly closer to Australia than is New Jersey, it's not like you can just hop on a ferry and spend the afternoon waltzing Matilda. Tokyo to Sydney is a ten-hour flight. Even more troubling than her sense of distance was her choice of pronouns: if *we* move to Japan. Rather than share my concerns, I decided to concede; it wasn't worth getting into a fight until I was offered the job—if I ever was.

"Yeah, that would be fun," I finally agreed with a modicum of sincerity. (The duck-billed platypus is my favorite egg-laying mammal.)

Annette smiled her beautiful smile and gave me a tender kiss; I nudged her toward the bedroom.

Inertia.

The next week was a pretty weird one.

Hillbilly Brad told Joe Motion he'd call from Chicago to let him know their decision once they'd finished with the Marlboro Men. They were interviewing from Monday through Wednesday, so I figured they'd let the winner know as early as Wednesday night or at the latest by Thursday morning. After all, they'd made their New York decision within moments of the final interview. (*They saved the best for last. I was the last. I am the best.*)

Angelica was the worst. It was as if she were on death row, waiting for the warden to peer through the bars of her cell and announce, "It's time." The phone startled her every time it rang.

"Why are you so jumpy?" I asked. "I'm the one with his ass on the line. You don't have anything to lose."

"I'm not jumpy!" she'd bark. "And what do you mean I don't have anything to lose? Who knows what kind of jerkoff they'll stick me with next! Yeah, you're a pain in my ass, but at least I can control you."

Despite a natural inclination toward cynicism, I couldn't help but share Angelica's inverted optimism. And it was driving me crazy. This whole thing had started out as a laugh, and now here I was, seriously invested in its outcome, my future in the hands of two Japanese men one might charitably describe as "kooky." Thus, I invoked the sour-grapes clause. That is, I didn't really want the job because the Japanese bombed Pearl Harbor; the Japanese invented Hello Kitty; I love dolphins and whales; there's no way I'm spending fourteen hours in a winged aluminum tube; and, if I fail, I won't have to tell Annette she's staying in New Jersey.

Wednesday came and went, and I did not hear from Joe Motion. Fuck.

Thursday came and went, and I did not hear from Joe Motion.

Fuck.

Oh well.

Fuck.

At least I still have Annette.

Fuck.

When I got home from work, that's exactly what we did.

And it was epic.

Complete catharsis.

The best sex we'd ever had.

So incredible that our connection transcended the physical.

As I was lying next to her in the wake of our lovemaking, it occurred to me that I still cared deeply for this beautiful Hungarian woman. That it would have been impossible to leave her behind. For the first time in months, we were holding each other and kissing and talking. Falling in love all over again. It was the perfect moment.

Then I noticed the blinking light on the answering machine.

"You didn't check the messages?" I asked her.

"What?"

"You knew I was waiting for a call."

Annette rolled on top of me and put her face two inches from my own.

"No, I didn't know you were waiting for a call," she said softly, "You said some pineapple man was supposed to call you at work."

"Pear," I corrected, "He's a pear-shaped man."

As Annette reached out for the playback button, I felt her breasts move against my skin. It was unspeakably erotic, and I wrapped my arms tightly around her.

"What's this?" she asked coyly.

"I love you," I said.

Although I would repeat this declaration several times over the next few weeks, this was the last time I actually meant it. Before Annette could reciprocate, and I'm certain she was about to, a nasally voice filled the room.

"This here's a message fer Max. I need to discuss somthin' with y'all."

I sat bolt upright in the bed, nearly propelling Annette to the floor, and stared at the answering machine as if the hillbilly's face were peeking out of it.

"Since y'all don't seem to be home, I'll call back in 'bout two hours."

I felt Annette staring at me.

"It's five-thirty now, so I'll git back to y'all 'bout eight-thirty."

That's three hours, you dipshit.

"I mean eight-thirty y'all's time; seven-thirty Chicago time."

Okay, not a dipshit.

"All right then…"

He let the last phrase hang in the air, and I imagined him sitting on one of those overstuffed hotel chairs with the barely noticeable stains, trying to remember if there was anything else he needed to say.

"Oh yeah," he continued a few moments later, "this is Brad."

I heard a click signaling the end of the message.

"He has a very funny accent," Annette said in the silence that followed.

I nodded.

"Oh my god," I said at last.

"Are you okay?"

"Yeah…I'm fine."

I was stunned.

"You look…funny."

I nodded again.

"What did he want?"

A categorical syllogism quickly formed in my mind:

Major premise: They call the winner.

Minor premise: They called me.

Conclusion: Fuckin' A!

"That was Hillbilly Brad," I told her, "one of the guys who interviewed me."

Annette's eyes went wide.

"Does that mean…"

She couldn't finish.

"I think so," I finally said.

"What should we do?" she whispered.

I looked at my watch.

"I could really use a doughnut."

She looked at me as if I'd just spoken Swahili.

"He's not gonna call back for an hour and a half. We have plenty of time."

"Doughnuts for dinner?"

"We can get some pizza, too," I said.

Annette loves pizza the way I love doughnuts.

"Oh my god!" she cried, "We're going to Japan!"

I found this sentence troubling on a number of levels.

Friday morning I told Angelica I got the job, and she seemed genuinely happy for me. "I can't believe it!" she kept saying, "You're going to Japan!" She had said the same thing on previous occasions, but always prefaced it with "You bastard."

Hillbilly Brad had called at eight-thirty, as promised, just as I was finishing my third doughnut. Annette and I shared the pizza, but she left all the doughnuts to me.

"Those things make you fat," she would always say.

As opposed to the slimming effects of Italian sausage and double cheese.

"Max, ah've got good news for y'all," he drawled after I'd said hello.

I looked over at Annette and nodded.

Even though I'd expected the confirmation, it was still overwhelming. I wanted to jump up and down and scream like some dildo who'd just won a blender on *The Price Is Right*, but I managed to maintain my composure. Hillbilly Brad went over the timetable and discussed the visa application procedure and told me I'd be receiving a FedEx package containing a contract and information about the job and other materials that would prepare me for the transition from East Coast to Far East. As I hung up the phone, I saw that Annette was crying. She might have been weeping for joy, but I suspected her tears were connected to a deeper realization that my good fortune portended the end of our relationship. I took her into my arms and rocked her gently. I know it seems like a loving gesture, but I recall wondering how long I should maintain this soothing embrace before sliding my hand into her pants.

About three and a half minutes.

7

This Is Not a Test

The Bible says, "Judge not lest ye be judged." I disagree. Survival depends on one's ability to judge. Take the college boy on spring break who jumps from the balcony of his hotel room, certain he can hit the swimming pool seven stories below. At the coroner's inquest, it is ruled that the unfortunate young man exercised poor judgment. But, one might argue, the verse doesn't prohibit the exercise of good judgement; it prohibits one from judging others. Tell that to yourself the next time you pass up a hitchhiker. No, Matthew got it wrong. Firesign Theatre got it right. What the Bible should have said is, "We're all bozos on this bus."

I share my ideas about judging others with Bernadette. It doesn't go well.

"But it's in the Bible," she insists.

"Yes."

"So it's God's word."

"They're actually Matthew's words," I correct.

"But Matthew was only saying what God wanted him to say."

"Okay, God's words. But it's still ridiculous."

"Oh, Mr. Max, please don't say that."

"What?"

"That God is ridiculous."

I can see Bernadette no longer wants to be a part of this discussion. That she'd rather make more coffee or go play with Joey. But that doesn't stop me.

"Because if I say God is ridiculous I'll go to hell?"

She looks down at the floor and shakes her head.

"Is that it? You think I'm going to hell?"

She continues to shake her head.

I go for the kill.

"Are you judging me, Bernadette?"

When she looks up, her eyes are filled with tears.

"Oh, Mr. Max," she sobs, "I would never judge you!"

As she weeps, I stand immobile, wanting to apologize but unable to find the words. Part of me takes comfort in the fact that I didn't actually intend to hurt her. The other part reminds me I'm a piece of shit.

Joey bursts into the room.

"Daddy, what did you do?"

Why does she automatically assume it was something I did?

"I accidentally made Bernadette cry."

"Oh, Daddy," she says disappointedly.

Joey runs to Bernadette and hugs her tightly. The sobbing stops.

Bernadette looks over at me, a painful expression on her face.

"I'm so sorry, Mr. Max," she says.

She's sorry?

Before I can forgive her, Joey says, "Don't worry, Bernadette. It's not your fault. Daddy's just an a-word sometimes."

A-word?

"Joey, what do you mean by a-word?" I demand.

Instead of responding, she takes Bernadette by the hand and leads her from the room.

"Judge not lest ye be judged!" I yell after her.

Later, Joey comes to me and says, "Daddy, we're going to the park."

"Okay, have a good time."

"I said *we*."

We?

"You're coming with us."

"I don't think so."

She gives me a look I've seen at one time or another on the face of every woman who's been in my life. It projects the following: *you were a total asshole, and now it's time to atone.* I have no interest in doing penance, but instead of simply refusing, I make the mistake of offering an excuse.

"Joey, I have a lot to do."

"What?"

"What do you mean?"

"What do you have to do?"

"Lots of stuff."

"Like what?"

"Like getting some work done."

"Work?"

"Yeah, work. That's what I do to earn money so you can live in this nice house and eat good food and play in the park that I'm not going to go with you to."

Despite the unwieldy number of prepositions, I believe my message is clear.

"You said you didn't have any work this weekend."

"I didn't say that."

"Yes you did! You said you were going to take it easy this weekend because you don't have any work."

"Well, I have other things to do."

"What?"

"They're none of your business."

"Why not?"

"Because they're private."

"Private?"

Joey looks genuinely confused.

It occurs to me that she might understand the word *private* in the context of *private parts*. I had recently introduced this term to her as I explained that there are certain parts of her body that no one else is allowed to touch. Her private parts. I had been encouraged to do this by Janice, a former co-worker who has a daughter about Joey's age.

"There's a lotta pervs out there," Janice informed me.

I consider expanding Joey's understanding of the p-word, but any explanation would surely lead to more questions.

"May I bring a book?"

My capitulation does not surprise her. I grab a paperback from the bookshelf and follow her out the door. It's a beautiful day, at least in terms of the weather: a brilliant blue sky, augmented by a tasteful assortment of fluffy cumulus clouds— the poor man's Rorschach test. I remember loving days like this as a kid, and had I been Joey's age, I surely would have been as enthusiastic as she was about a visit to the park. But, in accordance with the teachings of Paul the Apostle, I have given up my childish ways and thus would rather be drinking beer and watching reality television.

For such a nice day, there are only a few people in the park. A brother and sister play on the swing set, their devoted mother seated nearby, attentive eyes glued to her smartphone. Across the park, a young couple is arguing. I can't make out their words, but body language always gives it away. Particularly when it involves a slap to the face or a kick to the groin. Up ahead, a pudgy jogger bullies his way by Bernadette and Joey, forcing them to step off the narrow sidewalk. He's dressed from head to toe in yellow: yellow headband with logo; gauzy yellow singlet; crotch-hugging yellow running shorts with side slits up to the waistband; and high-tech yellow running shoes bearing a logo identical to the one on his headband. Unlike Bernadette and Joey, I refuse to give way as he approaches on the narrow sidewalk. He veers to the right at the last moment.

"Nice outfit, Banana Man," I murmur too softly for him to hear.

"Fuck you," he murmurs back.

I notice only two other people in the park. One is a neat-looking man, probably in his early thirties, wearing a pink polo shirt and khaki trousers. He's standing near a tree, holding an expensive-looking camera. The other is a very old man, late eighties or early nineties, sitting on a bench not far from the climbing gym. I smile when I see that he is smoking a cigarette.

I love it when old people smoke.

For more than half a century he's had to listen to endless warnings about the harmful effects of smoking, about cancer and emphysema and diabetes and arterial degeneration and bad breath and yellow teeth and smelly fingers and all the other caveats included in the nonsmokers' credo. Yet he's outlived most of his contemporaries and a fair number of his juniors. I watch as his trembling hand guides the tiny tube of desiccated leaves to his pale, dry lips. They clench as it comes to rest between them, and as he inhales, the cigarette's orangish tip begins to glow, brighter and brighter, until I must shield my eyes from its fiery brilliance. He draws the smoke deeper and deeper into his lungs, a process so oft repeated it is now involuntary. When they can hold no more, he suddenly freezes and remains absolutely still for several moments as the nicotine caresses and cajoles his alveoli, seeking access to the bloodstream, whereupon it will be whisked to his brain and transformed into a mild yet irresistible feeling of satisfaction that must be experienced to be understood. Transfer complete, his chest begins to fall and the smoke is expelled from his grateful lungs, a copious cloud of whitish gray that would seek out and engulf any nonsmoker in the immediate vicinity.

Bernadette and Joey have reached the climbing gym, but I am in no hurry to follow. The prospect of accompanying my daughter up the chain ladder, across the miniature wooden bridge, and down the child-size tunnel slide—for she will surely insist that I share her adventure—holds little appeal. Thus, I find myself walking over to the ancient smoker.

"Hey, old timer," I hear myself say.

Not once in my life have I used this particular term, and I wonder why I'm using it now. To the best of my recollection, I've never heard *old timer* said by anyone outside of a cowboy movie.

The old man looks up.

"Mind if I sit down?"

He slides to the far-right edge of the bench.

I like this old fella, I think to myself.

In my mind he becomes Walter Brennan, a peerless actor from the golden age of cinema who spent his entire career playing old men. His characters were inevitably cranky, womanless, and drunk—a profile with which I am vaguely familiar—yet he managed to instill in each of them an undeniably endearing quality. Such was his appeal that John Wayne, America's favorite heterosexual cowboy, gave him a tender kiss in the Howard Hawks masterpiece *Rio Bravo*.

"I see that you're smoking," I say to the old man as he sucks in a lungful of pleasure. He narrows his eyes, almost invisible beneath the sagging skin of his eyelids. Fearing he'll think I'm some anti-smoking crusader bent on eliminating the one remaining activity that lends purpose to his existence, I quickly add, "I think it's great. I think it's great that you're smoking. I like watching old people smoke." His expression does not change, and I begin to wonder if he's hard of hearing. "Yeah," I continue at a significantly higher decibel level, "I bet you're sick and tired of all those self-righteous nonsmokers telling you about the harmful effects of cigarettes." Still no reaction. I speak even louder. "I'm not like them. I used to be a smoker myself, but I quit. That doesn't mean I don't support your right to smoke. Hell, I'm more of a tobacco advocate now than when I did smoke. I love it when people light up. If fact, I encourage them to."

This is complete bullshit, and I have no idea where it's coming from. When I quit, I was extremely annoyed with anyone who failed to follow my example.

"Are you queer?" the old man rasps.

Surely I misunderstood.

"Are you queer?" he rasps a little louder.

Evidently not.

"What's the matter, you deaf?"

I keep waiting for the endearing Walter Brennen quality to kick in, but judging from the rage in the old man's squint, I'm guessing it won't happen anytime soon.

"No," I hear myself say.

My voice rises as I make the denial, so it sounds more like a question than a response.

"No, what?"

"Hunh?"

"No, you're not queer, or no, you're not deaf?"

As soon as he completes his mocking query, he takes another huge drag on his cigarette and then blows the smoke toward my face.

"I'm neither," I say a bit more convincingly, "and *queer* is a very offensive term in this context. If you want to question my sexual orientation, you should ask if I'm gay."

"So you're not queer, but you're gay, is that it?" He seems amused by this distinction.

"I'm neither. And how about showing a little civility, pops."

"Civility?" he repeats. I hear a note of sentimentality in his voice, as if the word has triggered a memory from his youth. He appears thoughtful for several seconds, and I see that my words have made a meaningful difference in this lonely old man's life.

"Gay. Queer. They're all a bunch of cocksuckers to me."

He breaks into a monumental coughing fit, the kind of full-body spasm that validates the phrase *coughing up a lung*. As I wait for it to pass, I'm fascinated to observe that even as his ancient body convulses and contorts, he struggles to get the cigarette back to his mouth.

"What's your problem?" I demand once the spasm has passed. "You should have learned a little tolerance by now. A little compassion. Maybe you should just mellow out instead of being such a cranky old bastard."

"Don't judge me, you son of a bitch!" he screams, although his voice is so raspy and weak it's barely audible. "I'm sittin' here mindin' my own business, then you slither up and tell me you like to watch men smoke. That seems pretty goddamn queer to me!"

"I didn't slither up, and I didn't say I liked watching men smoke," I correct. "I walked up and said I like watching old people smoke. I mean, here you are, what, ninety years old? And you're still puffing away. I think that's…"

"I'm fifty-eight years old, you four-eyed motherfucker!"

"Fifty-eight? Jesus!"

As he gets to his feet, I realize he doesn't look quite as old as I'd originally assumed. Late seventies, early eighties maybe. But fifty-eight? No way. I wonder if he has some latent form of progeria. Hoping we can part on good terms, I extend my hand in friendship. Instead of shaking it, he flips his saliva-soaked cigarette at me. It clings to my T-shirt for a moment and then falls to the ground, but the glowing tip remains embedded in the fabric. By the time I feel the heat, it's burned a hole just above my navel. He reaches into his pocket and pulls out an iPhone.

"I'm gonna call the cops on you if you follow me," he warns. He takes several steps backward and then turns and shuffles away.

"Have a nice day," I call after him.

I glance around until I spot Joey and Bernadette sitting at a picnic table. They are in the middle of a discussion, and Joey is pointing toward the swing set across the park. She runs toward it without seeing me approach. When I reach the table, Bernadette is wearing an expression of deep concentration, a look I've come to recognize as a prelude to her sharing something she finds difficult to articulate.

"Mr. Max, I…"

"It's okay, Bernadette. It was my fault."

A look of confusion appears on her face, which I take to mean she's caught off guard by my willingness to accept the blame.

"Yeah, it's okay. That whole thing about judging is just a matter of perspective, and I shouldn't have challenged yours. You have the right to believe whatever you want to believe, no matter how implausible I find it."

A moment later, recognition fills her eyes and she says, "No, it's the man…"

"Seriously, Bernadette, it's okay. Neither of us really did anything wrong. It was just a difference of opinion."

"I try not to judge him, but something is wrong…"

"You mean the old guy?" I interrupt.

Later, I will sift through the pieces of this conversation and wonder if I hadn't been so smug, if I had let Bernadette say what she was desperately trying to say instead of finishing her sentences for her, might the tragic turn of events have been avoided?

She is staring into the distance. I follow her gaze and see Joey walking from swing to swing, examining the chains that support the seats, as if she's trying to determine which will offer the most enjoyable ride. The smartphone family is nowhere in sight.

"The old guy?" Bernadette says, looking at me.

"Yeah, he was a real piece of work."

She is unfamiliar with the idiom.

"I mean, he was really...kooky."

Next to my temple, I make a circling motion with my right index finger, the universal symbol for kooky.

Bernadette nods and waits for me to continue.

"I was just trying to be friendly, and he got really angry just because I pointed out that cigarettes are harmful."

"The cigarettes are very bad," Bernadette agrees.

"Guess how old he is."

"Who?"

"The guy I was talking to. Guess how old he is."

Bernadette looks over at the vacant bench where we'd been sitting, as if she can still see the old bastard.

"Sixty?"

"Sixty! Jesus, Bernadette, that guy had to be at least eighty-five!"

"He's eighty-five?" she asks, genuinely surprised.

"No, he's fifty-eight."

"Fifty-eight," she repeats, "I miss by two years." She says this as if it were a failure.

"C'mon, Bernadette, that guy looked like he was in his eighties!"

"But you said fifty-eight."

"I did. I mean that's how old he is. But I'm talking about how old he looks."

"Sixty," she repeats, missing my point entirely.

I'm tempted to continue, to harangue her until she does see my point, but after this morning's fiasco, I decide to give it a rest.

"Maybe people age faster in the Philippines," I say by way of compromise.

"Oh, he definitely not Filipino."

I'm thinking about cigarettes now, about how, if I did smoke, this would definitely be the time to light up. I never have the craving, but I do recollect those moments when a cigarette could alleviate even the most unpleasant of situations.

"Did you ever smoke?" I ask.

She looks at me, and I'm amused to see a look of shame on her face.

"Bernadette?"

Her light-brown skin is suffused with red, but after several moments her guilty expression gives way to a shy smile.

"Once," she admits, "when I was eleven years old."

I smile back. I had my first smoke when I was about the same age.

"My friend Rizalyn and me sees an empty pack of cigarettes on the street, and she picks it up. There is still one cigarette inside. I remember it is American cigarettes. Kool. So we think it will be cool, like peppermint candy. We run to her house and get some matches. Then we go to the sea. We have a hiding place behind the rocks, and that's where we go to smoke the Kool cigarette. Rizalyn is first. She puts it in her mouth and sucks on it and then she's coughing. She's coughing and coughing and I'm saying, 'Is it good? Is it good?' But she can't talk. She hands to me the cigarette and I suck in the smoke and it's like fire. Now we are both coughing, but we are laughing, too. She tries again. But it's just as bad. Then my turn. Then her turn. And we keep doing that, laughing and coughing and laughing and coughing. But then I start to feel dizzy. And my stomach is dizzy, too. Like I'm gonna be sick. So I run out of the rocks and down to the sea and throw up in the water. It's horrible. When I was finish I see Rizalyn throwing up in the water just like me. I go over and we hug each other, and we are both crying. But then we are laughing. And then we go back home. And that's the only time I ever smoke a cigarette."

I'm still smiling. It's nice to hear a story from Bernadette's past that doesn't involve abuse or degradation. She shifts her eyes and looks across the park. Joey is sitting on a swing, her feet doing a little dance in the dirt as she tries to create some momentum.

"I never did much care for menthol cigarettes," I say.

Bernadette looks over at me.

"Did you smoke a lot?" she asks.

"I guess. About a pack and a half a day."

"Is that a lot?"

"Thirty cigarettes."

"Thirty? Oh, Mr. Max, you smoke a lot."

"Smoked. I smoked a lot. Past tense. I quit more than twenty years ago."

"And you never smoke again?"

"Not one cigarette. Or cigar. Or pipe. Or chewing tobacco. I gave it all up. I'm not like these people who only light up from time to time, when they're out with their friends. Out drinking. The social smokers. In my world, you either smoke all the time or you don't smoke at all."

"Like an addiction," she observes.

"Exactly."

"Like beer."

"And doughnuts."

"And I think you are addicted to coffee, too."

"Happily."

"Was it hard to quit?"

"Cigarettes? No, not really. Not if you really want to do it."

"Everyone tell me it's hard to quit smoking the cigarettes."

"Quitting isn't hard. *Trying* to quit is hard."

Bernadette looks confused.

"People who say they're trying to quit smoking never do."

"Why not?"

"Because when you *try* to do something, your goal is the attempt."

"I'm sorry, but I..."

"Think of it like this. Your hands are dirty. So you need to wash them. Now, do you say, 'I'm going to try to wash my hands' or do you say, 'I'm going to wash my hands'?"

Bernadette smiles. "I'm going to wash my hands."

"Right. Because it's not a question of trying. You just walk up to the sink, grab a bar of soap, and wash your hands."

"So if you want to quit smoking..."

"You just quit. You don't smoke any more. It's that simple. You experience some temporary discomfort, but it's not that bad. Not compared to lung cancer or emphysema. But when you *try* to quit smoking, what you're really doing is taking an uncomfortable hiatus, because deep down you know you're not really going to stop. So a few hours or a few days or a few weeks later, you light up again. But here's the ironic thing: you've succeeded. You've achieved your goal. You've done exactly what you said you were going to do: you tried to quit smoking."

"Do you ever miss the cigarettes, Mr. Max?" Bernadette asks me.

"You know, it's funny, I don't miss cigarettes at all, but even after all this time I still have dreams where I'm smoking. They're so real I can taste the tobacco, and I always tell myself it's okay if I have a few. I can stop anytime I want. But I never do. I just keep puffing away until I wake up."

"Does that mean you want to smoke?"

"No, dreams don't work that way. Freud believed…"

Bernadette's body stiffens so suddenly and completely that for a moment she is unrecognizable. When she comes back into focus, I say her name but she does not respond.

Something is wrong.

This is not a test.

Bernadette's eyes are huge and filled with dread, and I see that she is staring at the swings. Joey is nowhere in sight.

"Bernadette, she probably just went…"

"He's gone," she says, a sharpness in her voice that I've never heard.

"Who's gone?"

She is now looking over to the tree under which the man in the pink shirt had been standing.

"You mean that asshole in the Dockers?"

"He has a camera!"

"Yeah, I saw that guy. What about him?"

Tears are rolling down her cheeks, but she is not crying. Jesus!

"Sometheeng wrong. Sometheeng wrong with theese man."

Her accent is suddenly very strong.

"What do you mean?"

She hurries off toward the swings and I follow after her.

"Joey!" she cries, "Joey!"

Without realizing it, I'm calling her name, too. I hear the panic in my voice, although I don't know why I'm so afraid.

This is not a test.

"Who is that guy?"

Bernadette stops yelling and scans the entire park. Joey is gone. The man is gone. I grab Bernadette by the shoulders and force her to look at me.

"Goddammit, who is he??"

"He comes here and takes peekchures. Peekchures of the birds and the flowers. But sometimes I theenk he is taking peekchures of the children. He is very far away but he has the tele…telephoto."

"Telephoto lens."

"Tim-o-thee have one, too. That is how I theenk he is taking peekchures of the children. He is far away, but I theenk he is taking peekchures of Joey. I never talk to him. I don't know him, so maybe I might be wrong."

"Wrong about what?"

She shakes her head.

"What are you talking about? Why is he taking pictures of J…"

A wave of panic washes over me, and for a moment I lose my balance. I start to fall but manage a little half step and remain upright. I reach for my cell phone to call someone—the police, I guess—when I notice Bernadette is no longer by my side. It takes a moment to locate her, for she is sprinting away faster than I've ever seen anyone run. Her speed is Olympic. Unearthly. Unreal. In fact, nothing is real. I am trapped; unable to move. I don't know how long I stand here, watching someone else act while I remain frozen; probably no more than a few seconds, but certainly long enough to feel the humiliation. I lift my eyes and see a flash of pink. He's far in front of Bernadette, something struggling in his arms.

This is not a test.

I'm running now, but I can't actually feel my body. It's like running in a dream. You never seem to go anywhere. I'm catching up to Bernadette, so I must be moving despite my sense of immobility. But the man in the pink shirt has a huge lead. When he reaches the parking lot, Bernadette is at least fifty yards behind. I'm another twenty-five behind her. Joey is screaming. I can just hear her voice. She is calling for me.

Please, God.

I notice everything. Cigarette butts where the old man was sitting. My paperback on the bench where I'd left it. A child's footprint in the dust by the swing set. A squirrel. A leaf. A butterfly. Yet I never take my eyes from the man holding Joey. He runs to a newish Honda Civic and opens the back door. Joey is kicking and struggling, and he's having difficulty controlling her. For a moment I think she will escape, but he tightens his grip and thrusts her toward the car. He misses the opening and Joey's face smashes into the doorframe. Her head snaps back as if it were on a hinge, and her body goes limp. The man takes a step back and throws her into the back seat. Throws her like a sack of garbage. I'm certain I will fall apart later, but my emotions remain strangely muted. Every part of my mind and body seem to be fixated on going faster. On reaching my baby. He scurries around to the driver's side, opens the door, and jumps in. I see the car shimmy ever so slightly as the engine comes to life. A moment later he pulls the door shut. Now he will drive away and he will hurt Joey and he will hurt Joey and he will hurt my baby and oh god oh god oh god please god please god please god…

Bernadette reaches the parking lot and is only a few steps from the Honda when it races off, tires squealing. To get to the exit, the man must make a left turn. Bernadette instinctively cuts between two parked cars and races for the exit at an angle. *The square of the hypotenuse is equal to the sum of the squares of the other two sides.*

I'm almost to the parking lot when the car reaches the street. Bernadette is too late.

Please, God.

And then she leaps.

Like Superman when he takes off flying. Only Bernadette doesn't fly. She just slams into the side of the Honda. She gets her hands on the driver's-side door and, because the window is down, is able to hold on. Her unexpected arrival startles the

132 • MARC X GRIGOROFF

man, but he's too busy negotiating his exit from the parking lot to respond. He manages to complete the turn, but just as he accelerates, Bernadette reaches into the car and grabs the steering wheel. The Honda veers sharply to the left, towards the parked cars on that side of the street, but just before making contact, the man jerks the wheel to the right and they swerve back across the road. It sideswipes a light blue mini-van. Bernadette pulls the wheel back toward her, and the car shoots to the left. They almost smash into a white Ford, but once again the driver manages to wrestle the wheel in the opposite direction. I reach the street and am only twenty feet behind the swerving car. There is no sign of Joey, but I visualize her being flung around violently. The car continues to veer back and forth across the small road when the man finally realizes his mistake. Instead of fighting against the crazy woman clinging to the side of his car, he suddenly turns the wheel in the direction she is pulling. The Honda rockets across the street and sideswipes a beige Volkswagen Beetle. As Bernadette's body is crushed against it, I hear a sound that leaves a scar on my soul. She releases her grip and falls to the ground. When I race past, I do not look at her. The front end of the Honda has been badly damaged, and the man is having difficulty controlling it. Even without Bernadette pulling at the wheel, the car continues to veer back and forth. A few moments later, it turns sharply to the right and smashes into a light pole. I race to the driver's side of the car. In my peripheral vision, I see that the back seat is empty. Joey must be on the floor. I jerk open the driver's door with such force that it bounces back and strikes me in the left hip, nearly knocking me to the ground. The airbag has been triggered, and the man is lying back against the seat. I grab him by his pink shirt, which is now mostly red, and yank him out of the car.

I hit him in the nose as hard as I can.

He screams.

When I was twelve years old, I was playing baseball and some hothead threw his bat after striking out. It flew twenty feet through the air before smashing into my face. The doctor later explained that my nose wasn't broken so much as shattered. I still get shivers recalling the agony.

I hit him in the nose again.

Another scream.

I have no desire to hurt this man. I take no pleasure in his pain. I am not seeking vengeance. I'm not even angry. If anything, I'm scared. I only want to make sure he won't hurt Joey anymore. That he can't hit me over the head when I lift her out of his car. That he can't run away, then come back and do it again. To Joey. To some other child. He's barely able to stand, but I am concerned that he will find the strength to flee. I kick him in the left shin as hard as I can. Anyone who's ever banged a leg into a coffee table will understand just how incapacitating a well-placed shin kick can be. He falls to the ground. I am about to kick him again when he cries, "Don't…"

It sounds a little bubbly because of the blood accumulating in his mouth.

"Don't…" he gurgles again.

I stop.

Slowly, he turns his face upward.

"Don't…"

"Don't what?" I ask, surprised at how calm my voice sounds.

"Don't…judge me."

I glance over to where Bernadette is lying.

I feel his hand on my ankle.

"Only God can judge me."

I turn my eyes downward.

"Fine," I promise, "I won't judge you."

My next kick leaves him unconscious.

I grab the back door handle and jerk it upwards. Locked. Panic. The front door remains wide open, so all I have to do is reach inside to unlock the back door, but adrenalin and primal instinct have hijacked my ability to reason. I take a step back and kick in the window. Tiny pieces of safety glass fly everywhere, sparkling in the late afternoon sunlight. It's kind of pretty.

Joey is on the floor behind the driver's seat, her face a bloody mess, her little body twisted into a parody of the fetal position.

She is not moving.

Please, God.

This is not a test.

8

Takushī

The Japanese company that hired me provided a business-class ticket for my flight from Newark International to Tokyo-Narita. It was actually written into the contract. I'd only flown a few times—always domestic, always economy—and therefore had no idea how much less traumatic air travel could be when you weren't sandwiched—knees to chin, elbow to elbow—into a padded plastic seat along with the rest of the underprivileged. I was even more surprised to discover that the aircraft in which I'd be flying had a second floor. At the time, I didn't even know double-decker planes existed. Intrigued, I went for the additional elevation. This goes against my instinct for self-preservation, which is predicated on staying as close to the ground as possible, but since we'd be flying seven miles above the Earth, I calculated that the additional twelve feet would not significantly diminish my chances of survival should the plane fall from the sky. It turned out to be the right decision. Though mildly nervous through a good portion of the flight, I was never terrified. Flying is much more enjoyable when you aren't.

After a remarkably smooth landing at Narita Airport, we taxied for a few minutes before the plane finally stopped. Passengers sprang to their feet, suddenly desperate to escape the mighty vessel that had safely transported them nearly seven thousand miles. I remained comfortably ensconced in my seat, savoring the last few moments of my temporarily upgraded social status.

Exiting a commercial airliner after an intercontinental flight is much like leaving a cinema after a blockbuster movie. Before the feature begins, the freshly vacuumed aisles are neat and tidy, but when the closing credits roll, popcorn, candy, and flaccid, cheese-soaked nachos litter the floor; empty boxes and paper cups are wedged into every seat; the carpet is coated with a thickening patina of soda that pulls at your shoes as you struggle to flee. On my walk to the plane's exit door, I observed bizarrely stained blankets, used vomit bags, dog-eared magazines, discarded airline socks, broken headphones, half-empty snack bags, a soiled diaper, and so many wadded-up tissues that the floor appeared to be dusted with a layer of snow. As I approached the flight attendant manning the exit, her eyes were as lifeless as a lizard's. I looked for an alternate route, but she suddenly reanimated, her mouth twisting itself into the approximation of a smile.

"Buh-bye!" she chirped.

I hurried through the doorway and onto the gantry, glancing over my shoulder as I did. The flight attendant had already regained her reptilian mien. At the end of the gantry, the hall widened, and I stepped into Narita International Airport. Immigration notwithstanding, I was in the Land of the Rising Sun.

The first thing I noticed about Japan is that there are a lot of Japanese people. This might seem obvious, but it's one thing to know it and another to experience it. Japanese people were everywhere. And they looked confident. Most of the Japanese I'd crossed paths with in the United States did not. They were shy. Tentative. Deferential. But now they were on their home turf, and I was the outsider. I felt like that little chunk of lard in a can of Van Camp's Pork & Beans.

What's more, they all looked alike.

Oh, for fuck's sake.

When I say they all looked alike, what I mean is:

Virtually everyone had black hair.

And brown eyes.

Skin color was more or less uniform.

No one was particularly tall or short.

There were no fat people.

And everyone was in a hurry.

Thus, they all looked alike.

What does this really mean?

That I'm some white-trash bigot who strayed too far from his doublewide?

No, it does not. (Like I could afford a doublewide.)

What it means is that the physical characteristics I was accustomed to using as a means of differentiating one individual from another were unsuitable for Japan.

Still think I'm a cracker?

Okay, then let's take a bunch of white guys (a pack of wolves, a murder of crows, a pod of whales, a bunch of white guys) who are roughly the same height and weight, shave their heads and facial hair, and dress them in dark business suits.

Now try telling them apart.

What's that? They all look alike?

Or could it be that the physical characteristics you were accustomed to using as a means of differentiating one individual from another are no longer suitable?

Now, how does one solve this conundrum?

In my case, there was no eureka moment.

It happened over time.

One day I realized that instead of gazing at hair color and body girth, I was looking at the person. That is, I was scrutinizing faces. I was looking more closely at the features and expressions of my hosts; at their eyes and noses and mouths and teeth; their ears and eyebrows and chins and foreheads. These were the physical characteristics I found myself using as a means of individualizing the Japanese. And I daresay it would also work with a bunch of hairless white guys.

As I entered the main hall of the airport, I immediately spotted Yamakawa-san. Him I could differentiate. I hurried over, dragging my cheap, plastic suitcase behind me. He bowed, smiled, and then shook my hand.

"Welcome to Japan, Ma-ku-su-san," he said.

"*Arigato*, Yamakawa-san," I replied, having learned a few common Japanese phrases in the weeks leading up to my departure.

"Okie dokie," he replied.

He would not utter another syllable for the next hour and a half.

A man stepped forward and reached for my suitcase. I was about to protest but noticed Yamakawa-san was not alarmed and quickly deduced that this man (who looked like everybody else) must be a member of our party. In fact, he was the driver.

We followed him and my suitcase across the airport, down an escalator, through several doorways, and into a massive parking garage. Like its people, the cars of Japan express an aesthetic similarity: the Hondas, the Mazdas, the Mitsubishis, the Nissans. Ours was a Toyota town car, which meant that it stood out from the pint-sized vehicles surrounding it. As the driver struggled to heft my suitcase into the trunk, I started forward to help, but Yamakawa-san gently touched my arm. Without wasting a word, he'd made it clear that my assistance was neither necessary nor appropriate. Once the driver succeeded in stowing my luggage, he closed the trunk, and we got into the car. I was immediately taken with the décor: the seats were covered with white lace. There was something effeminate about it, though I had to admit it was kind of fancy. Later, I would learn that every taxicab in Japan was equally fancy. The driver started the car, put it in gear, and drove from the parking garage. Traffic was light, and we were out of the airport in no time. As we pulled onto a large highway, I turned to ask Yamakawa-san how far it was to Tokyo, but he appeared to be in a state of suspended animation. Okie dokie. I leaned back and let myself enjoy the moment. I'd made it, by god. I was in Japan. In a comfortable car. On my way to a new life. Although I didn't realize it then, the comfortable ride was costing someone a small fortune.

There are a number of non-invasive means of getting from Narita Airport to Tokyo, but town cars and taxis are not among them. I prefer going by train, either the Skyliner or the Narita Express. When I was living in Japan, they cost somewhere between twenty and thirty US dollars, depending on the exchange rate. The trip is about an hour, and you get a fairly comfortable reserved seat. You can save a few dollars and board a local train, but the ride is twice as long, and you might stand the entire journey. There are several inexpensive bus services, though you risk getting caught in traffic. A taxi, on the other hand, is stupidly expensive. Taxis in general are pricey in Japan, and with the highly efficient train and subway systems, they are easily avoided. But if you're ignorant, arrogant, or desperate enough to take a taxi to or from Narita airport, you can expect to pay somewhere between three and four hundred US dollars.

To put it bluntly:

Only an idiot would take a taxi to the airport.

Fast forward a year. I was sitting in a coffee shop in Ginza with a couple of friends, saying goodbye prior to leaving for a holiday in the US. My flight from Narita to O'Hare was not due to depart for another three and a half hours.

"Ma-ku-su-san," Mariko asked, "shouldn't you be on your way to the airport?"

I smiled at her naïveté. With just the right measure of condescension I replied, "Mariko, I know it's the Japanese way to follow a strict timetable and get to the airport with hours to spare, but that's not me. I'm going to have another cup of coffee, maybe two, because I have plenty of time."

She nodded politely, although I knew the cultural barrier would never allow her to see how much better life could be when you didn't take deadlines so seriously. My friend Steve-san, a tall Liverpudlian, lifted his glass to me. He understood. A few minutes later, Mariko bid us farewell.

I ordered another coffee.

I looked at my watch.

A little less than three hours to take off.

Still plenty of time.

My cell phone rang.

"Hello?"

"Are you at the airport?"

My sister, Mary.

"Heading there as soon as I finish my coffee."

"I thought your flight left at four fifty-five."

"It does. I've still got almost three hours.

"Where are you?"

"Ginza."

"And how long does it take to get from Ginza to the airport?"

"It's only an hour to the airport."

This is one of the things I hate about people who merely visit Japan, as opposed to those of us who live here and actually know something about it.

"It's an hour once you're on the train," she clarified.

"Well…yeah."

"So let me rephrase my question. How long does it take to get from Ginza to the station where you board the train?"

"Uhhh, about a twenty-minute walk to Ginza station, then take the Hibiya line to Ueno Station, twenty-five minutes, walk through the station to the Skyliner counter, another ten minutes or so…"

"So it'll take you almost an hour just to get to the train."

I did my own math.

A few seconds later I concurred.

"And then it's another hour on the Skyliner."

"I know that."

"So that leaves you a little over half an hour to get from the Skyliner platform to the check-in counter, and then through immigration and on to your gate."

"What's your point?"

(Despite mounting evidence to the contrary, I still clung to the belief that I had plenty of time.)

"Max," Mary said in a voice generally reserved for toddlers, "What time does the Skyliner leave for the airport?"

"I don't know. I didn't get my ticket yet. I'll buy it at the counter."

"But how long will you have to wait for the train?"

"Not long. They leave every half hour or so."

I felt a stirring in my brain. A thought was struggling to form. A moment later, it was complete.

"FUCK!!!!"

Steve-san looked up from his beer.

"Shouldn't you be at the airport?"

I ran from the coffee shop all the way to Ginza station, dragging my plastic suitcase behind me. Fortunately, my calculations had been on the high side. I made it to Ginza Station in just ten minutes; to Ueno Station in twenty-five; and then another eight to reach the Skyliner ticket counter. If there was a train leaving in the next five minutes, I would arrive at the airport with forty minutes to spare. I rushed to the counter.

"Next-o train-o," I said in flawless Japanese.

The man behind the counter shook his head.

"Train-o next-o," I ventured.

Again, he shook his head.

"Skyliner," I said, tapping my watch. "Next-o."

He pointed to a sign behind him.

Skyliner. 15:30.

"Next-o," he said.

After several tense moments, I was able to translate 15:30 into English: three-thirty p.m.

The next train would not leave for forty-five minutes.

FUCK!!!

I'm going to miss my fucking plane!

FUCK!!!

Unless...

I ran up a flight of stairs and out into the brisk Tokyo afternoon.

There were taxis everywhere!

It had to be an exaggeration, all that nonsensical talk of three-hundred-dollar taxi rides. I wouldn't listen to malicious gossip. A taxi could get me to Narita in less than an hour. And surely the ride wouldn't be more than fifty or sixty dollars. A hundred, tops.

"Do you speak English?" I asked the driver of the nearest taxi, shoving my suitcase across the clean white seat cover.

"A little," the driver said, looking disdainfully at the streak of dirt between me and the wheels of my suitcase.

"Can you get to Narita Airport in less than an hour?"

He stared at me for several seconds before saying, "No guarantees."

"Okay," I agreed, "no guarantees. But it is possible?"

"*Hai*," he said, taking for granted that I knew this much Japanese. "Possible."

"Okay, let's go!"

He put the Toyota in gear and pulled slowly from the curb.

"I'm really in a hurry," I said, keeping my voice as calm as possible.

"No guarantees," he replied without looking back.

Ten minutes later, we hit the expressway.

"How much longer?" I asked the driver.

He shrugged.

I waited.

"Depends on traffic."

The universal caveat for taxi drivers.

"No traffic, about one hour."

I looked at my watch. We would arrive twenty-three minutes before takeoff.

"No guarantees."

"Yeah, I got that, Ace," I replied, settling back into my seat, "no guarantees."

"*Hai.*"

I had no idea if twenty-three minutes was enough time. The usual policy is to close the boarding gate twenty minutes before takeoff, so it would be a miracle to check in, pass through immigration, and reach the gate before they locked me out.

I glanced at the meter.

Six thousand yen.

About eighty US dollars.

And we were just getting started.

I reached for the small pouch where I keep all my travel-related documents: passport, tickets, boarding passes, itineraries, extra cash. I pulled out my ticket—All Nippon Airways—and wondered if I'd have a chance to use it. I checked the time of departure, hoping I'd misread it and I actually had plenty of time. No such luck. The plane would depart at four fifty-five p.m. whether I was on board or not.

I glanced at the meter.

Seven thousand, three hundred and twenty yen.

As I was returning the ticket to the pouch, I noticed several phone numbers on the back of the envelope. Upon closer inspection, I saw they were numbers for ANA offices around the world. I found the one for Tokyo.

I almost didn't bother.

It's sure to be a recording.

Still…

I pulled out my phone.

As I punched in the number, the meter taunted me.

Seven thousand, seven hundred and eighty yen.

Seven thousand, seven hundred and ninety yen.

Seven thousand, eight hundred yen.

"ANA! HOW CAN I HELP YOU?"

The slightly accented female Japanese voice was loud and cheery.

"Oh…I…"

"Good afternoon, sir. This is ANA. How can I help you?" she repeated in a slightly softer voice, though it had lost none of its cheeriness.

"Sorry, I thought you'd be a recording."

"No," she said proudly, "this is me."

"That's good, because I really need to speak with someone."

"In that case, why don't you speak with me?"

If she hadn't been Japanese, I would have guessed her to be a smart-ass.

"Okay," I said. "The thing is, I've got a bit of a problem. I'm booked on a flight out of Narita at four fifty-five this afternoon, and I'm running late. There was an emergency, and I was delayed, so I won't get to the airport until…"

"Could I have your reservation number, please?"

I gave it to her and immediately heard the soft clattering of fingers on a keyboard.

"Are you at the airport now?" she asked a few moments later.

No, I'm not at the fucking airport.

"No, ma'am, I won't reach the airport for another forty minutes or so."

"Oh, that's not good."

No shit?

"Yes, ma'am, I agree, and that's why I'm calling. I was hoping you could…perhaps…tell them I might be a little late and ask them to wait for me?"

"No problem, sir. Of course we'll delay the flight until you arrive. We don't mind keeping the other passengers waiting and disrupting hundreds of international flights at one of the world's busiest airports, thereby increasing the likelihood of a mid-air collision. Now is there anything else I can do for you?"

What she actually said was, "I'm sorry, sir, the only thing I can do is alert the ANA check-in staff and let them know you'll be late."

"I appreciate that."

"But I have to warn you that the gate will close twenty minutes before departure, so…"

"No guarantees," I finished for her.

"*Hai*," the taxi driver agreed, "no guarantees."

I looked up and saw the meter had just cracked the ten-thousand-yen mark.

I began to accept the fact that I'd be spending the night in the airport lounge, having spent all my money on a futile taxi ride. Leaning back into the seat, I tried to relax, but the large quantities of coffee I'd imbibed made this impossible. I shut my eyes anyway and stubbornly kept them closed. A few minutes later, I opened them, blinked in the afternoon glare, and stared out the window. The city was far behind us, and we were racing along at a pretty good clip, though the meter had no trouble keeping up. It was now closing in on twenty thousand yen.

"How much longer?" I asked the driver.

Several seconds passed.

"Fifteen minutes," he finally answered.

I looked at my watch. We were ten minutes ahead of schedule!

"Great driving," I said happily.

"No guarantees."

Soon, signs of the airport were everywhere: outlying terminals, chain-link fences topped with razor wire, dozens of planes overhead, and increasingly heavy traffic. I checked my watch. Suddenly, I was optimistic. I would have at least thirty-five minutes to reach the gate. The meter was hovering at twenty-three thousand yen.

I closed my eyes and willed us onward.

Seven minutes later, we stopped in front of the arrivals gate. My fee was twenty-four thousand seven hundred fifty yen. About three hundred twenty-five dollars. I reached for my pouch. It was gone. At that point, it must have appeared that I was having some sort of seizure, frisking myself over and over, a look of terror on my blood-drained face. After several interminable seconds, the driver calmly pointed to a place on the seat next to me. I followed the trajectory of his finger.

Thank god.

I opened the pouch.

FUCK!

No money!

I'd been in such a hurry that I'd forgotten to go to the ATM.

"Do you take credit cards?"

The driver shook his head.

"Is there an ATM nearby?"

He had no idea what I'd just asked him.

"ATM-o! Money machine! Get-o money!"

I mimed putting my credit card into an ATM, punched in my PIN.

He pointed toward the terminal.

"Okay," I said, "I'll be right back."

I reached for my suitcase, but the driver shook his head.

"What? You think I'm gonna cheat you?"

"No guarantees."

I didn't see any ATMs near the entrance, so I started running down the long hallway. People with suitcases were everywhere, and they all seemed intent on slowing my progress. A Japanese man in an official-looking uniform was leaning on a nearby counter. The uniform suggested he might be some sort of airport administrator and would therefore know where I could find an ATM. On the other hand, in Japan, even garbage men wear official-looking uniforms.

"ATM-o?"

Nothing.

I mimed putting my credit card into an ATM, punched in my PIN.

"Ahhh," he said and pointed to a distant escalator.

"*Arigato!*" I yelled over my shoulder as I raced toward it.

Halfway there I spotted an ATM about thirty meters down another hall. The guy in the uniform was full of shit. I didn't have to go down some escalator. When I was still ten meters away, I realized it was a soft-drink machine. I should have reversed right then and headed back to the escalator, but inertia had me in its grip. When I got to the machine, I quickly looked over the selection. Boss Coffee. Pocari Sweat. Calpis. What the fuck am I doing?

I sprinted back toward the escalator.

As I approached it, I noticed the uniformed man motioning me onward with an encouraging smile. He was on my side after all. As soon as I reached the floor below, I saw the ATM. What's more, it sported the logo of the bank where I had my account. An elderly Japanese man was walking toward it, but I muscled in front of him, excusing myself with a half-hearted "*Sumimasen.*" I shoved my card into the machine, entered my PIN, and hit the fifty-thousand-yen button. Five ten-thousand-yen notes emerged a moment later. I grabbed them and raced through the building and out of the terminal.

The taxi was gone.

The son of a bitch had absconded with my suitcase!

But that doesn't make any sense!

He wants his money!

I ran back inside.

The correct door was on the other side of the terminal.

Twenty-seven seconds later the driver was counting his money. I grabbed my suitcase, creating another dirty streak across the seat cover, then raced back into the terminal.

I looked at my watch.

My plane would leave in twenty-three minutes.

At first I didn't see it because it was right in front of my face, but after wasting several precious seconds spinning my head around, I spotted a huge sign indicating the ANA check-in counter.

I sprinted toward it.

Two men and two women in ANA uniforms watched my approach. They seemed to be in some sort of defensive formation. As I got closer, one of the men ran out and grabbed my suitcase. The other took my passport, quickly scrutinized it, and handed it back with a boarding pass tucked between the pages. "*Kite kudasai!*" the man with my suitcase yelled as he hurried across the terminal. One of the women took my hand, and together we raced after him. I glanced over my shoulder at the other two. They waved and shouted, "Thank you for flying ANA!" The woman holding my hand was lovely. I was about to ask for her name when we reached the immigration checkpoint for airline crews. Apparently, they'd been notified about my late arrival, because the official merely glanced at my passport and motioned me through. I had no choice but to let go of the ANA woman's hand. Her male colleague stepped up next to her.

"*Arigato gozaimasu*," I said.

They bowed in unison.

I vowed that henceforth I would always fly ANA.

Unless one of their competitors offered a lower fare.

I hurried down the hall and reached the gate just as they were about to close it. A man took my shoulder bag and suitcase and put them through the X-ray machine. I emptied my pockets, walked through the metal detector, retrieved my bags, refilled my pockets, then hurried toward the gantry. There, a smiling Japanese woman ushered me into the plane. A minute later I was in my seat.

I'd made it.

I felt my face break into a smile.

Then I remembered the twenty-four-thousand-seven-hundred-fifty-yen taxi ride and felt a syllogism coming on:

Only an idiot would take a taxi to the airport.

I took a taxi to the airport.

Yeah.

When the town car reached the Tokyo hotel where I'd be staying, Yamakawa-san spoke for the first time since greeting me at the airport.

"Ma-ku-su-san, are you hungry?" he asked as we exited the car.

Suddenly I was.

"Well, hey there!"

I didn't bother to turn around.

"Hey, Brad."

He strutted up with his hand extended, but rather than shake it, I bowed. Yamakawa-san seemed amused. He'd asked the hillbilly to meet us at the hotel, figuring Brad could help me get settled and answer any questions I might have.

"Please take Ma-ku-su-san into the restaurant and buy him dinner," he said.

Brad suddenly looked stricken.

"Max probably just wants to hit the hay," he responded and then turned to me for confirmation.

"Nah, I'm wide awake, Brad. And I tell ya, I could eat a horse."

"But…"

"Ma-ku-su-san," Yamakawa-san interrupted, "Bu-ra-do-san will buy you dinner. Your hotel is in the same bi-ru-din-gu. He will show you."

After we exchanged bows, Yamakawa-san got back into the car. It pulled from the curb and was soon out of sight. I grabbed my suitcase and walked into the restaurant. Even in the US it would have been out of my price range; here, the prices would be astronomical. Brad staggered in behind me. A waiter said something to him in Japanese, and he said something back. We were escorted to a table not far from the entrance. The hillbilly sat across from me, a look of supplication on his face.

The menu was in both English and Japanese.

I glanced at the prices.

Jesus!

When the waiter came over, I ordered fettuccini carbonara and a glass of red wine.

"Aren't you getting anything, Bu-ra-do-san?" I asked innocently.

He shook his head.

I know he was relieved. The pasta was relatively inexpensive, at least compared to some of the other items on the menu. The Kobe beef would have set him back a month's salary.

Brad sat quietly as I stared out the window.

Suddenly, I was struck by a ghostly image. The face of a gorgeous woman seemed to be hovering before my eyes. Perhaps it was jet lag, but for several moments, I felt as if I were caught in a dream. And then the lovely apparition smiled. God, she was beautiful. Slowly, I turned from the window and saw her, not a ghost after all, but a stunning Japanese woman.

She held my eyes, and I managed to hold hers.

Brad was oblivious.

Her next smile was an invitation. I stood and walked to her table.

"I'm Max," I said, holding out my hand.

She took it in her own, a gentle touch that sent a shiver down my spine.

"Max." She didn't say it the Japanese way, Ma-ku-su. My name flowed from her lips as a single syllable.

"I just arrived from the US," I continued and then mentioned the company that had hired me. It seemed to impress her. But then she said, "I must go now."

What?

She rose and started to walk away.

"Will you…" I hesitated.

She stopped and waited for me to finish.

"Will you remember me?"

I have no idea why I chose those words. They seemed absurd even as I spoke them. Yet they had an effect on her. She lifted her hand and touched my face.

"I think I can remember you," she said softly.

A moment later she was gone, and I knew I'd never see her again.

But I was wrong.

I'd just met Joey's mother.

9

The Passenger

Please, God.

Yes?

Please, God.

Who is this?

Please, God.

I think you have the wrong number.

I don't know what time it is. After dark. I'm walking back to the hospital. The road is deserted. A hand grabs my shoulder. I should be frightened. Startled, at least. But I feel nothing. I have no fear left over for myself. I turn and see a man. He is smiling, but his smile is compromised by the absence of front teeth. He looks vaguely familiar. And then he looks very familiar. And then he is Milo Braggen. The last time I saw him he was rolling around on the floor of a trailer factory.

"What's with the teeth?" are my first words to him in thirty years.

He shrugs as if it were too trivial to mention.

"Cop," he finally answers.

Mary is a member of the police force, and she'd made no mention of a co-worker dabbling in orthodontics.

"Local?"

"Northern California. I live out there now. Got a little farm."

Milo. Farming. Northern California. It's a safe bet he isn't growing sweet corn.

"It's a good look for you," I say.

"Yeah," he agrees, "not everyone can pull it off."

Thirty years and we pick up right where we left off.

"What'd he hit you with?"

"Tactical baton."

"Any particular reason?"

"He believed I was displaying an insufficient level of respect."

I nod. I don't know what else to do.

"Look, Milo, it's nice to see you after all these years, and I'd love to catch up, but you caught me at a bad time. I gotta get back to the hospital."

"That's where I'm heading," he replies. "Mind if I walk with you?"

"That'd be great. Who you going to see?"

We take several steps in silence before he says, "You, ya dumb fuck."

I am nearly moved to tears.

Mary does not appear to have changed position in the hour I was away. She is sitting at Joey's bedside, leaning forward, and holding her little hand. I stand behind a crack in the doorway, listening as she serenades her niece in a soft and surprisingly pleasant voice. Joey is not responding, but the doctors and nurses insist it is crucial to surround her with familiar stimuli—a voice or a song or even a smell. Thus does Mary sing Joey's favorite lullaby, "The Passenger." I'm surprised she even knows it. Growing up, her musical preferences were never any more hardcore than The Mamas and The Papas. Of course, she often heard Iggy's masterpiece blasting from my bedroom and perhaps learned the lyrics because the volume made them impossible to ignore, the song getting stuck in her head, playing over and over no matter how hard she tried to exorcise it. Certainly, this is why I know all the words to fucking "Monday Monday."

I feel Milo fidgeting behind me, and a moment later his chin brushes the top of my head. He is standing on his tiptoes trying to see into the room.

"Take it easy," I hiss. I do not want to interrupt Mary's singing.

"She looks beautiful," he whispers.

Joey's head is wrapped in bandages; stitches run across her left cheek; a plastic shield is taped across her broken nose. Yet my old friend still manages to see her beauty.

"She looks just like she did in high school."

Oh.

I'd almost forgotten.

When we were kids, Milo would bug the shit out of me, asking about Mary and what she's like and if she ever mentions him. But he never had a chance. We were sophomores when Mary was a senior, so Milo was all but invisible. I doubt if she even knew his name. A two-year age gap might not seem like much when you're crowding fifty, but as a kid it's all but infinite. And now he's singing with her. My first impulse is to tell him to shut the fuck up, but a wave of emotion washes over me, and I go weak in the knees.

And then I'm singing, too.

Mary glances toward the commotion in the doorway, and before I realize what's happening, Milo ushers us into the room. I haven't shed a tear since lifting Joey from the floor of that car, but now they flood down my cheeks. My eyes are so watery I can barely see. My heart. My heart. It hurts so much. I start to fall, but Mary reaches out and grabs my arm; Milo takes the other. They lead me to my daughter's bedside, and there we stand: father, aunt, and toothless pot farmer from Northern California, singing:

La la la la la-la-la-la
La la la la la-la-la-la
La la la la la-la-la-la la-la la

"Please, God."

This is what I hear when I peek into Bernadette's room later that night. Father John is at her bedside, leaning forward and holding her hand. Yellow Converse high tops on his feet.

Bernadette is in a coma, too.

"This child has had so much pain in her life," the priest continues, "Why do you let her suffer so?"

It sounds like a prayer, but I discern a note of anger in his ragged voice. I wonder if he's a little pissed off at his Maker.

I know I'm a little pissed off at his Maker.

I watch as he extends his hand to the place where Bernadette's right leg should be. It is an enormously empty space, as all such voids are. Her remaining leg is in some sort of high-tech cast that runs from her toes to her upper thigh. The doctor had considered amputating that one as well, but I told him he'd better find a way to save it.

"She's related to the Marcos family," I improvised.

I let the implied threat hang in the air.

"Who's the Marcos family?"

What an idiot.

"Oh yeah," one of the nurses intervened, "that lady with all the shoes."

It's not uncommon for nurses to know more than doctors.

"Just save her leg," I commanded and then walked back to Joey's room.

I could have just as easily threatened him with the Mafia. On a whim, Angelica had called me from New Jersey—*I had a feeling something was wrong*—and when I told her what happened, she insisted she could arrange to have Joey's would-be kidnapper whacked. "I'll put a contract out on that sick motherfucker," she said through tears and anger. I declined the offer and assured her that Mr. Gladstone—that was his name, Francis Henry Gladstone—would have a much more unpleasant time in prison, explaining that pedophiles were considered the lowest of the low among prisoners, and that during their incarceration they were routinely beaten, tortured, and killed by the morally outraged murderers, muggers, and thieves with whom they shared accommodations. Only this promise assuaged my former colleague.

"Nice shoes," I say to Father John as I enter Bernadette's room. He looks up, surprised.

"Oh, Max," he says in a voice filled with despair, "how's Joey?"

He rises and takes a few steps toward me, the rubber soles of his yellow shoes squeaking on the tile floor.

"The same. The doctors say she should be okay. Apparently this kind of coma isn't uncommon after a blow to the head… the face. Her vital signs are all strong. And she's young. Anyway, they think she's going to be all right."

"I'm so glad to hear that."

And I'm so glad he didn't thank God.

The priest looks over at Bernadette and shakes his head sadly.

"You okay?" I ask him.

"I don't know what to tell her when she wakes up."

"What do you mean?"

"How do I explain what happened?"

"The guy who crushed her against a VW is the one who needs to explain."

"No," he says a few moments later, "I mean how will I explain that the God she loves so completely has allowed yet more tragedy to befall her? How do I frame the loss of her leg as part of our Heavenly Father's plan?" He stares at me for a long time after posing this last question. I assume it's rhetorical, so I make no attempt to respond. Without warning, he slams his fist into the wall.

"Goddammit!"

I almost feel bad for him, but the yellow sneakers are interfering with my ability to empathize. Seconds later, a middle-aged nurse with a pinched-up face rushes into the room. I've seen her around, the one who always looks as if she's about to slap someone.

"Sorry, I banged my shin on the bed," I say, covering for the priest.

She looks at Father John, who is cradling his right hand, then back at me.

"Well, just keep it down," she says testily.

I look at the comatose Bernadette, at the empty spot where her leg should be.

"Keep it down?"

"You heard me," she says like an angry schoolteacher.

I close my eyes for a moment. When I open them she is staring, waiting for an acknowledgement. Instead I pose another question.

"Why?"

Confusion clouds the nurse's eyes. Apparently, no one has ever questioned her command for silence.

"Because I don't want you disturbing the patient," she hisses and then leans over Bernadette and pretends to do something medical. I wait until she finishes her fake ministrations.

"Are you shittin' me?"

The nurse opens her mouth to speak but is unable to find her voice.

"She's in a fuckin' coma, Nurse Ratched. How are we gonna disturb her?"

Again, she looks from the priest to me.

"Don't speak to me in that manner, especially in front of a man of God."

"Leave me out of this one," Father John says, raising his wounded hand defensively.

"Isn't disturbing the patient the whole point?" I continue. "Wouldn't her waking up be a good thing? A positive development? A milestone on the road to recovery?"

"Are you a doctor?" the nurse demands.

"Are you?"

"I am a registered nurse," she says defiantly, "which means I have extensive medical training. Don't presume to lecture me on medical matters."

I start to retort but the priest gives his head a barely noticeable shake.

"Fine," I capitulate, "we'll keep it down."

She eyes me for a few seconds to confirm my sincerity, then nods authoritatively and walks out the door.

"She's actually very attractive," I muse.

"You'd make a lovely couple," the priest says wryly.

He walks back to Bernadette's bedside and takes her hand.

"She'll say it was God's will," I tell him.

He looks up at me.

"She will. Her faith will remain intact. Bernadette believes everything is God's will. But you already know that."

His eyebrows lift.

"So maybe it's *your* faith that's troubling you."

The priest offers a tired smile.

"My faith always troubles me," he replies, then closes his eyes and begins to pray.

As I step out into the hallway, I collide with Milo. The sharp clink of beer bottles is unmistakable. "I brought some refreshing beverages," he explains, holding up a medium-sized backpack. The thought of a cold beer suddenly sends my spirits soaring, a manic moment that quickly gives way to a more measured response.

"I don't think they allow beer drinking in the hospital."

"Max," he says as if I'm being obtuse, "they do morphine here." He has a point.

"Okay, but let me check on Joey first."

"I just came from her room. Mary said to tell you everything's okay and that you should drink a beer with me."

"She really said that?"

"Swear to god. She thinks you need to take it easy for a while."

I step back into Bernadette's room. Milo is right behind me.

"Shit," he said softly as he glances at the negative space created by Bernadette's missing leg.

The priest does not look up from his prayer.

"She saved Joey. It should have been me, but I didn't do a fucking thing."

Ignoring my self-pity, Milo reaches into his backpack and pulls out a Dos Equis. I wonder if he has an opener—Mexican brewers tend to eschew the wonders of twist-off technology— or if he's going to do his old party trick and open it with his molars. Even in his current state of dental compromise, I suspect Milo could pull it off. He gives me an I-know-what-you're-thinking smile and then whips out a church key.

"I've got nothing to prove," he says, popping the caps off of two beers with a quick flick of his wrist.

He hands me one of the bottles.

"What's her name?" he asks, nodding toward the bed.

"Bernadette."

"To Bernadette," he says.

"To Bernadette," I echo.

And then we drink.

I close my eyes as the beer slides down my throat. It's so good I actually quiver, but the pleasure I experience goes far beyond taste. My entire body responds, as if I'd jumped into a cool mountain spring after hiking through the desert. It brings to mind a beer moment I once experienced in Japan. It happened in Hakone, a charming little town southwest of Tokyo. Two young Japanese women, Hiromi and Yaeko, had planned for us to hike up a mountain. We'd met recently at a party, and when they revealed themselves to be avid hikers, I expressed interest in joining them on their next adventure. I thought they were kidding when they told me the rendezvous time: Saturday at seven-thirty a.m. As was my custom in Japan, I went out and got shitfaced Friday night. I slept until the phone rang.

"Wah?"

"Ma-ku-su-san, where are you?"

I looked around.

"Ugh…I'm here."

"Ma-ku-su-san, we are also here, waiting for you."

Again I looked around.

"No you're not."

"Yes, we are here at the station waiting for you."

Station?

"Who is this?"

Even as I asked the question, the answer popped into my head.

"Hiromi?"

"Yes, Ma-ku-su-san."

Struggling to sit up, I thought I might vomit. I forced the bile back down my throat.

"What time is it?"

"*Nana-ji han desu*," she said.

Hiromi was trying to teach me Japanese.

"Five o'clock?" I guessed.

"Ma-ku-su-san, it is seven-thirty."

"Really?"

I still wasn't sure where the conversation was going.

"Yes."

I waited for her to continue.

"Ma-ku-su-san?"

It was coming back to me.

Another ten seconds of silence.

Shit.

"Sorry, Hiromi, I guess I overslept."

Not that sorry. At least now I could go back to sleep and, with any luck, wake up after the worst of my hangover had run its course.

"We are waiting for you," Hiromi said patiently.

That doesn't make any sense. Unless...

"You still want me to come?" I asked incredulously.

"Ma-ku-su-san, we are waiting for you."

She said this as if I were the one for whom English is a second language.

"Okay, I'll get there as soon as I can."

I hung up the phone and decided I could sleep for five more minutes. As I rested my head on the pillow, I once again felt the urge to vomit. I crawled out of bed, took a quick shower, and threw on some clothes. I considered eating something, but my stomach made it clear that any attempt at nourishment would be rejected.

"Ma-ku-su-san, we are waiting for you," Hiromi had said.

The statement was certainly polite enough, and her tone had been sweet, but it would be a mistake to take it at face value. For years, American businessmen have been confounded by exceptionally polite Japanese executives who shower them with praise after a business presentation. The Americans, bloated with self-satisfaction, prepare for a windfall of lucrative sales, contracts, and partnerships. Thus, they feel a profound sense of betrayal when they discover the Japanese rejected their propositions and have no intention of ever doing business with them.

"But they loved us!" the baffled businessmen would exclaim.

In the words of *Luke*, "What we have here is failure to communicate."

This failure is exacerbated by the fact that many living in the Land of the Free and the Home of the Brave find it all but impossible to accept that the American way is not the only way. Japanese culture is built on a foundation of politeness that most foreigners are unable to grasp. The Japanese are sometimes so polite that—from an outsider's point of view—it seems masochistic. Take the word *no*. It's rarely used by the Japanese. They simply aren't that direct. And if it is spoken, it's probably out of humility—to decline a compliment. Thus, the American businessman might well have asked his Japanese counterpart, "Did you like the presentation?" To which the Japanese counterpart might well have responded, "It was incredible." Naturally, the American businessman is elated and follows up with, "So, do you think we can do business together?" The reply: "One would be honored to do business with you."

Success?

Let's take a closer look.

It is possible that the Japanese were impressed with the presentation and their respective companies will end up working together. Certainly, there have been many successful partnerships between Japanese and American businesses. It's equally likely, however, that the Japanese believe the presenter and his colleagues to be a pack of ignorant barbarians, totally unschooled in the ways of Japanese commerce, culture, and communication, and that their ideas are commensurate with their dismal levels of intelligence. In either case, the hosts' reactions would be the same: charming displays of politeness coupled with words of appreciation augmented by bows that seem to go on forever. Win or lose, success or failure, acceptance or rejection, the Japanese reaction would have been the same.

At least from an outsider's point of view.

There is, however, a difference.

Keep in mind, in a culture where extreme politeness is the norm, even the slightest behavioral nuance has profound significance: the bow is a few centimeters less deep; the eye contact is slightly less direct; the words of praise a shade less exultant.

Or so I assume.

I mean, I can't spot the difference.

But I know it's there.

When I joined my Japanese colleagues for presentations to Japanese clients, I came to understand that, regardless of the client's response, I had absolutely no idea what our hosts actually thought. I recall an important presentation in Hiroshima during which the top man appeared to be sound asleep, yet it turned out he was thrilled with our efforts and we won the account. Other times, clients seemed awed by what we showed them, when in fact they were thoroughly underwhelmed. So rather than draw my own conclusions, I'd sidle up to one of my Japanese pals and ask, "How'd we do?"

"Very well, Ma-ku-su-san, thank you for all your hard work," the response sometimes went. "Client-san is most impressed."

"So we won?" I'd ask just to be certain.

"*Hai*, Ma-ku-su-san," he'd nod, "we won."

Other times, the exchange went like this: "How'd we do?"

"Very well, Ma-ku-su-san, thank you for all your hard work. Client-san is most impressed."

"So we won?"

"Client-san has graciously decided to award the business to our competitors."

Thus, when Hiromi said, "We are waiting for you," in her patient, softly accented voice, I knew it didn't mean *Take your time, Ma-ku-su-san, we have nothing better to do than look forward to your presence.*

When I finally reached the station, it was nearly nine a.m. Since they'd almost certainly arrived early, it was a good bet that Hiromi and Yaeko had been waiting on that cold platform for more than two hours. Yet they greeted me with the radiant smiles and welcoming words that in America are reserved for the punctual. We caught the next train and rode it the rest of the way to Hakone. There we spent the day hiking up a beautifully forested mountain. The path was long, the ascent was arduous, and, because I was still hung over, the threat of regurgitation was constantly present. But, somehow, we made it to the summit. There, for the first time in my life, I beheld the splendor of Mt. Fuji. No postcard or *ukiyo-e* print can begin to capture the incredible feeling that ancient volcano inspires. By the time of our descent, my hangover had gone into remission, and I realized how fortunate it was that Hiromi and Yaeko waited for me. I apologized for my thoughtless tardiness, but they brushed it aside as if I'd done nothing wrong. Still, I sensed they were pleased I made the effort. At the base of the mountain, Hiromi turned to me and smiled. "Ma-ku-su-san," she asked coyly, "have you ever been to an *onsen?*"

"*Onsen?*"

"Japanese hot spring."

"You mean one of those outdoor baths?" I asked excitedly.

"*Hai,*" they said simultaneously.

Well, well, well. Bathing naked with two beautiful, young Japanese women.

"It would be a meaningful cultural experience," I said, picturing my companions without their clothes.

"*Hai,*" they agreed.

After hiking another fifteen minutes or so, we came to an unassuming building at the edge of a clearing.

"This is very famous *onsen*, Ma-ku-su-san," Yaeko informed me.

I'll be seeing you naked soon, I silently informed her.

After entering, Hiromi walked to the reception counter and spoke to the woman behind it. The woman bowed, and Hiromi passed her some money. Each of us then received a small white towel and a locker key.

"You go that way, Ma-ku-su-san," Hiromi pointed to a door.

"Aren't you coming with me?" I asked.

They looked puzzled.

"I mean...don't you..."

I let it hang in the air.

A few moments later Hiromi laughed. She said something in Japanese to Yaeko, who quickly joined in the laughter. "Ma-ku-su-san, there are separate baths for the men and the women," Yaeko explained once the laughter died down. "We have not bathed together since the days of our grandparents."

Apparently, General Douglas MacArthur, as supreme commander during the post–World War II occupation of Japan, put an end to the practice of co-ed bathing, as it offended his sense of propriety. No wonder Truman fired his ass.

I wandered through the door Hiromi had indicated and found myself in a mid-sized locker room. Several Japanese men and a few of their male offspring were sitting at benches removing their clothes. I checked the number on my key and walked to the corresponding locker. I felt several pairs of eyes on me. It was understandable. They probably didn't get many *gai jin* here. I had no idea how to behave in an *onsen*, so I looked around for someone to imitate. I saw a naked Japanese man close his locker and walk toward a row of tiny wooden stools neatly arranged in front of a series of faucets set close to the floor. He carried his towel in front of his genitals, so I did the same. I watched as he sat on one of the stools and proceeded to wash himself thoroughly from head to toe. I sat a few stools over and followed suit, mulling the irony of washing myself *before* a bath. The naked man rinsed off the soap and shampoo, rose from the tiny stool, and walked from the room, again holding the little towel in front of his genitals. I did the same. After passing through another doorway, my genitals and I found ourselves in a beautiful courtyard decorated with huge stones and dozens of pools of water. Some of the pools were only a couple of meters in diameter, while others were the size of a small swimming pool. In each of them were naked Japanese men soaking away, and each of these naked Japanese men had placed the genital-hiding towel atop his head. I put my foot into one of the smaller pools and was shocked. The water was scalding. I looked at the old man lounging in it, oblivious to the fact that he was being cooked alive. I walked over to one of the larger pools because there were kids in it, figuring their threshold for pain couldn't be any more developed than my own. I tested the water and found that it only marginally less unbearable. Nevertheless, I waded out a few feet until the heat started to make me uncomfortable. I was about to retreat when a Japanese man close to my own age stepped into the pool across from me. In a fluid motion, he whisked the towel from before his genitals and onto the top of his head, simultaneously bending his knees and sliding into a seated position. I attempted to imitate this maneuver but wound up dropping my genital-hiding towel. When that which my towel had been hiding made contact with the water, I nearly screamed. Oddly, boiling-hot water didn't feel all that different from freezing-cold water, and eventually it did become almost tolerable. I reached for my towel, which was floating just in front of my face, wrung the water from it, and placed it atop my head.

Now I looked like everyone else. I soon began enjoying the experience, despite the fact that I was separated from my lovely companions by a large, seemingly impenetrable stone wall. It really didn't make any difference; the volcanically heated water nullified any libido-driven impulses. All I wanted to do was sit quietly and relax. Later, I began exploring the other pools, all of which seemed to maintain a different temperature. After about forty minutes, I rose from the water and began walking toward the locker room. A disapproving look from an elderly Japanese man puzzled me, until I realized my genital-hiding towel was still atop my head. I quickly rectified this faux pas and walked inside. There I learned that it was time for another scrubbing session atop a tiny stool. After completing my third cleansing in less than an hour, I squeezed the water from my towel and used it to wipe residual moisture from my body. The air would have to do the rest. Eventually, I was dry enough to get dressed, and as I stood up, I realized I'd never felt so clean in my life. I felt…new.

Jesus, get to the point.

I'm still standing at Bernadette's bedside with the doubtful priest and the toothless Milo, that first gulp of beer just settling into my stomach. This entire Japan memory has taken maybe three seconds. It seems significantly longer because there's so much detail to cover, but inside my head it's basically been a single burst; that is, although I experienced the events sequentially, my memory serves them up simultaneously. It's similar to the way Tralfamadorians read a book. According to Herr Vonnegut, the individual pages don't make much sense, but because Tralfamadorians experience the past, present, and future concurrently, they effectively read every symbol on every page at the same time. Perhaps this is why our life flashes before our eyes at the very end—it doesn't make any sense until we experience it all at once.

Hiromi and Yaeko were waiting in a room with several other very clean people. They were all sitting or lying on the floor, which consisted of tatami mats, a comfortable straw flooring that is ubiquitous in Japan. Hiromi rose when she saw me, and though she looked exceptionally shiny and beautiful, I was too relaxed to entertain my usual litany of carnal thoughts. In fact, the extremely pleasant physical exhaustion I felt was decidedly post coital.

"Ma-ku-su-san," she said with a knowing smile, "did you like the *onsen?*"

"Yes," I said, voice cracking. I hadn't uttered a word in more than an hour.

She took my hand and led me to a beer-vending machine.

When I was living in Japan, they had vending machines for almost everything. Cold drinks. Hot drinks. Sake. Cigarettes. Telephone cards. French fries. Live bait. Umbrellas. Even used schoolgirl panties (or so the story goes).

Hiromi put a few coins into the slot and pushed the button twice. The machine clunked two times. She reached past the flap and pulled out two cans of Kirin Ichiban Shibori. Then my Japanese companion smiled mysteriously and said, "Ma-ku-su-san, I am going to give you the best beer of your life."

I was intrigued.

She handed me one of the beers. Its coldness against my still-warm skin was surprising. Hiromi continued to smile as I flipped open the tab and lifted the can to my lips.

And then I drank.

"Jesus."

"*Si*," Milo concurs, bringing me out of my Oriental reverie, "*La cerveza is muy fucking buena.*"

I glance cautiously at Father John. Evidently he doesn't *habla español*.

I take several additional gulps before lowering the bottle.

"Think the padre wants one?" Milo asks. "Hey, Padre, want a cold one?" he shouts before I can discourage him from interrupting the priest's prayer.

To my surprise, Father John looks up and says, "Oh, heavens yes."

Milo uses his church key to pop the cap off another Dos Equis and then passes him the bottle. The priest takes a huge pull, and when he lowers it, I can see from the expression on his face what he's thinking.

Jesus.

"Which do you prefer," Milo asks him, "beer or wine?"

Father John takes a few moments to consider the question, as if he's just been asked to clarify some major theological conundrum, and then declares, "Wine during Mass; beer at all other times."

Milo seems to appreciate this answer.

They continue to talk, but I tune them out and sit on Bernadette's bed. Her right leg ends just above where the knee should have been, and as I regard the stump, I think of Tony, a guy I knew growing up. He was a few years older than me, but we got to be friends after he came home from Vietnam. While he was there, his platoon was on patrol in some Vietnamese jungle, and the kid in front of him stepped on a land mine. That soldier lost his life; Tony lost both of his legs. Still, he managed to get around pretty well on two fake ones. So well, in fact, that people were often unaware of his prostheses. Once at a party, as Tony and I were climbing a flight of stairs, a pretty co-ed sitting next to the banister asked him, "Are you the guy with the sprained ankle?"

Without missing a beat Tony answered, "No, I'm the guy with two wooden legs."

The girl smiled, which seemed an odd reaction, and then I realized she thought Tony was kidding. One at a time, he hiked up his pant legs, revealing the artificial appendages that facilitated his mobility. The co-ed's expression did not change, she kept right on smiling, but tears were soon rolling down her cheeks.

"I'm sorry," Tony murmured as we continued up the stairs.

"Bernadette will be fine," I say, my voice a little too loud for the room.

When I turn, Milo and the priest are looking at me expectantly. I nod reassuringly and then hold out my beer. They clink theirs against mine, and then I drain the bottle. As I'm discarding the empty, Mary bursts through the door. She is out of breath, so she must have run all the way from the pediatric ward.

She ran.

Something's wrong.

Please, God.

"Joey's awake," she whispers.

And then she bursts into tears.

As I hurry toward the door, I see the priest step forward to comfort my sister. But Milo is quicker. He has his arms around

Mary before I make it past the bed. I run down the hall as fast as I can, doing my best to avoid the grim-faced nurses and sad-looking patients. When I reach Joey's room, Nurse Keep It Down is at her bedside. Joey's eyes are open, but she doesn't seem to recognize me.

"Where's the doctor?" I demand.

"He's on the way."

I reach out and take Joey's hand. She does not respond.

"Joey?"

She continues to stare blankly at me.

"Joey?"

"She's going to be disoriented for a little while," the nurse says, smiling encouragingly. "But I'm sure Joey is very happy to see her daddy."

Soon the doctor arrives, obviously preoccupied with some difficult dogleg on the back nine. He manages a politician's toothy smile and begins his examination. Taking a penlight from his pocket, he shines it into her eyes, then checks her reflexes and asks a few questions to which she does not respond. Finally, he makes some brief notations on her chart.

"This little girl's going to be fine," he declares as he moves toward the door.

"That's it?" I ask him. "Seriously?"

He turns to me and asks, "Are you a drinking man, Mr. Androv?"

"I've been known to indulge from time to time," I answer defensively, my breath reeking of the beer I'd just guzzled.

"Have you ever woken up with a really bad hangover after a heavy night of indulging? The kind where you have no idea where you are or how you got there? You can't think; you can't speak; and the last thing you want to do is answer a bunch of questions about how you feel. So you're essentially unresponsive. You're not brain damaged. You just need a little time to recover."

When the doctor finishes his analogy, I want to smack the smug smile right off his face. Instead, I look over at Joey and then back to him.

"So, what are you trying to tell me? She needs a Bloody Mary?"

This time his smile is genuine.

"I'll check back in thirty minutes."

After he leaves, Nurse Keep It Down checks Joey's blood pressure, pulse, temperature—the usual show those in the healthcare business put on for the relatives of patients.

"I'm just down the hall if you need me," she says sweetly.

"Thank you," I say, marveling at how our relationship has evolved.

I sit at Joey's bedside, holding her little hand, talking, and singing. She dozes off from time to time, but it's just sleep. Even I can tell the difference between a nap and a coma.

True to his word, the doctor stops by a half hour later, gives Joey a cursory once-over, and then leaves for the night. When Mary shows up, her eyes are still red from crying. I tell her to go home, that I will not leave Joey's bedside. She nods, kisses her niece, and then starts out the door. She's only taken a couple of steps when she stops and turns back.

"What's with your friend's teeth?" she asks, a little too self-consciously.

Are you kidding me?

"You'll have to ask him," I reply, having no desire to explain that one of her fellow law-enforcement officers smashed him in the mouth with a billy club. "Is he still here?" I ask hopefully. "I sure could use another one of those beers."

"He's in Bernadette's room with Father John. I'll see if he delivers."

The moment Mary says Bernadette's name I felt the tiniest bit of pressure from Joey's hand. I turn and see something new in her expression. Something that hadn't been there a moment earlier.

"Joey, are you worried about Bernadette?"

Nothing.

"Bernadette saved you, Joey."

Still nothing.

"I just stood there, but Bernadette...she saved you. She knew what to do. And she did it. I'm sorry it wasn't me. It should have been me. I should have reacted more quickly. But it was like...I don't know. Everything happened so fast. But Bernadette, she ran like the wind. Like a cheetah. She got to the car and she jumped on it and she held on and kept that bastard from taking you away." Somewhere in this monologue I'd started to cry. For a moment I thought it was Joey, but I realized they were my tears on her bandaged face. "It should have been me saving you, but I just wasn't fucking fast enough. Sorry, I shouldn't use that word. I...I was praying you'd be okay. Me, praying. Can you believe it? But it wasn't God who saved you, Joey. It was Bernadette."

Suddenly, Joey appears to be in distress. At first I think I've overwhelmed her with the story, that it's too much too soon. And then it hits me.

"She's here, Joey. *Ate* Bernadette is here in the hospital. She was...she got hurt, but she's going to be fine. She's going to be fine."

Milo bursts into the room. His silly smile quickly gives way to a more serious expression.

"Is she okay?" he whispers.

"Milo, I need your help."

"Oh yeah," he says, reaching for his backpack.

"No, not that. I need you to do something."

"Anything," he says with such sincerity I want to hug him.

He leaves as soon as I finish explaining.

Two minutes later, Father John shows up.

"Are you sure about this?" he asks. "I mean, don't you think the doctor..."

"I'm sure," I say, cutting him off.

"Do you mind if I say a prayer first?"

"Make it a quick one."

He crosses himself, kneels for a moment at Joey's bedside, then stands and says, "Let's do it."

I pull the sheets aside and carefully lift her from the bed. Father John wheels the IV stand around and takes the catheter bag with his other hand. He holds the door open, and I step into the hallway. As arranged, Milo is distracting Nurse Keep It Down. She is staring into Milo's toothless mouth as he points to where one of his canines had been. He's positioned himself so the nurse has her back to us. We slip by unnoticed. When we reach Bernadette's room, Joey's breathing is labored, and she still looks distraught. We step inside. She doesn't see Bernadette at first, but when I move closer to the bed, I hear the softest cry. I lower her to Bernadette's side. The priest positions the IV stand, hangs the catheter bag, then crosses himself; I almost do the same. Joey is calm now, her breathing less and less labored until I don't notice it at all. She closes her eyes. There is a knock on the door. For a moment I'm afraid it's hospital security, but it's Milo who steps into the room. He looks at Joey, nestled up against the comatose Bernadette and nods knowingly, as if he's just figured something out.

"Joey's the passenger," he announces.

Father John looks at me.

"It's a song," I explain.

"Ah," the priest replies.

And then he starts singing the chorus.

I look over at Milo. If he's surprised, he doesn't show it. Instead, he joins in. A moment later, we're all singing...

La la la la la-la-la-la
La la la la la-la-la-la
La la la la la-la-la-la la-la la

10

Sukiyaki

"Of course, God is the greatest philosopher of all." So declared President Richard Nixon. A Quaker. He also claimed, "Real men don't like soup." I wonder how he felt about oatmeal.

Hillbilly Brad delivered the bad news as I picked at my carbonara. I wasn't really paying attention to him or the pasta, reeling as I was from my encounter with the mysterious Japanese woman. Incredibly, Brad hadn't even noticed her. "Y'all gotta dress to the nines tomorrow," he drawled as I fantasized, "because Yamakawa-san's gonna be taking you 'round to meet the big bosses. If I were you, I'd wear one a my better suits."

This got my attention. It implied ownership of more than one suit—and that I'd be expected to wear the one I did own.

"Are you serious? I have to wear a suit?"

"Not every day. Just the first couple-a."

"Fine. I'll wear my suit."

He regarded me silently for several seconds, gauging my sincerity.

"That blue one y'all wore to the interview?"

It had been three months, and he remembered my suit.

"Where'd you git that thing, anyway?"

"I had it custom tailored at Brooks Brothers."

He let out a porcine snort.

"That's a good one, Max. But as it happens I do git my suits custom made, and that thing you wore is 'bout as off-the-rack as it gits!"

"You got me," I said, holding out my arms in mock surrender. "I bought it at J.C. Penney."

He shook his head sadly.

"So how many custom-made suits do you own, Bradley?"

"Fourteen," he said, perking up. "Eleven in regular rotation and three fer backup."

"You have backup suits?"

"Yup."

"Why?"

Again, the hillbilly regarded me questioningly.

"Well, in case I need 'em," he said as if I were the dipshit.

"Fourteen suits," I mused aloud.

"Not countin' the tux."

"You own a tuxedo?"

"Custom tailored."

"But why? Why do you need any kind of tux? Do you get invited to a lot of presidential inaugurations? Attend a lot of debutante balls? Is your girlfriend still in high school? And Jesus, Brad, fourteen suits?"

"Max, do y'all remember Richard Nixon?"

The non sequitur throws me.

"Of course I remember Tricky Dick. Thirty-fourth president of the United States."

"Thirty-seventh."

"Thirty-fourth. Right after Eisenhower."

"Dwight David Eisenhower *was* the thirty-fourth; Mr. Nixon was his vice. He ran fer president in 1960 but was defeated by that son-of-a-bootlegger John Fitzgerald Kennedy, who became the thirty-fifth. Lyndon Baines Johnson, the thirty-sixth, took over after that incident in Dallas in '63. In '64, LBJ ran fer re-election against the great Barry Goldwater and only won 'cause a that nuclear destruction propaganda. Then Johnson went and made a mess of Viet Nam, so he decided not to seek re-election in '68. It was his veep, Hubert Horatio Humphrey, who ran and lost to none other than Richard Milhous Nixon. It was and is the greatest political comeback of all time."

I had to admit, his knowledge of presidential middle names was impressive.

"What does that have to do with fourteen suits and a custom-made tuxedo?"

"RMN's one of my heroes!"

"Dick Nixon is your hero?"

"Yup," he said proudly.

"Watergate? Kent State? The bombing of Cambodia?"

"Footnotes. Historical blips. They don't begin to outweigh his definin' quality."

"Which was?"

"He was the best-dressed president of all time."

"Nixon?"

"He wore a suit relaxin' at home."

"And you find that heroic?"

"My philosophy is that the quality of a culture is determined by the way its members clothe themselves."

I suppressed an urge to slap him across the face, though not out of anger. I wanted to give him one of those therapeutic slaps, the kind you give someone having a mid-air meltdown.

"You know what happened to Nixon."

"What do you mean?"

"Jesus Christ, Brad! Nixon was the only president in the history of the United States forced to resign. Otherwise he would have been impeached."

"But he stayed true to the code."

"What code?"

"The dress code. When President Nixon walked outta the White House and got on that whirlybird, he projected an image of pride, power, and patriotism."

I was afraid he might tear up, but instead, he pulled himself together and announced, "Tell you what I'm gonna do: I'm gonna loan you one of my suits. We're 'bout the same size. And we can't have you wearin' that off-the-rack monstrosity more than once. Good lord, what'll people think?"

Now I was angry, though not because he insulted my suit. Not because he viewed me as a fashion charity case. I was pissed off because he used *loan* as a verb. It's a noun, for fuck's sake! And Brad is a copywriter, someone responsible for the quality of English advertising in Japan. I'll give him a break on *y'all* because he's a hillbilly, but there's no excuse for confusing the parts of speech. Rather than rub the faux pas in his face, I diplomatically paraphrased the sentence, substituting the proper word for the improper one and giving it noticeable emphasis: "You're offering to *lend* me one of your suits?"

"It'd be my pleasure."

Right over his head.

"Thanks, but no thanks."

"It's no problem. I'd be happy to do it."

"Not necessary. I'll just wear a different pair of pants and a different shirt."

"Yer gonna mix 'n' match?" Brad cried, as if he'd found a hairball in his soup.

The Japanese waiter was watching us. He looked nervous.

"C'mon, won't you take me up on my offer?"

"For the last time, you're not going to loan me a suit."

"*Lend* you a suit, Max. I wanna *lend* you a suit. *Loan* is a noun. You should know that."

Goddammit!

"Anyway," he said brightly, his mood suddenly lifting, "y'all best git some sleep. Tomorrow's a big day."

When he called for the bill, the waiter was visibly relieved.

"I stayed here too when I first arrived," he explained as we walked from the restaurant and into the hotel lobby.

"They said I could move into my place in a week," I replied. As part of my contract, the company provided an apartment in the heart of Tokyo. The rent was astronomical, but I didn't have to pay a cent. They even covered the utilities. "Why don't they just have the new employee come over *after* the apartment's ready?" I wondered aloud.

"I guess maybe they figure the transition's easier if y'all stay in a hotel fer a few days."

Finally, he said something that made sense.

We stopped at the check-in counter, and Brad asked for my passport. He spoke to the lovely Japanese receptionist for a few moments, then handed it to her. She typed something into a computer, looked at the passport, and slid a key card into a tiny folder. With a hotel pen, she wrote my room number on the back of it. The pen was even nicer than the one I'd stolen from the Essex, and I realized I'd soon be committing another act of larceny. She passed me the key card and my passport, then turned to Brad and said something in Japanese.

"Nah," he replied.

She bowed politely.

"What did she say?" I demanded.

Brad leaned forward and whispered, "She wanted to know if y'all are single."

"Really? But I *am* single!"

I waved at the receptionist and yelled, "I'm single!"

She looked nervously from me to Brad and then moved away to help another customer.

"Just kiddin'. She asked if y'all wanted help with yer luggage."

He walked away before I could call him an asshole. When we reached the elevator lobby, Brad pressed the up button and then extended his hand. "Welcome to Japan, Max," he said. "I'll meet y'all in the lobby tomorrow mornin' at nine. We can walk to the office from here." We shook hands, and he scurried away.

A bell announced the elevator's arrival, and when the doors opened I stepped inside. It was pretty much the same as all the other elevators I'd been in—only smaller. I assumed this was because the Japanese take up less space than their American counterparts. After a short ride to the seventh floor, the doors opened to a brightly carpeted hallway. There was a plaque on the wall showing the location of each room, so I had no trouble finding mine. I used the key card to open the door and stepped inside. It was pretty much the same as all the other hotel rooms I'd ever been in—only smaller. I opened the thick curtains covering the rear wall and revealed a large window overlooking the front of the hotel. Suddenly the room didn't seem quite so compact. I might actually enjoy staying here, I thought, adjusting to my new life in Japan until the apartment is ready. I walked to the mini fridge and looked inside. It was filled with Japanese beer. Yes, I was going to like it here.

Then the phone rang.

"Hello?"

"Max!"

Sometimes, even before a conversation begins, I know I'm going to be an asshole. Not intentionally. There's just no way of preventing it. Maybe it's because I'm in a bad mood or I'm tired or I'm hung over or I just met a mysterious Japanese woman and don't want to be reminded that I have a girlfriend.

"You made it!" Annette gushed, as if I'd just scaled the east face of K2.

"You were expecting the plane to crash?"

"No," she said, sounding wounded. "It's just that you're so far away."

Not far enough.

"What's it like?"

"What do you mean?"

"I mean, what's Japan like?"

"How should I know? I just got here."

"Why are you so grumpy?"

"I'm not grumpy. I landed like an hour ago and went from the airport to the hotel."

"Well, did you see anything interesting?"

"It's nighttime here. Tokyo is thirteen hours ahead of New Jersey."

"Oh, that's right," she said sadly. "It's day here, and it's night there. That makes you seem even further away."

Again, not far enough.

"Do you miss me?" she asked.

I hate questions like this; queries that put you in a moral quandary. Because the obvious answer—the logical, intelligent, courteous, commonsense answer—is the lie.

Yes, I miss you.

Easy.

But taking the moral high ground is never a question of ease.

It's a question of character.

It's a question of integrity.

"Do you miss me?"

"Jesus Christ, Annette, I just left. How the hell do you expect me to miss you?"

The long silence that followed yielded to a wave of sobs.

"Oh my god," she gasped before I could offer a fake apology.

"What?"

"Max," she said, fully recovered, "I'm going to ask you something, and I want you to be completely honest."

Sure. It worked so well last time.

"Are you having jet lag?"

Not what I expected.

"I don't know. I guess. Fourteen-hour plane ride. Thirteen-hour time difference."

"I knew it!" she cried gleefully.

"Knew what?"

"It's the jet lag!"

"Huh?"

"It's okay. I understand now."

"Understand what?"

"Why you're being such a prick. I read about it in a law enforcement journal. Some people become psychopaths when they're jet lagged. It's not really their fault. They get mean and violent and sometimes even commit crimes."

"And you think that's what's happening to me?"

"According to the article, some people are predisposed."

"You think I'm predisposed to being a prick?"

Annette laughed.

"I love you, Max."

Here we go again.

It was a ten-minute walk to the office, but it seemed much longer, thanks to Brad's non-stop narration. He described every structure we passed, including the one I'd be working in—an ugly gray monolith that stuck out like a sore thumb. Ironically, this made it perfectly compatible with the surrounding structures. As I was soon to discover, there is no logic to the architectural aesthetic of Japan's capital city. Walking down any given block, you might pass a thirty-story office tower; then a squat convenience store; followed by an impossibly narrow building with eighteen floors of restaurants; next a high-rise condo designed to resemble a rocket ship; and on the corner a century-old wooden house that miraculously survived the fire bombings of World War II. A few days later, you amble down that same block, and one of the buildings has disappeared. Next time you're in the neighborhood, a new one is in its place. This is because the land in Tokyo is far more valuable than anything one could possibly build on it. Thus, it's practical to demolish a perfectly healthy building and replace it with something more profitable. Like a parking garage. I once spent forty-five minutes pacing up and down the same three blocks, wondering if I'd finally lost my mind. I was attempting to return an overdue video, but the store had vanished. Finally, I realized the muddy gap between two of the taller buildings was the place where, five days earlier, I'd rented a VHS copy of *The Karate Kid Part III*. I still have it.

My first day went pretty well. Brad delivered me to the seventh-floor office where I'd be working and then excused himself, explaining he had a lot of things to take care of before he left Japan. I tried to look disappointed. The office was large, with several desks in two rows and a series of cubicles against a wall of windows. Yamakawa-san greeted me with a bow. I made sure to bow a bit more deeply, having learned this is expected of a subordinate. He indicated my cubicle and then introduced me to the other nine people I'd be working with: seven women and two men, all but one of whom were Japanese. As is my habit, I forgot each of their names even before the soundwaves had fully dissipated. It's hard enough to remember first names, but in Japan, everyone is addressed by his or her last name; everyone is Something-san. I once asked a Japanese co-worker if she knew the first name of a woman she'd worked with for over fourteen years. She didn't. In fact, she barely understood the question. While Japanese surnames aren't particularly difficult to pronounce, they often have several syllables, which further enhances my inability to recall them. Thank god for the *meishi*. In Japan, virtually everyone has a business card—a *meishi*—and the exchange of these cards is an important component of any business or social interaction where unfamiliar faces are present. After meeting my co-workers, I had an impressive stack that could be used as a learning tool, though I was able to remember one of the names without a mnemonic device: Derek. It belonged to a Welshman who worked as a proofreader. He looked like the undernourished member of a motorcycle gang: skinny, scruffy, vested, bearded, and booted—a relatively conspicuous presence in an office where every male, including me, was wearing a business suit. When I asked about his background, he told me he had a degree in animal husbandry and then shifted the subject to my tie.

"Da-fi-da-ku," I said.

He laughed and lit a cigarette. They still allowed smoking in offices when I was in Japan; in fact, they practically encouraged it. As I started to walk away, Derek called after me.

"Max," he said softly after I returned to his cubicle, "You shouldn't add *san* when referring to yourself." (I had introduced myself as *Max-san*.)

"Why not?"

"Because it's an honorific. You use it for other people's names, but never your own. Otherwise, you sound like an…"

"Asshole?"

"For lack of a better word."

"I doubt there is a better word."

"Next time just say, 'I'm Max.'"

"Thanks, Derek-san."

The Welshman bowed.

"Do you drink beer?" I was sure he did; I know a drinker when I see one.

"Recovering alcoholic," he said matter-of-factly.

"Ah, c'mon, what's a beer or two?"

He laughed. I knew we'd get along.

"So you like to drink beer," he confirmed.

"Every chance I get."

"The Japanese are gonna love you."

The rest of the day transpired pretty much as Hillbilly Brad had predicted, with Yamakawa-san and me going from office to office, paying homage to various bosses. It was perfunctory; the men I met—all of the bosses were men—offered little more than "Nice to meet you" or "Do you like Japanese food?" Yet they were all friendly and seemed genuinely welcoming. Yamakawa-san and I exchanged perhaps twenty-five words the entire afternoon, but I was surprised to discover how loquacious he could be with his fellow countrymen. He was funny and energetic and seemed well liked by his peers. It's difficult to get an honest read on people until you hear them communicate in their native language.

We returned to our office around five p.m. Yamakawa-san hurried over to a medium-sized TV on a stand near his desk and switched it on. Moments later, the screen was filled with enormously fat men, naked but for a band of cloth through their legs and around their waists.

"It's the second day of the *basho*," a voice said.

I turned to see Derek standing next to me, his eyes fixed on the TV.

"Sumo wrestling?"

"Yeah, a *basho* is a fifteen-day sumo tournament. There are six every year."

The office started to fill up with men and a few women from nearby offices, all of whom gathered around the TV. Their excitement was obvious. Then Yamakawa-san stepped over and put a cold can of Kirin beer into my hand.

"Ma-ku-su-san," my new boss said, holding up his own beer, "welcome to Japan."

I could feel my face smiling.

"*Kampai*," he said as we clinked them together.

"*Kampai*," I repeated and took a drink.

The TV crowd roared as a wrestler was pushed from the ring.

"So the object is to shove the other guy out of the circle?" I asked.

"*Hai*," Yamakawa-san said, then he turned and gave Derek a look.

Understanding the silent command, Derek elaborated: "Basically, there are two ways to win in sumo. You either push the other guy out of the ring or you force him to touch the ground with anything other than his feet."

Yamakawa-san nodded.

I took another drink.

For the next forty-five minutes, we watched the big men grapple and embrace and shove and slap and push and lift and force one another out of the ring or to the ground. As the matches progressed, I began to notice variations in styles and strategies. Some wrestlers depended on strength. Others relied on speed. And still others, guile. I watched one particularly mean-looking giant stare down his much smaller opponent, gaining a psychological advantage he clearly didn't need. There was never any doubt that these men were strong. How else could a contestant lift his 300-pound opponent off the ground? By six o'clock, the matches were over, and to my surprise, so was the workday. At least mine was. Yamakawa-san touched me on the shoulder and said, "Shall we go to dinner?" As I followed him out of the office, I noticed my new colleagues were paying no attention to our exit; so complete was their indifference, I suspected they were tracking our every move. Derek made no effort to hide his impending departure, strapping on a beat-to-hell motorcycle helmet and slipping into a pair of ugly yellow sewer boots.

"See you tomorrow," he said as he hurried from the office.

"*Sayonara,*" I answered.

"Damn," he said over his shoulder. "You're practically fluent."

Yamakawa-san and I continued down the hall to the elevators. He pushed the button, and we waited in silence for the doors to open. When they did, we stepped inside, joining several others already in the car. No one spoke on the downward journey, save for the girlish Japanese voice emanating from the control panel. The doors opened on the ground floor, and we walked to the exit. It was already dark, a November chill in the air, when we stepped from the ugly gray monolith. Yamakawa-san set off at a brisk pace toward Ginza, a few blocks west. It was surprising to see a man who spent much of the day in a state of semi-hibernation move so quickly. I kept falling behind, as I was fascinated by everything I saw. The lights. The shops. The signs. The buildings. The people. They all seemed so exotic. So beautiful. Even the unattractive ones. I thought of the mysterious beauty I'd met the night before, hoping to catch a glimpse of her. There are only about twelve million people in Tokyo, so I figured my chances weren't that bad.

"Ma-ku-su-san," Yamakawa-san called back to me as I hurried forward, "do you like *tempura*?"

"Yes," I said without knowing if this were true.

I assumed it was some sort of food, since we were going to dinner, but aside from that, I hadn't a clue. Whatever it turned out to be, I would eat it. Before leaving the US, I vowed to consume anything that was put in front of me. No matter how mysterious. Otherwise, I'd surely be seduced by the familiar and wind up taking all my meals at Ma-ku-do-na-ru-do. As the English-speaking waiter patiently explained a few minutes later, tempura is fish, prawns, and vegetables, battered and lightly fried. Our orders came with rice, miso soup, and some colorful pieces of leather Yamakawa-san referred to as *pickles*. The tempura was amazing. Each delicate piece had a beautiful, yellowish-gold coating that maintained a satisfying crunch, even after being dipped into the special sauce. It was light and flavorful and actually tasted healthy, a far cry from the fried fare to which I was accustomed: grease-soaked chicken thighs that allowed me to feel—in real time—the diminishment of my arterial blood flow.

Dinner conversation was minimal, at least from my perspective. Two or three words every ten minutes. But I didn't mind the silences. It was so satisfying to concentrate on the food. Although they would eventually become second nature, the chopsticks were problematic. The waiter offered to bring me a fork and knife, but I declined. Yamakawa-san nodded his endorsement. After an hour or so, far longer than I normally spend eating, he called for the check: *O-kanjo o kudasai*. I thanked him for the meal, and he gave me a slight bow. I bowed back, but he was turning away as I did, so I don't think it registered. As we meandered through the streets of Ginza, I continued to take in my unfamiliar surroundings, always keeping an eye out for the mystery woman.

"Ma-ku-su-san," Yamakawa-san said, breaking a seven-minute silence, "do you want to drink sake?"

Sake. Japanese rice wine.

"I would very much like to drink sake," I said earnestly.

He nodded silently, a silence that endured until we reached our destination, which turned out to be a non-descript building on a dimly lit side street. There was no indication that it housed a drinking establishment.

"This is my place," he said as we mounted a long, narrow flight of stairs.

"You own it?" I exclaimed, as I hurried after him.

At the top, we came to a small landing with a dark wooden door. Yamakawa-san smiled as he faced me, his way of answering my question.

"Oh," I said, "Your regular place."

The smile lingered for a moment, then he pushed open the door and stepped inside. I followed. It was very compact, just a small room with a couple of tables and a bar about two meters long—the kind of setup you'd find in a middle-aged couple's basement after the kids go off to college. It was a bit too bright for my liking, and the color scheme seemed soft, almost feminine. Behind the bar was an older Japanese woman. Older than I was, anyway. Probably in her fifties, although I'm as bad at determining ages as I am at remembering names. She was wearing a kimono, and for a moment I wondered if Yamakawa-san had brought me to a geisha house. But then I recalled having read that Japanese women often wear kimonos, particularly in social settings. Her eyes lit up when she saw Yamakawa-san, and she gave him a smile so strangely personal I felt like a voyeur. They bowed formally to one another.

"Hagiwara-san," he said, "this is Ma-ku-su-san."

She started to bow but had second thoughts. Instead, she extended her hand and said in a charmingly accented voice, "Nice to meet you, Ma-ku-su-san."

I took her hand. It was soft and gentle, yet I could feel strength in it.

"Nice to meet you," I echoed.

She held my eyes for a few moments, just as the mystery woman had, but this time I had to look away. I felt like a little boy caught checking out the babysitter's cleavage. I glanced over at Yamakawa-san, who nodded, somehow communicating that my reaction was perfectly understandable. He said something to her in Japanese. She bowed and walked behind the bar and through a small door I hadn't even noticed. Yamakawa-san led me to a table at the back of the room. As I sat, I realized I'd misjudged the interior. I now found the light to be gentle and friendly, the colors soft and comfortable. A reflection of the woman behind the bar.

"Do you come here a lot?" I asked.

"Twenty-three years," he said, answering his way.

"Wow, twenty-three years."

"Hagiwara-san opened this bar after her husband died. He was my friend."

This was followed by a long period of silence.

"How did he die?" I asked, surrendering to my impatience. "I mean, he must have been pretty young."

"*Hai*, a young man. Like you."

Before he could continue, Hagiwara-san arrived at our table carrying a ceramic bottle and two small wooden boxes. After carefully arranging them in front of us, she bowed and shuffled away without saying a word. I watched her go, realizing that her shuffle was necessitated by the kimono; it left little room for leg movement—just enough for the smallest of steps.

"Ma-ku-su-san," Yamakawa-san said.

I turned to see him holding one of the wooden boxes. "This is called *masu*. It is the old way of drinking sake."

"*Masu*," I echoed.

He reached for the ceramic bottle and proceeded to fill both boxes to the rim.

"It is filled to the top to show prosperity," he explained.

I watched as he raised the *masu* to his lips without spilling a drop. He took a sip and then set it back on the table. The moment

I attempted to lift my own box, sake splashed everywhere. Yamakawa-san nodded encouragingly, and I managed to get it to my lips without wasting any more. But the moment I tried to drink from it, sake dribbled from the sides of my mouth. I was a little embarrassed, but this was more than compensated for by the sake's exquisite taste. It was delicious and refreshing, as much a surprise as the tempura had been. I lowered the box, careful not to spill any more of its precious content.

"This is very good sake," Yamakawa-san said.

"It's amazing," I concurred.

For the next ten minutes, we drank without words. My technique improved as I watched Yamakawa-san, holding the box and drinking from it just as he did. It wasn't long before I felt a gentle glow of contentment. I was in Japan. I was drinking sake. I was happy.

"He died in a plane crash," Yamakawa-san said, breaking the silence.

I set the *masu* on the table and waited for him to continue.

"The worst in the history of Japan," he added after the silence had settled. "Five hundred and twenty people died, Ma-ku-su-san."

"Jesus," I muttered.

He took another drink. I did the same.

"Only two women and two girls survived."

Yamakawa-san stared into the distance, and I sensed this wasn't a story he often shared. The happiness I'd felt only moments earlier now seemed a distant memory.

"Hagiwara-san's husband was travelling with a famous Japanese singer. He was accompanying him to Osaka to discuss a project with the agency. The singer's name was Kyu Sakamoto."

My mouth dropped open.

Q Sakamoto.

I knew that name.

"Sakamoto-san had a very famous song that was popular even in America." Yamakawa-san explained. And then, in a beautiful, pitch-perfect voice, he began to sing.

I recognized the melody right away.

The "Sukiyaki" song.

I looked over and saw that Hagiwara-san was listening to her old friend's impromptu performance. How sad this song must make her feel, I thought. Or did it bring her closer to the young husband she'd lost all those years ago? When Yamakawa-san finished, he turned and, even though seated, bowed to her. A few moments later, she replaced our empty sake bottle with a full one. As she shuffled back to the bar, Yamakawa-san filled my *masu* to the rim. Without hesitation, I raised it to my lips and drank. Sake spilled from the sides of the box, from the corners of my mouth. It soaked my Daffy Duck tie, my ugly blue suit, my Sunday clothes, baptizing me in the name of the Father, and of the Son, and of the Holy Ghost...

11

A Miracle

She was groggy. Confused. Eyes unable to focus. Understandable, given that she'd been in a coma for two weeks. It took some time, but Bernadette gradually became aware of her surroundings, gradually became aware of Father John and me standing at her bedside. She smiled, a drowsy smile, as one does after a long, peaceful sleep. For a moment I was hopeful. But then her eyes filled with terror and she began thrashing in the bed as if she were being burned alive. My first thought was a seizure, but she was trying to rip out the lines and tubes, to escape from the bed. The nurse rushed forward and held her shoulders down, but the struggle intensified. How had two familiar faces frightened her so? How had...no. It wasn't the faces she saw that frightened her. It was the face she didn't see.

"Joey's all right, Bernadette!" I yelled. "She's all right! She's going to be fine."

My voice sounded strange, muddled, and I realized I was choked up, on the verge of tears. Once again, I was overwhelmed. How could this woman love so fiercely? After everything she's been through, how could she love at all? "Joey's fine. Joey's fine,"

I kept yelling. But she continued to struggle, and Father John had to step forward to help the nurse hold her down.

She fought even harder.

"GODDAMMIT, BERNADETTE! JOEY'S FINE!"

She was suddenly so still that for a terrifying moment I thought I'd killed her.

Slowly, the nurse and Father John released their grip. I'm sure they were relieved I'd calmed her, but I suspected they were a tad dismayed that I'd sworn at the woman who'd lost a leg while saving my daughter's life. The truth is, I was scared, and I tend to scream obscenities when I'm scared. It's usually *fuck*, but in this case I was compelled to take the Lord thy God's name in vain. In any case, it worked.

Bernadette was staring up at me. Wanting to believe what I'd told her.

"Joey is okay. I swear to God, she's okay."

She opened her mouth to speak but produced only a choking sound.

"Would you like some water?" the nurse asked gently.

Bernadette seemed surprised to see the nurse, who only moments earlier had been holding her down. Then she nodded, and the nurse held a flexible straw to Bernadette's lips.

"Just a little bit," the nurse said kindly.

Bernadette took a few small sips.

The room was calm now.

Serene.

Then the doctor arrived and kicked everyone but the nurse out of the room. Bernadette didn't mind. She had proof of life. But she had only one leg. We'd discussed it with the medical staff, and everyone agreed that Father John would break the news. When I returned to her room a few minutes later, he was already there, praying.

"Bernadette," I said upon entering.

She looked at me and smiled but didn't try to speak.

"We have to tell you something."

"Max," Father John said cautiously.

I tried to give him the look Yamakawa-san often gave me. A look that said everything if only you listened. I wanted it to say, *This woman saved my daughter. Was prepared to die for her. I'm the one who should reveal the cost of her love.*

The priest studied my face for several seconds and then returned to his prayer.

"Do you remember what happened?"

She nodded unsurely, as if not quite prepared for an exam.

"The park," I said. "We were in the park. You and me and Joey."

She nodded again.

"And there was a man. The man with the camera. He tried to take Joey away, but you ran after him. You chased him to the parking lot. He tried to put Joey in the car, but she was fighting. Because she's a fighter. Like you. And she almost got away. But the man was so much bigger, and he hit her face against the door."

Bernadette closed her eyes—whether to block it out or see it more clearly, I didn't know.

"And then you jumped onto the car to keep him from getting away. Because he was going to hurt her. He was going to...but you wouldn't let that happen. You pulled on the steering wheel so he couldn't drive straight. He was crashing into cars, but you never let go. You were amazing. You were...you were

Joey's guardian angel. (*Ever this day be at my side…*) Then he crashed into a car on the other side of the street, the side you were on, and you couldn't hold on any longer. But because of what you did, the man lost control and hit a pole. That's why I was able get Joey out of the car. Because of what you did. You saved her, Bernadette. You saved her. But you were really, badly hurt. So bad the doctors didn't know if you'd survive. But I knew. I knew you'd survive. Even though you were in a coma for almost two weeks."

Her eyes suddenly opened.

"You know what a coma is?"

She nodded.

"You were in a coma because your body had suffered so much trauma. Your legs, mostly. The damage to your legs was… extensive." I thought she'd look down at that point, that she'd assess the damage for herself. Instead, her eyes remained fixed on me. "The doctors did their best. They tried really, really hard."

The priest continued to pray, gripping her hand, though Bernadette seemed not to notice.

"They managed to save your left leg."

I hesitated, hoping the rest could be inferred, but she waited for me to finish the story.

"But they couldn't save the other. They had to amputate your right leg."

For a moment, the world was still.

Peaceful.

The calm before the storm.

And then she said:

"It's a miracle."

The priest stopped praying.

"Bernadette," he said gently, "do you understand what just Max told you?"

Now she did look down at her legs. First her right, its outline ending just above where her knee should have been. And then the left, immobilized in its high-tech cast.

"It's a miracle," she said again.

The priest turned to me, as if I had some special insight into her inexplicable reaction. I shrugged.

"I'm sorry, Bernadette," he pleaded, "but...how is this a miracle?"

She smiled in a way that is reserved for those on intimate terms with tragedy. "When we smashed into that car, I thought I was gone," she said, her voice soft and hoarse. "And I thought Joey was gone. And I thought God was gone." She paused to catch her breath. "But I am wrong. And it is a miracle."

The priest stared at Bernadette, his mouth quivering as if he was trying to put some inexpressible sentiment into words. After releasing her hand, he rose and stepped to the window. Using his fingers, he separated the slats of the white plastic blinds and looked through them, turning his head back and forth as if searching for something. I could tell by the way his shoulders trembled that he was crying.

The door swung open with such force that it would have knocked me over had I been standing a few inches closer. I turned, expecting to see the doctor but instead was greeted by the smiling face of Milo Braggen. Something had changed, but before I could figure out what it was, he looked over at Bernadette and said, "Well, hello, darlin'." She returned his greeting with a puzzled expression. Although he'd visited several times, Bernadette had never actually met Milo, having been unconscious. This detail seemed to have escaped him. He walked to the chair, sat down, and then took the hand the priest had been holding a few moments earlier. I was about to explain to Bernadette who this toothless…

That was it—the difference!

Milo wasn't toothless anymore!

"Kumusta ang pakiramdam mo?" he said, surprising me, shocking Bernadette. Father John continued staring out the window.

"Hindi ko alam," she said after several seconds.

"Ako si, Milo. Ako yong kaibigan ni Max at Joey at Mary."

Bernadette smiled.

"Wow, marunong ka palang mag Tagalog."

"Salamat. Medyo nakalimutan."

"Jesus, Milo," I said, "you speak Tagalog?"

Milo held up a finger: one moment, please.

"Mayron akong itatanong sau?"

Bernadette nodded.

"Marunong ka bang magluto ng adobong baboy?"

And then another miracle occurred.

She laughed.

Not a big laugh.

More of a giggle.

But it got the priest's attention. He turned from the window, a look of wonder on his face.

"He wants me to make him adobo pork," Bernadette translated, still smiling.

"What the hell, Milo?" I demanded.

"It's my favorite dish," he said, as if this explained everything.

I hadn't seen him for almost a week. He'd stayed around for several days—being extremely helpful and supportive, fawning over Mary—and then vanished as suddenly as he'd appeared. Now, here he was again, a full set of teeth in his mouth, speaking a relatively obscure Southeast Asian language, asking a woman who'd just awoken from a coma to find she was short a major appendage if she'd make dinner for him.

"You speak Tagalog?" I repeated.

He looked as if he didn't understand the question, as if he were thinking, *Doesn't everybody?* and then it seemed to occur to him that everybody does not.

"Oh, I had me a Filipina girlfriend. Amihan."

"Amihan," Bernadette repeated. "That's a pretty name."

"For a pretty girl." Milo added. "Though not as pretty as you."

It sounded like flirting, but Milo was just being honest. He tends to do that, to be naively truthful without considering the impact that truth might have. His expression became serious when he leaned in close and whispered, "I'm really sorry about your leg, Bernadette."

The priest glanced over at me, relieved I had already broken this news.

"Thank you," she replied, as if she'd just been paid a compliment.

Milo rose and stepped over to where I was standing. The moment he did, the priest slipped back into the chair.

"I see you made some improvements," I said to my unpredictable friend.

"Yep."

I waited for him to continue. He did not.

"Where'd you get 'em?"

"From a dentist."

"No dentist works that fast."

"They do in California," he said, "That's where I've been the past few days."

"You got a new set of teeth in five days?"

"Yup."

"Bullshit."

"I'd already ordered them. See, I was planning on coming back anyway, and I didn't want your—I mean, you know—didn't want people to see me without my teeth. But then I heard about your little girl and I said fuck it. That's why I had to go back to California. Pick up the teeth. Take care of a few loose ends."

"Loose ends?"

It sounded ominous, particularly when coming from someone involved in the illegal drug trade. Milo shook his head.

"I sold the farm."

"The pot farm?"

He frowned and then glanced at the priest and the patient to see if they'd heard my question. Though they hadn't, he led me out of the room, down the hall, and to a visitor's lounge that was deserted save for a man in yellow pants passed out across four of the plastic seats. I shook my head. Why the fuck would a grown man put on a pair of yellow pants? Milo walked to one of the soft-drink machines and returned with two cans of root beer; aside from water and coffee, it's the only non-alcoholic beverage I'm inclined to drink. I was impressed that he recalled this biographical detail. Then again, maybe he just wanted a root beer. We opened our cans and took a sip. Sweet and refreshing, but hardly a Jesus moment.

"Let's just say it supported a valuable cash crop," Milo continued after he swallowed his second gulp.

"Why'd you sell it?"

"My heart's not in it any more. Besides, competition was getting fierce."

"Competition? You mean like drug cartels?"

Milo laughed. "Nah, I never had any problem with drug cartels. It's the damn corporations."

"Corporations?"

"Yup."

"What corporations?"

"You know, the big boys."

I gestured helplessly.

"Big tobacco and such."

It took me a moment to get my head around what he'd just said. It somehow made sense, in the inexplicable way things make sense in Milo's world.

"You're saying the tobacco companies are growing pot?"

"Not exactly. It's more like they're preparing."

"Preparing? For what?"

"For when it's legalized."

I shook my head.

"Think about it. They've been decriminalizing marijuana for a long time now. Remember when we were kids? When gettin' busted with a joint could get you two or three years in prison? Now the cops don't even bother. A couple of states are gonna be legalizing it soon and not just for medical use. Pretty soon it'll be legal to buy pot just to get high. And the big corporations are gonna be there to take over production and distribution."

"I don't know…it just sounds…un-American."

"It's fuckin' apple pie! Who took over liquor production when they repealed the Eighteenth Amendment? It wasn't the bootleggers. They just diversified into other illegal enterprises. No, it was the corporations that reclaimed the liquor trade after prohibition ended. This is basically the same thing."

"How do you know all this?"

"You gotta know your business. And who knows the business of smoking better than the tobacco industry? The cigarette market is dying, so pot's gonna be their new lifeblood. All they have to do is make a few modifications to some of their factories, and they're ready to go."

He paused to take another gulp of root beer.

"I always thought the drug cartels would take over if it ever got legalized," I admitted. "You know, like they'd go legit."

"Nah, they'd never pay the taxes. The government wouldn't stand for that."

"But the cartels control it now, don't they?"

"Not as much as you might think. The hard stuff, maybe. But the pot trade is in different hands."

"The corporations."

Milo shrugged.

"So which corporation bought yours?"

"That's the good part. You remember when my old man lost the farm?"

It's not the kind of thing you forget: his father signed over the deed, then blew his brains out.

"Turns out the food conglomerate that bought the farm also owns one of the big tobacco companies. One of the big tobacco companies that's anticipating the decriminalization of a certain controlled substance."

Now I understood where Milo was going.

"You gotta be shittin' me."

"Nope, it's the same fuckin' company."

"Jesus, talk about history repeating itself."

"Not exactly repeating. When they bought the family farm, those pricks got it for a song. We got just enough to pay off the debts. But this time, they had to pay. Like I said, it's not a big farm, but it's a strip of land right in between two of their largest holdings. I was a huge pain in their ass."

"So you got a lot of money?"

"I got more than money."

Here Milo paused, a faraway look in his eyes. Then he stepped forward, placed his left hand on my shoulder, and said, "I got the farm back."

For a moment I was confused.

"You mean you got the *family* farm back? Jesus, Milo, that's a fucking miracle."

"Praise the Lord."

"You got the farm back!"

"Yup."

"So what are you going to do now?"

"I'm gonna live there."

"Will you work it?"

"Nah, I'm done with farming. I'll lease the acreage back to them. I'm just gonna drink beer and watch reruns of *The Twilight Zone*."

"And here I thought you'd lost your ambition."

His smile was so much more pleasant with incisors.

"What about money? You still gotta pay property taxes."

"The farm only covered half the price, brother. I took the rest in cash."

I didn't know much about the price of Illinois farmland, but Milo's family spread was easily worth ten million dollars. Probably a lot more.

"It only covered half the price?"

Milo smiled and took another swig of root beer. I did the same.

"So you're…"

"From now on, every pizza I order's gonna have extra cheese."

A thought suddenly occurred to me.

"I'll be damned."

"What?"

"It's you."

"It's me what?"

"You're the one paying for her room."

Bernadette had been moved to a private room, though her hospitalization insurance covered only the basics. When I'd questioned the administrators about this discrepancy, they offered vague but reassuring responses.

He shrugged. "I got my farm back and more money than I know what to do with."

"But you don't even know her. Or at least you didn't until a few minutes ago."

"So?"

I waited.

"I got a yearning for some adobo."

"Yeah, I'm dying to try it, too. What else?"

"I don't know. Maybe it's because she's a hero. A real one, I mean. Not one of those bullshit media constructs whose only heroic deed was saving his own ass. Man, that lady was ready to make the ultimate sacrifice. At the very least, she deserves her own room."

Though I believed him to be sincere, I wasn't convinced.

"You sure it doesn't have anything to do with Mary?"

He actually blushed.

I stood there watching him, this middle-aged man-boy who could artfully negotiate a multi-million-dollar deal with a mega-corporation, yet still become embarrassed over a high-school crush. An overwhelming force suddenly took possession of my body, compelling me to move forward and do something completely out of character: I hugged him. Milo was as surprised as I was, and for a moment his arms hung limp at his sides. And then he hugged me back. When we broke the clutch, neither of us said anything for a few moments. Then, lifting the root beer toward his mouth, Milo asked, "Was it good for you, too?" He took a massive gulp.

"It would have been better without the teeth," I replied.

I saw his eyes grow wide and his cheeks bulge as he tried to suppress the laugh that was forcing its way up through the liquid in his throat. Suddenly root beer was spurting out his mouth and nose, showering both of us.

"Jesus, Milo, what the fuck!"

I looked around for a napkin but didn't see any. Then I spotted a grayish towel lying on the floor near where Yellow Pants was sleeping. I used it to wipe root beer from my face and the lenses of my glasses. It had that nauseating smell towels get when they're used to clean up milk and then left in a heap to ferment as they dry. I was barely able to suppress my gag reflex.

"You done with that?" Milo asked, indicating the towel.

I tossed it to him.

He used it to wipe his own face but didn't seem to notice the smell.

"I should get back to the room," I said.

"Okay, maybe I'll get going then. I'm heading to the farm."

He offered the towel back, but I shook my head. The multi-millionaire looked around for a moment and, seeing no one other than Yellow Pants, stuffed it into the back pocket of his jeans. As I turned and headed back to the room, he yelled after me.

"Tell Mary I said hi."

That stopped me.

"Damn, I was supposed to call her as soon as Bernadette woke up."

"So, Mary's coming?" he said, making a transparent attempt to sound nonchalant.

"Man, you got it bad."

Milo shrugged.

"Does she even know how you feel?"

He considered the question.

"I don't know. Probably not."

"Why don't you tell her?"

"I can't."

"Why not?"

"I don't know. I kinda like not knowing. It means I still have a chance."

Milo logic.

"She asked about you."

His face lit up.

"Seriously? What'd she say?"

"She said, 'What's with your friend's teeth?'"

"Really?!!"

"Really."

"Why didn't you tell me this before?"

"Sorry, with everything that was going on, I guess your post-pubescent love life slipped my mind."

"That's okay," he said, "I understand."

It's okay. He understands.

"Look, if you're really interested in Mary, you're going to have to talk to her. Let her know. She's not seeing anybody. Hasn't for a long time. I think she's resigned to being alone."

Milo punched the air and mouthed the word *yes*.

"I'm glad you find her isolation so uplifting. But if you're serious about getting closer to my sister, you've got to be honest about what you were doing in California. I don't care if she is a cop. You start out with a lie, you don't have anything solid to build on." I believed these words to be valid, though my record with women hardly qualified me as a relationship counselor.

"I don't lie," he said with such sincerity that I almost believed him. "And by the way, she asked about you, too."

"Who?"

"Your sister."

"Why? There's nothing wrong with *my* teeth."

"It's your conscience she's worried about. She's thinks you blame yourself for what happened to Joey."

"I do blame myself. Jesus, I just stood there."

"That's not the way she tells it. She said you didn't freeze. It took you a couple of seconds to react because you had no idea what was going on. Bernadette just got a head start. Otherwise, it'd be you up there in that bed. She also said you were the one that immobilized the perpetrator."

"The perpetrator wasn't very mobile to begin with. I just wanted to make sure that motherfucker couldn't perpetrate anything else."

"Well, she's proud of you."

Proud of me?

"Really?"

"As a fuckin' peacock."

I sensed an opportunity.

"Mary's going to be proud of you, too, when I tell her you're paying for the room."

"Yeah?"

"Yeah. But if you really want to make her proud, there's something else you can do."

"I think maybe I already did it."

"Did what?"

"Did what you're gonna say."

"You know what I was going to say?"

He nodded.

"What are you, a mind reader now?"

"Not so much. But you're not exactly hard to read."

"No? Then what was I going to say?"

Milo glanced toward the soda machine; that last explosive gulp had ended his root beer. I offered him mine, expecting a polite refusal, but he took the can and drained it in one long pull. When he was finished, he handed it back to me.

"I talked to some people in California," he said, almost apologetically. "People in the medical community. They told me what Bernadette's gonna need: the treatment, the medication, the physical therapy, the prosthesis, and all that. So I, uhhh… made some arrangements."

He looked at me sheepishly.

"I hope that's okay. I mean, I probably shoulda asked her first."

"Asked her? How? She was in a coma, dipshit."

"Oh, yeah," he said happily.

"Is that it?"

"Well, they told me she's gonna need to have her house modified. A special bed, wheelchair ramps, hand railings, and such. I spoke to one of the contractors who's working on the farmhouse. He knows a guy out of Champaign who has experience with this kind of thing. I talked to him this morning, and he can start right away. I mean, if you think it's okay."

I nodded.

"I have to admit it, Milo, you are a goddamn mind reader."

"I fuckin' knew it!" he laughed.

In truth, I was going ask him to score some doughnuts.

"All that must be pretty expensive," I ventured.

"Nah," he said, shaking his head, "it's just extra cheese."

Mary's phone rang nine times before she answered. This irritates the hell out of me. It's a mobile phone, for Christ's sake. You carry it with you. Wherever you go. Are you so stuffed into your pants that you can't squeeze a wafer-thin electronic device out of your pocket?

"Hello?"

"Jesus, Mary, nine rings?"

She knows how much I hate waiting for her to pick up. I could just see her holding it in her hand, feeling it vibrate, knowing I was on the other end of the line getting exponentially annoyed with each passing ring.

"I was bathing your daughter."

"Yeah, I figured it was something like that."

"Hi, Daddy!" I heard Joey shout from somewhere in the distance. She was doing much better now. There had been some pretty awful dreams her first few nights at home, but she'd slept through the past few like a baby. In my bed, of course. She refused to sleep in her own. This was fine with me, as long as she didn't complain about my reading light.

"Tell her I said hi."

"Your daddy says hi," Mary yelled back to Joey. "Now dry yourself off, hon." Then in a much lower voice she asked, "Is everything okay?"

"She's awake."

"Oh, thank goodness," Mary sighed. "How is she?"

"She was a little freaked out at first."

"That must have been horrifying, waking up and finding out your leg had been amputated."

"No, it wasn't that. She thought...you know...Joey..."

"Oh God," Mary said, heartbreak in her voice. "She thought Joey was gone?"

"Yeah. It took some effort, but I finally convinced her she was okay. Once she realized that Joey was fine, she didn't seem that concerned about her leg."

"She's a saint," Mary said after a brief pause. I'm pretty sure she was praying in the gaps. "Did Father John tell her?"

"I told her."

Another pause. Another prayer.

"And she took it well?"

"Like a saint."

Mary made a sound I recognized as a prelude to tears. Joey must have recognized it too, for a moment later she cried, "I wanna talk to Daddy!"

I heard a shuffling sound as Joey grabbed for the phone.

"Is *Ate* okay?"

"She's awake, Joey. She's fine. I was just going to…"

"Then why is Aunt Mary crying?"

"Because she's a big baby."

"No she's not!"

"You want to come to the hospital?"

"Yes! I want to see *Ate*!"

"She wants to see you, too."

"Will you come and get me?"

"Mary can drive you. I'm kind of busy here."

"I'll pick 'em up!"

Milo's voice came from behind, startling the shit out of me.

"Jesus, Milo, I thought you left."

"Had to take a piss."

"Daddy, Aunt Mary said you're not supposed to say Jesus's name unless you're praying."

"I told you, she's a big baby." Before she could defend her aunt, I said, "Milo will come and get you."

He gave me a friendly slap on the back and ran for the door. I could see the filthy rag flapping in his back pocket.

"He'll be there in ten minutes, so you'd better get dressed. And make sure your hair's dry."

"Okay, Daddy," she said in a way that expressed appreciation far more clearly than a thank-you.

Mary came back on the line.

"Milo will be by to pick you up in ten minutes."

"He's back?"

"Oh, so you remember him."

"Your friend with the missing teeth," she said more evenly.

"Yeah, that's the one, only..."

"Only what?"

"You'll see. Ten minutes. Make sure Joey's hair's dry."

I pulled the phone away from my ear but put it back when I heard Mary say my name.

"Max?"

"Yeah?"

"I'm so glad she's okay."

"Yeah."

"Joey loves her so much. Like a..."

"Yeah."

I hit the end-call button and slid the phone back into my pocket. I started walking back to Bernadette's room but hadn't gotten five steps when the phone rang again.

Jesus, Mary.

"What?"

"Max?"

My name flowed from her lips as a single syllable.

"Max?"

I hadn't heard her voice in three years.

"Max, how is our daughter?"

Our daughter.

"She's…she's fine," I said after several seconds, my voice shaking.

I heard a deep sigh.

"I saw Steve-san. He told me she was hurt."

"You saw Steve? You're back in Tokyo?"

"She was hurt badly?"

I wanted to hang up, to tell her she had no right to ask me about "our" daughter after she'd abandoned her, left her with a father far too self-absorbed to raise her properly.

"She got her head banged pretty badly, a concussion, and there's a cut on her face. But she's…she's okay now. The doctor said the scar should be almost invisible in a few years."

A long silence.

I knew what was coming. It was inevitable. Naoko had had an epiphany. She'd finally realized how much she loves our daughter, how much she wants to be a part of her life. Maybe she wants custody. Maybe she wants to take her back to Japan. Her family is extremely wealthy and could hire a crack legal team, while I'd be represented by some dipshit who passed the bar on his twenty-seventh try.

"I'm so happy to hear that," was all she said.

Another long silence. Now I wasn't sure what was going through her mind. I steered the conversation away from Joey.

"Why did you leave South America? I thought you loved it there. Didn't you open a yoga school or something?"

"Yes."

Nothing more.

I was missing something. She was communicating in that frustratingly Japanese way. Through silences.

"Naoko?"

"Yes?"

"How long have you been back?"

Another long silence.

"Almost a year."

A year?

"I don't understand. Why'd you come back? Did what's-his-face come back with you?"

For fifteen seconds I listened to her breathing.

"I am alone now."

This elicited no sympathy. In fact, I registered a slight surge of pleasure.

"Are you staying with your family?"

Nothing.

"Why did you call me?"

"Because our daughter was hurt."

Our daughter.

"That's it?"

"Yes."

A Japanese yes.

"What is it, Naoko? What is it you want me to know?"

"I don't have much time," she finally said.

This was vintage Naoko. When we were together, she'd instigate an argument and then claim the upper hand by saying she didn't want to fight.

"Well, don't let me keep you," I said angrily.

"Oh, Max," she sighed, "you are so much the same."

I don't think she intended it as a criticism, but I couldn't help taking it that way.

"What's that supposed to mean?"

Another long pause.

"Impatient."

"Really? I'm impatient? Well, I had the patience to stay with *our* daughter."

"Yes," she whispered.

Nothing more.

This time I waited. (*Impatient, my ass.*)

"I don't have much time."

So hang up the fucking phone!

"Does she know about me?"

(I don't have much time.)

"She knows she has a mother."

The problem with impatience…

"Max?"

…is that it gets in the way of understanding.

"Does she know about me?"

My legs gave out, and suddenly I found myself sitting on the floor next to Yellow Pants. I could see patches of dried blood on his face, as if he'd decided to shave just before passing out in a hospital lounge. I watched his chest rise and fall and realized his respiration was in sync with Naoko's, breathing into a phone eight thousand miles away.

"She knows her mother is Japanese and that she lives in South America," I finally managed to say. I knew she needed to hear more, but I was finding it very difficult to talk to her about Joey. About our daughter. "She knows…"

Yellow Pants gave an indignant snort, as if I was disturbing his dream state. I lowered my voice.

"She knows her mother is…beautiful. When I told her that, she insisted on seeing a picture. So I showed her the only one I could find. It's from that trip we took to Nikko. You're standing in the snow in front of the waterfall. There's a smile on your face, but I remember you were angry when I took the photo. I didn't tell her that. She looked at it for a long time without saying anything. When I asked for it back, she wouldn't give it to me. She must have hidden it or something, because I never saw it again."

I waited for a few moments, hoping that would be enough, but Naoko's silence told me it wasn't.

"She knows her mother loves to sing. I told her how you used to sing her to sleep when we brought her home from the hospital. How pretty your voice was. But the songs always sounded so sad. I didn't tell her that, though. She knows about the scar on your left knee, and she knows you got stung by a jellyfish when you were a little girl and your brother peed on it to make it stop stinging. That made her laugh so hard."

I wondered if it made Naoko smile.

(Joey's smile.)

"Let's see...she knows your favorite food is sashimi and your favorite dessert is green-tea ice cream. And...yeah."

Naoko remained silent. I strained to recall other anecdotes I'd shared with Joey, but there was nothing more.

"That's about..."

Before I could finish, an unforgettable image stumbled its way into my consciousness. It was one of my clearest memories of Naoko, yet it had nearly slipped my mind.

"She knows about the birthday present. About the time you gave me nine hundred and ninety-nine origami cranes, even though it takes a thousand to bring good luck. How you told me this is what made the gift so special. No one else has ever received nine hundred and ninety-nine paper cranes. Only me. So I was the lucky one."

Now *I* was smiling.

"It's Joey's favorite story about you."

Still, Naoko remained silent. I knew what she wanted to hear.

"She never asked me why you left us...why you left her... but I could tell she wanted to know. I could see it in her eyes sometimes, even when we were talking about something else." I had imagined this conversation with Naoko on countless occasions, but in none of those scenarios was I sitting on the floor next to an unconscious drunk in yellow pants, unable to vent the anger I'd always insisted was there. "She knows her mother had a terrible sadness, a sadness that just wouldn't go away. And she was afraid her little girl would catch that sadness, which made her even sadder. That's why she had to leave. So she could find a way to make it better, to make it go away. And that someday, when the sadness was finally gone, maybe then her mother would come back."

(I don't have much time.)

"So Joey asked me... she asked me what made you so sad. And I...I told her I wasn't sure. That sometimes people get sad for no reason. That it's like catching a cold. But it wasn't enough. She kept looking at me...waiting for me to tell her the rest. Waiting for the truth. So I told her that...it was me. I made you sad. I didn't mean to, but I did. It was my fault. I was the reason you went away."

I was crying now. But at this point it didn't matter.

"And then I told her I was sorry. Because I was afraid that she would be angry with me for driving her mother away. But she just smiled and said, 'I'm glad you stayed with me, Daddy.'"

I wiped my eyes with my sleeve.

"What's wrong with you, Naoko?"

Silence.

"Goddammit, what's wrong?"

"Thank you, Max."

Her voice was calm. Stoic.

"For what?"

"For telling our daughter such a beautiful story."

"I did it for her."

"Yes," she said sadly, "that is the reason for my gratitude."

"What's wrong, Naoko?"

"I don't have much time."

"What does that mean? C'mon, I'm not Japanese! I don't know how to translate what you're not saying!"

Nothing.

"Is it cancer?"

(It's always cancer.)

"Your family's got money. Jesus, you can get the best treatment in the world. There're all sorts of new medical protocols out there now."

(It's a miracle.)

When she finally spoke, her voice was barely a whisper.

"Tell our daughter...tell Joey...."

Yellow Pants snorted again. It was a disgusting sound, phlegmy and desperate, but it broke Naoko's suffocating spell of sadness. I stood up and looked around me, at the hospital walls, at the stained floor, at the empty root-beer cans, at the dried blood on the drunk's face. It all seemed coherent now. All that had happened in the past two weeks, in the past four and a half years. A scar for Joey. A wooden leg for Bernadette. A bruised ego for the self-absorbed father. A terminal illness for the absent mother. So fucking what? It adds up to life. In *The Deer Hunter*, Robert DeNiro screams at John Cazale for forgetting his boots. He said something I never quite understood, but at that moment, it resonated. That's what I wanted to say to Naoko; that's what I wanted her to understand: *This is this.*

This is this.

But, of course, I didn't.

Joey's mother.

God, she was beautiful.

"Naoko?"

Soft breathing.

"She looks just like you."

Silence.

But I could hear the tears running down her face.

12

Perfect World

Lunchtime. I was walking along Ginza Dori searching for the *shabu-shabu* restaurant where I sometimes ate. The ugly gray monolith was only a few blocks away, so Ginza was a convenient place to have a meal, at least in terms of selection. The prices weren't at all convenient. This restaurant was an exception— the food was amazing and the lunch prices affordable. As was the case with many restaurants in Tokyo, dinner prices were exponentially higher than their midday counterparts. At a popular Tokyo steakhouse, an identical cut of meat will cost you five times as much in the evening as it did in the afternoon, even if it came from the same cow.

Shabu-shabu appeals to me for reasons beyond taste. There's the name: *shabu-shabu*. It repeats itself. The audacity of that: you can't have it unless you ask for it twice. Coincidentally, I'm partial to foods that echo: couscous, mahi-mahi, M&M's, HoHos, pizza pizza. I'm also drawn to *shabu-shabu* because it's an audience-participation dish. You are served two plates of raw food: one filled with vegetables, mushrooms, tofu, and other ingredients from the plant kingdom; the second is covered with thin slices of raw tissue from the animal kingdom. You're also given a pot of boiling water and an extra-long pair of chopsticks. With those chopsticks, put some veggies and tofu into the boiling water. Next, pick up a slice of beef or pork and swirl it in the water until it transitions from pinkish red to dull brown. When the desired hue is achieved, dip it into one of the several sauces arranged before you. The Japanese are very specific: there are sauces designated for meat, others for vegetables, and still others for items that defy classification. I never remember which sauce is for what, so I dip randomly and ignore the scathing looks from my fellow diners. At some point, you will notice an odd-looking spoon and container among your utensils. These are for removing and storing the scum that accumulates along the periphery of the boiling pot. How the scum gets there is beyond me, but the Japanese are insistent that it be removed. I don't actually have a problem with scum, so I tend to ignore it. Eventually, one of the waiters will come along and remove it for me, shaking his head sadly as he does. One thing diners should always remember—as I sometimes do—is that when food is removed from the simmering water, it should not be immediately ingested. It looks harmless enough, clenched between the tips of your chopsticks, but it's dangerously hot. The sauces help cool it down, but it won't be ready for ingestion until you blow on it for several seconds. Extra precaution must be exercised with tofu, as this soy-based time bomb holds heat the way nuclear fuel rods hold energy. I once swallowed a chunk of tofu that was cool to the touch, but a quarter of the way down my throat it broke apart and unleashed the volcanic fury stored within. The pain was explosive—far worse than the burn you experience when molten pizza cheese cleaves to the roof of your mouth. I couldn't talk. I couldn't breathe. I couldn't reach for the ice-cold beer a few inches from my left hand. As the fiery mass slid slowly down my throat, it blazed a trail of misery and didn't stop scorching the lining of my esophagus until it settled in my stomach.

I was searching for the *shabu-shabu* restaurant because I couldn't find it. This happened to me a lot in Tokyo, even on repeat visits. Many areas of the city are laid out in a way that make sense only to a schizophrenic; additionally, the addresses aren't always sequential. Even if you do find your building, you might have to pass through several labyrinthine floors, basements, and subbasements before you either reach your destination or give up and go to Ma-ku-do-na-ru-do. Of course, all this has changed with GPS and Google Maps, but when I was in Tokyo, you might as well have used a sextant. I was standing in front of a building I was certain contained the *shabu-shabu* restaurant—I'd already felt this certainty twice—when I heard a soft, feminine voice behind me say, "Max." (My name flowed from her lips as a single syllable.)

She was looking at me with an amused smile, and I must have been gaping like an idiot. It didn't seem real, any more than bumping into Madonna would have seemed real. Then there was a shimmer, and the world disappeared. I found myself in a tiny universe, alone except for the woman I'd been thinking about for the past year and a half. We stayed like that, suspended in our private little space-time continuum for what seemed like minutes, though it was probably no more than a few seconds. Then I did something that further separated me from reality:

I stepped over and—without the fear of rejection that plagues the initial rounds of my relationships—put my lips to hers. The two of us were floating in a magical bubble somewhere near Cassiopeia. First kisses can be sublime, but this one was utterly transcendent. I could have died at that moment and…no, that's ridiculous. Dying would have sucked. What I mean to say is that, at that moment, I was beyond the reach of death. Not exactly immortal, but certainly not beholden to the temporal constrictions faced by a mere human being.

A few light years later, our lips separated, but I continued to hold her, careful not to squeeze too tightly. (Annette often complained that I hugged like a wrestler; she also insisted that professional wrestling was real—a sport, she called it. We'd broken up about a month after our phone conversation at the hotel. She dumped me when I refused to buy her a plane ticket to come and see me. "Why don't you buy your own ticket," I'd suggested. "Why don't you go fuck yourself," was her counterproposal.) I felt the mystery woman return my embrace but sensed a hint of restlessness. Then I remembered we were standing on one of the busiest streets in Japan, a country where public displays of affection are generally considered offensive. (Oddly, public vomiting is cheerfully tolerated.) We released our holds and gazed into each other's eyes. I know it sounds corny, but that's what you do in this sort of situation: you gaze. At that moment, I truly believed what I saw in her eyes was what I felt in my heart. But, of course, love is blind. It took a while, but once I regained my sight, I realized it hadn't been love in her eyes. It had been surprise. She was surprised I'd kissed her; surprised she'd kissed me back; surprised she'd surrendered control. But love? I don't think so. In fact, I don't think she's ever loved anyone. Love involves a profound connection, and the soon-to-be mother of my child steadfastly refused to be profoundly connected to anyone.

I had no such qualms.

I was as connected as a conjoined twin.

Hand in hand, we began walking down the street. Every once in a while I'd glance at her, but no words passed between us. She stopped abruptly and pulled her hand from mine. Something was wrong; it was too good to be true. I tried to read her expression, but she was staring straight ahead. I followed her eyeline; nothing stood out. Finally, she turned to me and said, "Are you hungry?"

Food was the last thing on my mind. Nonetheless, I heard myself saying, "Actually, I was on my way to a *shabu-shabu* restaurant."

"Yes," she agreed, "do you like sashimi?"

"Of course."

I do like sashimi, though I would have said yes to anything.

She grabbed my hand and we continued down the sidewalk, but now everything felt more real. We had a destination.

Once again, we came to an abrupt stop.

This time it was my doing.

"I don't even know your name," I said.

She smiled. (A beautiful smile.)

"My name is Naoko," she replied.

"Naoko," I said reverently.

She nodded.

"Naoko," I said again.

With every step, I repeated it.

Naoko.

Naoko.

Naoko.

In my head, of course.

Naoko.

Naoko.

Naoko.

Though I was not obsessed.

Naoko.

Naoko.

I just didn't want to forget it.

Naoko.

It was during that first meal together I learned of her love for sashimi. I probably had a couple of slices of the raw fish, but I wasn't interested in food—cooked or otherwise. Instead, I watched Naoko. She'd look up from chewing, see me staring, and then offer me a slice. It wasn't until much later that I found out we were dining in one of the most exclusive restaurants in Tokyo. Normally, it takes a month to get a lunchtime reservation, but for Naoko and her family, this sort of formality was unnecessary. When I started for the front to settle the bill, she said there was no need to pay. Fine with me. I found out later our lunchtime meal would have cost anyone else at least five hundred dollars.

We continued walking through Tokyo, though it felt like floating. Then Naoko broke the spell: "Don't you have to go back to work?"

Somehow, I'd forgotten about my job as a copywriter for a gargantuan Japanese advertising agency. It was as if my world had been reset and previous experiences and obligations were no longer relevant. Only Naoko mattered. (Recalling this sentiment never fails to make my stomach turn.)

"Yeah, I guess I do," I replied sadly.

Naoko nodded.

"Do you…"

I knew what I wanted to say but wasn't sure how to phrase it without sounding pathetic. She probably understood but waited for me to continue.

"I mean…can we meet later? I get off work about six."

"Six?" She sounded surprised.

"Yeah, well, I'm a *gai jin*. They don't expect me to work as hard as the Japanese."

She laughed. (A beautiful laugh.)

"Do you remember the restaurant where we met?" she asked.

Do I remember the restaurant where we met.

"I'll be in the hotel lobby behind it."

"Okay," I said evenly, "I'll be there at six fifteen."

I stepped forward to kiss her goodbye, but she leaned away. This puzzled me, for we'd already gotten past the awkward initial embrace. Perhaps she doesn't want to make another spectacle on the sidewalk, I reasoned at the time. Looking back, I'm certain it had nothing to do with social mores; rather, it was her way of reacquiring the control she'd surrendered when I first kissed her. As I would soon learn, Naoko is not comfortable unless she's holding the reins. My momentary confusion gave way to clumsiness, and I stumbled as I stepped back. When she turned and walked away, I wondered if these last few moments had negated an otherwise perfect encounter. The way waking up negates a wet dream.

Though I'd sounded nonchalant when Naoko mentioned work, I was actually facing an important deadline. A Japanese creative team was waiting for me to deliver a name for an airline seat that could recline to one hundred eighty degrees. This was after I told them the name they came up with didn't work. The name they came up with was *Crash Bed*. A copywriter on the Japanese team discovered that *crash* was slang for sleep, so, from his point of view, *Crash Bed* was both edgy and descriptive. It took some doing, but I managed to convince them that using *crash* in the context of air travel would be problematic. Thus, it was now my responsibility to conjure a name that wasn't associated with a massive loss of life. This sort of thing was common in the agency: asking a native-English-speaking copywriter to check English copy written by a native Japanese-speaking copywriter. Having been on the job for more than a year, I'd provided this sort of advice to numerous creative teams who felt perfectly capable of writing English slogans, despite the fact that they were barely able to speak the language. Sometimes they followed my advice; often they didn't. Any English speaker who has spent time in Japan has seen a plethora of signs, banners, T-shirts, products, commercials, advertisements, and countless other forms of public communication that involve a stunningly inept—and endlessly entertaining—use of English. A sign in a Japanese train station reads, "For Restrooms, Go back toward your behind." On the corporate level, consider Kanebo Cosmetics' former slogan, "For Beautiful Human Life." Or Hitachi's "Inspire the Next." After a little head scratching and some thoughtful contemplation, it's possible to discern what these signs and slogans are attempting to communicate—just as one can eventually make sense of the seemingly incoherent ramblings of a precocious two-year-old.

I was once asked to evaluate a name that had been chosen for a no-frills automobile stripped of all but the barest necessities. Naturally, the Japanese team decided to call it *The Naked*.

"No one outside the porn industry will purchase *The Naked*," I counselled.

"But it's the concept of the car," my Japanese colleague explained.

"As a concept it's fine," I countered. "As a name it sucks."

"Sucks?"

"Uhhh, it's inappropriate. Doesn't work."

"But the engineer came up with it."

"You let the engineer name the car?"

"Yes."

"Why?"

This question seemed to confuse him.

"So it's already been decided?"

"Yes."

"Then what difference does it make what I think?"

I knew the answer. He had expected me to confirm their choice, as a Japanese team player would have done. You don't rock the boat. "The nail that stands up gets hammered down," the Japanese adage warns. But I'm not Japanese, so hammer away.

He started to leave, but I wasn't quite finished.

"Why don't you call it the *Supponpon?*" I asked, using a word I'd learned from a Japanese woman I'd met at a bar in Roppongi.

He looked at me as if I were demented.

"Oh, Ma-ku-su-san," he explained after his laughter had ebbed, "we could never name a car *Supponpon.*"

"Why not?" I pressed.

"Because it means…"

A thoughtful look crept over his face.

"…naked."

He bowed and left without saying another word. Ultimately, they did name the car *The Naked*, but only for the Japanese market. The export models would be called something else. (*Supponpon* has a nice ring to it.) But the most incredibly inappropriate English slogan of all time nearly happened on Derek's watch. A Japanese automobile company had decided to market one of their best-selling cars—call it the Honda Prelude—as much more than a mere mode of transport. The Prelude would become an integral part of your life, both public and private. A beloved member of the family. A friend that supports your happiness. A partner that helps you achieve your dreams. Given these lofty objectives, particularly for an inanimate object, it was no simple task for the Japanese creatives to come up with an English slogan that would express them. Yet they did. They were able to assemble a sublime selection of words that redefined the very concept of the automobile. It went like this: "Honda Prelude. We want to come in your privates."

A few blocks from the office, I realized I was hungry. Being with Naoko had suppressed my appetite, but since she was no longer present, my stomach was reasserting itself, making it clear that ingesting a few slices of raw tuna did not absolve me of my responsibility. So I did what I always do when I need healthy, satisfying food that can be eaten and enjoyed quickly—I hurried to the nearby Mister Donut. For the short while it took to devour two glazed and a Bavarian cream, I was relatively content; the consumption of doughnuts tends to push all negative thoughts from my consciousness. A biochemical reaction—endorphins without the exercise. But the moment that last swallow clears my taste buds, life reasserts itself, and in this instance, I was left to wonder if Naoko would actually meet me at the designated time and place.

As soon as I stepped into the office, Derek walked up to me and demanded, "What's the matter with you?"

"Huh?"

"You look like you just saw a ghost."

"I did, kind of."

"Japanese girl? Nice ass? Strange face?"

"How did you…"

"I bumped into her outside the building right after you left. I guess she figured we were acquainted since we're both of the Caucasian persuasion."

I found this somewhat disconcerting—not the revelation that Derek and I are white people; rather, it was the discovery that my chance encounter with Naoko had had nothing to do with chance.

"What'd she say?"

"That she lost touch with some guy named Max but thinks he works here. Asked me if I knew him."

"If she knew where I worked, why'd it take her so long to find me?"

Derek cocked an eyebrow, something he tends to do when he feels I'm being obtuse.

"So what'd you tell her?"

"That the only Max I'm acquainted with is a coprophiliac."

It took a moment to get my head around what he'd just said.

"The fact that you even know that word is suspect."

"Yeah? Well, it seems to be in your lexicon, too," he answered.

"I stumbled across it in an article about Chuck Berry. What's your excuse?"

"I'm obsessed with words."

"You sure you're not obsessed with something else?"

Derek ignored the question.

"Okay then, what were your actual words?"

"He's on his way to Ginza. You can probably catch him if you hurry."

I nodded. It all seemed to fit.

"Hey, do me a favor and keep this to yourself."

I didn't mind Derek knowing about Naoko, but I had no desire to share my personal life with the rest of the office. People tend to gossip, even in Japan. Of course, Hillbilly Brad had been present when Naoko and I met, but he was so preoccupied with how much my meal was going to cost him, he didn't notice her. Brad had since returned to Bull Shoals, Arkansas, where he'd embarked on the next phase of his career: operating a clothing store. "Brad's Fads," he called it.

"And what do you mean she has a strange face?"

"I mean her face is slightly different from the female Japanese faces to which I am accustomed. I'm not saying she's unattractive…"

"Unattractive? Jesus, that woman is gorgeous!"

"Max, you have a unique taste in women. The ones you're attracted to don't necessarily attract me."

"Bullshit! She transcends the finicky distinctions of individual taste. She's *universally* gorgeous."

Derek regarded me as if I were a child throwing a tantrum.

"What's wrong with her face?"

"Nothing. It just seemed a little…asymmetrical or something. Maybe it's her eyes."

"Her eyes are amazing!"

"Then she's the girl for you."

"But not for you?"

Derek shrugged.

"You know I've been looking for her since I got here."

"Really? She's the one?"

He made it sound like he couldn't understand what all the fuss was about. I was starting to get angry, something that never happened when I talked to Derek. I opened my mouth to deliver a scathing rebuttal, but it snapped shut as realization slapped me upside the head.

"You're fuckin' with me."

He shrugged again.

"So you like her face?"

"What do you think?"

"I think you're fuckin' with me."

"Only partially. I was serious about her ass. That thing could stop a train."

I had no idea what this meant, but it sounded vaguely complimentary.

"I've got to tell you, Derek, she could be the one. I've never been so completely mesmerized by someone."

He looked unconvinced.

"What? You don't believe me?"

He smiled knowingly and said, "I believe you want to come in her privates."

By the time I stepped into the lobby of the hotel behind the restaurant where Naoko and I had met, I was twenty minutes late. Of course I was. All afternoon I'd been counting down the minutes until I'd see her again, yet I managed to miscalculate the amount of time it would take to get from the office to the restaurant. This happens on a regular basis, and it seems to be one of those mistakes from which I cannot learn. The problem stems from the fact that I make perfect-world time estimates: every calculation is based on a best-case scenario. Unfortunately, as exemplified by my taxi ride to the airport, the scenarios that constitute my life are seldom best case. In this one, I calculated it would take no more than fifteen minutes to walk from the ugly gray monolith to the nearby hotel lobby. Keep in mind, I lived for a week in that hotel and had made the trek to and from work at least a dozen times. So I knew how long the journey would take. In a perfect world. Unbeknownst to me, one of the four elevators was being serviced that day. Another had been hijacked by several employees of the Black Cat moving company who were in the process of transferring furniture from one office to another; they were working so slowly it was impossible to tell which direction they were going. That left two elevators to service all twenty-seven floors of a building where more than three thousand people spent the better part of their lives. Thus, it would be an excruciating five-minute wait before the doors opened on the twenty-fifth floor. I was tempted to run down the two dozen flights of stairs, but I knew the moment I stepped into the stairwell, the elevator would arrive. I even tried to bluff it, taking several steps toward the emergency exit, but it wasn't fooled. When the elevator finally did arrive, it was bursting with humanity. I managed to shove myself in backwards using the top of the doorway to gain leverage, as one does when boarding a crowded train. I heard several people let out their breaths, ostensibly to create more space.

The ride was neither pleasant nor brief. We stopped at every floor, and from time to time, more people got on, managing to squeeze themselves into spaces that weren't there. Seven minutes after I boarded, we arrived at the ground floor. Up to that point, the passengers had been perfectly composed, but once escape was imminent, patience gave way to panic and we shot from the car like projectile vomit. A serious-looking fellow in a dark suit (virtually every male in the building other than myself and Derek) fell to the floor and was nearly trampled. I wasted several seconds helping him to his feet. He was still bowing as I raced from the ugly gray monolith. By the time I stepped into the lobby of the hotel where I was to meet Naoko, I was twenty minutes late.

She was nowhere to be seen.

Fuck.

Fuck!

Fuck!!!!!!!!!!!

A minute and forty-four fucks later, I spotted her. Now all I had to do was apologize and convince her it would never happen again. Before I could speak (I was still a little breathless), Naoko said, "I was held up."

Held up?

"Somebody robbed you?"

She laughed.

"No, I was delayed."

"Oh," I said, feeling foolish but thankful I wouldn't need to apologize.

Looking back, I realize Naoko didn't feel the need to apologize either. As I would discover, this was another way she exercised control—by making others wait for her. In the weeks and months to come, I managed to frustrate this control mechanism on numerous occasions, so inaccurate were my travel calculations. But however preventable, my tardiness was never intentional.

"So, what do you feel like doing?" I finally managed to ask.

Had Naoko said she wanted to see an über-boring, five-hour kabuki performance, I would have been thrilled. Had she insisted on attending a four-hour lecture on plate tectonics, I would have jumped for joy. Had she demanded that we spend the next several hours exploring the Museum of Ballroom Dancing, my heart would have soared. So when she said, "Why don't we go to your place and watch a movie or something?" I nearly lost control of my bowels.

"Yeah," I said after I'd recovered, "why not? Is there any movie you'd like to see? We could stop by *Tsutaya* and rent one."

"No, anything is fine. Whatever you have at your house."

"Great," I said, taking her hand.

As I did, she leaned in and kissed me on the lips. Again, I was forced to tighten my anal sphincter. Naoko smiled at my expression, unaware of the muscle group I was activating. Anyway, she was happy. She was orchestrating the scenario. She was in control. None of this occurred to me at the time, nor would it have mattered if it had. What did occur to me was that my Welsh co-worker was right: I did want to come in her privates.

13

Omiyage

Oh my God, I am heartily sorry...
Sorry.
Sorry.
If there's one thing Catholicism taught me,
it's how to apologize.
How to say
Sorry.
Over the years, it's become a reflex.
Something I say without thinking.
How do you do?
Sorry.
Was Steve-san thinking when he apologized to me?
When he called me from Japan in the middle of the night.
Woke me from a nightmare and said,
"Sorry."
"For what?"
"Naoko died."
Japanese Buddhists tend to process their dead very quickly. Naoko's funeral would begin twenty-eight hours from the moment Steve-san apologized. If I was going to attend, the

ordeal would begin the moment I hung up the phone. I'd have to book a ticket, drive three and a half hours to O'Hare in my piece-of-shit Chevy, check in, go through customs, board the plane, spend fourteen hours in the economy-class section of a winged aluminum tube, wait forty-five minutes to get through Japanese immigration, ride an hour on the Narita Express, and then go ten stops on the Yamanote Line to Shibuya station, where Steve-san would meet me.

He'd gotten a call from Naoko's brother.

Then he called me.

Sorry.

Fifty-three hours after beginning my funereal journey to Japan, my return flight touches down at Chicago O'Hare International Airport. Eighty-seven minutes later, I find myself standing across the counter from a skinny girl at the Krispy Kreme doughnut shop in Elk Grove Village. After ordering a dozen glazed, I ask her, "How do you do it?"

She looks at me blankly.

"I'd gain fifty pounds if I worked here."

"Oh, I'm blessed with a high metabolism."

"Praise the Lord," I say as she hands me twenty-two hundred calories.

Half the doughnuts are gone before I hit Kankakee.

Only two remain when I pull into my driveway.

One is for Joey.

I always bring her a gift.

The other is for me; I can't let her eat alone.

Milo is on the porch. I'm not surprised. He'd taken my advice and come clean with Mary, providing her with a detailed account of his agricultural adventures in California. At his request, I was in attendance when he made the confession. I'd expected Mary to question him, to draw out incriminating details as she would with a suspect. Instead, she listened silently, sometimes nodding, sometimes shaking her head in disbelief. When he finished, Mary made two inquiries. The first was, "Are you completely out of the marijuana trade?" To which Milo responded with a single syllable: "Yes." So far, so good. And then she asked, "Were you ever arrested?" Milo's eyes widened. He looked over at me and then back at Mary. Oh shit, I thought, what the hell did he do? "Well," he began uncertainly, "one time me and Max…"

"Jesus, Milo," I interrupted, "she means were you arrested in relation to your pot plantation. She doesn't give a shit about…"

"You were arrested?" Mary asked, looking at me.

"He sure was," Milo said.

"When we were fifteen. Christ, Milo, why'd you even bring that up?"

"You told me to be completely honest."

"I meant about you, dumbass!"

"Why were you arrested?" Mary demanded.

"It was nothing."

"Criminal trespass," Milo yelled, as if he were on a game show.

"We were swimming at the Holiday Inn."

"The Holiday Inn?" Mary said, surprised. "You were in a motel?"

"We weren't actually guests," Milo clarified.

"It was nothing!"

"I scored some beers from my brother," he continued, "and after we drank 'em we decided to go for a swim."

"At the Holiday Inn?"

"It was Max's idea."

"Yes, it was my idea. Guilty as charged. We got arrested thirty years ago. Can we move on, or should I call my lawyer?"

"Wait a minute," Mary said, ignoring my indignation. "It doesn't add up. Why didn't they just kick you out? No, you did something else to get arrested."

"We didn't *do* anything," I argued. "Okay, we were trespassing. But nobody else was in the pool. Then this lady and her two daughters came out for a dip. The girls were about our age, kind of pretty, so we decided to show off a little bit. Do some flips off the diving board. Problem was, we were so drunk we forgot we were skinny dipping. So when we got out of the water, their mom started screaming."

"We could've got away," Milo maintained, "but the manager ran out and grabbed our clothes. Only thing we could do was jump back in the pool."

"What happened then?" Mary demanded. "And why haven't I heard about it?"

"Oh," Milo said, "my dad came down to the police station and sorted it out. We apologized to the old lady and the Holiday Inn guy, so the cops decided to let it slide."

Hearing Milo mention his dad always makes me uncomfortable.

"'Boys will be boys,' is what he said. Remember, Max?"

There was no nostalgia in his voice.

"Yeah," I said carefully. "I remember."

"Boys will be boys," he repeated, much more slowly this time. His eyes focused inward, and he sat quietly for several seconds. Mary looked over at me, puzzled, then back at Milo.

"The cops told me I was lucky to have such an understanding dad," he said, his voice barely above a whisper. "Yeah, lucky me. As soon as he got me alone, he smashed me in the face. And I went down, boy. I should have known better. I should have seen it coming."

Milo almost never spoke about the abuse he and his brother suffered at the hands of their father. I knew about it, but the subject was essentially off limits.

"Then he grabbed me by the throat and shoved me up against the wall so hard my head punched a hole in the drywall. I blacked out for a couple of seconds, but he held me up against that wall and never said a word. His grip kept getting tighter and tighter. And he had this look on his face. Man, I'll never forget that look. It was so full of rage. And I knew right then, I knew he was gonna kill me. I knew...I knew I was gonna die." When Milo looked up at my sister, his eyes were moist. "And I swear to God, Mary, I swear to God, all I could think of was you."

Milo steps off the porch and walks across the lawn, hands in pockets.

"You okay, man?"

I start to answer but am distracted by the arrhythmic ticking noises emanating from the Chevy as its cooling metal parts contract. I've heard that sound hundreds of times and never given it a second thought. Now it seems significant. I touch the warm hood, feel the vibrations of its death rattle.

"Max?"

"I'm fine."

He reaches for the nearly empty box of Krispy Kremes.

"Any left?"

A look through the cellophane window confirms the presence of two glazed.

"Give one to Mary."

He thanks me and walks into the house.

I listen to the ticking for another minute or so, then slide back in and drive fifteen miles to a truck stop on the interstate. I need to buy something for Joey now that I've given her gift to Milo. Truck stops sell an incredible array of merchandise. Cowboy hats and boots and belts with big buckles. All manner of pornography. Millions of country music CDs. And a coffee-table book, cover slightly sun faded, with photos of Japan. I have no idea what such a book is doing in a truck stop halfway between Chicago and Memphis, but it is a better gift for Joey than a Krispy Kreme, particularly since her doughnut gene has yet to express itself. I pass my purchase to the cashier, who looks as if she hasn't seen a book in a good long while—certainly not one that extolls the virtues of the Orient.

"Doin' a long haul in my Peterbilt," I tell her, "Reading about the Far East keeps me alert on the open road."

"Oh really?" she says, one heavily plucked eyebrow arching upward.

"Better than a crystal meth suppository," I add.

I figure she'll tell me to go fuck myself, not that I would blame her. She has to deal with assholes all day long.

"Well, you have a safe trip, cowboy," is all she says.

I count nine Peterbilts as I retrace my steps across the massive parking lot. When I reach my car, it's still ticking, but the urgency is no longer there.

I drive home.

I go inside.

Mary's embrace is so constricting, my breath catches. (You hug like a wrestler.) When she releases me, I notice Father John smiling from the couch. Milo sits next to him, and they're each holding a bottle of Dos Equis. Milo has doughnut glaze crusted around his lips. I check Mary. Her mouth also sports a sugary halo.

"I see you enjoyed the *omiyage*," I said.

"You don't buy *omiyage* in a doughnut shop," Mary says dismissively.

"What's *omiyage*?" Milo asks.

"It's a customary gift Japanese people bring back for friends, relatives, or co-workers when they travel," Mary explains as if she'd memorized the answer to a test question.

"Well, here's some *omiyage* for you," Milo says, pulling a beer from the small cooler at his feet. He wields his trusty church key and then hands me the bottle. It vibrates with cold.

I drink.

Jesus.

"Where's Joey?"

"Asleep in your bed," Mary answers.

I glance at my watch. Past midnight. Of course she's asleep. "She's been sleeping in my bed?"

"Just tonight. She knew you'd be coming home."

I look over at the priest, at his feet. Goddamn yellow Converse.

"Are you tired?" he asks. "That's an incredible journey you just made."

"Actually, I'm kind of wired from all the coffee."

"Well, the remedy is in your hand," Milo says, raising his beer.

I set mine on the coffee table.

"I'm going to check on Joey."

I step into my room and see a tiny shape angled across the bed. I watch her until I'm satisfied, until I confirm the subtle movements of her breathing. When she was younger, I'd put my hand on her abdomen, holding it there until I could feel the expansion and contraction of her diaphragm. Sometimes it was scary. With a baby, there can be long intervals between breaths. I put a knee on the bed and scoop her into my arms. She's getting heavier. I move her close to the wall and place a pillow on the other side. A barrier. This is both a safety measure and a means of ensuring she doesn't kick me in the face. I rise and begin walking from the room. I stop and turn back. "I love you, Joey." The voice is raspy, unfamiliar.

"Is she okay?" Mary asks.

"Sound asleep. How's she been?"

"Fine. She spent a lot of time over at Bernadette's."

This doesn't surprise me. She's been helping out a lot since Bernadette returned home. I am amazed at how mature Joey has become since the accident. Some kids regress; others progress. That's what the pediatric psychologist told me. When I broke the news of her mother's death, Joey stared at me for a long time. Like she does when she's trying to decide if I'm joking or not. Though she didn't remember Naoko, I assumed there would be tears, tantrums. Instead, she asked if I was okay.

"Did she want to know about her mom?"

"She talked about it a little bit, but you were the one on her mind."

"Me?"

"She missed you. Her mother is an abstract concept, but you're real. The moment you said goodbye, she started counting the hours until you'd get back. I don't know why this always surprises you so much."

"How's Bernadette?" I say, changing the subject.

Milo and Mary turn their faces toward the priest.

It takes a moment, but once he realizes the spotlight is his, he stands and addresses the room. "She's doing very well, getting stronger every day. As you might imagine, her spirit remains undaunted, despite the loss of her leg. Joey's visits mean the world to her and are surely as salubrious as any drugs or physical therapy she's receiving."

Milo frowns. "Salubrious?"

"It means well lubricated." I tell him.

Mary smacks my shoulder.

"Good for her health," she corrects.

"I know what it means," Milo says, "but it stood out. Salubrious. It's a good word."

The priest waits to see if he has anything else to say.

Milo nods. *Please continue.*

"Thanks to Milo's generosity," he continues, "which is also having a salubrious effect, Bernadette has been fit for a prosthesis, which she'll begin using as soon as her…her…" He lets out a sigh. "Sorry, I'm uncomfortable with that term."

"What term is that?" Milo asks.

"Stump," I say. "They call what remains of an amputated leg a stump."

"It's not a very nice word," Mary agrees.

"When the stump heals…"

"How about just calling it her leg?" Milo offers.

Father John gives him an appreciative look.

"When Bernadette's leg has properly healed, she'll begin using her prosthesis. She's doing physiotherapy three times a day and can't wait to start walking on her own. Every day, I take her out in her wheelchair, which she finds a little embarrassing. It's not that she's embarrassed to be *seen* in a wheelchair; she's just not accustomed to having people take care of her. Joey loves to push the chair when she comes along but sometimes gets on Bernadette's lap, and I push them both." He opens his mouth to continue but decides he's said enough. He sits back down on the couch.

Quiet settles over the room. It ends with the whoosh of a bottle cap flying off a beer bottle. Milo hands me another cold one.

"What about you, Max?"

"Yeah," Mary says, "how was your trip?"

How was *my trip?*

"I don't know. I didn't even have time to get jet lagged. Now that it's over, I'd say it went by really fast. But there were times when it seemed to go on forever." I can see from their expressions they've all experienced some version of what I just described. "I got bumped up to business class on the way there, which was nice. I don't know why they did it. Maybe they knew why I was going. I did ask about the bereavement discount. Anyway, I managed to get a little sleep so I wasn't dead tired when I got to Tokyo. Steve-san met me at the station, and then we walked over to the wake. It was very solemn. Lots of solemn people. Lots of incense. Lots of chanting. Naoko in a box surrounded by flowers."

I took another swallow of Milo's remedy.

"How was her family?" Mary asked. "You'd never met them, had you?"

Mary was right. I'd never met the family, though I had despised them. According to Naoko, they were fascists who didn't want anything to do with a half-breed granddaughter or her worthless *gai jin* father. Now they were burying their daughter. I don't believe in karma, but if I did…

The moment Steve-san and I walked into the wake, we became the center of attention. The scrutiny wasn't nearly as obvious as it would have been at an American funeral; no heads swiveled; no mouths dropped open; no one leaned over to a wife or husband or girlfriend and whispered a little too loudly. But we could feel their eyes on us. I looked around and saw that we were the only *gai jin* in attendance. This seemed odd. I'd always assumed Naoko had a posse of international friends, though I'd never met any of them. Aside from Carlo, her Peruvian-Japanese partner. He was nowhere to be seen, thank god. A youngish man in a dark suit was moving rapidly in our direction. As he neared us, I noticed his resemblance to Naoko. Her brother, no doubt, the boy who peed on her jellyfish sting. Just before she died, Naoko had told him to contact a *gai jin* named Steve-san—he should be the one to inform me of her death. (Sorry.) Upon reaching us, the brother bowed deeply, as we did in return. Then he shook Steve-san's hand and said, "Thank you for coming." Steve-san gestured to me and said, "Jiro-san, this is Max-san."

"*Hajimemashite,*" I said, leaving out the part where I begged him to do everything he could for me.

Jiro looked at me for several moments before speaking. He appeared to be overcome with emotion, which made me anxious. I had no idea what emotion he was feeling or what it portended. Was he going to thank me for coming? Or would he light into me for knocking up his sister, blame me for her death? I took a step back, but as I did he stepped forward and grasped my right hand in both of his. "Ma-ku-su-san," he said, "it is my honor to meet you."

I did not know how to respond to this, so I bowed. You can't go wrong with a bow.

"Would you mind coming with me? My parents would like to meet you."

I glanced at Steve-san.

He nodded.

"I don't want to trouble them in their time of sorrow," I protested.

In fact, I didn't want to trouble Naoko's parents in their time of anything.

"It is no trouble, Ma-ku-su-san. They are very eager to meet you. When Steve-san called to tell us you were coming, my mother cried. It was the first time since Naoko died that she had shed tears."

This made absolutely no sense and left me even more reluctant.

"Really, I'm afraid I'll be disturbing them."

"Ma-ku-su-san, please, they must see you."

They must see me.

"Okay," I agreed. "I'll meet your parents."

Jiro's expression radiated gratitude.

"Su-te-bu-san, I'll be back in a moment."

"Take your time," Steve-san replied.

Jiro turned and began walking back across the room.

I followed a few steps behind.

The crowd parted gracefully as we made our way across the large room, a choreographed scene from a movie whose title I could no longer recall. We came to a small room with sliding doors. Jiro indicated I should wait. I stepped back, and he disappeared inside. After the doors slid shut, I stood there, uncomfortable, anxious about what I was going to face when I crossed the threshold. I caught the eye of a young Japanese woman in the company of a much older man. Daughter? Girlfriend? AV idol? I bowed in her direction, and she gave me a coquettish smile. Daddy-o scowled and then led her away. The door slid open.

I stepped into a small, sparsely furnished room. There was a beautiful *ukiyo-e* print on the wall and an antique table with four intricately carved chairs around it. Standing just to the right of the table were Naoko's mother and father. There was no mistaking them; the daughter resonated in the faces of her parents. Normally the inverse is true—we see the parents in the children—but at that moment, it was Naoko peeking out from behind their sad expressions. Her father was slightly stooped and appeared to be about seventy. Although probably as old as her husband, Naoko's mother was absolutely stunning. When her daughter and I were first together, when I had yet to relinquish the silly notion of growing old together, this is how I imagined Naoko would one day look.

The mother smiled.

(A beautiful smile.)

"Max-san," she said softly.

Only it sounded more like "Ma-ku-su-san," the way a Japanese woman would say it.

For a moment, I didn't know what to say.

And then I said it.

"I'm sorry."

Her husband stepped forward and shook my hand. There might have been tears in his eyes. They motioned me to the table, and the three of us sat. I looked over at Jiro to see if he'd be joining us, but he bowed and said, "*Shitsurei shimasu,*" then left the room.

There was a beautiful porcelain tea service on the table, and Naoko's mother began pouring.

"*Arigato gozaimasu,*" I said, as she placed a cup before me.

"*Dō itashimashite.*"

I waited for her to finish filling three cups before taking a sip. The tea was warm and delicious, and I was glad for the distraction. Neither of them touched theirs. We sat silently for several moments, but it was the sort of Japanese silence to which I was accustomed. They had asked to see me. They would speak when they were ready.

"Ma-ku-su-san," Naoko's mother finally began, "I must apologize for my poor English."

Her English was excellent, her accent charming.

"Your English is wonderful," I contradicted politely, "and it is infinitely better than my Japanese."

A nod.

More silence.

"Ma-ku-su-san," Naoko's father asked, "how was your flight?"

His heavily accented voice was hoarse, as if he hadn't used it in a while.

"I got bumped up to business class, so it was actually quite good," I said a little too enthusiastically.

Even before the final syllable faded, I was aware of the stupidity of my words. A man this wealthy, this prominent, had probably never flown coach in his life—never needed an upward bump—and would not understand the pleasure of such unexpected bounty. Additionally, emphasizing my airborne comfort as he was preparing to cremate his daughter was surely a faux pas in any culture. It wouldn't be overt, but I braced myself for the rebuke that would surely follow.

(I'm sorry.)

Naoko's father looked up and smiled. "I love when that happens."

Another long period of silence ensued. Naoko's parents were looking at me with such hopeful expectation that it was painful to witness. They suddenly seemed very young, almost like children. Like Joey waiting for me to continue a bedtime story.

"She'll be five next month," I began.

They both nodded.

"May twenty-sixth," Naoko's mother said softly.

"That's right," I said, "May twenty-sixth."

I took another sip of tea.

"She's very smart and very…"

I stopped myself, once again realizing that I was committing a grievous cultural no-no. One does not brag on one's child in Japan. But how else could I describe her? I started to apologize but stopped when I saw how they were looking at me—the way people lost in a desert might look at someone who's about to give them a drink of water.

"…and very beautiful. Like her…mother."

Their eyes remained fixed on mine.

"Like her grandmother."

She glanced down shyly, making her seem even more childlike.

"You all have the same smile."

Naoko's father nodded. He knew it was true of his wife and daughter, and now another had inherited this lovely trait. I told them about their granddaughter, everything I could remember. This made me feel generous, magnanimous even, sharing intimate details about the life of a child in whom they'd shown no interest until the death of their daughter. But I knew it was the right thing to do. When at last I stopped speaking, the room seemed a bit less sorrowful.

"Ma-ku-su-san," Naoko's mother asked softly, "what is her name?"

What's her name?

They don't even know their granddaughter's name?

"Joey," I said.

"Joey," they said in unison, making it sound like a liturgical response.

Again, they were looking at me expectantly.

"We couldn't think of a name. I don't know why. Nothing seemed to fit. Then one day Naoko said the baby looked like a little kangaroo."

They looked at one another, shook their heads.

"Kan-ga-rū," I said slowly, pronouncing it the Japanese way.

"Ahh, kan-ga-rū," they repeated in hushed tones, as if they'd just been let in on an important secret. Still, they were confused.

"The thing is, Naoko-san said the baby looked like a little kan-ga-rū, and that's when I had the idea of calling her Joey. You see, in English, a baby kan-ga-rū is called a joey." Although I'd made this same explanation to Mary and Bernadette and a few others, in present company it sounded idiotic. I'd named their granddaughter after a marsupial.

"Joey," they repeated with undisguised delight.

I took a sip of tea, emptying the small cup, and Naoko's mother immediately refilled it. I lifted it to my lips and let my mind drift for a few moments. By the time I placed the delicate vessel back on its saucer, another silence had descended on the table. It was immediately clear that this one was different. It had a discomforting quality that darkened the room, and I could see that Naoko's parents felt it as acutely as I did.

"Our daughter explained to us that you had given the baby up for adoption," Naoko's father began, ending the awful quiet. "She told us that a wealthy American couple had taken our granddaughter and that we could never see her. She said that is what you wanted, Ma-ku-su-san. That it was best for everyone, but especially for Joey. And she told us you didn't ever want to speak with us. That you hated us because of the way we treated her. We are ashamed to tell you this and hope you can forgive us for believing it."

When I got over the shock of their revelation, I didn't know what to say.

So I said it again.

"I'm sorry."

When Naoko's mother looked up at me, there was such sadness in her eyes. But there was something else. Something hopeful.

"Ma-ku-su-san," she began, "we…"

She was unable to continue.

Then again, some requests shouldn't have to be voiced.

"Joey would love to meet her grandparents."

For a moment, they didn't react. Then Naoko's father bowed deeply. Her mother leaned over and took my hand, a surprising gesture for an old woman in Japan, and all the more touching for that.

"How could that bitch be so cruel?"

Mary seemed to have even fewer qualms than I did about speaking ill of the dead.

"I don't think she was trying to be cruel."

"Bullshit!"

My sister almost never swears, and doing so in consecutive sentences is a milestone.

"She decided she didn't want anything to do with her daughter, and that meant her parents couldn't have anything to do with their granddaughter. She lied to them. She lied to you. She lied to everyone."

"Well, she won't be lying anymore."

"I'm sorry she's dead, Max, but she was a horrible person."

"She was a miserable person."

"Horrible because she wanted everyone else to be as miserable as she was."

"Yeah, she would have made an excellent Catholic."

Father John looks up at this point.

"No offense."

He responds by taking a drink of his beer.

"Look, Mary, I'm not going to sit here and defend Naoko. When I was with her, I knew who she was. And she knew who I was. And for whatever reason, we decided to stay together... for a while."

"I don't know why *she* stayed. But *you* stayed because you wanted to fuck her."

I had never heard Mary use the F-word.

Milo's eyes are on the floor. Father John is also staring at the floor, though I'm almost certain he's laughing.

"I won't deny I was physically attracted to her," I say, admitting the obvious, "and that perhaps this attraction superseded other, less agreeable, aspects of her personality."

"No kidding."

"But you know what? Joey is the result of that attraction. She is the consequence of that relationship. So I won't apologize for it."

"That's not what I meant."

"I know it's not. And I don't really disagree with the things you said. But she's Joey's mother. Alive or dead, she always will be. And that little girl seems to have gotten the best of both of us. Maybe even more than the best, if that's possible. I'm telling you, Joey would have loved Naoko, no matter what. She would have recognized the pain. She would have understood the weakness. She would have forgiven her without even thinking of it as forgiveness. She has that much love in her."

I look over at Father John.

"And don't tell me it came from God," I pre-empted.

"I was going to suggest it came from you."

"Well, it sure didn't come from her mother," Mary snaps.

"You don't know that." I snap back. "Who knows what passed between them in that little time they had together. Jesus, if you'd ever met her parents, you'd know there was love in that family. It was worth the trip just to meet them."

"Who cares where it came from?" Milo intervenes. "The fact is, she's an angel."

Words slightly slurred.

"An angel," he says again. "And so is Bernadette. And so is Mary…"

"Oh, shut the fuck up."

"You're an angel too," he says, reaching out and patting my head.

"Just give me a beer."

He pulls a Dos Equis from his cooler.

"Last one."

"Way to plan ahead," I say ungraciously.

"I mean it's the last one in the cooler. I've got a fuckin' case in the fridge."

"I'm glad you finally had a chance to straighten things out with the grandparents," Father John says. "Joey will always be a connection to their daughter, the miracle she left behind."

"They want to meet her."

The room goes quiet.

"Of course I agreed," I say, annoyed that it wasn't obvious to them.

Father John looks relieved. "I truly believe you've made the right decision."

"It really wasn't much of a decision. They're nice people in a lot of pain. And she is their granddaughter. It came down to being an asshole or not."

"Don't be modest, Max," Mary says sweetly, "You choosing not to be an asshole must have involved a great deal of soul-searching."

Milo, his right hand in the cooler, laughs at his girlfriend's wit.

"Hey, Einstein, you gave me the last one, remember?"

Milo snaps his fingers as if he'd recalled this detail himself. He picks up the cooler and takes it into the kitchen. I turn back to Mary.

"When you meet them, you'll understand. She hurt her parents as much as anyone else. Probably more. They don't know why she did the things she did. Or why she didn't try to set things straight before she died. She was a cipher to them. But it's not about Naoko any more. They want to see their granddaughter. They want to meet Joey."

"So they're coming here?"

"No, we're going there."

"We?"

"Me, Joey, you if you want. They want to meet her family— everyone who's important to her."

"Well, I'd love to visit Japan again, but I can't just..."

"You don't have to worry about that," Milo says as he walks back into the room carrying the cooler, several beers heavier now.

"We discussed this, Milo. You're not paying for me every time..."

"Milo's not paying for anything, and neither are you," I interrupt. "And neither am I."

After a few moments, Mary's mouth forms an "Oh."

"Yeah. Joey's grandparents are loaded. And I mean seriously loaded. They'll be buying the tickets. They wanted to put us in first class, but I told them business class was just fine. Besides, we can sit in the upstairs part of the plane."

"The upstairs?" Milo says enthusiastically, "Man, that sounds cool. Can I come too? I'll buy my own ticket."

"Milo!" Mary practically shouts.

"Of course you can come," I say, "You're more or less family now anyway."

Father John rises from the sofa.

"You upset because we didn't invite you?"

"I'll get over it. But for now, Nature calls."

Once he's out of earshot, I turn to my sister and Milo and demand, "So, what's up with you two?"

They both appear puzzled by the question.

"Are you happy? Are you serious? Are you aware of the consequences of unprotected sex?"

"Yes," Milo answers gravely.

Mary smiles. I expect her to tell me to mind my own business, particularly after alluding to the exchange of bodily fluids, but she nods thoughtfully and says, "Milo wants me to move to the farm with him." Before I can respond, she rises from her chair and walks into the kitchen. Her revelation is unexpected, though it shouldn't have been. I'm just so used to thinking of Mary as permanently single. The way I think of myself. She returns carrying a soft drink, and it dawns on me that I've not seen her take a drink all night. She must be on standby. Mary never drinks alcohol when there's a possibility of being called into work.

"It'd be great, don't you think?" Milo says to me.

"What would be great?" Father John asks as he walks back into the room.

I notice his hands are glistening with water. I'm always happy to see this, people coming out of the toilet with freshly washed hands, as it means I won't inadvertently be shaking hands with their genitals.

"Mary moving to the farm with me," Milo answers.

"That *would* be great," the priest agrees.

"I don't recall Vatican II offering dispensation to couples living in sin," I can't resist saying.

"When we live together it won't be in sin," Mary clarifies.

I could almost feel Milo's disappointment: no sin equals no sex. Mary shakes her head.

"I know what you're thinking, Max."

"It's Milo who's thinking it," I say.

"No, that's not what he's thinking," she says confidently.

Mary turns to Milo and smiles. (A beautiful smile.) And in that moment, my sister is more radiant than I've ever seen her. Not a word passes between them, but now Milo is also glowing. He stands and starts toward her but trips over the cooler and falls into my arms. Before I can push him away, Mary throws her arms around both of us. And then I understand. Mary has just agreed to become Milo's wife.

I feel a hand on my shoulder and turn to see Father John indicating we should move to the porch. I manage to extricate myself from the scrum and follow the priest through the front door. Amazing, I think to myself, thirty years after his initial crush, Milo's dream comes true.

"I've never seen Mary so happy," I say to the priest.

"Love is transformative," he replies.

"Well, those two are going to be transforming the hell out of each other."

He smiles, but there's something on his mind.

"What is it?" I ask him.

"I'm going through somewhat of a transformative period myself," he says after a moment of reflection.

"Crisis of faith?"

"It's not really a matter of faith, though many will see it that way," he says, looking toward Bernadette's house. "I've decided to take a leave of absence from the priesthood."

"You can do that?"

"Of course."

"For how long?"

"Indefinitely."

"That sounds permanent."

He shrugs.

"And you're taking this leave of absence because…"

"There are a number of reasons."

"Does one of the reasons live in that house?"

I've seen the way he looks at her. The way he was with her in the hospital. The way he cares. Still, he's a priest and they're supposed to minister to the infirm. Maybe he's confused about his feelings. Transference, that's what the psychiatrists call it. When the patient falls for the doctor. Or in this case, the doctor for the patient.

"How does Bernadette feel?"

"We haven't discussed it."

"But you must have some idea."

"My decision wasn't predicated on whether or not Bernadette has feelings for me. It's enough that I have them for her. They've helped clarify so many of the issues that have troubled me my entire life in the priesthood. From the earliest days in the seminary, we're taught to deal with such human feelings. How to deconstruct them. How to suppress them. How to seek counsel. How to pray for strength. And I have the ability to do all these things. I simply don't have the will."

"So you *have* lost your faith."

"I'm not turning my back on God. I'm choosing to serve Him in a different manner. To follow a different calling."

"As Bernadette's toy boy."

The priest shakes his head, laughing quietly.

"You will never let me take myself too seriously."

"In this case, maybe you should take yourself seriously."

He begins pacing the porch, his expression thoughtful.

"I've been considering this for several years. Long before I met Bernadette. She's simply helped crystallize my thinking."

"Oh my god," I say, "she gave them to you."

He stops pacing.

"The yellow sneakers. They're from Bernadette."

"Yes, they were a gift."

"Now it makes sense. I mean, why else would you wear them?"

"What is it with you and yellow?"

"I find it offensive. Not the color, *per se*. I don't have anything against bananas or mustard or submarines. But yellow pants and shoes? Come on."

He glances at his feet and smiles.

"Anyway, I'm convinced," I tell him.

"Of what?"

"That you do love Bernadette."

"Because I wear the shoes?"

"Because you wear the shoes."

I chance a look into the house. Milo and my sister are cuddling on the couch.

"I'm going to grab another beer before they get started. Want one?"

"I think I'll call it a night."

He extends his hand.

"Thank you, Max. I always enjoy our conversations. And I am deeply sorry about Joey's mother."

I start to say something, but the words catch in my throat.

"Are you okay?"

Am I okay?

"I'm kind of sad, Father," I hear myself say. "I didn't expect to be, but I am."

The handshake has run its course, but he doesn't let go. I feel like I'm back in the confessional, trying to recall one last sin.

"I did love her, you know."

14

La Petite Mort

I've never understood the male obsession with virginity—the desire to have sex with someone who's clumsy, frightened, embarrassed, uncertain, restricted, reluctant, restrained. I'm not saying the first time can't be good, just that it gets a whole lot better.

"I was her first," I've heard men brag, as if this entitles them to the place of honor in a woman's biography—as if all subsequent lovers will have to settle for the consolation prize. I think the real desire for female virginity stems from insecurity. Presumably, a virgin won't be able to compare your tiny dick to anyone else's; won't be disappointed that you came thirty seconds after penetration; might not yet realize a thoughtful, caring lover will bring her to orgasm—multiple times. This is certainly why I hoped Naoko was a virgin. Though it wasn't so much the size issue. I was concerned about endurance. My body tends to rush things the first few times I'm with someone—when I'm clumsy, frightened, embarrassed, uncertain, restricted, reluctant, restrained. Besides, I'd practically deified her. Is it even possible to satisfy a goddess?

Naoko was not a virgin, but thanks to her no-nonsense approach to sex, I managed not to be a disappointment. When we arrived at my apartment, I did all the things one does when hoping to fornicate. I made her a drink, put on seductive music, lit some candles, gave her the tour. I was slow and methodical. She was impatient. *I thought we came here to fuck,* her expression seemed to be saying. So I kissed her. And it was transcendent. Until she became restless. So I moved on to more serious foreplay. Again, sublime. Again, impatience. So I took off her clothes. Her body was absolutely breathtaking. And I mean that in a literal sense: I struggled for breath. After getting my respiration under control, I didn't touch her. It was enough to behold her perfect body, as one would a natural wonder or a priceless work of art. My beholding made her impatient, so I got down to business. I grabbed her ass with both hands and started kissing her lovely breasts, as delectable as two perfectly formed scoops of ice cream. We continued this way for some time, the frozen dessert and I, but when I glanced up, she was looking at me with—let's call it anticipation. Ah, I thought, she's anticipating my descent to her nether regions. It was a journey I would have been thrilled to undertake, but before I could embark, she rolled from beneath me, placed her hands on my shoulders, and mounted me like a monkey on a bicycle. I slid in ever so slightly, daring to go no further lest I pull the ripcord before jumping from the plane. Naoko had no such reservations. She began applying pressure at once, causing me to move deeper and deeper inside her. Then she wiggled her hips, and I was in up to the hilt. Don't move, I begged her silently, don't move! Please, just remain still for a while. This is good. This is amazing. This is…she began bouncing up and down like a bull rider at a rodeo. It was a spectacular sight, hips thrusting, breasts undulating, mouth gaping, eyes bulging. But unlike a bull rider, I wanted her to stay in the saddle significantly longer than the requisite eight seconds. I closed my eyes and conjured images I hoped would prevent a premature release: vomiting drunks, maggots, The Bee Gees, testicular cancer, Christmas music. "Oh, Max!" the angel screamed, throwing herself forward so that we were lying chest to chest, cheek to cheek. As Naoko gasped and quivered, I congratulated myself for having made it through round one. God knows how many more rounds remained—how much longer I'd have to hold out—but I was determined to do whatever it took to satisfy this divine creature sent down from the hea…

"Can you come?"

The voice sounded impatient.

"I'm sorry, did you say something, Naoko?"

"Can you come?"

"You want me to come?"

"Yes."

"Now?"

"If you can."

If I can?

The unpleasant images running through my mind were immediately washed away by the choral movement of Beethoven's Ninth Symphony. I executed a graceful rollover without compromising penetration, and in ten hearty thrusts I was…wait!

"Naoko, are you on the pill?" I asked breathlessly.

Apparently she wasn't paying attention, for I had to repeat my question.

"Don't worry. I can't get pregnant," she said impatiently.

Now it was my turn to gasp and quiver.

The little death, the French call it.

When the Earth finally stopped shaking, I remained still and held her in my arms, basking in the dreamy calm that lay in the wake of our passion. Our little death. This is not always the case after making love. Once the dam bursts, thoughts of escape often flood my mind. But not with Naoko. We shall remain as one, our bodies entangled, our souls en…

"I have to go."

She pushed me off her, sat up, and swung both legs over the side of the bed.

"Really? You have to go?" I asked pathetically.

"I'm meeting a friend this evening."

"Oh," I couldn't hide the disappointment in my voice. "I was hoping we could get something to eat. Watch that movie we were talking about."

She seemed genuinely moved.

"You really want me to stay?"

"Absolutely," I begged.

"Okay, I'll meet him for a few minutes then come back. Can I spend the night?"

"Oh yeah, that'd be the bee's knees."

What the fuck did I just say?

"Beezneez?"

"Sorry, yeah, the bee's knees. It's an old expression. It means…it's perfect."

"The bee's knees," Naoko said, trying it out.

She leaned in and gave me a long, tender kiss that almost got me going again.

"Was that the bee's knees?"

"Oh yeah," I said, "knees, elbows, hips, ankles."

She laughed.

(A charming laugh.)

I watched as she put on her clothes, an activity nearly as erotic as their removal. She started toward the door but abruptly turned, stepped back to the bedside, and took my face in her hands. "Bee's knees," she said, looking into my soul. Then she left, promising to be back within the hour. I didn't see her again for two weeks.

Naoko called three hours later and explained that her friend Carlo was upset and needed a shoulder to cry on. Thus, she would not be spending the night. Later I learned that Carlo, a bisexual yoga instructor in his early thirties, was her best friend and taught at the yoga studio she had opened in Shinjuku. He was born and raised in Peru—Japanese father, Peruvian mother—and met Naoko when she was traveling through South America. Together they climbed Machu Picchu, and when she returned to Japan, Carlo followed. According to Naoko, they were in the process of opening a second studio in Osaka. Unfortunately, a number of problems had arisen, and they would be travelling there via Shinkansen the next day.

"How long will you be gone?"

"Just a couple of days," she promised. "I'll come and see you as soon as I get back."

A couple of days became a couple of weeks, and not once did she contact me. I was depressed, angry, impatient, and, whenever the situation allowed, intoxicated. Not even doughnuts could bring me respite. Then one day I came home from work and found her sitting outside my apartment. A large suitcase was next to her.

"You just got back?"

"A few days ago," she said.

I glanced at the luggage.

"I brought a few things with me. I was hoping I could stay with you for a while."

It took a moment to make sense of her words. Stay with me? For a while? Though elated, I tried to appear contemplative. Two weeks without a word, I reminded myself. For the first time, Naoko looked unsure of herself. Vulnerable. She stood and fixed me with a heartbreakingly hopeful expression.

"Bee's knees?" she said softly.

I took her into my arms. It was several moments before I realized she was weeping. It would be several months before I understood why.

At the time, she'd been living in Aoyama with her wealthy parents, though I didn't learn the extent of their wealth until much later. Her family owns a string of businesses, including that pricey restaurant where Naoko first appeared and the adjacent hotel where I spent my first week in Japan. She and her parents had had a major falling out, and Naoko insisted she could no longer stay with them. They were ultratraditional, firmly set in their ways, and contemptuous of anyone who wasn't Japanese. Worst of all, they despised Carlo. So Naoko moved in, and my life became something else. At first, I welcomed the changes. We were together. What else mattered? As predicted, the lovemaking got a whole lot better, although her approach was somewhat mannish. I don't mean she favored a strap-on. Rather, she climaxed very quickly and considered our coupling complete once she achieved orgasm. (Can you come?) In the end, we were both more or less satisfied, though I looked forward to breaking the five-minute mark. As time passed, something else began to gnaw at me. I'd fallen for Naoko the moment I met her, but her feelings for me were ambiguous at best. When in love, one can stick one's head pretty far up one's ass, but even from that vantage point, I couldn't help feeling it would end badly.

Naoko's relationship with Carlo soon became problematic. The two of them spent hours together every day, and although she insisted they'd never been lovers, they shared an intimacy far deeper than our own. He was very friendly to me, flirty even, but I never trusted the son of a bitch. I recognized him as a user, someone who latches on to a person of means and then rides the gravy train until it runs out of track. Yet if I even suggested he was less than she made him out to be, we got into a fight. She insisted I was jealous, and maybe I was, but I know an asshole when I see one. The accuracy of my assessment was verified one evening when, after downing an entire bottle of very expensive chardonnay, Naoko told me why the yoga studio in Osaka had never come to fruition. Carlo was supposed to put up half the money for the venture, and Naoko (her parents, actually) would put up the other half. It wasn't until the papers were about to be signed that Carlo admitted he didn't have the funds. This was only a temporary setback, he assured her, and he would have his half of the investment in a few months. At first, it looked as if mom and dad might cover the entire sum, but at the last minute, they changed their minds and the deal fell through. This is why she wept in my arms after returning from Osaka; this is why she decided to move out of a multimillion-dollar condo and into my humble abode. It's also worth noting that Naoko learned of Carlo's financial shortcomings the day before our "spontaneous" reunion in Ginza—a year and a half after our brief encounter in the restaurant. Why then? I always wondered. After so long, what made her decide to come for me? Simple: she was on the rebound.

Once the two of them made up, they were closer than ever. He became a fixture at my apartment and often joined us for dinner. It got so bad I found myself staying later and later at the office, hoping he'd be gone by the time I got home. Inevitably, I'd find them sitting on the couch sipping wine or sake and laughing like two schoolgirls. It was even worse when Carlo wasn't around. He'd sometimes disappear for a few days—even Naoko didn't seem to know where he went—and she'd become morose and listless. I, of course, was thrilled to have her to myself, but during these periods she was curt and argumentative and resistant to any suggestion that we get out and enjoy ourselves—that we go to a club or try a new restaurant or watch a movie. These were also periods of profound sexual inactivity. Of course they were. Nonetheless, I still hoped we could work things out. I was in love with Naoko and more than willing to make compromises. But after a few months, the only feelings I registered were nervousness or anger or confusion. I was miserable.

Finally, I worked up the courage to confront her.

It was Carlo or me.

I wasn't optimistic.

I called Naoko from work and told her we needed to talk when I got home. I made it clear that under no circumstances was what's-his-face to be there. (I'd taken to referring to Carlo in this manner, as if refusing to say his name somehow diminished his significance to my life.)

"You won't have to worry about what's-his-face anymore," she said angrily and then hung up on me.

I stared at the phone. What the hell just happened?

When I got home that evening, Naoko was sitting on the couch. She appeared to have been in that position for a long time, perhaps since we'd spoken on the phone. I wasn't sure what to make of her appearance: tastefully matched skirt and blouse, hair neatly combed, legs crossed at the ankles, hands resting demurely on her lap. She looked like a hopeful job applicant. I set down my backpack and walked slowly toward the living room, ignoring an impulse to grab the bottle of Maker's Mark beckoning from atop the refrigerator.

"*Genki?*" I asked. She did not respond, so I figured my Japanese pronunciation must be even worse than usual. "Are you okay?" Again, she remained silent.

"We are fine," she eventually said.

We?

Carlo and I?

You and I?

"That's good," I said, wondering if it was.

Several moments passed. It was obvious we were playing by Japanese rules, so I decided to respect the silence. It was Naoko's to break.

"Carlo is gone."

She said it evenly, giving no indication as to where or why or for how long. I was straining the leash that tethered my curiosity but knew better than to ask.

"He went home to South America," she finally clarified. "He won't be coming back."

It wasn't easy, but I managed to maintain a neutral expression as a chorus of flappers danced the Charleston on my amygdala. With that asshole out of the picture, we might actually have a chance.

More silence.

"He was unhappy with a decision I made."

I waited.

And waited.

Fuck patience.

"What decision?"

A single tear appeared at the corner of her left eye. I watched as it rolled down her cheek, leaving a shiny track in its wake. It was followed by several others. I moved to the couch and put my arms around her. She leaned into me and began sobbing. I made Mary cry like this once when we were kids, after I'd hit her in the face with a roller skate. It was an accident, but I'd been reckless. My father held Mary in his arms, and she cried and cried and cried, and all he said was, "There, there." Over and over. So that's what I said. "There, there." But only once. Because it sounded moronic. Nonetheless, Naoko eventually stopped crying. She stayed tucked into me for some time, then gradually sat up and looked into my eyes.

"I decided to keep the baby."

Baby?

Wait a minute.

Baby?

"It's yours," Naoko said, answering a question I wouldn't have known how to ask. "I know you've wondered about Carlo and me, but we're just friends. More like sisters than anything else. The most erotic thing we ever did was paint each other's toenails."

I wasn't sure if this was good news or bad.

"It wasn't a lie when I said I couldn't get pregnant. The doctor told me it was almost impossible—that over ninety-three percent of women like me remain childless. As it turns out, I'm in the lucky seven percent."

Lucky?

"I'm just over three months. I didn't want to tell you until I was sure that everything was alright with the pregnancy."

Our first coupling was just over three months ago. Lucky, indeed.

"I understand you have to make a decision, too. I don't expect you to be a father just because I've decided to be a mother. Whatever you choose to do is okay with me."

Yeah, I have a choice, all right. I can opt for immediate induction into the Asshole Hall of Fame by dumping a beautiful woman with whom I'm in love, abandoning our child even before it's born, and ensuring that I'll be shot in the scrotum should Mary ever find out about it. Or I can attempt to be a decent human being.

Still I struggled.

One thing puzzled me, though.

"Do you really want to have a baby?"

She nodded.

"But you've never even talked about kids."

"It was too early in our relationship."

Good answer.

"But what about your dreams? What about the yoga schools? What about going to India and studying with that pot-bellied guru in the diaper? You want to give all that up?"

"Carlo is gone."

"So? You don't need that asshole. You're smart. You're talented. You're hard working. You can do it without him."

"I meant what I said," she sounded impatient. "You don't have to stay."

"Do you want me to stay?"

The room was suddenly very quiet.

"Yes, I want you to stay."

Naoko's pregnancy wasn't obvious until around the fifth month, which is about the time Mary dropped by for a visit. Back then, my sister was working for the Illinois State Police and had earned a spot on the governor's personal protection detail. In an effort to court the female vote, the governor's re-election committee had insisted that at least one female be on the team keeping the state's highest-ranking official safe. Mary was a crack shot, had no trouble navigating the testosterone-laden world of law enforcement, and could look pretty good when she wanted to, which wasn't very often. Her selection was a no-brainer, yet somehow, she got the job. When the governor attended an agricultural conference in Tokyo, Mary received permission to remain in town for a week after it ended. I explained to her that my apartment wasn't very big, hoping she'd take the hint. Naturally, she accepted my offer.

Mary disliked Naoko the moment she met her. My sister never said or did anything overtly hostile, but I could sense the energy she was expending to keep herself in check. Naoko had an even stronger aversion toward Mary, but, being Japanese, she was much more adept at concealing it.

"She's a flake," Mary told me the evening before her return to the States, "and I can tell you, she has no interest in being a mother."

"How can you say that?"

"She doesn't even acknowledge the baby, other than in the abstract. As a burden. Everything is about her. About how much discomfort she's in. How fat she's getting. How she can't do her yoga positions any more. How she has to do everything on her own."

"On her own?"

"That's what she said."

"Those exact words?"

"No. Her exact words were, 'Max is useless.'"

"Oh, that's just a Japanese thing. Yamakawa-san told me all Japanese wives talk about how useless their husbands are."

"How charming."

"It's one of those cultural things."

"So, do you plan to get married?"

"I don't know. We really haven't talked about it."

Mary snorted.

"You really don't think she's excited about the baby?"

"Excited? I don't even think she wants it."

"You're wrong. She told me she does. She made the choice to keep it. She said even if I took off, she'd have the baby."

"And you believed that?"

"Yes, I did."

"Do you believe it now?"

"Jesus, Mary, why are you doing this? Why do you want to screw everything up?"

"Everything is already screwed up. You just don't see it. Normally I wouldn't care, but this time there's a baby in the mix. You're going to be a father. She's going to be a mother. And neither of you are taking it seriously. You don't seem to get that this is a lifelong relationship. You can't break up with your child like you do with one of your floozies."

Floozies?

"For the rest of your life, you'll be a father. The only question is will you be a good one or a bad one. You can be other things, too. It's not exclusive. But for the next eighteen years or so, fatherhood should be your priority. That child will depend on you for everything."

"It's not just me. Naoko is the mother, and she'll…"

At that point I just ran out of words.

"I hope so," she said sadly. "I really do."

The next morning, Naoko and I walked Mary to the train station. It was a beautiful day, so clear you could probably see

Mt. Fuji from my office window. Despite the weather, I was feeling melancholy. Mary's words from the evening before had shaken me. When we reached the turnstile, she hugged me again and said she had confidence that I'd be a good father.

"I'll do my best," I replied, wondering if that were true.

She stepped over to Naoko, who looked decidedly uncomfortable. In fact, Naoko always looked uncomfortable around Mary. I think it was because her beauty held no sway over my sister, no basis for control. Mary wasn't affected by Naoko's train-stopping ass or the magic of her smile or the sensuality of her touch. She was just her brother's flaky girlfriend. Still, it looked as if Mary was about to give her a hug. Abruptly, Naoko bowed, ensuring that Mary would keep her distance. I waited for my sister to bow back, but she didn't. Instead, she stepped forward and placed both of her hands on my pregnant girlfriend's swollen belly. I'd never seen Naoko look so utterly helpless. Then Mary leaned down, whispered something I couldn't hear, and gave my unborn daughter her first kiss.

After Mary left, things began to deteriorate. Naoko became increasingly taciturn. She spent more and more time in bed and refused to leave the apartment for anything other than a doctor's appointment. She felt she was too unattractive to be seen in public. Although I'd never found the pregnant-female form particularly appealing, Naoko was ravishing. Unfortunately, sexual intercourse was even less likely than social intercourse. "How can I have sex with you when I look like this?" she demanded. I offered a number of clever responses to this obviously rhetorical question, each of which was met with stony silence. I knew she was pregnant; I knew her hormones were all over the place; I knew it was difficult for her. Yet, despite all this knowledge, she was starting to piss me off.

Then one day everything changed.

I came home from work and found Naoko floating above her yoga mat, an expression of serenity on her face that had been absent since Carlo's exit. Okay, she wasn't exactly levitating, but the effect was nearly as dramatic. She was clad in her favorite Divine Goddess yoga wear and looked utterly beautiful, her rounded tummy adding yet another sensual curve to her body. I watched silently for several minutes, careful not to disturb her. Eventually she came out of her trance and looked up at me.

"Why are you staring?"

I felt embarrassed, as if I'd just been caught peeking through a keyhole.

"Sorry, I just…I'm just happy to see you doing something."

A cold smile.

"Well, I'm glad you're happy, and I apologize if my misery has caused you discomfort."

"C'mon, that's not what I meant. It's nice to see you active for once. It was like you'd given up."

"Given up?"

"Yeah, given up. I was worried. You haven't looked this good in weeks."

"You were worried that I didn't look good enough for you?"

"Jesus, Naoko, all I meant was…"

"Please," she interrupted, "I don't want to argue."

I didn't want to argue either, so I stood there trying to think of something that wouldn't further escalate the situation.

"I'm sorry," I finally said, but she didn't hear me, having already drifted back to serenityville or wherever it is yoga people go when they're in the groove.

She worked out every day after that, sometimes more than once. I'm hardly an expert on prenatal care, but I cautioned her about overexerting herself lest she damage the baby. I figured if we were going to have one, it might as well be born intact. Naoko assured me the doctor approved of her yoga regimen. In addition to her workouts, she also started taking long walks, and occasionally I would accompany her. These were probably our best times together. We never argued on our walks, not that we talked much. Most often, we would move along in silence, holding hands, enjoying the sights, sounds, and smells of Tokyo. I sometimes wondered what had facilitated Naoko's dramatic transformation, but I never dared ask. Because it really didn't matter.

It really did matter.

I came home one evening and heard her talking to someone on the phone. Normally her conversations are in Japanese, so I don't have any idea what she's saying or to whom she's saying it. But this particular day she was speaking Spanish. I still didn't have any idea what she was saying, but the only person she ever spoke Spanish with was Carlo. When the call ended, she stepped out of the room and saw me waiting. Whatever pleasantness had accumulated over the past few weeks drained from her face, leaving behind a look of anger so intense I knew it would be suicidal to say anything.

But I did anyway.

"Let's go to Tonki for dinner."

Tonki was a traditional *tonkatsu* restaurant where well-trained chefs prepared delicious cuts of breaded, lightly fried pork; mounds of freshly shredded cabbage; flavorful Japanese rice; and miso soup seasoned with tiny clams. Naoko loved it. Her angry expression faded, and we went on to have a very pleasant dinner. On the walk back to the apartment, I decided to broach the subject of the phone call, because the elephant wasn't just in the room, it was taking a dump on the carpet.

"Naoko, I know Carlo's your friend," I began. I could feel her body tense through the hand I was holding, but she did not pull it away. "I just want you to know I think it's great you're talking again. No matter what, I want you to be happy."

When she looked at me, I could feel the tension dissipating. Normally, this would induce me to continue talking, to augment my statement with additional support until I said something that would negate all the goodwill I'd just established. This time, I managed to keep my mouth shut.

"Thank you, Max." She put her head against my shoulder, and my heart started beating so fast I thought it would explode.

After that, she spoke to him every day. Sometimes in Spanish. Sometimes in Japanese. Never in English. But Naoko was happy, and what's-his-face was six thousand miles away. What difference did it make?

I was not in the delivery room when Joey was born. There were several reasons for this. The fact that I was the father but not the husband confused the hospital administrators. Moreover, the impregnator was a *gai jin*, making the situation even more atypical, and atypical always presents a challenge in Japan.

Finally, while it was increasingly common for Japanese fathers to be present in the delivery room, it was by no means compulsory.

This is all bullshit.

The only reason I wasn't in the delivery room when Joey was born was that Naoko didn't want me there. She was adamant that no one but the doctor and nurses bear witness. So I did what expectant fathers do in the movies: I paced back and forth in the corridor. After a few minutes I tired, so I sat down and fell asleep. A Japanese nurse awakened me some time later. She'd clearly been coached on how to communicate with foreigners: "Mah-mah oh-kay. Bay-bee oh-kay." Her verb-less sentences were punctuated with the *okay* sign: index finger on the thumb forming an *O*, while the middle, ring, and pinky fingers formed the *K*. In some countries this gesture is the symbol for anus. I couldn't recall if Japan was among them. "Mah-mah oh-kay. Bay-bee oh-kay," she repeated.

Baby.

Naoko had been obviously pregnant for several months, and we'd come to the hospital in order for her to give birth, yet the *fact* of a baby came as a surprise to me. I was trying to get my head around this fact when I noticed the nurse hadn't left. Perhaps she needed confirmation that her message had been understood. I lifted my right hand and made the anus sign. She answered with another gesture, the one that says *come with me, you dipshit*. I struggled to my feet and followed her down a long corridor. Eventually we came to a wall of glass, behind which was a city of babies. They all looked pretty much the same, wearing little hats and mittens, swaddled in little blankets, resting in little bassinets. The nurse pointed to one of them—third row from the front, fourth bassinet from the left—and said, "Doh-ta."

Doh-ta?

Daughter?

It didn't sound right.

Not that *son* would have been any more coherent.

I stared at this "doh-ta" for some time, and as I did, my heart began to beat faster. Eventually it was pounding with such ferocity that I might have just run a marathon. I found it increasingly difficult to breathe. The nurse noticed my distress and stepped forward to offer assistance—apparently, a panic attack isn't all that rare in the maternity ward. Once again, I invoked the anus sign and then staggered to a chair. As I sat there getting my breathing under control and willing my heart to slow the hell down, I considered the human reproductive system. My mom had explained it to me when I was nine years old: sexual intercourse involves a sperm (provided by the man) fertilizing an egg (provided by the woman), which will then grow into one of those tiny beings behind the glass wall. Once I hit puberty, it was necessary to reinterpret this information, because the last thing I wanted to do was fertilize the egg of a high-school classmate. Ergo, sexual intercourse was about a sperm (provided by me) *not* fertilizing an egg (provided by any girl willing to go all the way with me), which would *not* grow into a baby, so I would *not* have to get married and *not* have to quit high school and *not* get a minimum-wage job and *not* live in a trailer park on Route 130. In other words, the purpose of sex was to *not* have a baby. So when Naoko told me I was going to be a father, I wondered, how is that possible? All we did was fuck.

She and the baby came home two days later. At first, we just called her "the baby." Naoko had chosen Pablo for a boy, her desired gender, but gave little thought to girl names. I suggested Björk, but this was quickly vetoed. Then one evening as I was holding "the baby," her back against my stomach, Naoko said she looked like a little kangaroo. A joey.

Those first few days were chaotic, but then something of a routine emerged. Naoko cared for Joey while I was at work, and I was responsible for the night-time feedings and diaper changes. She'd decided against breastfeeding for fear of not having enough milk. Mary insisted this was bullshit, but I was raised on formula, so I didn't have any problem with the decision. Things were going pretty well, though I was always tired. Naoko, on the other hand, had endless reserves of energy. I'd come home in the evening to find her working out, which presented a kind of symmetry, since she was often working out when I left in the morning.

"Don't overdo it," I told her, "You just had a baby."

"I need to get back in shape."

"There's no hurry. Besides, you look amazing."

I didn't see it coming.

After two weeks, you could barely tell she'd been pregnant. It seemed unnatural. Naturally, I was horny. It was only when I attempted to satisfy my desire that she played the postpartum card: "What are you doing? I just had a baby!"

I didn't see it coming.

When we first brought Joey home from the hospital, Naoko sang or hummed to her almost constantly, old Japanese melodies that were both soothing and melancholy. After a couple of weeks, she did this less frequently. And then not at all.

I didn't see it coming.

At the end of the third week, she walked into the bedroom where I was feeding Joey and said, "I'm leaving."

I looked up and waited for her to continue.

"Do you understand what I'm saying?"

I nodded.

"I'm going to Peru. Carlo and I are opening a yoga studio in Lima."

I probably should have felt something—anger or sadness or fear or any of the other emotions that correspond to the sudden death of a relationship. (Maybe I did see it coming.) But I didn't feel anything. Except certainty.

Certainty that we were finished.

Certainty that whatever we had was gone forever.

In this, I found a measure of peace.

Certainty gives you closure. It allows you to avoid the humiliating self-deceit. All the pointless hope. All the meaningless pain. You don't have to forgive. Or be forgiven. You don't even have to say goodbye.

(This is this.)

I held up Joey for her to see.

"Why?" I asked.

"This has all been very traumatic for me," she began, "and I just need some time..."

"No," I interrupted, "that's not what I'm asking. I get why you're leaving. I really do. What puzzles me is why you decided to have a baby in the first place. You didn't have to get pregnant.

You didn't have to carry it to term. But you did. You made that choice. Why?"

For a long time, she just stared. At some point, she began to cry. This pleased me. I wasn't being sadistic; I just wanted to know she felt something.

"I hoped it would make me happy," she finally said.

Naoko waited for me to respond, but I had nothing to add. Without acknowledging her daughter, she turned and left the room, closing the door behind her.

Joey lay silently in my arms.

"I'm sorry," I said to no one in particular.

15

Happiness

Original Sin. God said don't eat the fruit of the Tree of Knowledge. Eve ate the fruit of the Tree of Knowledge. The Creator was disappointed but hardly surprised, being omniscient and all. Yet I wonder if He was hoping to be wrong, hoping that things would turn out differently despite knowing the outcome—the way you re-watch a tragic movie, desperately clinging to the possibility that it will somehow end differently. That Thelma and Louise escape to Belize in their flying car. That Old Yeller won't die. That Rambo will. If nothing else, the story of Adam and Eve offers insight into God's attitude toward temptation. Clearly, His thinking is at odds with those who've made it their duty to censor and suppress—to ban or burn that which challenges their Christian sensibilities: books, movies, TV shows, magazines, plays, critical thought, and virtually every scientific discovery ever made. These folks believe they have a divine duty to eliminate temptation, despite the fact that it was God who created it. Yes, He planted that tree.

But why?

Why would God devise a test He knew we were going to fail?

Maybe He thought Paradise was too good for us.

Maybe He didn't want us to be happy.

Two weeks after I return from Naoko's funeral, Joey climbs onto my bed, pushes her face against mine, and declares, "Daddy, I don't want to be baptized."

I open my eyes.

Hers have melded into one.

"Let me sleep."

"Did you hear what I said?"

Something about not wanting to be baptized.

And here I had my outfit all picked out.

"Why not?" I ask, rolling onto my back so she won't be repelled by a blast of morning breath. "I thought you were excited about it."

No reply.

"Is it because of what happened to your mom?"

She blinks.

"Bernadette?"

Another blink.

"And you? Because you got hurt?"

"I'm almost five."

"So?"

"I think baptism is just a phase I was going through."

"A phase?"

She nods.

"What about Original Sin?"

"You said it wasn't real."

"Did I?"

"You say it all the time."

"Well, it's not about what I believe. It's about what you believe."

Joey suddenly looks thoughtful, wise beyond her years.

"It's bullshit," she says.

"As your parent, I'm obliged to tell you not to use that term."

"Bullshit?"

"Joey."

"You say it all the time."

"I'm entitled."

"Why?"

"Because I'm a grown-up."

"So I have to wait until I'm a grown-up?"

"No, just until first grade."

This seems to satisfy her.

"*Ate* told me I need to have faith."

Of course she did.

"Do you know what that means?"

"I should believe what the Bible says?"

"It means you should believe without proof."

"Oh," she says tentatively.

"If I told you there were elephants dancing in the front yard, would you believe me?"

She smiles and shakes her head.

"What if I said I'm your father and I know what's best for you? You have to believe me. You have to have faith. And if you don't, you're going to be punished. Would you believe in the elephants then?"

Slowly, almost apologetically, she shakes her head.

"Of course not. Because it's bullshit. When something is unbelievable, the only way to believe it is to have faith. You don't need faith when something is believable. If I took you to the window and opened the curtains and there were elephants dancing in the yard, would you believe me then?"

She smiles. A beautiful smile.

"Yes."

"Why?"

"Because I can see them."

"Exactly. Your belief is based on evidence instead of faith."

"So faith is bad?"

"It depends on how you define bad. Faith inhibits critical thinking, and to me, that's a bad thing. Of course, the Church says critical thinking is bad, because it inevitably compromises faith."

"But *Ate* has faith."

Of course she does.

"In her case, I don't know. I look at Bernadette and think if this is what faith does to you, then fine, be faithful. But faith seldom brings out the best in people. It usually brings out the worst. Some of the cruelest people in history were inspired by faith. Just ask any woman who was burned at the stake."

Another period of contemplation.

"Will *Ate* be mad if I don't get baptized?"

The question surprises me, though I should have seen it coming.

"She could never be mad at you, Joey. Bernadette wants you to have faith because she loves you and thinks it will bring you closer to God. But she knows there's more than one way to do that. She'll understand if you don't want to get baptized."

Joey stares at me for several seconds.

"Daddy, do you believe in God?"

"Sure I do. Now go feed the elephants."

When I was fifteen, one of my best friends and two of his brothers were killed in an automobile accident. This event brought a new dimension of reality to my life: death. I'd been immortal up to that point, but when I found out George was dead, I knew it was only a matter of time. The funeral was surreal—grief so thick it was hard to move, yet people kept insisting the boys were in a better place. The more religious they were, the harder they tried to put a positive spin on it. *They're at peace. They're in their heavenly home. They're having supper with the Lord Jesus.* A few even sounded sincere, but if you looked in their eyes, you could see the desperation. It was at that point I realized it wasn't faith that sustained these people. It was hope. That's what they were clinging to. The kind of hope that leads you to buy a lottery ticket: you know you're not going to win, but until they announce those numbers, you can sure pretend to be rich. After George died, I couldn't pretend anymore. I was still going to church, of course, still displaying the outward signs of faith, but inside I was a holy mess—terrified, certain every day would be my last. But after several months of not dying, I began to believe survival might be possible. If I could just make it to twenty, there was a chance I would live to be old, and at that point it wouldn't matter if I died, because an old me wouldn't really be me at all. From time to time, I even managed to forget about mortality. Then some kid would be killed in a farming accident or a car crash or a drowning or even a homicide, and once again, death would grab me by the throat and squeeze so hard I couldn't even scream.

I did make it to twenty.

The fear subsided but did not go away.

Then at twenty-two I was offered a fresh perspective on death. Theo, one of my best friends, found out he had cancer. I was devastated, but better him than me. Or so I thought. One day I visited him in the hospital, and he told me something so utterly extraordinary that I would have, at that moment, traded places. According to Theo, there are women who find the terminally ill irresistibly attractive—women who will sneak into a dying patient's room and fuck his socks off. "They'll do whatever you want," he swore. At the time, Theo was pale, emaciated, and on some serious painkillers; thus, I was skeptical. Five minutes later, an incredibly beautiful young woman danced into the room. She apologized when she saw he wasn't alone, and Theo gave her a dismissive wave. "I'll come back later," she said, looking at him the way I might look at a Playboy centerfold. Jesus Christ, I thought, some people have all the luck. Theo died two months later, and although the mortician had done a number on him, there was no covering the look of satisfaction on his face. I hoped to see the mystery woman at his funeral, but she wasn't there. Probably too busy banging some other soon-to-be-dead guy. Good for her, I thought. Good for him.

So either I'd be killed instantly and not know what hit me, or I'd be fucked to death.

I could live with that.

"You okay, Max?"

Milo is at the kitchen table drinking coffee and looking at a book. He and Mary had stayed over again. Joey sits to his right, a bowl of doughnut-shaped cereal in front of her.

"I'm fine."

"You're holding your side again."

I look down. I'm holding my side again. I've been doing this for the past couple of weeks. There's a dull pain that won't go away. It's ruined my appetite. Which probably explains why I've been so tired. Felt so weak.

"No, I'm not."

"You've been doing that the last few days. Like you've got a cramp or something."

I drop my hands.

"I think you've got a cramp in your brain."

I turn away, pour myself a cup of coffee.

"You've lost some weight, too."

I have lost some weight.

"Where's your concubine?" I ask, ignoring his observation.

"She had an early shift," he says, smiling. He likes being asked about Mary.

I sit across from him. Acknowledge my daughter.

"Morning, Joey."

"Morning, Daddy."

Milo turns a page.

"Hey, I really like this book," he gushes. It's the *omiyage* from the truck stop. "Can I borrow it?"

"You'll have to ask her," I answer, nodding toward Joey, who spoons a massive load of soggy cereal into her mouth.

"Oh, sorry, Joey," he says sincerely. "I didn't realize it was yours."

"Mmmmaaass…"

"Easy, you're going to choke," I say in my artificially paternal voice.

She sits back in her chair to concentrate on swallowing. It happens in stages, but eventually she manages to coax the mush down her throat.

"It's my very favorite book," she says to Milo.

"In that case, you'd better take it," he says, sliding it to her.

"It's okay, you can look at it."

"I'm all done for now."

Joey pushes her bowl aside and starts flipping through the pages. A photo of the famous red lantern at the Asakusa temple catches her attention. She leans closer, eyes the caption beneath it.

"Max," Milo asks in an odd voice, "is she reading that?"

"I suppose."

"Isn't she a little young? Hell, I didn't read until halfway through first grade."

It was the same for me. I knew the alphabet and could spell my name by the time I was five, but I didn't become literate until after entering grade school. Our first books were breathtakingly insipid, a series featuring a perfectly Caucasian family with three perfectly Caucasian children: Dick, Jane, and Sally. They had a dog named Spot and a cat named Puff, also Caucasian. The prose was riveting: "See Dick run. Run, Dick, run. Run, run, run." It had the literary force of the multiplication tables. Nevertheless, I learned to read.

"You taught her?" Milo asks.

"Not really. I used to read to her, but then she started picking out words herself. Pretty soon she was reading *Green Eggs and Ham* to me."

"I love that book," Milo gushes.

Joey looks up.

"What book?"

"*Green Eggs and Ham.*"

"It's a little childish."

Milo looks crestfallen.

"I think it has an important message," he counters.

Joey glances at me to confirm the authenticity of his statement.

"What message is that, Milo?" I ask.

"That you shouldn't close yourself off to new experiences. The whole narrative is based on the fact that Sam-I-Am can't get that other guy to try something unfamiliar. He's shut himself off from new experiences, and Sam-I-Am is committed to helping him break free from that self-limiting pattern of behavior."

"Is this from your doctoral dissertation?"

He laughs, and then his expression turns serious.

"You're doing it again."

I don't know what he means until I see where he's looking. I'm holding my side, pushing against the dull pain. A headache is coming on. I pick up my cup, change the subject.

"Joey's decided not to get baptized."

"No kidding?" he says, turning to Joey. "How come?"

She looks up from a photo of the Kabukiza Theatre.

"I just...it doesn't make sense."

Milo glances at me and then back at Joey.

"Me and your dad went through all that," he begins. "We both got baptized and made our First Communion and did all the other stuff good Catholics are supposed to do. Not that we had a choice. We had faith shoved down our throats. Especially in catechism. Hey Max, remember Sister Mary Cherry?"

"Sister Mary Cherry?" Joey repeats.

"She was our catechism teacher. And, boy, she hated your dad."

"Why?" Joey asks, though she doesn't seem particularly surprised.

"I asked too many questions."

"Well, you were kind of a smart-ass, too."

"Did she hate you?" Joey asks Milo, pushing her book back across the table.

"Darlin', Sister Mary Cherry loved me."

"Why?"

"Because I just nodded my head and kept my mouth shut."

"Yes," I agree, "at six years old, Milo had already perfected the art of looking stupid."

"Better to look stupid than to be stupid."

I can think of no rejoinder.

"Besides, it's a useful talent that's served me very well over the years," he adds.

"How?" Joey asks.

"People are a lot more inclined to show you who they really are—and what they really want—if they don't think you're smart enough to be a threat."

"So I should look stupid?"

"No, Joey, just be yourself. For Milo, looking stupid comes naturally."

He nods as if I'd just given him a compliment. The room is silent for several seconds, and I can see something is troubling Joey. Finally she mumbles, "*Ate* says we all have to believe in something."

"She's right. We all do believe in something. It's just not necessarily what we're told to believe. Life is complicated, and it's hard to know what's true and what isn't, but it's exciting to explore all those ideas and philosophies. To engage in critical thinking. Our beliefs should change as we learn and grow and discover new things. But most religions won't let you do that. They see change as a threat. So they force you to believe their narrow, antiquated view of the world."

"You cannot force a man to believe," Milo says in a voice not quite his own. "You can only force him to pretend to believe."

Joey and I look at him.

"Pindar Plifner wrote it," he explains.

Milo loves quoting Pindar Plifner.

"Who's Pindar Plifner?" Joey demands.

Milo smiles. "He's an outlaw theologian."

"A theologian is a person who studies and writes about religion," I explain. "And an outlaw theologian is a theologian who pisses off all the other theologians."

My head has started to pound, so I excuse myself and walk to the bathroom, where I down a handful of ibuprofen. I wash my hands and flush the toilet to create a subterfuge. When I return, Milo is still discussing his outlaw theologian.

"Pindar met God in the desert, then started the Church of the Sacred Sand. And believe it or not, I'm a member in good standing." From beneath his T-shirt, he pulls out a fine chain with a small silver cross dangling from it. Upon closer inspection, Joey sees that it's not a cross.

"Is that a cactus?"

"Sure is, a saguaro cactus. Symbol of life in the desert."

"As opposed to death on a cross," I interject.

"Do you go to the sand church on Sunday?" Joey asks him.

"Nah, there's no church. The only thing Sacred Sanders are supposed to do is be happy and facilitate happiness in others. And even that's voluntary. God told Pindar He has no desire to be worshipped or feared or loved. And He won't get involved in our lives. He just likes to watch. We're like a big reality TV show. Before people came along, God was bored."

I know the story well, having read *Sacred Sand*, the book Pindar wrote after crashing a stolen Cessna in the Sonoran Desert, where he had a face-to-face with the Creator of Heaven and Earth. It wasn't a big seller, though it did cause a stir—particularly among the Catholic hierarchy—and Pindar was duly excommunicated. (He saw this as an honor, noting that most pedophile priests remain members in good standing.) Pindar's teachings are based on a single premise: God was bored. Eternity, it seems, is a long time. Ergo, the universe and everything in it are byproducts of the Supreme Being's ennui. There's no mention of life after death, though you get the feeling anything's possible. As God put it to Pindar, "Everything that hasn't happened, hasn't happened yet."

Milo met Pindar and his wife, Yvette, when they visited the farm to score pot. Yvette, a talented harpist, had stage-four non-Hodgkin's lymphoma and knew Milo through a fellow cancer patient who told her about some "goofy angel" who gave free marijuana to anyone undergoing chemotherapy. The couple wound up staying several days, during which, in addition to getting high, Yvette played the harp and Pindar spoke of his adventure in the desert. Milo especially loved his account of God's departure, when Pindar thought to ask if there was some message he might deliver to humanity. The Supreme Being thought for a few moments and then replied, "Tell them not to be afraid."

I'm afraid.
Not because of the symptoms.
I've had mysterious pains in the past.
Discovered ominous lumps
Noticed unusual spots.
They all went away.
But this time it's different.
This time I'm happy.
And that is troubling.
For, unlike Pindar Plifner, I believe happiness is the harbinger of disaster.
The intermediate state between tragedies.
The hole in the doughnut.
As long as my life is shit, I have nothing to fear. As long as I might appreciate a premature exit, I'm indestructible. But once everything falls into place—once my neighbor trades her

leg for my daughter's life; once Joey's future is financed by her billionaire grandparents; once my sister marries one of the few truly decent men on the planet; once I finally embrace the horrifying beauty of life—that's when I get fucked to death.

"Max!"

Mary's cop voice startles me.

I hurry to the front door.

"Didn't you hear me knocking?"

My sister is wearing her police uniform, looking crisp and fresh even after her early-morning shift. I do a double take when I see Bernadette standing next to her, leaning on a pair of crutches, smiling like an angel.

"My God, Bernadette, I didn't know you were getting around on crutches!"

"Hello, Mr. Max! Yes, I been practicing!"

She is wearing a pair of blue jeans, the right pant leg rolled up and pinned neatly beneath the abbreviated appendage formerly known as Stump. Her left foot, extending just beyond the end of the other pant leg, is bare. She has on a T-shirt purchased for fifty cents at a church rummage sale; I know this because I inquired as to its origin the first time I saw her wearing it. My curiosity had been piqued by the words emblazoned across the front, a parody of the Nike slogan that reads "Just Do Me." I explained that the alteration of the final two letters had rendered the message somewhat less than wholesome, but Bernadette didn't seem to mind. It came from the Church, after all.

"Can we come in?" Mary says, pushing past me.

I shift my weight, preparing to assist Bernadette, but she glides into the room without effort.

"Where is everybody?" Mary asks.

Before I can answer, Joey bursts into the room.

"*Ate!*" she yells, throwing her arms around Bernadette's waist.

Bernadette lets her left crutch fall against the couch and hugs back with her free arm.

"Hello, my angel," she coos.

Mary offers to help her sit, but Bernadette manages to lower herself to the couch unaided. Joey sits beside her. Milo walks in and looks over at Mary. For several moments they regard each other like a pair of teenaged virgins, and then gentleman Milo steps over and kisses her chastely on the cheek. Noticing Bernadette, he says something in Tagalog that makes her laugh. He then volunteers to bring out the coffee. Mary slides in next to Joey and gives her a ferocious hug. Goddamn happiness. When she releases her, Joey is smiling. But the smile disappears when Mary says, "Bernadette showed me your baptism dress. It's so beautiful! I can't wait to see you in it!" Suddenly, Joey looks frightened. Mary reaches for her, but she recoils. When Bernadette takes her hand, Joey brusquely pulls it away.

"Joey, what's wrong?" Bernadette asks.

Her mouth opens, but no sound is issued. I know what's coming. She hasn't done this since she was a toddler, but I recognize the prelude to a massive sob.

"What's wrong, sweetie?" Mary pleads, her voice shaking.

The room fills with the sound of anguish. Mary looks up at me, shocked and confused, wondering why I appear to be so unconcerned. Her eyes darken with suspicion. I shake my head.

"Joey, please tell me what's wrong!" Bernadette pleads.

"It's okay, Bernadette," I say, stepping toward the couch. "Joey has something she needs to tell you."

This is exactly the wrong thing to say, for the moment I do, Joey screams as if she'd stuck her finger into my car's cigarette lighter. She jumps from the couch and runs across the room just as Milo enters carrying a tray of coffee. Instead of dodging him, she throws her arms around his waist. Miraculously, he manages to keep the tray steady as Joey sobs into his shirt. I hurry over and take the tray from him. Mary is on her feet, and Bernadette is struggling to rise, but I tell them to sit down as I put the tray on the coffee table. Milo stands patiently as Joey cries, gently rubbing her head. Finally, he squats down, looks her in the eyes, and says, "Let's blow this pop stand." I have no idea if Joey is familiar with the phrase, but she takes his hand as he rises, and they walk to the front door, not once looking in our direction.

"What was that all about?" Mary demands the moment the door shuts. Now, this is more like it, I think. Discord. So much more familiar than happiness. Still, the ache in my abdomen does not abate.

"I've never seen her so upset. What did you do?"

Bernadette is looking at me, eyes pleading for an explanation.

"I think..."

"You think?" Mary repeats mockingly. "You think, therefore you're an asshole?"

Although she is wrong to judge me so harshly, I can't help but appreciate the Descartes reference.

"You brought up the dress, Mary."

"Yeah? So?"

"So she changed her mind about getting baptized, and now she's afraid of losing Bernadette."

"What?" Her whisper is a shout.

Bernadette begins struggling with her crutches, trying to rise from the couch.

"I've got to see Joey," she says, her voice choked with tears.

I move to the couch and drop to a knee, genuflecting before her. Carefully, I place my hands on hers and say her name. My voice sounds strange, gentler perhaps, and Bernadette becomes still. "Milo's got this." I see Mary nod, and a moment later Bernadette does too. Why Milo? My guess is Joey chose to be comforted by the only other child in the room. We sit quietly and drink our coffee.

After ten minutes, the door opens and Milo steps inside. Joey follows a moment later. She glances at me, her expression betraying no emotion, and then walks over to Bernadette.

"*Ate?*" she says, her arms dangling at her sides.

"Yes, Joey?"

She looks at Milo and then back to Bernadette.

"I don't want to be baptized."

Her voice trembles as she speaks, and for some reason, I find this heartbreaking. I want to hug her, but I figure my place is on the sidelines.

Tears well in Bernadette's eyes.

When Joey sees them, her mouth begins to quiver.

Then Bernadette smiles.

A beautiful smile.

"Oh, Joey. You are such a wonderful person, and God loves you so much. You don't have to be baptized."

She reaches for her, and this time Joey steps into the embrace.

"What about Limbo?" Joey asks over her shoulder.

Bernadette gently pushes her back until they are face to face.

"When I grew up, they taught us Limbo is where babies that weren't baptized had to go. But I don't know anymore. And if there is a Limbo, I will ask God to send me there, too."

"What about Daddy?"

Before Bernadette can respond, Mary declares, "Oh honey, your daddy will be very lucky to make it as far as Limbo."

At last, Joey smiles.

"Milo had an idea," she says.

We all turn to Milo. He shrugs.

"He said I can wear my baptism dress to his and Mary's wedding."

Goddammit! Why hadn't I thought of that?

"That's a wonderful idea!" Bernadette exclaims.

Mary is looking at Milo as if he just won a spelling bee.

Everybody's happy.

Fuck this shit.

16

Nihon

This is what Japan is like. This is what the Japanese are like. Anytime you hear someone make such statements, it's safe to assume that he or she is full of shit. Generalizations about any country, its culture, or its people are dubious, as they're typically based on faulty inductive reasoning: the Parisians won't speak English to me, hence, the French are rude; I got laid in Toronto, ergo, Canadians have low standards. But generalizations about Japan are especially absurd. This became glaringly evident during World War II when Japanese prisoners of war exhibited behavior that completely flummoxed their American captors. Hoping to gain insight into their unpredictable detainees, the United States Office of War Information commissioned anthropologist Ruth Benedict to do an analysis of Japanese culture. Her findings were later published as *The Chrysanthemum and the Sword*. In it, Benedict posits that every cultural trait attributed to the Japanese is contradicted by the fact that the opposite trait is equally prevalent. Ironically, the book became a bestseller in Japan.

Rather than tell you what Japan is like, I'll tell what I like about Japan. Three random things. Let me see…okay: fugu, cherry blossoms, and the *Kanamara Matsuri*. I've never eaten fugu and don't intend to; I just like the fact that a deadly poisonous fish responsible for killing dozens of diners a year is among the country's greatest delicacies. Cherry blossoms are pretty, but what happens beneath them is even more attractive: in a tradition known as *hanami*, friends, family, and coworkers gather beneath the *sakura* to eat and drink—often excessively—and welcome the coming of spring. Speaking of coming, the *Kanamara Matsuri* is a festival celebrating the penis. Yes, that penis.

A few weeks into my new job, Yamakawa-san pulled me aside and said, "Ma-ku-su-san, please do not return to America until I retire." I was touched. Apparently, he believed the levity I brought to the workspace was good for office morale. I got along well with my Japanese co-workers, and the fact that we could watch sumo and drink beer while still on the clock kept me perpetually ebullient. Moreover, I enjoyed the work. In the US, I'd written print, TV, and radio ads for a few regional clients, but most of the copy I was responsible for supported ad campaigns created by elite writers. That is, I wrote brochures, leaflets, in-store product signage, and other supplementary promotional materials collectively known as collateral. It's an appropriate designation, for those of us mired in this banal segment of the advertising world—those deemed unworthy to work on glamorous *above-the-line* campaigns—are indeed collateral damage. "It's a stepping stone," the creative directors will tell you, "a tremendous learning opportunity that will hone your writing skills, so that when you finally do get your shot, you're truly prepared." Of course, by the time you're truly prepared, they decide to go with a younger writer, an up-and-comer far more conscious of the current zeitgeist. But as soon as I arrived in Japan, I stepped into the big time. Suddenly, I was writing ads that would appear in newspapers and magazines all over the world. I was working with teams that were creating multimillion-dollar TV commercials. Best of all, I was coming up with inspirational quotes that would be printed on the sides of beer cans. (Several times a year, Japanese beer companies produce seasonal versions to complement their regular offerings. This involves tweaking the formula just enough to capture the spirit of the season, designing a limited-edition can, and emblazoning it with a quote—in English—that defines the mystical qualities of the beverage it contains. Something like, *Experience the flavors of the season with each sip of this crisp, refreshing brew—ideal for intimate moments with a special friend, unforgettable family gatherings, or simply listening to the wind whispering through the lovely fall foliage.*) As far as I was concerned, I had made it to the pinnacle of the advertising world. So I heartily agreed to Yamakawa-san's request that I not return to America until his retirement two years hence. Honestly, I was so content I wasn't planning on leaving until *my* retirement.

And then I had a kid.

And then I became a single parent.

And then I discovered being a single parent is difficult.

Especially in Japan.

Especially when you're not Japanese.

Or even if you are.

To wit, my status as a single parent did not diminish my work obligations; I was obliged to spend at least eight hours a day in the ugly gray monolith. This created a dilemma, for in Japan one does not bring a baby to the office. It's just not done. So that's what I did. Eventually Cha Cha, one of my favorite coworkers, helped me find a reliable babysitter, but for the first few weeks after Naoko left, Joey came with me to the office. It was such a shocking departure from Japanese reality that no one knew how to respond. So they didn't. At least not at first. Eventually Yamakawa-san ambled over to my cubicle, looked down at the baby nestled in a cardboard box (a makeshift bassinet), and bowed. Cha Cha ventured over a few minutes later, presumably to ask if I needed any office supplies. Her official name is Takahashi-san, but I called her Cha Cha because she once told me she liked salsa. Later, I realized she was talking about the condiment rather than the Latin-American dance, but the name stuck. Cha Cha was the office manager, and part of her job was to make sure I had sufficient stationery supplies.

"Ma-ku-su-san, you brought your beautiful baby to the office today," Cha Cha told me.

In Japan, one often points out the obvious. It's a way of avoiding controversy.

"Yes," I replied, not wanting to rock the boat.

"Do you need any pens?"

"No, thank you. This one still has plenty of ink."

She bowed and went back to her desk.

Over the next few days, Joey's presence did produce a reaction, but it turned out to be a pleasant one. Female coworkers would stop by my cubicle to discuss something or other and then turn their attention to the baby. At first they just marveled over her—as people are wont to do with nascent dogs, cats, and humans—but soon they were holding her, singing to her, giving her the bottle. Even the men began showing an interest. My smitten coworkers looked after Joey when I was out for a meeting, and if she cried, someone rushed over to see if she was okay—even when I was sitting next to her. Most helpfully, Watanabe-san, who had a child of her own, relieved me of diaper-changing duty. Although I might have been misinterpreting the signs—this was Japan, after all—I believed the office was a happier place when Joey was there. At home it was just her and me, and that brought us even closer. Not so much as father and daughter; more as fellow human beings caught up in a series of unpredictable circumstances over which we had very little control. (We're all bozos on this bus.) Ultimately, my sister was right: caring for an infant on your own is a lot of work and costs a lot of sleep and kills any chance of a social life. But I managed.

Eventually, Cha Cha found a Japanese woman to look after Joey during the day. Her name was Suzuki-san, and she lived nearby. She'd raised three children of her own, one of whom worked just down the hall from our office. After that, I took Joey to her apartment on my way to work and picked her up on the way home. Suzuki-san didn't speak English, but at that point, neither did Joey, so it didn't affect their ability to communicate. I, on the other hand, knew just enough Japanese to confuse the poor woman. But we managed.

Once I stopped bringing Joey to work, the office seemed a little less joyful—like the end of summer vacation. I'm certain my co-workers missed her, but no one ever said a word to me. Occasionally, though, I'd find a package on my desk, and in it would be a toy or a romper or some other thoughtful gift. There was never a note, so I always stood up and thanked the entire office, bowing. They stood and returned the bow, and then we all got back to work.

When Joey was eight months old, Yamakawa-san had his *sobetsukai*, the Japanese version of a retirement party. It was a surprisingly raucous affair, with dozens of people, loads of food, and an incessant flow of sake. No matter how restrained Japanese salary men are during the day, after work they let it all hang out. In fact, after-work drinking sessions are a job staple. During these outings, the hierarchy disappears and suddenly you and your shitfaced boss are singing "Dancing Queen" in front of your equally shitfaced coworkers. You're free to express personal feelings and concerns you wouldn't dare bring up at the office. And your shitfaced boss actually listens, unoffended. But at work the next day, the hierarchy reasserts itself and you reassert your humility. Like a one-night stand with your neighbor's wife, there is no mention of the fun you had the night before.

Many of the guests were about the same age as Yamakawa-san, and when I mentioned this, he explained they were all in the same class; that is, they'd all started working for the Agency at the same time. Every spring in Japan, a new batch of eager young college grads begin their careers on the same day. Forty-some years later, they'll have their own *sobetsukai*. Lifetime employment with a single company was once a defining characteristic of the Japanese work ethic. It's changed over the years, and it's no longer uncommon to encounter a professional with several previous jobs listed on his or her resumé, but in Yamakawa-san's day, it was pretty much until death—or retirement—do you part.

"You can go home now, Ma-ku-su-san," he told me at the party.

For a moment I was confused. Go home? But I haven't even tried the *otoro*. Then I realized he was referring to my promise.

Yamakawa-san was retired.

I could go home now.

But what did that mean?

Where would I go?

By then, I felt at home in Japan, but I knew it would be easier to care for Joey in the US. Going back to New Jersey wouldn't be any more convenient than staying in Tokyo. It would probably be worse. I'd have to find a different Suzuki-san. And I was more than a little afraid of running into Annette. No, I would break the promise I'd made to myself and return to my hometown, Carver, Illinois. Mary was there, and that made all the difference. She'd help take care of Joey and be the female presence in her young niece's life. As for employment, I had no idea. They don't have advertising agencies in Carver, Illinois. And I sure as hell couldn't go back to the trailer factory, even though my steel-toed shoes remained functional; I still owed them for that trailer I'd destroyed. I was pondering my dilemma when Yamakawa-san said, "I have spoken to my replacement,

Koji-san, and if you would like, you can continue your job working from the United States on a freelance basis."

I was somewhat intoxicated, which greatly amplified the gratitude I felt and put me on the verge of tears. I bowed until I could pull myself together. "How about you?" I asked once my bowing spree had ended. "What are you going to do with all your free time?"

Yamakawa-san shook his head.

"No free time," he said.

"You took another job?" I asked, surprised.

This made him smile.

"My wife and I will be golfing all over the world. This is our dream, to travel and to play golf."

Like a lot of his countrymen, Yamakawa-san was obsessed with golf, a sport that can be extremely expensive in Japan. Enthusiasts often combine vacations with golf outings, because even with airfare and lodging factored in, it's not that much more costly than playing domestically. And god help you if you hit a hole in one. Japanese golfing tradition mandates that after an ace, the lucky linksman must throw a lavish party for his or her golfing buddies and club members—instead of the other way around. Indeed, acing a hole can put you *several thousand dollars* in the hole. Thus do many Japanese golfers purchase hole-in-one insurance, which offsets the cost of any potential good fortune. Yamakawa-san and his wife—both of whom carried hole-in-one policies—would spend their retirement years doing what they loved on some of the most beautiful courses in the world. Good for him. Good for her.

I put in my notice the Monday after Yamakawa-san's *sobetsukai*. It was agreed that I would work for another three months, up to the third anniversary of my arrival. Koji-san had already begun preparing the paperwork and told me I would earn at least half my salary as a freelancer. In Carver, half my Japanese salary would be a significant raise. He also asked that I help find a replacement, which involved interviewing several native-English-speaking writers currently residing in Japan. This became unnecessary when a copywriter from the Osaka office, a Canadian named Keith, asked to be transferred to Tokyo.

About a month before my own *sobetsukai*, Koji-san asked me to speak at a seminar the Agency was hosting. The event was part of an effort to resolve an issue that had long plagued Japanese businesses abroad. The Agency had satellite offices throughout Southeast Asia—in places like Thailand, Vietnam, the Philippines, Malaysia, Singapore, and Indonesia—and, inevitably, problems would arise between the Japanese staff sent down to run these offices and the locals who actually did the work. The issue wasn't language; it was culture. The locals simply didn't understand the Japanese way of doing business. Moreover, the Japanese staff tended to stick together, eat at Japanese restaurants, and engage primarily with those who speak Japanese—just as they would in Japan. In most cases, they weren't being aloof or chauvinistic; like most human beings, they sought the comfort of the familiar. Nonetheless, the sense of separation sometimes caused misunderstandings and engendered a toxic work environment. Thus, the Agency decided to fly a few employees from each of the satellite offices to Tokyo for a seminar. There, they could express their grievances and gain insight into Japanese culture, which would improve office morale and elevate productivity. The seminar was hosted by Tomaru-sensei, a well-known professor from one of Japan's top universities. He asked the attendees to call him Tom. I was invited to share my experiences as an American ex-pat living and working in Japan. The opportunity delighted me. I'd been in the ugly gray monolith for almost three years and managed to do my job well, get along with my coworkers, and have a baby out of wedlock. I could teach these yokels a thing or two.

My hour-long summary of life in Tokyo was well received. Tom was incredibly articulate and insightful, occasionally asking questions that revealed knowledge I didn't even know I possessed. Afterwards, he asked me to stay and participate in an exercise with the attendees. I readily agreed, for I was basking in the glow of my new-found celebrity. The exercise turned out to be a card game. I love card games.

When I lived in New Jersey, I'd sometimes drive down to Atlantic City and play blackjack. It's one of the best games in the casinos, and if you learn the basic strategy and follow it religiously, you can reduce the house odds to a little over fifty percent. In other words, if you play every hand exactly the way the basic strategy stipulates, you will, over time, only lose a portion of your money. Of course, this doesn't take into account the science of luck. I enjoyed the excitement for a while but decided to quit cold turkey one night after realizing I was never satisfied. If I won, I was disappointed that I didn't stay longer and win more. If I lost, I was disappointed that I didn't stay longer and win it back. Gamblers call this flirting with addiction. Which is fitting, because it's a good way to get fucked.

Tom divided us into groups of four and seated us at five tables, labeled A through E. He designated table A as the highest and table E the lowest, giving some players an unfair advantage. But hey, it's just a game. On each table was a deck of cards and a set of rules that we were to read silently. Every game would have two winners, who would move up one table (unless they were already at A). The two losers would move down one table (unless they were already at E). The object of the game was to be sitting at table A after the final hand was played. Before beginning, Tom added a final stipulation: there was to be no talking. All the better for my concentration, I thought. I won the first game easily and moved up from table D to table C. (I could teach these yokels a thing or two.) Unfortunately, some of the yokels at table C were violating the rules. I tried to point out their mistakes, but it was difficult without words. Sadly, I lost. Then I was back at table D with a new group of people, who proved to be even more clueless than the previous bunch. My gestures became increasingly aggressive, yet I lost again. Now I was relegated to the shit table, where the stupidity continued. An honest man doesn't have a chance with these people, I lamented, losing for the third time. At last, Tom said the fun was over and gathered the cards. Then he asked us how we felt about the game. None of the attendees said anything, so I decided to air my grievances. "It appears that many of you didn't understand the rules," I said, attempting to be diplomatic. "I play a lot of cards, and I know rules can sometimes be confusing, but these were so simple. I guess I'm a little disappointed."

Tom listened thoughtfully, and I could tell he appreciated both my candor and my accurate assessment of the situation.

Then he asked if anyone else had a comment. After several moments of silence, a young woman from the Philippines raised her hand. Tom recognized her, and she said quietly, almost regretfully, "The rules were different." She glanced at me, then turned back to Tom and clarified, "The rules you put on each table were different." It took me a few seconds to understand what those words implied, but when I did, I felt as if I'd been hit in the face with a sushi platter. After three years of living and working in Japan—of learning and growing and becoming an openminded citizen of the world—I had failed to understand the most fundamental truth of all: the rules were different. I'd never felt more American.

My last few weeks at the office consisted mainly of being taken to lunch. Since Keith from the Osaka office had already arrived, there wasn't much for me to do. He was a good writer, and I told him so. Yet I got the impression Keith didn't like me very much—especially after he revealed that he was a graduate of Trinity College, and I told him I'd never heard of it. "It's the Harvard of Canada!" he cried indignantly. "Oh," I sympathized, "it's in Canada."

A few of the higher-ups took me to ridiculously expensive restaurants, where the food was ridiculously good. Many opted for places with affordable lunchtime specials, also ridiculously good. Cha Cha led me to a humble shack that served *katsudon*—a breaded pork cutlet, fried and served in a bowl of rice with egg and onion—and it, too, was ridiculously good. Over the course of these lunches, I received many compliments on how well I used chopsticks. The first time I earned this praise was shortly after my arrival in Japan, and I swelled with pride. But after three years, it's about as meaningful as a participation trophy. I thanked them anyway. Each of the meals was memorable, not only for the food, but also because it was a wonderful way to say goodbye to people whose talent I admired and friendship I valued. And they were paying.

My *sobetsukai* was much smaller that Yamakawa-san's. I had no classmates to celebrate with—only my office coworkers and a few artists and writers from other departments with whom I'd grown close. Though no one requested it, I brought Joey along because I knew they all wanted to see her. Derek, now working for a different agency, dropped by. He shook his head when he saw Joey. To him, she was just another rug rat, and Derek detested rug rats. The fact that he made no exception for my own child greatly elevated my respect for him. I received a dozen gifts, all of them pens. Everyone oohed and aahed as I unwrapped one writing utensil after another. They were expensive—not stupidly expensive like the snow-capped phallic symbols corporate douchebags display in the pockets of their monogrammed shirts—but expensive compared to the Bic medium-points I typically used. I appreciated all twelve but have yet to take them out of their boxes. Maybe when this one runs out of ink.

Two days later, the movers came and packed up my apartment. I hadn't accumulated much, but they dutifully wrapped everything—including pencils, bottle caps, and loose change—before carefully placing the precious cargo into reinforced cardboard boxes. Moving expenses were written into my contract, so I didn't have to lift a finger or pay a thing. Nonetheless, I tried to be helpful, offering packing tips to men who spoke no English and would have ignored me even if they'd been fluent. Joey was at Suzuki-san's, so after the movers left I sat alone in the empty apartment and contemplated my future. I got as far as the upcoming trip to Narita Airport and then lost interest. The future would arrive whether I contemplated it or not. A humming sound caught my attention. It was coming from the refrigerator, resonating in the empty apartment. I walked over and opened it for the final time. Inside was a very cold bottle of Asahi Super Dry. I used a door jamb to pry the cap off and then sat on the floor and drank. Jesus.

Yamakawa-san died five months after I left Japan.

One morning, his heart just stopped beating.

I flew back for the funeral.

"We were so happy," his wife sobbed. "Our whole lives, we looked forward to his retirement, to when we could do all the things we wanted to do."

I looked into her eyes.

They were void of happiness.

You're safe now, I thought.

17

The End

The left-wing engine explodes, sending shrapnel through the fuselage. There is a horrible whooshing noise as the air leaves the cabin, and magazines, vomit bags, papers, pillows, blankets, and anything else that isn't bolted down whirl violently around our heads. It stops as suddenly as it begins. After a moment of silence, a collective scream fills the void. Oxygen masks drop from the ceiling and dangle before our eyes like giant spiders. The screaming dies down as passengers struggle to put them on, far more difficult to negotiate than the pre-flight safety demonstration would have you believe. As I reach for mine, I look across the aisle and see that Bernadette is putting on Joey's mask before saving herself. Several people are covered with blood. One man has a chunk of metal protruding from his left temple. He is not wearing his mask, and no one is assisting him. The plane descends rapidly, though we're not yet falling. Joey looks at me from behind her mask, and I can see that she's smiling. She could be on a rollercoaster. An elderly couple two rows up are struggling, trying to help each other, but in their frenzy are making things worse. I inhale deeply and remove my mask. I can hold my breath for well over a minute, so I feel confident as I step into the aisle. From behind, an authoritative female voice orders me back to my seat. For some reason, this makes me smile. When I reach the couple, I take the mask from the woman's hands. She looks up at me, horrified, as if I'm responsible what is happening. I fit the mask over her mouth and tighten the strap behind her head. I do the same for the man, who is weeping. I caress the top of his head, the way I sometimes do with Joey when she's upset. The plane shudders violently, and I have to grab his seat to keep from falling. Joey is still watching me, still smiling. I give her the thumbs up. She returns the signal. As the plane continues its rapid descent, the angle becomes even more pronounced. I'm walking uphill as I move back to my seat. Bernadette has her arms around Joey and appears to be frightened, but I'm certain she is not afraid for herself. Another shudder, more violent this time, and the screams intensify. Joey continues to smile. Everyone screams on a roller coaster. I look back at Mary and am not surprised to see that she's stoic. There are tears in her eyes, but fear is absent. Noticing me, she places her hand over her heart; I reciprocate by nodding. Milo sits next to her, holding her hand. He looks sadly resigned but, like Mary, does not seem to be afraid. They're just disappointed they won't have more time together. With his free hand he flips me the bird. I do the same. This is how we say goodbye. My lungs are starting to hurt, so I take a breath. The air is cold and only vaguely satisfying, but it holds enough oxygen for me to remain conscious. I struggle back into my seat and put on my mask. I strap myself in, just as the safety demonstration has taught me, and wait for the end to come. I feel so calm, so peaceful, as if I'm in a warm bath. It will all be over soon. I look across the aisle at Joey and see that her eyes are no longer smiling. She's terrified, and I wonder why. Is it death? Can someone so young fear death? Bernadette tries to hold her, but Joey is screaming for me, trying to unfasten her seatbelt. I don't understand her motivation. I can't protect her. Any more than I could that day in the park. I can only say goodbye. I reach across the aisle. Our fingers touch, and I manage to take her hand. "Daddy!" she cries. *It's okay*, I want to tell her, but I can't make a sound. She continues to struggle, fighting the seatbelt that won't release her. She beats on the buckle with her little fists. Tears at the strap with her fingers. Her eyes are pleading. Why won't you help me? Why won't you help me? I'm sorry, Joey, I say over and over. I'm sorry. But she doesn't hear me. Because I no longer have a voice. "Ladies and gentlemen, this is your captain speaking. I'd like to apologize for the all the drama. It seems one of our passengers, Max Androv in 57B, is having a nightmare. As soon as he wakes up, I'll turn off the fasten seatbelt sign and you'll be free to roam around the cabin. As always, thank you for flying United."

"Daddy?"

I open my eyes when I hear Joey's voice. I look to my right and see her across the aisle, kneeling in the expansive business-class seat. Bernadette is asleep in the seat next to her.

"What time will we get to Japan?"

I shake the sleep from my head.

"Do you mean our time or Japan time?"

"I don't know."

"Japan is thirteen hours ahead of Carver."

"Why?"

"Because the Earth is round, and the sun can only shine on one part of it at a time. When it's daytime in Japan, it's nighttime in Carver." I watch a series of expressions transform her face as she struggles to understand.

"Oh," she finally says. "What time will it be in Japan?"

"Three p.m. in the afternoon," Milo declares, squatting in the aisle between us.

I hate when he does this. Not the butting in—that I can live with. I hate the redundancy.

"In Carver, it'll be two a.m. in the morning," he adds.

"Jesus, Milo, when is two a.m. not in the morning?"

He looks at me blankly.

"Because a.m. *means* morning. It's the abbreviation for *ante meridiem*, which is Latin for *before midday*, i.e., morning. So just say two a.m. Or two in the morning. But not both. Don't add unnecessary words to your sentences. Christ, you talk enough as it is."

"What about p.m.?

"*Post meridiem.* Same thing, only *after* midday."

"You explained that very well," Milo says.

"I'm glad you learned something."

"Can you tell me how magnets work?"

"Why don't you go play with your fiancée."

"Good idea. I can share this new knowledge with her."

"I'm pretty sure she graduated from high school."

"You doing okay, Joey?" he asks, ignoring the barb.

Joey nods her head.

As Milo stands, he spots a half-eaten bag of pretzels on my tray.

"You done with those?"

I pass him the bag. He shoves several pretzels into his mouth and then shakes his head. "Air travel hasn't been the same since they stopped serving peanuts. These are okay, but they're a poor substitute for the ultimate airline snack."

"Why don't they serve peanuts?" Joey asks.

"A lot of people are allergic to peanuts," I explain. "They decided to ban them so no one would get hurt."

"People are allergic to peanuts?"

"Yeah, and it can be pretty severe. Some people go into anaphylactic shock just being near a peanut. They could even die."

"Then I'm glad they don't serve peanuts," Joey says defiantly.

"I still miss 'em," Milo insists as he pops another pretzel into his mouth.

He holds the bag out to Joey, who searches until she finds an unbroken one. She examines it closely before taking a small bite. When she's finished crunching, she turns to me and says, "Are people allergic to pretzels?"

"I don't know. Some people probably are—the gluten intolerant. But the peanut allergy is a lot more serious."

"Be great if it were the other way around," Milo said wistfully.

"Man, I swear, as soon as we get to the duty-free shop, I'll buy you a bag of peanuts."

"It's not the same as those little packets the stewardesses handed out."

"They're called flight attendants now."

"Yeah, but they were stewardesses when they handed out peanuts."

Milo logic.

He walks down the aisle and plops into his seat next to Mary. They look so happy. So unaware. When I turn back, Joey is studying me.

"Daddy, are you okay?"

I start to speak but can't find that first syllable. Deftly, she unfastens her seatbelt then hops across the aisle and onto my lap.

"I'm fine. Why are you asking me that?"

She stares into my face.

"You look sad."

"Really?"

"Yes."

"Well, that's Milo's fault."

"No, you look sad all the time."

"Do I look sad now?" I say, grinning.

"That's not what I mean."

"What do you mean?"

"You look sad when you think nobody can see you."

When Catholics need to unburden themselves, they talk to a priest. So it stands to reason that when former Catholics need to unburden themselves, they talk to a former priest. I just happen to have one in my Rolodex. John Franklin, former priest. I gave him a call. He was still staying at the rectory, showing the ropes to his replacement celibate. Father John offered to stop by, but I explained it was a private matter that necessitated a clandestine rendezvous. He was intrigued. We arranged to meet at the truck stop where I bought Joey's *omiyage*. They had a restaurant, but it was frequented primarily by truckers and travelers—no one who'd know me.

As Father John walked over to the booth I occupied, I noted he wasn't wearing his beloved yellow Converse. Instead, he'd chosen a pair of Birkenstocks, opting for comfort over style. He'd further distanced himself from the dictates of fashion by pairing his German sandals with white gym socks. "What's the matter?" he asked, responding to what must have been a disgusted look on my face. I started to explain, but the man was doing me a favor. "Thanks for coming."

"It's my pleasure," he said with a friendly smile.

A middle-aged waitress came over, and we both ordered coffee. She seemed tired, as if she'd worked all night, but was nonetheless friendly and patient. Her nametag said Doris. A good waitress name, I thought. Doris asked if we wanted something to eat and stood by as we scanned the menu. Though it wasn't listed, I asked for a doughnut. She apologized and suggested a cinnamon roll. I asked her if they were any good, and she feigned indignation. "Tell you what," she said, "if you don't like it, you don't have to pay for it."

"In that case, we'll take two."

Doris made a note on her pad and then hurried off, returning just a few moments later with two cups of coffee. "I'm gonna heat those rolls up just a bit, if you don't mind," she said. "In the oven, not the microwave."

"Wonderful," Father John said.

"I like Doris," I said after she walked away.

"You'd make a lovely couple."

"She was wearing a wedding ring."

"Was she?"

"I don't know."

He grinned.

We both tried the coffee.

Classic truck-stop brew. Nothing fancy, absolutely perfect.

Silence settled over the table, despite the fact that we were in a noisy truck stop. Father John seemed perfectly content to sit quietly and enjoy his coffee. It felt very Japanese.

"I think I have cancer," I said to get the ball rolling.

His expression did not change. He simply nodded for me to continue.

"I…I've been having these pains. These symptoms. And I looked them up on the internet."

He stirred ever so slightly.

"Yeah, I know it's stupid to self-diagnose over the internet, but what other choice did I have?"

There were any number of other choices, but he let the comment slide.

"I'm…uh…pretty fucking scared."

He shook his head.

"You dragged me all the way out here just to tell me that?"

I literally felt my jaw drop.

Then he gave me that friendly smile again.

"Good one," I said.

He took another sip of his coffee.

"Milo already came to see me."

What?

"Milo? What's he got to do with anything?"

"He told me about your cancer scare."

Again, my jaw dropped.

"That can't be. He doesn't know anything. You're the first person I've told."

"I know that, but Milo came to me…"

"I swear, I didn't tell him."

"Not in words. But he's very perceptive. Especially when it comes to people dealing with cancer. Milo knows the signs, and I don't just mean symptoms; he seems to understand how people react to cancer. The nuances. That's how he realized, not that you have cancer, but that you think you have it."

I sat back in the booth, stunned but, all things considered, not all that surprised.

"Apparently, he spent a lot of time helping cancer patients when he lived in California," Father John explained.

"He sounds like a very nice man," Doris interjected as she set two large cinnamon rolls on the table. They commanded my full attention: golden brown, beautifully coiled, icing slightly melted, the aroma of cinnamon surrounding us like an aura. Doris placed the check on the table and then left without waiting for a response. She knew when to let the food do the talking. I wanted to grab that gorgeous pastry and take a huge bite but, following Father John's lead, used my knife and fork to cut off a reasonably sized morsel. It tasted as good as I'd expected, and I'd had very high expectations. Three bites later, I set down my utensils and took a sip of coffee.

"Yeah, Milo was a regular Albert Schweitzer when it came to marijuana."

"He's a remarkable man," Father John concurred. "And he loves you as much as he loves your sister."

"So why did he come to you? Why didn't he tell me himself?"

"He seems to think you're a bit stubborn and that had he said anything, you would have told him to fuck off. His words."

"Yeah," I admitted, "that's probably what would've happened."

"He came to *me* figuring that, sooner or later, you would too. And here you are. As I said, he's very perceptive. And if you didn't, then I could approach you, because you'd be reluctant to tell *me* to fuck off."

"I've never heard a priest say *fuck* so much."

"I'm not really a priest anymore. And we *are* in a truck stop."

"Okay, so now you know and Milo knows. What the hell am I supposed to do?"

He took a piece of paper from his jacket pocket and handed it to me. Written on it was the name Ray and a phone number.

"Milo asked me to give you this. It's the phone number of an oncologist Milo met in California. He has a practice in Champaign, and he's expecting your call. Whenever you're ready. But please be ready soon. Because if you do have…"

"I know, early detection. So Milo set all this up?"

"Yes."

"He really should've come to me."

The priest raised an eyebrow.

"Yeah, I would have told him to fuck off."

Fourteen days later, I called Ray. Two full weeks. Why did it take so long for me to make an appointment that would almost certainly increase my chances of survival? Why would I put off a decision that would help prolong my life?

Simple.

I didn't want to have cancer.

And I believed the only way to remain in a state of grace was through the power of ignorance—by prolonging my blindness to the mutated genes, the corrupted mitosis, the billions of renegade cells destroying my life even as they seek immortality for themselves. Until this nightmare scenario is confirmed, there is plausible deniability, a mental loophole far more precious than most people understand. It supports the possibility of a future not filled with pain and sorrow and pity and fear and rage and self-loathing and vomit and hair loss and diarrhea and constipation. It gives you a chance to witness your daughter grow into the person you weren't strong enough or smart enough or good enough to be; to see your neurotic sister and her childlike husband grow old together; to watch your beautiful neighbor continue to brandish her smile despite life's best efforts to rip it from her face. Until the moment some overpaid, under-feeling son-of-a-bitch with a god complex stamps a sneering, hollow-eyed skull on your diagnostic chart, there is a possibility that you'll continue to inhale and exhale and sleep and wake up and eat and shit and love and hate until you're so old and tired and weak that you've finally had enough, and you can give the finger to cancer and AIDS and drunk drivers and terrorists and tornados and murderers and muggers and plane crashes and anything else that tried and failed to shorten your journey, and off you go to heaven or hell or oblivion or anywhere else, as long as it doesn't involve being reborn as some brand-new asshole who has to go through this shit all over again.

No.

That's not it.

I waited two weeks because I was weak and selfish and afraid.

A sudden burst of turbulence causes the plane to drop several feet. It feels like falling. In that moment, my heart races and I'm terrified. But why? I've already accepted the imminence of my death; a plane crash would simply hasten the inevitable. It would be a blessing. I look over at Joey, laughing, enjoying the rollercoaster ride. Bernadette is laughing with her. Of course, I wouldn't want to take them with me. I don't want to take anyone with me. This is *my* fate, not theirs. Then again, what if I could pass it on? What if I could make some sort of celestial bargain and have someone die in my place? Would I do it? Would I trade my life for Mary's? Milo's? Angelica's? Iggy's? No, I wouldn't allow anyone to take my place. Well, some asshole maybe, but friends and family get a pass. From this perspective, one could argue that I'm being heroic. It's a nice thought. I always wanted to be a hero. To be that guy who dives on a hand grenade to save the entire platoon. But I wanted to be that guy and survive. I wanted to enjoy the perks of heroism. The honor. The glory. I had no interest in being a dead hero—in being honored posthumously. Where's the fun in that?

I've been thinking about death a lot lately.

Now that I know I'm going to die.

Yeah, yeah, we're all going to die.

But once that countdown starts—once you hear the ticking—you get it.

You know.

Mortality.

It's infuriating.

And sometimes it isn't.

Sometimes it's a good idea. Because one day I'll have had my fill of life. I'll want to move on to something else. Or nothing at all. Stay alive long enough and it begins to feel like incarceration. Like you're a prisoner. And death is freedom. I'm speculating. I haven't yet reached that stage. Maybe in a couple thousand years.

A lot of people in my position find religion.

They turn to God.

So they're no longer helpless.

They can pray.

Pray for a miracle.

Please, God, take the cancer away.

Like He wasn't the one who gave it to you in the first place.

"All prayers are selfish," Pindar Plifner wrote. He wasn't being judgmental. He was stating the obvious. You want something, so you ask God for it. A new bicycle. A cure for childhood leukemia. A deeper understanding of the Bible. A set of Ginsu knives. "What about world peace?" one might counter. "That's not selfish." Yeah, like you wouldn't benefit from world peace. "Religion by its very nature is selfish," he insisted.

I once dined with a beautiful woman, Claire, a former television personality and born-again Christian who, I think, was interested in rescuing me from the dark side. I, on the other hand, was hoping to give her a tour. Also at the table was one of her friends, a missionary who'd spent years in Africa setting up desperately needed health clinics and spreading The Word of the Lord. I was about halfway through my carbonara when Claire lifted her wine glass and said, "God is good."

"Amen," responded the missionary, raising his own glass.

They both looked at me.

At that point, I thought I still might have a chance with Claire (I'd even said a little prayer), so I elevated my glass a couple of inches. Yet I couldn't help feeling a little annoyed by her declaration. In spite of my lust, I asked, "Why did you say that?"

"Because God *is* good."

"Yeah, but isn't that kind of a given?"

"Of course."

"Then why say it? It's redundant. It's like saying water is wet or ice is cold or the sun is hot. If you know it and you believe it, you don't have to say it." Claire's expression hardened, but she let me continue. "When I hear people say God is good, it makes me wonder if they're trying to convince themselves. They want to believe it, they're trying to believe it, and if they say it often enough, eventually they will believe it. Like The Little Engine that Could: I think I can, I think I can, I think I can."

The missionary bobbed his head as I invoked the train's mantra, but Claire's eyes had turned stone cold.

"God is good, Max," she said sweetly, though it felt like a threat. "God is the source of all goodness."

Fuck.

I would have acquiesced to God is good but making Him the source of *all* goodness galled me. Rather than respond immediately, I filled my mouth with pasta, chewed, swallowed, then had a drink of wine. Claire never took her eyes from me.

"All goodness comes from God?" I asked, releasing my wine glass.

"Amen," she declared.

"You believe that too?" I asked the missionary.

"Amen," he echoed.

There, you see? Claire conveyed with a condescending smile.

I nodded and then frowned, as if a thought had just occurred to me.

"But what if God didn't exist?"

"God does exist," Claire snapped.

"Yeah, I know. He exists and He's good. I'm not challenging that. But hypothetically, in a world where there is no God, would there be goodness? Would people still look after one another? Would they do the right thing? Would you still be a good person, Claire?" I looked over at the missionary. "Would you still go to Africa and set up health clinics?"

The missionary deferred to Claire.

"What would be the point?" she said.

I wanted to slap them both, the way Moe would slap Larry and Curly, consecutively and with exaggerated sound effects. But, to borrow Claire's phrase, what would be the point? I wasn't going to change any minds. On the other hand, I was enjoying the pasta and the wine. So I nodded thoughtfully, as if she'd said something worth considering. In fact, Claire was validating Pindar Plifner's assertions about religion and selfishness, making it clear she was motivated by one thing: a reward. Goodness is merely a means to an end, and if there were no God to give you that reward, then fuck humanity.

So I won't be begging God for forgiveness on my deathbed.

I might be a self-absorbed asshole.

But I'm not *that* selfish.

When Naoko's parents invited Joey and me to visit them in Japan, they had no idea I'd take them up on their offer so quickly. But I wanted to travel before the diagnosis was confirmed—before I was officially terminally ill. They explained that not only did they want to meet their granddaughter, they were also eager to get to know the others in Joey's life, which is why Mary, Milo, and Bernadette are on the plane. This struck me as exceptionally generous and perceptive, and I wondered yet again how Naoko could have grown up to be so bitter and dejected. Her brother Jiro seems happy and relatively well adjusted, although my opinion is based largely on Steve-san's assessment. Since the funeral, he and Jiro have been getting together regularly, as they've discovered a shared passion for professional wrestling. They meet at an *izakaya* to drink beer and eat *yakitori* and discuss the Flying Clothesline and the Arm Twist Ropewalk Chop and other artful moves until they're both good and shitfaced. (Annette tried to have such discussions with me, but they never ended well.) Jiro will meet our little entourage at the airport, and we'll make the trip to his parents' home in Aoyama—an extremely wealthy neighborhood in Tokyo—in a full-sized limousine. When I mentioned this to Milo, he couldn't wait to find out if it had a bar, "like they do in the movies."

"Jesus, Milo, as soon as we clear customs, I'll buy you a six-pack."

"Thanks, Max, but it's just not the same as havin' a martini in a limo."

I mentioned this exchange to Steve, who mentioned it to Jiro; the limo will have a fully stocked bar.

I reach over and slide up the plastic shade, then glance through the window. I'm sitting on the left side of the plane because it offers a view of Mount Fuji, which should be visible soon. Not long after takeoff, I'd asked the flight attendant to let me know when we're close, so my daughter could get a good look at it. She smiled at Joey and said she'd check with the captain. Mount Fuji is a breathtaking mountain, and it's easy to understand why it holds such a special place in Japanese hearts. There's a rumor that during World War II, Fujiyama was one of the proposed targets for the first atomic bomb. According to legend, some believed that destroying the sacred mountain would so demoralize the Japanese, they would lose their will to fight. In the end, it was decided that killing eighty thousand men, women, and children would be a more effective means of demoralizing the populace. And so it goes. Mount Fuji is best seen in winter and from a distance. In winter because it loses a good deal of its charm without the snowcap; from a distance because when you're up close, the gravelly gray basalt isn't all that attractive. It's kind of like a comic book: at arm's length, everything looks great. But up close? It's just a bunch of dots.

"Hey, Max," Milo says, slipping past me and into the window seat. "You're not dying."

I hear him, and I recognize the individual words, but I am unable to find meaning.

"You're not dying," he says again.

I take a breath.

Then another.

Suddenly, my heart is racing.

"I spoke to Ray before we left. The tests were all negative. You don't have cancer. Ray thinks your symptoms are due to stress. Maybe some guilt. And the fact that your ex died of cancer probably sweetened the pot."

"What the fuck, Milo?"

"I can't stand to see you like this. And there's no point. You've got Mary worried sick. And Joey, she knows something's wrong. Christ, she just lost her mother. I didn't want to say anything, but I…I couldn't let you suffer like this. Couldn't let them suffer."

"What the fuck, Milo?"

He shrugs.

I punch him in the face.

Hard.

I draw my arm back to hit him again, yet he does not try to defend himself. There are tears in his eyes.

"You're gonna be okay," he manages to say.

I drop my arm.

Now I have tears in my eyes.

"What the fuck, Milo?"

He puts his hand on my shoulder.

"You're gonna be okay."

I try to make sense of it.

"That son of a bitch told you? Ray? Is he even a doctor?"

"Yeah, but he was pretty high."

"I could sue you both for violating doctor-patient confidentiality."

"We'd just deny it."

"What the fuck, Milo?"

He rubs his jaw where I hit him.

"You got any more of those pretzels?"

I shake my head.

"Maybe I'll ask one of the stewardesses."

"Flight attendants."

He scans the aisle and then looks back at me.

"You feeling better?"

"No," I tell him honestly. "Not yet."

He nods, then rises from the seat.

"Sorry," he says and begins walking toward a flight attendant. He speaks to her for a moment, and then she disappears behind the bulkhead. A moment later she reappears with several bags of pretzels.

I don't have cancer.

I'm not dying.

I'm going to have to rethink everything.

"Ladies and gentlemen, this is your captain speaking. There's a little girl named Joey sitting somewhere among you, and she has her heart set on seeing Mount Fuji." I look over at my daughter, who is both surprised and delighted to hear her name mentioned over the intercom. "Well, I'm happy to tell you, Joey, that if you look out the left side of the aircraft, you'll soon have a wonderful view of one of the world's most beautiful mountains."

Suddenly, everyone on the left side of the plane is attempting to look out a window. Everyone except me. My eyes are on Joey. She unbuckles her seatbelt and moves quickly across the aisle. Bernadette is beaming at me, sure that I had something to do with the surprise. I might have mentioned Joey's name when I spoke to the flight attendant, though I certainly didn't expect a public announcement. Joey climbs onto my lap and then over me and into the empty window seat. She pushes her face to the glass, and a few moments later I hear an astonished "Oh!" After several seconds she turns and looks at me, an expression of wonder on her face. She moves back so I can see for myself. As I stare through the glass, I think about Milo's revelation. I still don't quite understand it. I'd worked hard to come to grips with my death. To believe it. To accept it. Now it seems wrong. Like the rules have been broken. Like I'm being cheated. Still, I feel a muted joy. Before long, it will engulf me, and I'll dance in the aisles. But for now, I just look out the window. At first I see nothing but clouds, white and fluffy and solid enough to stand on. I scan the horizon but am unable to locate the mountain. Joey pushes her face next to mine, and together we stare out the window. I feel her smile against my cheek. And then I see it. More beautiful than ever. Its magnificent snowy cap shining in the afternoon sunlight. Joey and I stay this way, cheek to cheek, for several minutes, gradually turning our heads to the left as the plane leaves the breathtaking landmark behind. When it finally disappears, we move away from the window and sit back in our seats. Joey is gazing at me with undiluted happiness. Suddenly, I reach out and pull her into a tight embrace. She hugs me back. Tears are streaming from my eyes, so I dare not let her go. I close them tightly, hoping this will stem the flow, and eventually the tears abate. After running my sleeve across my face, I release her and quickly turn away. I pull my knees inward so she can slip by me and over to her own seat next to Bernadette, but she does not move. When I turn back, she is buckling herself into the window seat. My Joey. Not a word has passed between us, but I feel as if we've just had the most important conversation of our lives.

The joy has come now.

I'm not dying.

The ticking has stopped.

But I try to keep the feeling in check.

Joy is just an extreme form of happiness.

And happiness is the harbinger of disaster.

But is there more to it than that?

Pindar Plifner believes it's the only thing God wants from us. Not devotion, not sacrifice, just happiness. Though he never defines it. He does compare it to love, but only insofar as they are both easily mistaken for other psychological states. "Likewise, happiness is frequently confused with euphoria, a highly intense feeling that can be sustained only for short periods of time," he wrote. "Ironically, those who insist on maintaining this ephemeral state are the most unhappy and disillusioned of all, for in their pursuit of ultimate bliss, they are immune to any pleasure that falls short of it."

There is a stirring in the cabin, a sense of anticipation. The perky voice of a flight attendant fills the air. "Ladies and gentlemen," she begins, "as we will soon be landing at Narita International Airport, the captain has asked me to remind you to fasten your seatbelt and secure your personal belongings. Please stow your tray table and put your seatback upright. At this time we also ask you to turn off all electronic devices, as they can interfere with the navigation system." (You can practically see the airport, but we'll wind up in Kamchatka if someone plays Candy Crush.) "Thank you for flying United."

Joey is struggling to get her seat into the upright position, but she doesn't have enough body mass. I reach over and pull as Joey holds down the release button. It slides forward, and she smiles.

"Mr. Max?"

I turn and see Bernadette leaning toward me, a curious expression on her face.

"Is everything okay?"

"Yeah, Bernadette, everything's okay."

She nods.

"It's just that you look…you look so…"

"I know."

I know.

Happiness isn't a whole.

Nor is it the sum of the parts.

It *is* the parts.

Joey.

Mary.

Milo.

Bernadette.

Doughnuts.

Beer.

Bacon.

Coffee.

Baseball.

Duct tape.

Iggy Pop.

The Three Stooges.

Bing Crosby.

Life.

I look out the window. The land looks so neat and orderly at this altitude. Perfectly planned and executed. From this perspective, it would be easy to believe that the universe was created by a supreme being—by a god of infinite power and wisdom and goodness. But it's much harder to accept that when you get up close.

Up close, it's just a bunch of dots.

The captain's electronically amplified voice instructs the flight attendants to buckle themselves into their seats in preparation for landing. They dutifully oblige him. Joey slides her hand beneath mine, and I squeeze her fingers gently. For a few moments, nothing happens. Then the flaps are extended, and we begin our inevitable descent.

A Word from the Author

I began writing this book because I was frustrated with life. Not just my life. Everyone's. Then it occurred to me: if I write a book, I can end the frustration. I can create a world in which I control everything. Thus, I began writing. And quickly discovered that I was in control of very little. It seems the characters have far more say in what happens than one might think. They don't consult their creator before they act. They do whatever the hell they want. I tried to wrest control from them—to make them bend to my will—but always failed. The words just didn't ring true. So I had to rewrite. And rewrite. And rewrite. Until they got their way. It doesn't really seem fair.

Marc X
October 2024

I Could Have Done It Without Them.
(It Just Wouldn't Have Turned Out as Well.)

I hadn't seen Brenda Byers in 15 years, but one day we got to texting about prepositions. I mentioned that, a few years earlier, I'd written a book that included a passage about those pesky parts of speech. She asked me to send her the passage. I emailed the entire chapter. She liked it a lot but pointed out some questionable punctuation. And a clumsy phrase or two. It turns out Brenda is an editor and proofreader. She asked to read the rest of the book. And if I didn't mind, she'd continue to point out questionable punctuation and clumsy phrases. Because she believed in the book. Thank you, Brenda. Lina Sion believed in the book. Lina is a literary agent who advised me, encouraged me, and became my friend. Thank you, Lina. I must also thank Barney Karpfinger, who took time out of his busy schedule to read an early draft and offer insights and encouragement. A special thanks to T, a brilliant microlepidopterist with an unerring eye for detail; nothing gets by T. And a well-deserved *merci* to Sébastien Teissier, my friend, confidant, and author of the award-winning French thriller, *X*. There are so many more, including Georg Schneider, Lisa Purcell, Bede Scott, Casey Anderson, Lily Tung, Georgia Cobble, Gina Goss, Steve Walsh, Atsuko Ozeki, Kurt Schorsch, Agnès Zabeth, and a few I've surely forgotten who read early drafts and made me feel as if I were doing something right. Others who helped me along include Alison Lester, Fran Rittman, Tom Adelman, Gary Goh, Veronica Phua, etc. If your name should have been included here—and I'm almost certain that is the case—please forgive my memory lapse and know that the Latin abbreviation is intended for you.

Miss Marta

She was many things—history teacher, mother of five, sibling to seven, friend to countless—but when I think of my sister Marta, the first descriptor that comes to mind is *librarian*. At an age when most settle into retirement, she accepted a position at the Tuscola Public Library. It was fitting, because books were sacred to her—not for their physical essence but for what they contained. Marta had a lifelong passion for reading, and that passion could be contagious. It certainly was for me. And for many who ventured into the library. To them, she was *Miss Marta*, an enthusiastic bibliophile who always seemed to know just which story would appeal to them. At her funeral, those same young people and their parents came to pay tribute to the person who'd made reading so enjoyable. There were many. The line seemed to go on for hours, and each mourner had a story about how Miss Marta strengthened their bond with the written word. Marta read *Well I'll Be Damned* when it was just a bunch of laser-printed pages in a binder clip. She loved it. It's difficult to express how much this meant to me. And how much I miss Marta.

About the Author

Marc X Grigoroff spent over three decades in Japan and Singapore creating ad campaigns and indulging in some of the finest cuisine on the planet. He wrote and directed *Salawati,* an award-winning feature film; composed the musical, *A Quiet Moment;* authored the children's book, *The Other Side;* is a prolific voice-over artist; and has had short stories and flash fiction featured in online literary publications. Before all this, he worked as a garbage man. *Well I'll Be Damned* is his first novel.

About the Author

Made in the USA
Monee, IL
01 February 2025

75870853R00215